NO IRISH NEED APPLY

A NOVEL ABOUT NEW YORK CITY'S HELL'S KITCHEN DURING THE MID–1800'S

OTHER BOOKS BY JOHN FINUCANE

WHEN THE BRONX BURNED

THE USUAL

TOMORROW, MICKEY, TOMORROW

NO IRISH NEED APPLY

A NOVEL ABOUT NEW YORK CITY'S HELL'S KITCHEN DURING THE MID–1800'S

BY

JOHN FINUCANE

EDITED BY JOHN VEDDER

www.bookstandpublishing.com

Published by
Bookstand Publishing
Morgan Hill, CA 95037
4261_5

ISBN 978-1-63498-098-2

Printed in the United States of America

Inspired by my brother FDNY firefighter Jim Barry, and his tales of the Barry family that fled from Ireland during the Great Hunger and settled in New York's Hell's Kitchen.

PART I

CHAPTER ONE

JUNE 1855, NEW YORK CITY – The sad-eyed little girl sat in her dim kitchen and massaged her callused hands with the tips of her fingers. She kept looking up at her mother who stood in front of a jagged piece of a mirror that was hanging somewhat precariously from a badly splintered wall in the kitchen. Their dismal, two-room, one window flat was one that begged to be patched and painted.

Mom's perfect body was wrapped in a tight-fitting green dress. Her striking face was made even more beautiful by her green eyes and red hair. The little girl watched as her mom did a last minute touch up of her hair. The dress her mom wore was a gift to her from the acclaimed artist, Dion Frazer, for whom her mom had once posed.

Nine-year-old Angie was a perfect reflection of Angela, her mother—she too had green eyes and red hair, and a few freckles. She sat with her upper body completely exposed, just like a boy, which her mother did not like. Of course she had nothing to hide; she was only a child.

"Angie darling, you're not a three-year old. You shouldn't walk around like that. Cover yourself," said her mom. "You're a young lady now. And why do you always got to wear your father's old work trousers? Why don't you wear that damn dress I got you? I went all the way down to Jew town to get it."

"I gots nuttin ta cover!" She slapped her hands where her breasts should be. "Anyway, I build like a guy. A strong guy." Which she was, for she had the lean muscular body of a hard-working young man rather than the petite soft-skinned nine-year-old girl she was meant to be. She liked walking around shirtless in her apartment. Every chance she got, she'd

1

stand before the piece of mirror and flex those muscles just like boys did. Her arms, chest, and shoulders, including her calves and thighs, were lined with well-defined bulging muscles. Or she'd be posing with her *dukes up*, throwing punches and mimicking her favorite prizefighter Yankee Sullivan. She still adored him, even after his defeat by Tom Hyer, the hero of the nativists, in a much-heralded fight. Yankee was the favorite of immigrants.

"Wish I wuz a boy," she said.

"Yeah, I know. I wish you'd stop saying that. What am I gonna do with ya?" her mother muttered.

The child reached her arms across the table, tightly gripping its far edge, flexing the many muscles of her strong arms. "When ya gonna learn mees to read?" she asked, looking her mom in the eyes through short bangs.

Her mom's mouth moved, but said nothing, silenced by a rush of guilt.

Letting her off the hook, the child changed the subject. "Look," she said, flaunting the palms of her hands. "My blissers is all healed. Guess I won'ts be gitten anymore a dem."

Her mom's face was a picture of heartache. "I never wanted you working with that father of yours. But we needed the money, honey."

Her daughter's hardened hands were the result of two years of hard labor, working six and seven days a week with her dad, digging out cellars for the tenant houses, factories, and warehouses being built along the Westside. The same reason she was stacked with muscle. Some people thought she was a freak of nature. They couldn't understand how such a pretty face could be attached to such a muscular body, a body that belonged to a young man of fifteen or sixteen, who did the same laborious work. Her strange appearance made her the target of ridicule, forcing her to become a tough little street fighter. Often enough, her pretty little face was flawed by a swollen lip, bloody nose, or a black eye, and on some occasions, all of the above.

She and her father were inseparable. Often times they were seen together without her mom. "Was he abusing her?" the gossipmongers asked over and over. But that speculation ended abruptly one recent morning when he up and disappeared, leaving the girl and her mother destitute. The contractor who employed them would not keep her on without her dad, and her mother was unemployable.

The only job Angela could get was that of a *seamstress* that paid $1.00 a week. Her rent was $6.00 a month for a ramshackle tenement that stunk of shit and dirty humanity; where the cold winds of winter came howling through cracks in the walls; where the heat of summer was unbearable. The only option left for this husbandless woman of exceptional beauty who had a body *that drove men crazy* was prostitution. Against all she stood for, she began selling herself to men for a living. Her plan was to prostitute herself just long enough to get the two of them back on their feet. And if she were lucky, she would again pose for artists.

Several months earlier, a well-known painter was hired in complete confidence by a super-rich client of hers, to paint her portrait; in the words of that important man; "To capture forever her unique Celtic beauty." For this she was paid $50. The artist also painted a full body likeness of her, in a provocative tight fitting dress—the one she wore tonight— "to capture the perfect form of her body." This painting the painter kept for his studio. For that she received $45 and was permitted to keep the dress.

But for Angie, who just couldn't understand the *whys and whats* of her mother's new line of work, it was confusing and hurtful. Angie was especially hurt when her mother's work called for her to be out three or more nights a week, sometimes working into the early hours of the morning.

"Doan go, mommy," the angry girl snapped, shoving a book in her mom's face. "Ya shud be here learnin mees ta read."

"Darling, please. Don't start that again. You know I gotta work. Mommy gotta feed her beautiful daughter. Pay the rent," she said while dabbing perfume on her neck. Angela then asked he daughter, "How do I look?"

"Weal nice. Ya teaches me to read da morra? Will ya?"

"I'll be leaving now and be home by morning," Angela said. They hugged and kissed each other. "Mommy loves you, baby." Without another word, her mother was out the door.

Those pretty but sad green eyes stared from behind a once-white, drab curtain that hung over the apartment's only window. She watched an all-too-familiar scene on the muddy street below. The big black stallion and the *one-of-a-kind* Brougham carriage it pulled were parked out front of the wooden tenement in which she lived. She couldn't understand why there was nobody about the street. Usually, at that time, the women and their children would be all over the street.

From behind that curtain she watched her mother descend the stoop presenting a most confidant image. She was adorned in her skimpy lace garb that accented the *drive-men-crazy* curves of her body. Angie also saw the tall, well-dressed owner of that beautiful horse and carriage that regularly picked her up, step out of the white carriage. But this time he looked different. Instead of his hair *pony-tailing* from the back of his head, it hung wildly down over his shoulders, covering his face. She chuckled, thinking he looked like a madman.

Something else didn't look right. The chauffeur was too tall, too burly, and much too young to be the regular driver. She admired his size and strength, but when he stepped down from the driver's seat and joined the other man. The two of them began clobbering her mother until she was unconscious. Angie was horrified. She watched as they picked up her mother's sagging body like it was a sack of meal and threw her into the carriage.

The nine year-old flew down the stairs, *I gotta save my mudda,* but the beating and abduction were over in a matter of seconds. The crime happened in total silence, so as not to draw anybody's attention. The big black stallion and the *one-of-a-kind* Brougham carriage bolted down the street. All the while Angie's eyes were stuck on the image of the black stallion painted on the carriage door, with the word Blackie spelled below it. After that, her mind shut down and she retreated back upstairs to the kitchen.

Dawn's light had started to break over the city when the nine-year-old awoke to an empty house. A strange sense of loss overcame her; she knew she would never see her mom again. For almost two more days she sat by the window, watching for her. By then she was finally convinced that her mom had abandoned her. And why not? Her father had done the same.

But there were some doubts. Why did she leave a few pieces of clothing she owned and a handful of silver dollars?

In the early morning hours of that third day, she slipped out of the flat for the last time, bringing with her their few possessions: her father's Ulliean Pipes, the silver dollars, a family photograph, and a photo of Yankee Sullivan dressed in boxers' tights. Included were the few threadbare trousers and shirts she had worn while digging cellars with her father.

Barefooted, she descended the gloomy dark stairs down to the street, where she vanished into the night.

* * * * *

Every Sunday when possible, Angie had spent a lot of time with her folks down by the North River. There, they could isolate themselves from the cruel world and relax in a peaceful surrounding. She enjoyed the flocks of seagulls and loved being in the water, eventually becoming an exceptional swimmer. During the warmer months, she spent much of her off-work time swimming in that river.

Knowing the river shoreline as well as she did, she already knew where her new home would be: the old, rickety shed on the unused MacAdams property, as long as it was okay with Battle Axe, the undeclared leader of the area's vagabonds.

All she had to do now was clean out the long vacant dugout beneath its wooden flooring. And she was pleased with its isolation.

The wooded area that surrounded the shed kept her out of view of the workforce at Macon's slaughterhouse. If her presence were known, the pretty little thing would definitely have occasional, unwanted male visitors, whom she feared, having witnessed too often her mother, and even herself, being abused by the male species.

She quickly settled in to her damp and chilly abode. Her first order of business was to figure out a means of income. The muscular young girl chose to work the ferry terminals for tips, carrying people's luggage to their waiting carriages. The regulars did not welcome her, but after a few punch outs, they left her alone. Eventually, her peers came to admire the gritty little tiger with the broad shoulders. Her choice of work wasn't easy. She was jumped twice and the baggage stolen. On both occasions the owners accused her of being part of a team of thieves.

After a while, the few dollars she earned lugging people's luggage no longer cut it for her. She wanted more than just enough for a couple of skimpy meals a day. Only on rare occasion could she afford the pleasure of a play in the Bowery and the cost of the fare to get there.

She had known for a long time how to up her income. The *pickings* were good at the ferry terminals. Like everything was up for grabs: watches, jewelry, wallets, handbags, briefcases, and light luggage. Whatever, you name it. All she had to do was sharpen her pickpocket and grab-and-run skills. She already had the gall. Once she made the decision to *change jobs*, she began visiting the different ferry terminals to familiarize herself with their schedules.

Shortly afterwards, she started bringing home the receipts. At first she lifted items of little value: hats, umbrellas, and articles of clothing. Not long thereafter, what she brought home had great monetary value: jewelry, watches and wallets with money in them. She even brought home a diamond studded gold watch. While these items began to accumulate in her hovel, she had no regular fence that she could count on for a fair price. But she knew whom to turn to for that information. Her neighbors also dealt in stolen merchandize, especially things that glittered in the sunlight. She would speak to Battle Axe, who advised her, "Thomas Brogan is your man. And when you deal with him, nobody will mess with you."

CHAPTER TWO

JULY 1860--Pure strength is what it took the gymnast-like thief to shimmy up the thick, fifteen-foot marble pillar that stood at the right side of the entryway to the Tower Building. One slip and his brains would be splattered on the granite steps far below. That same great strength enabled the burglar to lock his short legs around the top of the pillar and grip the outer lip of the ledge that sat on top of the pillars. That feat enabled him, in one fluid motion, to flip himself up onto that ledge. He moved like a cat: silent and undetectable. The cat-like burglar, dressed in black attire that hugged him, blended in with the night shadows. And at the slightest sound, he froze in place, becoming part of the edifice. No way would he allow himself to be seen in the deserted business district.

For a moment his eyes studied the window in front of him, every detail of its ornamental, cement block framing. When satisfied the frame was secure, he once again pulled himself up using the frame's many built-in ridges for support. Like a snake, the burglar slid his way through an open window on the third floor and into the offices of Langrem & Sons.

Twelve hours earlier he had been in Langrem's disguised as a delivery boy with the wrong address. He wanted to reaffirm the location of the cash box. While there, he planted an escape rope in the janitor's room, should he need it. He crept like a cat to the desk with the cash box, opened the drawer, then the box. He cleaned it out. Wow! Five ten dollar gold pieces and one five, and three silver dollars.

Oh shit! He dropped to the floor. Somebody was tampering with the office doorknob. *Who the hell is that? What do I do?* He lay low and listened. After a few twist of the doorknob, he determined it had to be the night watchman. Through the many glass panes of the walls along the hall, he watched the watchman continue on down the hall and turn the corner at the end of the long hallway. The happy thief escaped down the interior stairs to the lobby, always moving with caution. On opening the large entryway door, he removed his mask and quickly vanished into the night.

* * * * *

The horse's hooves pounded the cobble stones, galloping at full charge, as the Young Immigrant Engine Company's fire truck sped along Tenth Avenue racing toward the shimmering red glow that lit up the evening sky. *It's got to be a good one,* thought Johnny O'Hara. He was fifteen years old and one of the youngest members of the fire company. His gut tightened, at the thought of the danger that lay ahead. Still a few blocks away from the blaze, he could already smell it: burning wood, paint and tar. The two-fisted fifteen-year-old, outfitted in his fireman's helmet, fire boots, and red shirt, could see the thick smoke clouding the street up ahead.

"Look at them fuckers," he shouted, as he pointed down the unpaved side street towards Ninth Avenue, where he saw their rivals and avowed enemies, Know Nothing Hose Company No. 1, speeding to the same fire. He knew they were determined to beat his company to the conflagration.

"There's the enemy! Go! Go! Move it! Move it!" he yelled, his adrenalin pumping. Instinctively, he waved his fist at them.

"We gotta beats dem," somebody shouted.

The red-shirted firemen tightened their grips on the fire engine and relaxed their bent knees upon seeing the large excavation blocking the road up ahead, knowing there was going to be one hell of a bump when the engine jumped the curb. Seeing the charging horses fast approaching the sidewalk and hearing the metallic clanging of the heavy, steel covered wheels rolling along the cobblestones and then hitting the curb, the shaken citizens ran for their lives, narrowly avoiding being crushed.

"No matter what! This is our fire!" ordered their foreman, Thomas Brogan. "Is that understood?" His voice bellowed over the noise from the pounding of the horseshoes on the cobblestones, the clanging of the wagon's fire bell, and the cheering of the young runners and gathering crowd chasing after them.

Young Johnny continued shouting at the top of his lungs: "Hurry! Hurry! We gotta beat dese bums!"

The first fire company to reach the water hydrant gets the water. That fire company gets the honor of putting the fire out. Those were the acknowledged rules.

One block to the east, their American counterparts were also all charged up, but for a different reason; they were readying for a slugfest. Knowing the immigrants would beat them to the hydrant, they prepared to fight them for possession of the hydrant. They wanted to steal the Yimmies fire. And they knew the immigrants would put up a hell of a fight. And the big, hard-brawling Johnny O'Hara would be right in the middle of it. This was his first fire as the pipe man—the man who will extinguish the blaze— his first opportunity to show his stuff as a fireman.

"Shit! There's those *potato heads*. Those *sauerkrauts*," roared Batesy, his eyes glaring. "We have to beat 'em, one way or the other." Batesy, the foreman who sat with the driver, had been baptized Millhouse Bates. He led the local chapter of the anti-immigrant Know Nothing Party.

8

Although the immigrants were welcomed by federal law, the Know Nothings hated them, not just because they were a threat to their job security, but also because they were mostly Roman Catholic.

"The plug is on our end of the block," said Big Mike Brogan, another large man, the younger brother of the leader of the *Young Immigrant* gang, Thomas Brogan. Thomas was also foreman of their unchartered fire company: The Young Immigrant Engine Company.

A great cheer erupted from the crowd when the Yimmies turned into the street ahead of the Know Nothings. Seemed everybody in the neighborhood had turned out for this one. Looked like a good fire was waiting for them; heavy smoke gushing from the entrance doorway and two nearby windows, one of which was beginning to show fire.

In the crowd of firewatchers were two young, ragtag members of the Yimmie fire company. One was Battler Quinn, an aspiring lightweight pugilist. The other was a short, broad-shouldered fourteen-year-old dude named Red Hester. They weren't just watching the fire. No, the two young brawlers were *guarding* the fire hydrant. Red Hester had been many blocks away, walking along the shoreline of the North River. When he spotted the column of smoke, he broke into a run. He ran the long distance to claim the nearest hydrant to the fire. He dumped a city trash can and placed it over the hydrant. "Nobidy gonna take dis from us," he shouted to Battler, his buddy from the fire company.

The Know Nothing's fire engine rumbled into the street from the other end of the block, followed by a cloud of dust. Their tall, strapping blond-headed driver Chuck Jansen, was on his feet, shouting, "Outta the way you thrash!" This was his favorite reference to immigrants. He raced the horses right at the milling crowd. The cursing throng ran for safety. A few hardy souls took after him, heaving whatever missiles they could find. But he ignored the flying objects, including a bottle that bounced off his helmet.

Expletives came from everywhere. They came from nearly every mouth, from every window, from every stoop, and from every roof of every immigrant-filled tenant house and shack on the block.

"Stop here," ordered Batesy. He yelped and covered his face when a flowerpot shattered right between the two of them. But not Jansen. He laughed uproariously.

Fists flew, feet kicked—some were barefooted and some wore boots with sharpened, metal edges. Mayhem surrounded them. Fireman fought against fireman, runner against runner and even a handful of the irked public that Jansen had tried to run down.   Meanwhile, the fire had worsened. Flames were lapping up the front of the building, and nobody paid it any attention.

At the hydrant, Red Hester and Battler Quinn took on two of Batesy's men. The four rolled around on the ground, fingernails clawing and fists pounding at each other's face as they fought for possession of the fire hydrant.

Red sprung to his feet. He threw left, left, right, then another left jab, keeping his taller opponent at bay. Then, taking advantage of his short stature, he stepped in on his taller opponent and landed a left hook—backed by the power of his bulging, broad shoulders—and dropped him.

When Chuck Jansen jumped to the street to get into the fray and saw the face of the redheaded guy fighting by the hydrant, he felt a sudden queasiness. "I know that face," he said.

"Who?" said Batesy.

"The redhead."

Jansen deflected a wooden crate heading for his head.

Still nobody was paying any heed to the fast spreading flames that were lapping higher and higher. Nor did anybody notice what looked like a person trapped on the third floor, trying to open a window.

Defiantly, Red and Battler, who were being cheered on and sometimes helped by spectators, stood their ground. They easily outpunched a second group of attackers. Just when they were weakening from the overwhelming odds, the Brogan *monsters* and several other company members came to their aide. They brought with them a length of hose, which the leader threw to Red. "Hook it up," he ordered.   With that, the Brogans and the two McCarthys, Vinnie and Timothy, turned and joined in the brawl, throwing punches at Batesy's men, who were also heading to the

10

water plug, with their own lengths of hose. Thomas Brogan's knees buckled when an equally big man punched him in the jaw. But that didn't stop Thomas Brogan for a moment. His opponent's look of victory and loud laugh were dashed by a Brogan right to the jaw that sent him to the floor. He struggled to rise, but collapsed unconscious.

The crazed-looking Jansen worked his way toward Red, shoving people aside like weightless objects. He continued his advance—his stomach tightening—until he got a good view of Red's face. *Hester. That's a Hester.* Turning on a dime, the ashen-faced bruiser disappeared back into the crowd.

The Yimmies, as the Young Immigrants were known, had hooked up their pumper to the hydrant. They controlled the water and therefore would be the ones to put the fire out.

With strong arms, they yanked lengths of hose from the hose tender. They were anxious to put the fire out, but they continued fighting pitched battles with Batesy's men, who still hoped to steal the fire. Finally, those hopes were dashed when Johnny O'Hara got the spectators to join in the melee against the attackers.

By then, the entire building frontage was shrouded by smoke, the flames whipping amidst and quickly spreading up the fascia. And just like that, as if an Army sergeant roared a command to his troops, the fighting ceased. Suddenly, everybody was concerned with the shouts and squeals coming from behind the smoke rolling up the front of the building.

Wiping the blood from his eyes, Red sprang into action. He grabbed the center rungs of a heavy wooden ladder, and yanked it from the side of the pumper. He dropped the twenty-five footer to the ground. In one quick motion, he pivoted the ladder, placing the butt end against the building. Then with a burst of super strength, the little guy flipped it up over his head and with a hand over hand motion, he ran the ladder up flush against the building. While still in motion, he braced the ladder with his powerful shoulders and walked the butt end back near the curbstone, where he rested it. And up he went, like running up a flight of stairs, he disappeared into the twirling smoke.

"I'ma gonna droppa the baby," the woman shrieked from above, hidden somewhere within the smoke cloud.

Red cringed at the thought of the baby splattering on the slate sidewalk, and he shouted back, "Wait for me."

Red emerged through the smoke just in time to snatch the baby from the outstretched arms of the terrified mother who was about to drop it. The fourteen-year-old fireman backed down the ladder to a point where he could see Vinnie McCarthy, who was butting the ladder. He dropped his charge into McCarthy's waiting arms. Red rushed back up the ladder, shouting, "Wait for me! Wait for me!" He returned to the window and wrapped his powerful arm around the woman's waist, then yanked her from the window.

Red did not see the proud look on Brogan's face. As a matter of fact, he was oblivious to everything, almost missing Brogan's command over the speaking trumpet, "C'mon Red! Get your ass on down here! Let's get this fire out!"

CHAPTER THREE

With the fire pumper hooked up to the hydrant, the pumper crew started pumping and cranking, building great water pressure. The Yimmies were ready to move in on the fire. Red fell in behind Johnny, who had the pipe. They opened up the powerful stream of water against the front of the building, saturating it, knocking down much of the outside fire. The crowd cheered them on, shouting, "Go to it boys! Go to it!" Their chants invigorated the firemen on the hose line.

Their adrenaline pumping at max, Johnny, Red, and the others then began moving in on the fire, ready to enter the blazing hallway. But just then, the whole right side of the wooden three-story structure flashed over with fire, quickly reigniting the front. The shouting and cheering became louder as the fire grew in size. Another fire engine turned into the block from the other end, its bell clanging wildly.

"Give it another shot, lads," Brogan directed. They again drenched the front of the building, again putting out much of the fire on the outside. In short order, these crazy kids were entering the hallway, following their stream of water, burying themselves in the scorching heat and smoke, apparently protected by Brogan's *homemade* fire coats. Young Red kept pushing Johnny with his shoulder, shouting, "Keep moving, Johnny! Keep it moving!"

Johnny felt confidant with Red at his back. He knew Red would be as tough fighting a fire as he was fighting with his dukes. He also knew he could count on Red, no matter what the circumstance might be.

"C'mon! Move dat line in!" shouted Vinnie, leaning his shoulder into Red's back.

The knowledge of the trapped people scared Johnny. *I gotta get this fire out before it gets them.* He inched himself along the red-hot, smoke-filled hallway. "Oh shit, it is hot!" he shouted, wondering how long he could endure the heat.

With his eyes closed, he moved in on the wall of fire and smoke that awaited them. No sooner had he opened his eyes than he saw right before him an orange glow. *Oh great. Now I can put this thing out.*

"Go get it, Johnny!" shouted Red, who leaned hard against Johnny's back. And likewise, Vinnie McCarty pressed hard against Red's back.

"You know, you got some ass there, kid. Like a broad's ass," said Vinnie. In the middle of all the gagging and coughing, a hardy round of laughter erupted.

"Why don't ya kiss it, McCarthy," retorted Red, to another round of laughter.

The banter boosted Johnny's courage, just what he needed to keep him moving in against the dreaded Red Devil.

"It is hot!" Johnny again shouted.

"Cool it down, Johnny!" shouted Red, still pushing hard against O'Hara's back. "Over ya head and all around." Red sighed when the water finally cooled and showered down on them, providing some relief from the scalding steam.

On all fours, they advanced along the hallway. Red continued coaxing him: "Dat's it, Johnny. Straight ahead, all around and overhead." He knew all the expressions firemen used to encourage each other; he'd heard them many times before.

Johnny kept the water aimed high, slamming off the ceiling. The remaining air in the hallway was still superhot, but the flames were diminishing. "More pressure!" he shouted. He could hear his call for more water being repeated by others. He even heard Brogan outside shouting through his speaking trumpet, "More pressure!"

Finally, Batesy's men started stretching their own hose line as a precaution, should the fire extend to adjoining structures. Once he knocked the fire down in the hallway, Johnny hurried to the base of the stairwell and shot a stream of water right up the well, knocking down any visible fire. He then rushed back to the apartment, where the fire had originated. With the protection of the new coats, they moved in on the fire, dousing it to a point where they saw no more flames. And they knew the fire had been extinguished when they heard loud cheering erupt from the crowd outside on the street. The people always cheered when the water started showering them, when the flames had ceased to be.

With the fire extinguished, Johnny, Red, and the others rushed outside to suck in some of that fresh air. Jansen also rushed there, not to suck in the air but rather to again closely check out Red. What was it about Red that had him so spoofed?

"Bastards, bastards," Batesy shouted, slamming his helmet against his pumper. The fact that the Yimmies put the fire out so quickly and that his men weren't able to take control of the hydrant had him livid. He then roared for all to hear, a threat to Thomas Brogan and his men, "You scum, you! You'll pay dearly! This is not over!"

* * * * *

The Yimmies were back in their *unauthorized* firehouse, a *rickety old shed*, rubbing down and feeding the horses and cleaning their equipment, preparing for the next fire. Brogan used the time to critique the fire, which is done after every fire. The critique included praise where it was due. He congratulated Red and Battler for saving the hydrant. He would also use the opportunity to discuss weaknesses displayed if there were any. But he found none this time.

The men had nothing but praise for the *homemade* fire coats. They were elated with the protection the coats afforded them against the heat and hot water, and how they were able to move in on the fire much faster.

"One more point and then you're dismissed. Except for O'Hara here, who I want to see in me office." He then commended Red Hester and Vinnie McCarthy for their life-saving heroics on the ladder. "See you at the next fire." With that said, the members departed and Johnny and Brogan stepped into the makeshift office, an area about 10' by 15', separated from the rest of the station by a crude wall made of wood planking. In the so-called office was a wood plank table/desk, a couple of chairs, two file cabinets and other odds and ends.

The smiling Brogan grabbed Johnny's hand and shook it. "You did a great job at the fire. You guys proved to me that my fire coat does make a difference. And now I know that it will prove to be helpful in saving lives."

"Yes, it sure did. Not once did I feel the hot water through it. And as far as me doing a great job, well, I couldn't have done it without Red at my back," insisted Johnny.

"You know, for a kid, you displayed true leadership. Yer instincts. The way you led the team, or should I say kids, into the fire with the hose line. And I know Red was damned good. But it was you who displayed the leadership, Johnny. The kind of natural ability most people don't possess. You got a future if you use yer head."

Johnny was red-faced with embarrassment. "I . . . I learned that from you, Mr. Brogan. You're my idol; my hero. When I grow up, I wanna be just like you."

"I'm your hero? You wanna be like me?" said Brogan, really taken aback. "But why?"

"Because you got all the money. You're the real American hero. Just like all the rich people. Like the big shots."

Brogan smiled as he looked up. "Yer kidding me, aren't you?"

* * * * *

Charlton Bimsbey sat at his desk in his spacious office located on the fifth floor of *The Bimsbey Building,* an office building on Fifth Avenue, which he owned. A copy of the morning issue of the *Herald* was spread across the cluttered desktop. On the wall directly behind the large mahogany desk were two sizeable paintings. One painting portrayed a young woman with beautiful, flaming red hair. The painting was bordered in a thick, hand-carved gold frame that distinguished itself on the dark, floral wallpaper. Hanging next to it, in an equally attractive frame, the other painting had the same size landscape but of an unusually large black stallion pulling an unusually large white coach.

English-born Charlton Bimsbey was one of New York's leading bankers, with large investments in many of America's leading industries, including the insurance business. While hardly known to the public, he was prominent and powerful in financial circles throughout the nation.

"Looks like it will soon be the north against the south," he said, turning his head, glancing at the woman's portrait.

"You really think so?" asked Bailey.

"Yes," continued Bimsbey. "Those South Carolinians are threatening to leave the Union. My senses tell me they will."

"If so, it will be a short thing," said Bailey, speaking with confidence.

Bimsbey told him to take a seat, pointing to a cushioned armchair, a twin of the one Bimsbey sat on.

"That's not what I see. Be long and bloody," said Bimsbey. "Painful for the cannon fodder, the warriors that is. But it'll be very profitable for those of us who will supply the warriors their weaponry. On both sides, mind you." He chuckled. "That's why we are investing in a war."

"Your insight is generally accurate," said Bailey.

"Now for business. You still have that Batesy fellow working for you?"

"Yes, Charlton. Why?" asked Bill Bailey, a well-known restaurateur, financed by Bimsbey.

"Still a firebrand stirring up those Know Nothings?"

"Very much so, sir," answered Bailey. "He led the charge at yesterday's battle royal at that fire on the west side."

"True he utterly despises all foreigners?" Bimsbey hardly looked at Bailey, refusing to take his eyes off of the young woman's portrait.

"Absolutely. He'd have them all shipped back. Especially the donkeys."

Bimsbey then asked, "Is he a good shit-stirrer? I mean, can he incite people to the point of fighting? Taking the law into their own hands?"

"The best, sir. A true leader with both brawn and brain. And at twenty-two, he's already foreman of the fire company."

"Do you hold much sway over him?" Bimsbey's gaze at the young redhead gave way to a pleasant smile.

"Yes. As long as he works for me. Especially, if he wants to run this place, which I've promised him. A position he'd do anything for."

Just what Bimsbey wanted to hear.

"Is that big blond-headed lad still his right-hand man? The one Mason. Or is it Jason?" Bimsbey's pretense not to know Jansen didn't fool Bailey. He knew he knew him; that Jansen carried out some nasty deeds for him. Of course, Bailey did not know the nature of those deeds, nor did he ask.

"You mean Chuck Jansen. Yes. Still alive and kicking. Literally. Kicking people's asses," said Bailey. Although Bailey wanted to challenge him on his Jansen charade, he thought it best not too. "Still terrorizing the immigrant community." He chuckled as did Bimsbey.

"Listen to this," Bimsbey read from the *Herald.* "'. . . Immigrant Fire Company Saves Three Going Where Yanks Would Not . . .' The *Herald's* saying the foreigners got more balls than their American counterparts. The editorial also stressed that in the fight for the hydrant, the foreigners beat back the natives."

"That'll boil Batesy's blood. He'll want revenge," said Bailey.

Bimsbey smiled, pleased with that knowledge. "To what extremes will he go?"

"To any, sir." Bailey's look hardened. He put a cigarette to his lips.

"Don't light it. Smoke outside," Bimsbey reprimanded.

"Batesy will go to any extreme necessary."

"This is our opportunity to keep them at each other's throats," said Bimsbey, forgetting himself.

"Keep who at each other's throats, sir?" queried Bailey.

"Oh, nothing. Nothing at all, just talking to myself."

Bailey's eyes narrowed while thinking hard about what Bimsbey meant. *Does he mean to keep our American lads constantly at war with the foreigners?*

"I see you're thinking about what I said . . . it's a necessary evil for capitalism to survive and thrive. We must pit them against each other. Our boys," he laughed, his hand over his heart, "and the foreigners. To have them always attacking each other. Or else they will be attacking us. Their employers, that is."

"Sounds like you wrote that divisive editorial in the *Herald*," Bailey paused; a look of devilment in his eyes.

Bimsbey grunted, but did not answer him.

"Now I know what you mean, Charlton."

Bimsbey descended from the Marquis of Hastings, a past leader of one of the richest trading companies in the world, the British East India Company. The Marquis dispatched Bimsbey's father, also named Charlton, to America in 1812 to act on behalf of the company, for business building purposes. He arrived shortly before war broke out between the two countries. No problem for him. His loyalty belonged to the company's ability to profit. Didn't really care who won the war, England or America. Young Bimsbey had remained in England to finish his education, which he completed at the University of Oxford in 1827. Then, at 21 years, he joined his father in the States. For business reasons, through a tutor, he softened his "harsh" English accent.

"Would he be crazy enough to organize an assault on their community?" asked Bimsbey. "I mean burn down an establishment that hires only foreigners?" He opened a cigar box, offering one to Bailey, which he took. Bailey wondered why he offered him a cigar when he just told him not to smoke in the office. Then Bimsbey took from the cigar box a diamond-studded cigar cutter. "Use this," he said. "There'll be no loose tobacco floating around in your mouth. And do me a favor. Smoke it outside."

"Why did you give me a cigar if you don't want me to smoke it?"

"An opportunity to show off my new cigar cutter," said Bimsbey with a chuckle. Bailey's answers concerning Batesy had pleased him immensely. "Can he get his people to assault them?" He finally took his eyes off the redhead, anxious to hear his response.

"Yesterday, he just about said that at that fire. Didn't like losing to the foreigners who he calls *Yimmies.*"

"It's all good," said Bimsbey. "Such a confrontation would be wonderful. It would go a long way to achieving what has to be done."

"Yes. Yes it would," Bailey replied. Without being told what to do by Bimsbey, he knew what he wanted done and would make sure Batesy would carry it out. "I have one question, Charlton. You've been staring at that painting. If you don't mind me asking, who is she?"

"A beautiful woman. That's who. I'd have married her if things went my way. Poor thing. She disappeared five years, two months, and thirteen days ago. Could even be dead."

CHAPTER FOUR

SUNDAY AFTERNOON, JULY 14 – From the top floor landing of the tenement where he lived, Johnny O'Hara heard that sound he loved so well coming from the roof; the haunting music of the Ulliean Pipes. Playing the pipes, he knew, was his good friend Red Hester. The heart-wrenching sound drifted through the open roof door, down the stairs to his ears. Quickening his pace, he darted up the remaining flight of squeaky steps, two at time, towards the daylight on the other side of the open bulkhead door.

"Oh, shyte man," said Red, bursting with laughter. He couldn't help but laugh at the look of disgust on Johnny's face as he stepped out onto the roof only to be hit on the forehead with pigeon shit.

"Ach," grunted Johnny, wiping his forehead clean with a swipe of the back of his hand that he then wiped clean on the leg of his trousers. Although preoccupied with the bird shit, it didn't stop him from noticing that Red's feet were again wrapped in rags. It bugged the hell out of him that his friend did not own a pair of shoes. When hanging around the firehouse, Red often wore his fire boots.

Red enjoyed it when his biggest fan, Johnny, would plop down beside him, rest his head against the parapet wall, then close his eyes and let his mind drift. The sound—similar to but not the same as bagpipes—always brought back those lingering and disturbing memories of his short life in Ireland. Johnny would remember the local Ulliean piper playing at the burials of his siblings, relatives and friends, all victims of the *avoidable* Great Hunger. From what Johnny could remember, the piper was always playing.

But this time he didn't plop himself down. He decided that first he would get a birds-eye-view of the block from his corner rooftop, high above many crudely constructed shanties. He tramped toward the roof's edge, his thumping boots making splashing sounds as he stepped in scattered puddles of rainwater from the recent downpour.

"Oh fuck no! Not again," Johnny swore, repulsed by the sight at the other end of the block, at the corner of 33rd and Ninth Avenue.

"Wots da matta?" Red sprang to his feet to join Johnny at the wall.

A large group of Batesy's thugs were lining up to do battle. To Johnny they seemed to fill the intersection. Many of them wore black pull-over masks with eye openings. They all carried a weapon of some sort: clubs, brickbats, or pipes, including a few who boldly flaunted pistols. Pedestrians, fearing for their safety, rushed from the area.

They maneuvered in what looked like a disciplined military formation: five men across and nine rows deep, with the obvious leader out front. Johnny could see them but not hear them. The leader, a tall blond man, directed them with silent hand signals.

Red handed Johnny the pipes, shouting, "Hold dis 'til I gets back," then bolted for the roof door.

"Where ye going?" asked Johnny.

"Get de boys. Weez gonna kick sum asses," Red answered in his child-like, tough-guy voice, taking off in a flash.

"Why the hell you have to be fighting all the time?" Johnny yelled after him.

Johnny continued watching with revulsion the all too familiar scene: a gang attacking his neighborhood. They spilled into his block, like disciplined soldiers, trotting on the soles of their shoes—a few being barefooted—through the putrid mix of compressed horse droppings, garbage, soil, and water puddles that covered the earthen roadway. One of them carried a fireman's axe, the sight of which scared Johnny. Visions of the man driving the pointed edge of the axe into Red's head flashed through his mind. Grinding his teeth, flexing his arms until they shook, he repeated himself, giving out with a boyish roar, "Why the hell do you got to all the time fight?"

Around the corner on Tenth Avenue, where they were returning from the grocery, Johnny's mother strolled hand in hand with Katie. Mrs. O'Hara had young Katie giggling with tales from the *old sod;* the kind of stories the young one loved. Suddenly, from behind, she heard the sounds of excited men and boys running and shouting. When she turned and saw them, some of whom were carrying weapons and gathering to fight, she could not help being petrified. *Mother of God, there's going to be another fight*, she shuddered. She yanked Katie, pulling her like a rag doll, out of the way of the young men. "Ah bejasus! I hope it's not dem Yanks agin," she shouted.

The blond giant kept to the fore of his gang of street fighters as they rushed into Young Immigrant turf. Pointing with his right hand, he commanded three of his mates, whispering with his uniquely deep voice, "Go, go." Peeling off from the group, the three thugs ran through an empty lot of waist-high lush green brush. Two of them were able to avoid the deflated remains of a once-large hog, but the other was not so fortunate. He stepped right into the stinking carcass. He *phewed*, cringed his nose, and closed his eyes all at once. In his hand he carried a long-handled bolt cutter—the kind used by firemen—while each of the others carried two large bottles filled with paraffin.

The young ruffians, who were members of the *Young Immigrants*—a local gang made up mostly of the sons of Irish, German and Italian immigrants—charged into 33rd Street, immediately making contact with the attackers who were howling, a tactic used to scare their opponents. Fists flew, clubs cracked heads and crunched bones, blood splashed as knives slashed and gunfire crackled. Those who were knocked unconscious fell upon the fetid mixture that covered the street. Some landed face down, but most of them were quickly revived by the horrid stench.

* * * * *

"Gentlemen, I called this meeting for our mutual benefit," said Charlton Bimsbey, looking down his nose at his associates. "We are part of a group of people who controls the wealth in this nation. Together, we create the jobs. Can you imagine the power we could wield if we worked together?"

His colleagues liked very much what he said, which they demonstrated with raised eyebrows, glee-filled eyes and a simple nod of the head.

"And by going it alone," he continued, "as we have been doing, we are hurting ourselves and our interests, both present and future."

Bimsbey, a 49 year-old free spirit, had a full head of long, black hair that he kept in a tail at the back of his head, when going about his normal routine. When necessary for him to be in public, he would wear his hair down, all around his head, so as not to be recognized.

"We must work together and consolidate our efforts here and elsewhere. Our good friend Jacob," he pointed to Jacob Bosh, New York's foremost textile producer, "is already doing business in several states. Branching out, as we say. He's also linked to the gold mining industry, which I am heavily invested in. That too, we will eventually control. As for myself, I have recently added to my assets some war related industries."

"Very wise indeed," agreed one of his guests while others nodded their heads in agreement, with the exception of Jacob Bosh.

"Let me finish," he said. "We must also give greater support to the effort underway to establish a paid fire department here in the city. The volunteer system has to go. It's no longer efficient. Costing us fortunes. The city is too big. Too many people for a volunteer fire department."

Jacob Bosh, from wealthy English stock, had successfully expanded his textile operations into New Jersey and Pennsylvania. He also supplied equipment to the mining industry in Colorado and California. Wisely, he brought everything to the miner rather than the miner having to go to him. Everything! From shovels and picks to the rail tracks and bucket cars needed to transport the precious metals to the earth's surface. And once up top, it was his equipment they used to separate the gold and silver from the rock. Bosh also believed there would be a nasty war, but his conscience forbade him to profit from it.

"We want to control all the major industries," Bimsbey continued. "Control across the nation will increase our wealth and influence a hundredfold, to say the least." He paused, studying the reaction of the others, then said, "And control the workingman."

"What do you mean, control the workingman?" asked an irritated Jacob Bosh.

"Just as I said. It is we who must set their pay scales and work conditions. Not those rebellious upstart unions they have speaking for them." Bimsbey stared coolly at Bosh, never raising his voice, which he never did, especially when doing business with people whose cooperation he sought.

Speaking softly, Bosh replied, "And what are these *rebellious* ones asking for?"

"You know what they want, Jacob? To break us. To take our wealth for themselves. The drunken swill." He cringed his nose and gasped, as if reacting to a repugnant odor.

With the exception of Jacob Bosh, the other empire builders Jules Rothchilder, Prago Santan, and Leonard Morgan agreed wholeheartedly with him. Rothchilder, the only son of the Rothchilder's, would inherit their financial empire that controlled considerable wealth in Europe. Santan, an American-born descendent of the Santans of Sweden, operated and built railroads in several states. He too operated with wealth from abroad. Leonard Morgan specialized in investment banking. One of his specialties was raising venture capital for major, proven investments. His firm ran several coal mining companies in Pennsylvania and West Virginia. Not in attendance were the Rockfelts and Astorias, the giants of the oil and insurance industries. Not only were they in full support of Bimsbey's proposals, but were leading the charge for him in Albany to get rid of the City's volunteer firemen. This idea was originally proposed by Leonard Morgan who wanted a paid fire department to replace the volunteers. He estimated that change would save their underwriting interests many millions of dollars each year.

"I know what the unions want," Jacob said. "They don't want the working man to work seven days a week, fourteen or more hours a day and still go hungry. They want quality time at home with their wives and children. To make a decent wage. To sum it all up, they want to be treated with a little dignity. And we want to deprive them of that? Is that right, Charlton?"

"Yes, Jacob."

Bimsbey carried on the business of the British East India Company. The company wanted to spread its tentacles throughout the United States, from coast to coast, from border to border.

Much of the wealth of the English-dominated Company was originally derived from illegitimate trading and coercion. The East India Company long monopolized India's exporting business, entirely controlling its tea trade. The company got a cut on everything shipped from Indian ports, including Indian opium.

In the early 1800s, when the company had financial problems, it sold Indian grown opium to dealers in China. China's Qing Government had declared opium use, which was in big demand, illegal and made every effort to stop the trade. Emperor Qing sent a commissioner to Guangzhou to put an end to the illegal opium traffic. The commissioner took possession of the opium stocks owned by Chinese dealers, then detained the entire foreign community and seized and destroyed tens of thousands of chests of British opium. But England's governmental leaders retaliated with a punitive expedition, thus initiating the first Anglo-Chinese war, known as the Opium War (1839-42). The unprepared Chinese were disastrously defeated, resulting in The Treaty of Nanjing (1842) where China ceded many concessions to the English, including the island of Hong Kong and made the British opium trade legal throughout China.

* * * * *

From his rooftop perch, Johnny watched the three young men running through the lot until they disappeared behind another crude tenant house. Then he ran to the corner of the roof, still watching. For a moment the sight of so many men brawling so violently blurred before him: bloodied men clubbing and punching each other while other men were being knocked to the ground and stomped on. He saw screaming mothers dragging their children to safety. He heard the dogs in the lumberyard growling and barking above the dull thudding, slapping sounds of hand to hand combat. And, of course, the gun shots; several of them. At the same time he could clearly see that the three men who had run behind the tenant house were now sprinting across the street to North River Lumber.

One of them ran to a new firehouse that was near completion in the lot adjacent to the lumberyard. That structure was being built and paid for compliments of the owners of the lumberyard. It would be the first all-immigrant fire station in the city and would house the fire company to which Johnny belonged.

Using a hammer, the thug broke the door's single windowpane, through which he poured paraffin. He then splashed the remaining fluid on the building's wood facing and ignited it. A red-orange blaze flashed inside, quickly spreading across the wooden flooring and walls, rapidly producing a lot of smoke that began to fill the inside of the building. The fire then lapped from the window, creating a fast-expanding column of black smoke that rolled skyward.

The nervous man rushed to join his two comrades at the lumberyard gate. Just then one of the men got off three deadly shots at the attacking dogs. The first snapping mongrel that had his snout pushed through the space where the chained yard gates joined was shot right through the top of his snout between the eyes.

With the dogs silenced, they used the fireman's bolt-cutter to cut open the padlock that secured the chain. They ran around to the rear of the structure that housed the offices on the second floor and a shed downstairs, where they again used the bolt cutter to snap another lock.

By this time a growing ball of fire was consuming the façade of the new firehouse, greatly adding to the people's agitation and sorrow. The huge column of smoke from the fire that rolled up to the heavens was visible for miles around.

Johnny doubled back across the roof to watch the raging battle on the street. He was just in time to see his broad-shouldered friend, little five-foot-tall Red Hester dive from a flatbed wagon onto the back of a much bigger opponent. He caught him around the throat, locking him in a choke hold. It wasn't long before the wildly swinging opponent passed out and collapsed. Red then turned on an attacker, not much taller than himself. Red stepped to the side to avoid being hit, at the same time threw a hard left hook that caught the attacker flush on his jaw, dropping him on one knee. As Johnny admired his buddy's fighting abilities, Red drove his foot into his stunned rival's privates. "Ouch," muttered Johnny, thinking of how much that must have hurt. With that guy out of the way, the over-confident Red jumped on the gang leader's back, clawing at his throat, immediately drawing blood. This blond-headed monster, who must have weighed over 220 pounds—almost three times Red's weight—gave out with a deep roar and flipped Red from his back. Red landed face down into the muck-covered street, making a thudding, splashing sound. He planted his shoe on Red's back and pressed real hard, causing him great pain.

"Get off me," Red screamed.

"I'm saving your ass for another day, Hester," shouted the gang leader, startling Red.

Oh shit! Red needs help. Johnny bolted from the roof.

The man with the fireman's axe attacked the water plug in front of the lumberyard, the only hydrant on the block. With one powerful over-the-shoulder blow from the hammerhead of the axe, he severed the hydrant's hose connection, making it impossible for a fire engine to hook up to it for a water supply.

The three men who lit up the firehouse were now on the second floor in the offices, dousing the place with paraffin. They saturated the whole place with the combustible liquid, then backed out through the rear exit.

"Dese bums really tink dey gonna take our jobs and git away wid it?" whispered one of them. He then ignited a rag and threw it inside. With a sudden boom and a flash of light, the place lit up. Fire raced across the floor and up the stairs. In a matter of moments, both floors were ablaze.

When Mrs. O'Hara heard the gunshots, she shoved her daughter, Katie, behind a parked *dung wagon*, then used her trembling body to shield her daughter's petite form, screaming at her, "Stay behind me!" A couple of bullets pinged and popped around them, splintering the wagon's wooden siding. The horse bucked, then took off in a gallop, pulling the objectionable smelling wagon with it, exposing Mrs. O'Hara and Katie to the gunfire. Without warning the horse collapsed, its legs jerking then going limp.

As everybody's attention turned to the fire inside the office/shed complex, an explosion blew out many of the windows on the second floor, sending burning debris out into the street, some of it hitting the combatants. Immediately thereafter, fire burst through the second-story's front windows. Still the skirmishing continued.

More gun blasts followed, one of which dropped another brawler on the seat of his pants, holding his bicep. He could not hide the pain he felt.

Still protecting Katie with her body, Mrs. O'Hara ran for the corner, pushing the little one in front of her. Katie kept looking back, watching the shootout and the rapidly progressing fires, rather than where she was going.

CHAPTER FIVE

"Charlton, please. Get to the point," insisted Prago Santan, as he slid his hands into a pair of white linen gloves and then lit a Cuban cigar. Immediately, the smoke wafted, turning the clear air into a smoky haze.

"Is it necessary for you to smoke that thing in here?" asked Bimsbey, who normally forbade people smoking in his office.

"That's hypocritical for you to be concerned the smoke will contaminate the atmosphere, when it's already polluted with your evil intentions," interjected a sour Bosh.

Prago smiled, but said nothing.

Morgan and Rothchilder chuckled, nodding agreeably to Bosh even though they were part and parcel of Bimsbey's *evil intentions.*

The five of them looked lost sitting at the huge conference table that could comfortably seat upwards to 20 people. And as usual, Bimsbey sat at a chair that gave him an unobstructed view of the painting of the beautiful young redheaded woman.

Believe it or not, this table top came right through that window there." Bimsbey directed their attention to one of the many windows that ran across the street-side front wall of his office. Inlaid dead center on the table surface was a life-like image of a nude woman.

"I am glad you all want to hear more," said Bimbsey. "First, I want us to work together to monopolize our industries, thereby enabling us to control pricing and wages."

"But the Feds frown on such monopolies. They're already grumbling about it in Washington," said Jacob Bosh. "And also, is it honorable to do such a thing? I mean, how much wealth do we have to control?"

Bimsbey's smiling eyes again narrowed. "To answer your second question first, as much as possible. And as far as the Feds getting involved, we have many powerful friends in Washington." He then shouted, "What's honorable to you, my dear friend, means nothing to them. It's all about putting money in their pockets. That'll get them to do our bidding."

Jacob, who rarely smiled or laughed, this time roared with laughter, "Leeches! Yes, leeches. They're everywhere." He gave out with a high-pitched cackle, bringing a chuckle from the others. "I can see it now," he continued. "From this day forward, we will no longer be a democracy of the people, by the people, and for the people. It will be a capitalistic democracy, a democracy of the rich, by the rich, and for the rich. "That's not what our founding fathers had in mind."

"So as you can see, Jacob, it's business as usual. We're capitalists first. We want to make money, not lose it or give it away," said Morgan.

"But there is also an emerging problem we must deal with, or we will certainly have to share *our* wealth," said Bimbsey. "Our wealth," he reiterated loudly, becoming much more serious in tone. "And that is the working scum. More and more they are demanding higher wages and better working conditions."

"They should thank us for providing them with jobs," insisted Jules Rothchilder. "Lousy ingrates, I tell you."

"You too, Jules." Bosh shook his head, demonstrating his displeasure with Rothchilder's view. Although all of Bosh's business enterprises were successful and his peers admired his brilliance in business, some even idolized him; he never ill-treated his employees. He believed in a fair wage, for a fair day's work and that one's employees must be treated with dignity. "But don't we need them as much as they need us?" Bosh continued.

"How do we counter this pending revolution?" asked Morgan. "What do you propose? If you haven't already begun the counter offensive."

"First, let me spell out the solution," Bimsbey said. "The immigrants that we are supposed to hate." He paused and smiled. "Actually we all love them. Right?" He again paused and looked at the other smiling, nodding faces.

Morgan laughed aloud. "Yes, how we love the cheap labor."

Bosh cut in, but he wasn't smiling. "And we *encourage* an atmosphere of hating immigrants. Just to keep the people divided. What hypocrites. What kind of Christians are you?" He pointed to Rothchilder and asked, "And what kind of a Jew are you, Jules?"

"Please, Jacob. Enough of your spiritual rhetoric. Let me continue," Bimsbey insisted. "Right you are, Leonard. Cheap labor. And immigrants will always guarantee us cheap labor. And we'll keep the immigrants in line by using the coloreds. And when the North prevails in this war, which it will, there will be a huge surplus of cheap colored labor. And through the cheap labor we will keep the workers at each other's throats: natives fighting the immigrants and the immigrants fighting the coloreds. "And

29

you're right," he continued. "*Our* plan of attack," he laughed, "is already underway."

"Our plan, as you call it, seems perfect," chuckled Prago, who had no input into the plan, just like his counterparts, and that's the way they preferred it. Let Bimsbey do the planning and scheming.

"What have you done?" asked Bosh.

Bimsbey replied, "Right now our American boys are attacking."

"What!" Bosh jumped to his feet, cutting Bimsbey off. "Attacking . . . attacking! What the hell are you talking about? Attacking who?"

Grinning, Bimsbey replied in a soft tone, "The foreign trash who is taking the jobs from our American boys." Again he laughed. "Those terrible foreigners who do the work for less money."

"What do you mean *attacking*?" Bosh repeated.

"Just as I said, Jacob. Attacking. By now *our* boys are beating the pants off of that immigrant scum over by 33rd Street. And they're probably readying to burn down that illegal firehouse the Golden Brothers have built for the neighborhood at their riverside lumberyard, in which they plan to move into shortly. I don't know exactly when, but very soon. And the lumberyard will also be burned. The Golden's, those Irish bastards, only hire immigrant help. For less money." He laughed hardily. "Can you imagine that? They hire cheap labor." His face reflected the pleasure he felt.

"Isn't that the height of hypocrisy?" snapped Bosh.

"No! It's capitalism at its best," said Bimsbey.

"No," snapped Bosh. "Capitalism at its best is when an employer treats his employees with respect and gives them a fair wage for a fair days work."

"Yes, Charlton. I like what I hear," said Rothchilder. "We will be using both sides to our mutual benefit. I love that. And they'll be too busy fighting each other."

"And so do I," said Morgan. He laughed aloud. "Charlton, Charlton. You are good. I know exactly where you are heading with this."

"Good. Then let me continue," said Bimsbey. "This is only the beginning. When we have the workers warring with each other, they won't have the time or the energy to go after the real culprits." A smile broke on his face. "Need I say who they are?" He laughed aloud. "Just as Jules said. The truth of the matter, native or immigrant, it makes no difference. Those dumb things will never figure that out. And to make sure they don't, we will have our agents involved with all the groups." Bimsbey paused to look at the smiling faces of his evil counterparts, with Bosh being the one exception.

"Don't like this at all," shouted Bosh. "I repeat myself? What kind of Christian gentlemen are—" He stopped abruptly, glancing at Jules Rothschilds the Jew. "I should say, God-fearing gentlemen are we? To take advantage of, or should I say, to rob the poor workingman that can hardly feed himself. His family."

"You don't have much of a choice, Jacob. The scum will take everything from you if you let them. Rob them before they rob you," Bimsbey shouted back.

* * * * *

Mrs. O'Hara was petrified by the fire and the intensity of the heat on her body. She feared the whole block would burn. "God help us," she screamed.

Stacks of lumber burning out of control gave off great columns of smoke. No sooner had Johnny O'Hara's mother and sister, Katie, found safety around the corner when gunfire again rang out. *Ping! Pang!* The bullets slammed off the sidewalk, chipping away the wall of the building where they crouched. Mrs. O'Hara's body jolted, and without a sound she buckled, slamming to the ground. Her eyes rolled back in her head.

Johnny rocketed down the four flights of dimly-lit creaky stairs to the main entrance, taking three steps at a time, where he witnessed one final shootout through thick smoke and a shower of embers raining down from the raging blaze across the street. A member of the attacking gang dropped on his back. Another man was hit in the arm. He ran off, screaming in pain.

"Shit! We hit the woman," the blond-headed gang leader yelled while gripping the collar of his wounded friend and yanking him to his feet.

That was when Johnny saw his ashen-faced sister Katie, who just last week celebrated her ninth birthday, standing dumbfounded over the still body of their mother, her head laying in a spreading pool of blood. Without regard for his own safety, he ran to them. He pulled Katie down flat on the muddy street. At that same time, he heard the blond-haired, blue-eyed man shout in his unusually deep voice, "No big deal. Probably a dung cleaner's wife."

The man then aimed his pistol at O'Hara. Freezing in place, O'Hara glared into the man's eyes for a few seconds that seemed like an eternity—a face he'd never forget—waiting to hear the gun explode. Instead he heard the repeated clicking sound of a pistol misfiring. At the same time, he heard Red's voice shouting, "Run, O'Hara, run!" The blond-headed leader then faced Red and grinned. "When I'm ready, I'll get you," he shouted, jabbing his finger at him.

"You and what army?" challenged Red.

Oh no. Not Red too! Losing his cool, O'Hara lunged at the blond-headed man, reaching for the pistol. But he sidestepped O'Hara and hit him a glancing blow on the head with the pistol handle. Again he smiled at Red. "When I'm ready, Hester."

The man rushed off with his wounded comrade, practically carrying him, with O'Hara yelling after him. "I'll get you. I'll get you. I swear I will." His heart sank and his eyes filled with tears. His stomach felt queasy, devastated by the sight of his mother lying dead in her own blood.

"Sorry, O'Hara?" said Red, himself on the verge of crying, feeling genuine hurt for his friend.

"He killed me mom." Wiping the tears from his cheeks as if to hide the fact that he was crying, O'Hara grabbed Red's shoulders. "Thought he was going to shoot you. My best friend." He wanted to embrace Red, but thought better of it. "If anything happened to you," he continued, "I'd shit. Why'd he call you Hester? How's he know you?" Rubbing his eyes, he gagged on the low hanging smoke.

"Yeah," Red replied. He was also baffled about who this guy was.

O'Hara felt strange, wondering why he wanted to hug Red.

From the back of the yard, behind the two-story building that housed offices upstairs and a shed on the main floor, came a loud crashing sound—like an explosion, sending a huge ball of fire shooting skyward. With it came a great roar from the spectators.

Young O'Hara often found himself envious of Red's looks, and would often tease him, saying, "With those looks, you should have been a girl," which would piss Red off to no end. And as soon as Red would come at him with his fists ready, O'Hara would back up in a fit of laughter and take it all back.

And most times Red would say, "One a dese days ya gonna get it," as he threw a punch at the air. O'Hara considered Red the toughest little guy he ever met: utterly fearless. And capable of punching harder than most guys he knew.

He often thought he worried too much about Red's welfare. Like it bothered him that Red's feet were often wrapped in rags, or plain shoeless, and that he never wore a decent stitch of clothes; always wearing frayed clothing. Often his knees were through his pants and his elbows through his shirtsleeves. Once, Red had a hole in the seat of his pants that showed flesh where there should have been underwear. That made him curse Red's mom for neglecting him so. Then he cursed himself for thinking about Red when he should be mourning his own mother's horrible death.

* * * * *

"Right about now, our boys ...." Bimsbey stopped and ha, ha ha'd, heartily. "Our boys. Oh how I enjoy saying that."

As the others chuckled, Jacob Bosh lodged his protest. "Shame on you. I don't even know what I'm doing here."

"You're here for the same reason we are. To protect *our* financial interests," replied Bimsbey without looking his way. "Now, if I may continue. Right about now, our boys should be finishing up their assault on the Yimmies, and the burning of the lumberyard and the firehouse should be well underway." Jumping to his feet all excited, Bimsbey shouted, "Look! Look there." He motioned with a velvety hand for them to look out the large windows that lined the front of his office. Getting to their feet like thrilled children, his associates saw the huge column of rising smoke off in the distance.

"Who are *our boys*? These fine Americans you speak of?" asked the agitated Bosh. His arms were trembling.

"A mix of Bowery Boys, Know Nothings, and volleys, of course. All dedicated to saving America." Again Bimsbey laughed.

"The firemen," shouted Bosh, "the very men whose greatest joy in life is the Volunteer Fire Department that you want to destroy. You have them carrying out your dastardly acts? You hypocrite, you."

"It's business, my good friend."

"They'll be busy attacking each other, blaming each other for their economic woes," said Prago with a chuckle.

"The critical point here is that we get agents into every possible group," said Bimsbey. "To keep them at each other's throats. Otherwise, they'll unite and be at our throats. Then we'll *have to* share the wealth. That's *not* an option."

"Exactly," said Prago.

"That's it. Keep them at each other's throats," said Morgan, with a snobbish *phew* and a wave of the hand.

"And killing? Is that part of it too, Charlton?" snapped Bosh.

Bimsbey raised his shoulders. "Accidents happen. And we wouldn't be causing such accidents. Would we ever give such an order to kill someone?" He paused to stare at Bosh, no longer able to hide his annoyance with him. "Look at it this way, Jacob *my friend*. Without us, there would be no jobs to speak of. They'd not be able to provide for their families."

"Provide what?" shouted Bosh. "The lowest form of housing, minimal food. Many of the unfortunates wear rags and have no shoes. Is this what you call providing?"

"What would you propose, Jacob?"

"To share a little more of our vast fortunes, so that they could have a little more comfort. A little more quality time with their families."

"Don't be so naive, my friend. They'd only want more."

"But Charlton," Jules cut in. "What if things go wrong and somebody does die? We would be responsible."

"First of all, Jules, we'd never be directly involved. Others, not associated with us, would be responsible. And they're the ones doing the planning. Not us. We'll be far removed. If someone has to go to prison, it will not be us. And secondly, we'll use our established clout with the newspapers and city council. Once in a while, however, some lower level agent will have to pay dearly. I should mention too, that the police department will do our bidding."

"Sure. They'll have their hands out too. The corrupt so-and-so's," Bosh wouldn't let up. He kept looking them in the eye, hoping to gain an ally.

"Jacob, please." By then Prago Santan's tolerance of Bosh's continuous challenges began to deminish. "Tell him, Charlton. The city needs us." Prago removed his linen gloves after crushing out the lit end of his cigar, causing an even fouler odor drawing a sour look from Bimsbey. He slid the thin gloves up under the cuffs of his shirtsleeves.

"That's correct, my friend. We are the economic survival of New York City. So you see Jacob, our wealth is our protection. And that is all I have to say on the matter, my friends." Before anyone could reply, Bimsbey, sounding annoyed, growled, "Prago! Why do you wear gloves when you smoke those stink bombs?"

"The discoloration of the fingers." Prago gently fluttered his cigar holding fingers.

* * * * *

By now the conflagration had extended to several large structures. It created its own howling windstorm that spread the fire to the lumber storage sheds and even threatened the tenements that lined the other side of the street. Fortunately, the fiery embers that filled the air were blown to the west, out over the North river.

Repeatedly, the crowds of firewatchers were driven back and forth by the constant shifting heat and smoke, producing a great choir of shouts. The only people to run *towards* the heat and smoke—which they did with

35

great bravado—were the volunteers of the Young Immigrant Fire Company, who were still arriving to assist in putting out the conflagration. But there wasn't much they could do as the fire trucks had not yet arrived at the scene.

Needless to say, O'Hara was not helping with the fire. He and his sister were kneeling by their mother's body, as if guarding it. They would not leave it. With his powerful arms, he enveloped his sister, hoping to console her as she bawled hysterically; tears covering her childish face. Then when the smoke cleared for a second and she saw her mother's prematurely gray hair resting in a pool of her blood, she gave out with a spine-chilling wail and collapsed in his arms.

"My dear Katie," he whispered, cradling her in his arms. "I will take care of you. I promise." He stared at the backside of the blond-headed man, watching him hurrying away; pledging to himself: *And I will take care of you, too.*

Suddenly the fighting ended; the invaders took off. They had accomplished their mission. The firehouse and the lumberyard and all the jobs that went with it were gone.

"My joba, my joba," cried an Italian-accented man. "Where the hella the firemana?"

Some people cursed aloud and shouted threats to vent their upset. Others, especially the mothers, stood by while some wailed aloud and some silently wept, but all watched as their sole source of income burned up in flames.

"For sure it doesn't even matter if the firemen ever get here. The whole place is lost," said a man, speaking with a thick Irish lilt. He watched the heat waves fluttering through the air, reaching across the yard to the last two sheds back by the river. He watched as a light film of quivering smoke crept upwards along the surface of the structure's walls, then in an instant flash over igniting them. And just like that, the whole complex was in flames.

Chapter Six

It would be a while before any fire companies would arrive. Several blocks to the east on Broadway another group of mask-wearing attackers waited in hiding for the *Young Immigrant Engine Company,* that they knew would pass that way responding to the fire. Boldly, they didn't even try to hide from the public, some of who stopped to see what the masked men were up to.

The Young Immigrant Engine Company was the only fire company in the city made up *almost* exclusively of immigrants and their sons. All of its officers were foreign born and had planned to relocate permanently to the new firehouse no later than 6 pm this day. The dilapidated shed the *unchartered* fire company called their firehouse had been condemned and set to be demolished that evening, compliments of their Yankee opponents.

"Stop them at all costs," shouted Batesy when the fearsome-looking horses that pulled the fire engine came galloping up busy Broadway. Batesy was the attackers' young-looking leader, a man whose cold-dark eyes glared out from under his mask.

"You heard the boss," one of the gang members shouted as they brazenly stepped out in front of the oncoming horses, blocking their passage.

"Clear the roadway," the German-accented assistant foreman Hans Hauser, bellowed through his speaking trumpet, as his driver pulled hard on the reigns. The horses came to a sudden stop, two of them rising on their hind legs and one of them slipping on the muddy street, almost losing its footing.

"Fuck you, Yimmie garbage," a masked attacker shouted back.

Two of the thugs grabbed at Hans' red fireman's blouse, yanking him from his seat. Vinnie and Timothy McCarthy ran to his aid, along with the other firemen, only to be attacked by the hooded mob. Many an alarmed civilian stood by in wonderment, shaken by the riotous behavior.

Batesy then ordered, "Release the horses and break up the pumper . . . cut the hose. We'll put these donkeys and krauts out of business."

A major brouhaha erupted on the street, but the hard-fighting firemen, about ten strong and three young followers, were pummeled by about twenty of the attackers. Hans Hauser and Timothy McCarthy were knocked down and bloodied by blows from clubs. The remaining combatants banged away at each other—some wrestled on the muddy cobblestones. The punks then whipped out knives and started slashing at the firemen, holding them a bay.

Not long after the boys began smelling the fire did they see the smoke drifting over their heads, across Broadway.

"Whoa! Look at dat. Must be the whole place," shouted one jubilant attacker.

Another shouted, "Dere goes ya jobs ya scabs, ya."

As one group of thugs held the firemen at bay, the remainder of the gang lined up alongside the pumper and hose tender. One wagon at a time they rocked them higher and higher until the engines flipped over, spilling their contents on the roadway.

Several outraged spectators tried to rally their fellow citizens to help the firemen. But they were easily deterred from doing anything by the sight of a couple of revolvers suddenly pointed in their direction and the sound of a single shot fired into the air.

Then with their own axes and axes from the flipped engine, the assailants hacked away at the hose, at the brakes and pulleys on the pumper; then proceeded to chop away at the wagons. By that time, the thick smoke from the fire had begun banking down on the firemen and their attackers. Some of the masked men inhaled the smoke as if they enjoyed it; something only a fireman would do.

"You scab, Yimmies! That should put a halt to your gallop. Yoose took our jobs. If we can't get 'em back, hell, you ain't *gonna* have 'em either," one of the attackers shouted, bringing on a loud cheer from the rest of them.

"Where the hell are the coppers when you need them?" shouted a spectator, who shook with rage.

"So that's what it's all about, you Yankee shit, you," said one of the firemen, speaking with a German accent.

38

"Who are ye? Why ye hiding ya faces?" shouted Vinnie McCarthy, helping his brother to his feet.

"Shut your yap. You try to stop us, we'll cut you," the gang member shouted, waving a large shiny blade. The two gang members with the pistols again pointed them at the spectators, who were again edging forward.

"Let's go! Our work here is done," shouted the masked Batesy, with a wave of his arm.

* * * * *

It was common knowledge at the city council that the Young Immigrant Engine Company had never been accepted by most of the rank and file of New York's volunteer fire department. The immigrant volunteers were despised by the surrounding volunteer fire companies, the very companies it worked with at conflagrations. Hence, the reason the immigrants were never granted an official charter from the city, which they had long sought through legal channels. This discord between the fire companies contributed to the eventual decision to disband the volunteers and create a paid, professional department. Too often, fights between responding companies caused major delays in putting fires out, leading to untold destruction, meaning large losses for insurance companies.

Many times the city warned the so-called immigrant firemen—many of who were first-generation—to *cease and desist forthwith* (to disband their illegal fire company), which they did not. Consequently, the city ordered the demolition of the dilapidated shed they used as a firehouse. But the city did not know that the immigrants had a new firehouse. Only Batesy knew that and kept it to himself so the council would not interfere with his evil plans.

The volunteers and the gangs they associated with knew well that the immigrants—most of whom were members of the Immigrant Volunteer Fire Company—made up over ninety percent of North River Lumber's workforce and that was accomplished by working for lesser wages than their American counterparts, all part of Bimsbey's master plan. This, and the fact that they belonged to the Young Immigrants street gang, angered the Americans to no end.

That the attackers destroyed everything on the fire engine, including the engine itself, led the Young Immigrants to suspect that firemen were involved by preventing their company from getting to the fire, guaranteed that the fire would burn uncontrolled, doing maximum damage.

"Jesus, Mary, and Joseph! How will I feed me family," cried one teary-eyed lumberyard employee, who cringed from the heat.

"Fuck 'em where they breathe," shouted one laughing Yankee volunteer to another, who directed a weak stream of water at the fire. But they didn't laugh for long. A local man walked up behind the offending fireman, tapped him on the shoulder, and when he turned around, punched him in the mouth and knocked him out cold. Fortunately, the police stepped in just in time to prevent another large-scale brawl. By the time peace had returned, the big fellow that threw the punch had disappeared and the coppers were not able to make an arrest.

The neighbors were furious with the Yanks, knowing they made no effort at all to save any part of the lumberyard or new firehouse, which would save their jobs. There were several more scuffles between the locals and the firemen, and again the police had to separate the brawlers.

A police carriage that carried three plainclothes officers parked unnoticed at one end of the street. These stern-faced coppers were not there to keep order, but to put together a story acceptable to the public about the free-for-all and killing and the disastrous fire. They stepped down from the wagon and went their separate ways; their eyes scanned everyone and everything; their ears perked, listening to every voice and sound.

* * * * *

By the time the newly ordained priest had arrived right in the thick of the smoke to give O'Hara's mother her Last Rites, she had already turned blue. He could hardly see, rubbing his burning eyes uncontrollably. He coughed and gagged. He was on the verge of panicking and preparing to run from the smoke when Johnny said, "Drop to the prone." The priest did as he was told.

"That's so much better," he coughed out. He would give her Last Rights lying on the street under the smoke, which had not yet banked down to the street level.

The overly-enthusiastic, sweat-drenched young priest had run all the way from Holy Cross's rectory on 42nd Street. His frock stuck to his sweat-soaked back.

Somebody grumbled matter-of-factly, "What the hell took you so long, *fadda?*" The priest ignored him and continued to pray. Johnny nodded to the man, who he recognized as a friend of his mother, but said nothing. Red tugged at Johnny's shirtsleeve, asking, "Where ya gonna put her out so dat da peoples kin say goodbye?"

"You mean wake her. So the people can pay their last respects. Mr. Brady will probably let us use the backroom of the Shamrock."

"Ya tink dats respecting enuff?" asked Red.

"Yes. And it's think and respectful, not tink and respecting," Johnny corrected him.

"How 'bout ya place?" asked Red, ignoring Johnny's lesson in proper English.

"Whadda ye think?" said Johnny.

"Ah, ya do better askin da fadda. Dat Solomon's a weal bum. Ya want I do a job on dat bum?"

"No, Red. Don't do that. They'd put you in jail. You me best friend."

Red's face lit up. He idolized Johnny. "I your bess fren, Johnny?" he asked.

"You bet," said Johnny, speaking softly. "You always were. And I need your friendship now more than ever."

When the priest finished and got to his feet, he asked Red if he were Mrs. O'Hara's son. "No," said Johnny, stepping forward. "I am. I'm Johnny O'Hara. And Red Hester here is my best buddy."

"I'm Father Brian Rafferty from Holy Cross. On behalf of all at the parish, I want you to know we are deeply upset and hurt by your mother's passing. Your mom gave so much to the parish, I am told. She'll be missed immeasurably."

Red's eyes strained. *Wot da hell's dat word?*

"We must pray that the authorities get the man who did this horrible thing."

"Do you really think so, father?" Johnny asked in a not too convincing tone.

The priest nodded as if guaranteeing he'd be caught. "Sure. Look. The police are already investigating. Son, I must ask you—"

Johnny started crying and said, "First Father, I have to know why God let this happen to my mom. Why he took my father, my brother, and my beautiful sister during the Great Hunger? My mom was such a good person. Always praying. Always helping someone. And she always helped the church." Again Johnny sobbed, trying hard to control himself.

"It is God's will. You must believe that. And you must believe, too, that she is in a better place, in the hereafter with God our Father. Where we will all be one day. You must believe, son."

Johnny just shook his head.

"A funeral mass is being arranged for tomorrow."

"Father. Would it be disrespectful to use the back of the Shamrock Inn for the wake? If they cleaned it up? You know, looking nice. Mr. Brady said he'd keep it nice and respectful."

The Shamrock Inn was a run-of-the-mill neighborhood tavern on the corner of 33rd Street and Tenth Avenue. Father Rafferty knew of the place. "Why not hold the wake in your apartment?" he asked.

"Solomon will put us out today. Just like he did the Burgers and Malloys."

"That—" The priest shook his head. "The Shamrock will do just fine. We'll have the hearse come out to pick up her remains," Father Rafferty spoke softly, "right after the wake and take her to the church for tomorrow's mass. Ten o'clock. The driver will then take her to Potters Field."

"Bullshyte, fadda. Not Johnny's mudda," Red snapped. "She gotta git bedda dan dat."

"Hisst, Red," Johnny cut in, putting his finger to his mouth.

"That's okay," the priest said. "If you mean by the church that will be costly."

"Ey, wasn't she always helping da people who go to ya church? Why ya can't treat her special? "

"I can't make that decision. I'm very sorry."

"How much?" Red asked in an aggressive tone, rubbing his fingers together.

"At least forty. Maybe more," said the priest.

"Eeegads! Dat's a bunch," Red said.

"Well there's a coffin and a gravesite. Then the hearse and two men. And, of course, the hole to be dug," said the priest. "How would you pay for that?"

"Doan worry 'bout it, fadda. I git it," Red whispered, making sure nobody could hear. "Just doan go askin questions. Okay, fadda?"

The coroner's van pulled up with three men sitting on the driver's seat. Two of them wore white, peaked caps and blue uniforms and the other one wore a dark suit of civilian attire. Solemn faced, the three of them stared at the inferno, their eyes reflecting the horror they felt at the sight they were witnessing. Already the smoke started to affect them.

"Let's get this business done and get the hell outta here. Before we get our asses all burned," one of them insisted.

"Hold your horses, will ya," the man in the dark suit shouted back. He stepped from the van. "Wait around the corner, if you have to." He knelt down by the group, expressed his condolences, then introduced himself. "I'm Dr. Leonard Pole, assistant to the coroner."

Wasting no time, Dr. Pole put on a pair of skin-tight, rubber gloves. He physically verified the bullet's entry point on the forehead, probing the area with his fingers. Then gently, he turned her head for a look at the cranium under her blood-soaked hair, where he probed with the tips of his index and middle fingers that suddenly sunk slightly into the exit hole, the size of a silver dollar.

"Who's responsible for the body?" he asked.

"I am. I'm her son." Johnny nodded. His face showed his dislike for the men in the white hats, but he knew they were only doing their job.

"Sign here," the doctor directed, being considerate of Johnny's sensitivities, handing him a clipboard. "We won't be taking your mom to the morgue. I have confirmed for the coroner, as requested by Alderman Mulvihey, the tragic circumstances of Mrs. O'Hara's death. You may proceed with her wake and burial.

A chorus of excited screams and shouts of "run for it" came from the crowd as they scrambled for their lives. The front section of the two-story building, some fifty-feet wide, collapsed, shooting flame and scorching heat across the street at the fleeing spectators.

"At the wake, you can pay the hearse driver, Mister VonSharp," said the shaken priest as he cringed from the heat. "He'll make sure Mrs. O'Hara's interment is proper and respectful."

Shhhhhh! Red put his finger to her lips. "Why you talken so loud? Wot dat word means, fadda?"

"You mean interment?"

"Yeah."

"Buried. It means buried. If there's nothing else, I'll see you at the wake." The priest made the sign of the cross and departed.

Johnny shook his head. "Where you getting all that money?"

"I gots it, Johnny. Awright," Red insisted, staring teasingly into his eyes. "And soon I show you how you can gets money."

"That's 'I got it.' Not 'gots it, and 'get money,' not 'gets money.'" Johnny smiled. Again he felt an overwhelming fondness for his buddy, a strange feeling he didn't understand. He felt like he was too close to this kid, like he's not his brother.

The coppers meandered unnoticed through the preoccupied crowd, studying faces and listening to conversations. They questioned several among them, including the owners of North River Lumber: two Irish Catholics, whom they asked many questions that seemed to suggest they might have started the fire to collect on the insurance. That, of course, didn't make sense. Their business was thriving. They also questioned several firemen and a lone worker from Macon's Beef.

When finished interviewing the firemen, the police simply disappeared.

Two more companies of firemen and their fire trucks raced into the block. They came from each end, their bells clanging relentlessly, putting on one hell of a show like they were interested in putting out the fire. But the native sons didn't fool anybody.

"Where da hell dey been," said Battler. "Sure took dair time gitten here, da bastards."

"Yeah. Sure. They making sure the place destroyed first, before they *cuminzee*. Bastards. Bastards," agreed Hans. His German accent prevalent, speaking through swollen lips.

When the police moved on, Big Mike Brogan, the twenty-two-year-old, second in command of the Young Immigrants, called everybody together. "Who'd those sneaky coppers question?" he asked. Nobody acknowledged him.

"You mean those dirty booly dogs didn't talk to any of you guys? What kind of an investigation was that? They don't speak to the people who are going to suffer dearly?"

"They spoke to that guy there," said Battler, pointing at a bald-headed man wearing a blood-covered apron.

"Hey mister," Big Mike shouted as he approached the man. "What'd they ask you?"

"The dumb cop. You know what he want? To know why I was working on Sunday. He's a Know Nothing. And he had one of those pins on his jacket; those *idiot pins*. Asked me if I knew which one of you guys started the fire."

"Which one of us! The nerve of that son-of-bitch," barked Big Mike, nearly drowned out by a flurry of angry outbursts from the gang. "What did ya tell him?"

"Told 'em I wasn't there when the fire started. How would I know who did it? But it pissed me off. So I said, 'Why would they start the fire? Some of them work there. That's when they moved on."

"Fucking booly dogs. What are they up to? They know damn well we didn't do it. They know our people that work there. What else he ask?" Big Mike continued.

"Wanted to know which one of you shot the lady. Said you were all drunk and fighting. That some of you drew guns and fired shots. That you hit that poor lady."

"Oh they're setting us up, those bastards," roared Big Mike.

"I know that," said the man. "But he didn't wanna hear what I had to say."

"Rotten bums," shouted Johnny, bursting into tears—Katie began bawling again. "Why are they doing this? The blond guy shot my mom."

"They can't do that. Right Big Mike?" another voice shouted.

"Dey can do whatever dey wants," said Battler. "I'd likes to duke it out wid one a dose fucks. I'd whips him good." He held up his two fists. Then he turned to the gang, speaking softly. "Now Johnny has nobody but a very young sister. What's he gonna do?"

Then came an urgent shout over the bullhorn: "Clear the street, clear the street," a panicky voice shouted over a speaking trumpet. The fire officer waved frantically at the people standing opposite the firehouse. "Get out of the way," he continued. *Vavhoom!* Down came the firehouse on top of itself, shooting a gush of flame, embers and intense heat across the street. Shouts and screams came from the panic-stricken crowd as they ran to get clear. This time several slow-moving bystanders suffered serious burns. One woman's hair actually flamed for a second before Timothy McCarthy slapped it out with his hands.

"Everybody okay?" Big Mike shouted, checking his own men. The fact that nobody responded to him meant his boys were okay. "Damn! That was a close one," he said, shaking his head. Then he motioned the gang to follow him over to the body of Mrs. O'Hara. He wrapped his arm around Johnny's shoulders. "If there's anything ya need, Johnny, *anything.*" After a pause, he said, "We're all here for you. You're one of us, always."

46

Johnny nodded appreciatively.

The rest of the gang followed Big Mike's lead, extending their sympathies to Johnny and his sister, Katie. Some of them stepped forward for a look at his mom, but Big Mike waved them off, shaking his head. "Gather 'round," he said, directing them to assemble around him.

"Listen up, everybody," he uttered. "We gotta talk about this." When he had their full attention, he shouted, "Who were they? Did they set the fire?"

"Yeah," sobbed Johnny, as he and Red joined them. "I *saw* them start the fires."

"Anybody recognize them?" Big Mike again asked. He scanned their faces for a response, getting nothing but blank stares and shrugs. "God dam, ye. Don't ye know anything?" he roared.

Then the cocky little redhead stepped forward, pushing out his chest and getting everybody's attention. He shouted, "Hell, wez too busy *fightin*. But I knows one a da fuckers. I doan forget his ugly face." Then in a mournful voice, he said, "Da one dat shot Johnny's mom."

"Ya didn't do a good job, I see," said Big Mike, shaking his head while looking over at Johnny and Katie. "I won't even ask how you got that blinker, Red."

"Yeah. One a dem punched me eye, but I got another one a good kick." He looked apologetically at young Katie, then shouted, "Right in the nuts! And he gots some of dis too." Red waved his fists, flexing his muscular arms and broad shoulders.

"You got guts, kid. I like that," said Big Mike, asking again if anybody recognized any of the attackers.

"I thought they were the *Bowerys*," said Battler. "But den I reckoned one from the *American Guard*. Den an *Americus* guy. Den I was all confused. Who da hell dey are?"

Somebody else said they saw two guys from the *Washington Fire Company*.

"So that's it," said Big Mike. "They joined together against us. The foreigners. Heck, most of us were born here, just like them. And that still don't mean anything to them bums."

"Why?" somebody asked.

"Jobs," said Big Mike. "Remember the guy that said we work for less money. Called us scabs. That's why they burned down the lumberyard. Get rid of our jobs."

Vinnie McCarthy interjected, "The other day when those bums tried to take the fire from us. That guy Batesy made a threat. Said we'd pay dearly. I bet ya this is the payback."

"And they made sure our fire company wouldn't get here. The only guys that would give a damn about our people." Big Mike couldn't hide his anger. His jaw tight, he rubbed his clenched fist then punched his palm.

"We need our own firehouse. Right here," said Battler. He glanced over at the burning remains of the firehouse and lumberyard.

"Oh yeah, smart guy. Where's the money gonna come from?" Big Mike shot back.

"You guys are a disgrace. All you're doing is making it tough for all of us," shouted their fast-approaching Alderman, Sean Mulvihey, pointing to the smoldering wreckage. Although short in stature, Mulvihey feared no one, especially when representing the needs of his large immigrant constituency. He wore a freshly-pressed dark suit with white spats, and a bowler that sat on his eyebrows.

"What the hell you talking about, Mister … Alderman?" demanded Big Mike, rubbing his irritated, blood shot eyes.

"I'll tell you jerks what I'm talking about. A *Herald* reporter told me a bunch of drunken Irishmen, you guys," he pointed his finger angrily at them, "destroyed the fire engine and shot the horses. Some of me peers at the council said it was the result of a drunken Irish brouhaha that started right here. A fact just confirmed to me by the coppers that just left."

If the rage in Johnny's eyes could kill, Mulvihey would have been dead. Picking up on his anger, Big Mike stepped between them. "I guess the booly dogs said we shot Johnny's mother. That we started the fire that destroyed our jobs," Big Mike replied in a cool manner.

"Exactly," growled Mulvihey. "They suspect she was shot in the crossfire. And the firemen reported that when they arrived, a bunch of Young Immigrants tried to stop them from putting the fire out."

"All lies," said Big Mike. Looking Mulvihey in the eye and pointing at the burning lumberyard, he challenged, "We did this? Is that what you're saying?"

"You on their side, mister?" shouted Johnny, lunging at him.

Big Mike stepped in front of Johnny, absorbing the impact of his big frame. "Easy there. He's one of us."

Mulvihey shouted, "Kid, you ever raise your hand to me again—"

"Wait! Wait a minute," shouted Big Mike, wrapping his arm around Johnny, like a big brother would do. "Calm down, will yiz. We don't need to be fighting among ourselves." He did not want his guys attacking Mulvihey, the man who disseminated part-time jobs to many of the locals. The man who secured fulltime employment for others. And with all the jobs wiped out for many of the Young Immigrant's and their fathers by the fire, they will need him now. Besides, Big Mike's brother, Thomas, had a good relationship with Mulvihey, who protected his sometimes *shady* operations.

"You'll what, mister?" Johnny screamed, as Big Mike continued to hold him back. "I'm not afraid of you. Or anybody. You're some friend to be blaming us!"

Red stepped beside Johnny, fists clenched as if ready to rumble. "Hey boss. Ya fuck wid Johnny and I do to ya wot Yankee Sullivan shoudda done to Hyer." Red did not mean to be funny, but he provoked a stifled laugh from his gang mates.

"I saw my mother's killer. A big, blond-haired fuck from outside." Again tears formed in his eyes.

"And he tried shooting Johnny, too," Red sounded off. "Whyn't ya askin us wot happen? Why ya believe dem coppers?"

"Let's settle down here," said Big Mike, a politician in his own right.

"Maybe I jumped the gun," said Mulvihey, apologetically. "Guess I should have known better."

"It's okay to kill a *lowly* Mick, isn't it?" said Big Mike.

"Surely looks that way," continued the alderman, looking at Johnny. "And I'm sorry, kid, for what I said." Grabbing Johnny's hand, he shook it, a move Johnny and his friends appreciated. "The bastards," he continued. "But that's the way it is, and looks like it'll always be. I stopped at the precinct house. Got a promise from one of our own. A good man, Sergeant Desmond O'Connell, promised he'd investigate this matter. But made it clear that no matter what he finds, if it's a cover-up, there's nothing he can do. Looking at his timepiece, Sean Mulvihey said, "He should be here momentarily."

"Where'll you stay?" Mulvihey asked the O'Haras. "I can get you into Holy Cross."

"No, no! Dey stay wid me," insisted Red, thumbing his chest."

"That's fine by me," said Mulvihey, raising his hands. Then stepping close to Johnny, he whispered, "I think the young one should stay at the home. It is a good place."

Although still ticked at Mulvihey, Johnny agreed, adding, "I like that. She already goes to school there."

The alderman looked across the street at the smoldering ruins, picturing the faces of the many men he knew who just lost their jobs there. He shook his head in disgust, listening to the Yanks as they joked about the fire and the jobs that were lost. Oh, he could understand their bitterness at losing jobs to immigrants and their sons because they'd work for less, just as the immigrants resented the Negroes who would work for less than them, but he could not accept the destruction they inflicted.

"And lad," he continued, "it's there for you, too, if you want it." Tapping his chest and speaking loud enough to be heard over the noise of the firefighting operations, he said, "That's why I am here. To help you." He paused making sure he had everybody's attention. "If you take me up on my offer, go see Father Peter. Tell him Sean Mulvihey sent you."

"Ya needn't worry. I take care a dem," insisted Red.

Johnny thanked Mr. Mulvihey for the offer, but insisted he'd go with his friend.

Suddenly Johnny rubbed his stomach with his hand. *Whadda we gonna do for food. Gotta feed Katie.* None of them had eaten all day. Not since yesterday.

"Here come the coppers now," said Big Mike, tensing up. "Hope they're not gonna give us a bunch of shit."

Broadly grinning, Alderman Mulvihey faced the two approaching police officers. "Sergeant O'Connell. Glad to see you. And yourself, Officer Zelle."

"This them?" the sergeant asked in a whisper. When Mulvihey nodded yes, O'Connell shook Johnny's hand then held Katie's for a moment. He could feel everybody's eyes on him, like a hawk's on its prey. "I am so sorry," said the sullen-faced officer, with a hint of an Irish accent. Katie began to cry.

"Ah, don't cry now, young lady," said Mulvihey, handing Katie a silver dollar, which she snapped from his hand.

"Did anyone see who did the shooting?" asked Sergeant O'Connell as he guided Johnny and Katie away from the others. "We need to speak privately."

"Yes," said Johnny, a tall lad for his fifteen years: burly, strong, and dangerous looking when he wanted to be. "Yes. And I will take care of him myself."

"Now, young man," the sergeant said, shaking his head disapprovingly. "I know if I were you, I'd want to do the same. And I don't blame you. But that would only get you in big, big trouble. You would be destroying your life to revenge the lowly coward that did this terrible thing. Please," he strongly urged, "let the police department handle it. The last thing I'd want is to see is a fine lad like you, who I know is a survivor of the Great Hunger, destroy his life."

The sergeant eyed Johnny up and down, impressed by his size and apparent strength. "You'd sure make a fine police officer, you know." His words brought a smile to Johnny's face.

Sergeant O'Connell, a seasoned police officer who could be as tough as the toughest of coppers, and surprisingly compassionate, gave a damn about the immigrant communities, especially the Irish, knowing full well what they had been through. He too, with his family, suffered the tragedy of the Great Hunger, having lost several family members to it. And he also knew what it was like to want to kill the responsible "English bastards." Since becoming a police officer, he has sought out and guided many an immigrant lad or immigrant's son, to the Police Department—young lads that would have otherwise gone bad. He'd even tutored individuals who were preparing for the entry exam.

Johnny respected the sergeant—his mother brought him up to respect the authorities—and gave him credit for even venturing into the neighborhood, which most cops did not do unless they were part of a squad. The sergeant's appearance and size impressed Johnny. He was clean-shaven, had freshly-cut short hair with an equally short and neat beard, and wore a spotless uniform. He had a reputation throughout the 20th Precinct to be *one hell of a fighter*. One of the few coppers respected and feared by most members of the various gangs in the precinct. His uniform fit his fine physique perfectly, no room to spare around his massive biceps, bulging chest, and hulking shoulders.

By now the firemen had surrounded the lumberyard and were drowning it with water streams from at least nine different locations. Several of the pumpers were sucking water directly from the river.

Everybody had to look up to make eye contact with Sergeant O'Connell, including Johnny O'Hara and Big Mike, both six footers. The sergeant's partner, Patrolman Ernest Zelle, was also a bull of a man. Both men were part of a so-called *goon* squad, a special squad used by many precincts to combat the street fighters. Officer Zelle maintained a business-like demeanor.

"Did anyone else see who did it?" Sergeant O'Connell asked, scanning the group.

"Me," barked Red in his cocky way, tapping his chest.

"Would you mind describing him to my partner?"

"Sure, Boss." He nodded, then stepped up to Patrolman Zelle.

Again facing Johnny, the sergeant asked, "What did the shooter look like?"

Johnny started his description, "Big like you, but with blond hair."

"What color were his eyes?"

"Blue. And he had a deep, deep voice."

The sergeant recorded everything Johnny said in his black memo book, including the fact that he aimed the pistol at Johnny and Red, but that it misfired. He also questioned other gang members.

Sergeant O'Connell again gave his condolences to the O'Haras, then bid them farewell, giving a thumbs up to Red.

Red looked puzzled. "Dem coppers okay. Gotta remember dem."

Sergeant O'Connell, Mulvihey, and Big Mike conversed briefly before parting. O'Connell asked, "The O'Hara kid looks like a tough case. A broken nose already. Scars on the face."

Mulvihey replied, "From what I hear, he's not a bad kid. Smart. Very smart. Is protective of his mother and sister. He's been the man of the family since '47, when his *Da* died on one of the coffin ships. He motioned towards Red. "Look at the sweet face on that kid. The picture of innocence; like a child. But the scars take away the innocence."

"It breaks my heart to see these kids like this," said O'Connell. "What hope is there for them? They're hated . . . sure we're all hated, aren't we? Because we're Irish."

"And German immigrants," stone-faced Officer Zelle interjected.

"And Catholic," added the alderman.

"Well what'll yuz do about Mrs. O'Hara's killer?" asked Big Mike.

"I'll push hard on this case. That I promise. But for now, I'm certain he'll disappear off the face of this Earth."

* * * * *

With a bar cloth in hand, shinning glasses, Mr. Brady leaned over his crude wood-plank bar. "Now lads, would ye be so kind as to take the body upstairs?" he asked Battler and a friend. "The landlord had a change of heart after Mulvihey spoke to him," he added with a wink of the eye. "I'll buy ye a drink."

"Yeah. We'll sure need one after dat. But first ya gotta tell me *someting*?" said Battler.

"And what's that?"

"I thought a person killed like dat, they gotta go to the morgue? Didn't dey have to know how dat person wuz kilt?" asked Battler, taking a drag on his cigarette then letting it drop a couple of feet into a spittoon.

"For the most part that's correct. But on occasion, someone with authority, such as the alderman, can have that step bypassed. On the QT of course." Again Brady gave him a wink. "But, you see both the coroner and O'Connell have confirmed and recorded the incident and all the details."

"One more queskin," said Battler. "How'd dey git the landlord to let Johnny and Katie stay up dere long enuff for the wake?"

"Mulvihey leaned on him. Threatened that the city would take action against him for the many violations that exist in the building. So he relented. The O'Haras can use the flat for the wake, but gotta be out by noon."

* * * *

That night many, many people turned out to pay their respects. The upstairs two-room, one-window flat was hot and muggy—oppressive actually—just big enough for people to stop at the corpse, say a quick prayer while standing, then leave. Refreshments were available at the Shamrock, compliments of Mr. Brady and Thomas Brogan. The haunting banshee-like wails of keening women were heard throughout the building.

Many of Mrs. O'Hara's friends turned out. Also paying their respects were more than a hundred volunteer firemen and gang members. The volleys wore their red fireman's blouses out of respect for Johnny. Most notably, a great many of the firemen and gang members in attendance were bruised or bandaged from the day's fighting. The waiting line extended down the stairwell and out onto the street.

The hearse driver, Mr. VonSharp, and his assistant entered the apartment just before nine, as the last of the visitors were leaving. "Hey good-looking face," he called to Red in a strong German accent, "you have money for me, yes?"

"Yeah," snapped Red, placing the counted and recounted money in the man's hand. "Yeah, I gotten it."

VonSharp smiled, placing the money in his pocket. "You not talk to a gingster. You talking to a man who worken for the Church. I respects the dead."

Red's fists were clenched, having mistaken the German for a wise guy. Fortunately, before there could be an incident, Johnny detracted Red, wrapping his arm around him, gently forcing him into the other room.

That's when Johnny first noticed under Red's loose-fitting vest what looked like small braless breasts. Innocently he joked, "What's that?"

"What's what?" asked Red, hardly paying him any heed.

Red-faced with embarrassment, Johnny quickly pointed to Red's chest. "What's that?"

Red replied with a chuckle, "I doan knows. Muscle? Or maybe I is 'posed to be a gurl." He laughed again, then grabbed his crotch. "Dis what makes da man. Right Johnny O'Hara?"

"C'mon Katie. We gotta get our things together."

"I'll help," offered Red.

The three of them gathered up the few rags of clothing they possessed, placing them and a few cooking utensils into two old sacks.

Johnny invited Red to stay with them for the night, which he accepted.

"You can sleep there," he said, pointing to his bed. "Katie and I will sleep in the other one."

"Where we gonna go tomorrow? Huh, Johnny?" his anxious sister asked.

"Katie, yuz guys kin stay wid me. Right Johnny," said Red. "I gots a real cool place, kid. Like a hideout. Wez have a lotta fun dere."

With that, Katie's teary eyes sparkled. "You mean it, Red? Is it really a hideout? Nobody knows where it is?"

"Dat's right. Nobody but me."

"Where yuz gonna leave ya stuff when wez at church?" asked Red.

"It's you. Not yuz.' You got a lot to learn, Red." Johnny shook his head. "Brady said I could leave these things in his place."

"Good. After dat we can bring it to my place."

"Won't your folks mind?"

"Heck, man," Red paused, turning away, looking out the window. "I gots no folks. I been alone since my mudda left."

"Gee, I didn't know that. I thought—"

"Oh dats awright. I kin truss ya. Ya keep a secret, right Johnny?"

"I'm your friend. And I mean it," he insisted. "Where you live?"

"By da river. In dat ole shed, just behind the McAdams place. And da peoples there doan bodder me. But I takes no chances. Dat's why I carry dis." Red flashed a knife. "I got udda tings too, ya know. And tell me, boss. Ya gonna see dat priest dat guy toll us about?"

"Yeah, I'll see him. Because of my mom. She worked for them. Besides, Katie goes to school there. Make the guy feel good." He looked around the room, sizing it up, then asked Red, "Your place bigger than this?"

"Nah."

"What do you do about food?"

"Doan ask," said Red.

* * * * *

No longer the sad-eyed nine-year old, Angie was now fourteen and living alone having lost both of her parents. Her father, who had been a hard-drinking musician by night and a cellar digger by day, simply disappeared. People considered him the finest Ulliean Pipe player in the city. But, unfortunately, he could never organize performances because of his drinking, denying himself and his family a great source of income. And the few dollars he did earn performing, he quickly spent on drink. If word got out that he'd be playing the pipes in a neighborhood tavern, it wouldn't be long before people filled the place to capacity, if not to overflowing. They loved his music.

Hearsay had it that Angie's father drank himself to death. But more often than not, people said he simply abandoned her and Angel, her mother, leaving them destitute. Having no skills to speak of, Angie's mother put her beauty to work, turning to prostitution. She did her work mostly at night or in the evening, which Angie hated. She wanted her mom to stay home and teach her how to read and write, which never happened. Angie found herself getting very angry with her mom for leaving her alone so often, usually until the early hours of the morning, for which she always forgave her. But she told herself she would never forgive her mom for abandoning her, just like her father did.

It was a Sunday night and Angel Hester had promised to stay home, to finally help her daughter learn to read and write. But she broke that promise, too. Instead, she spent the better part of an hour putting on her face.

"Wot ya doing? Ya s'posed to stay home wid me," the kid complained.

"Sorry honey. There's been a change of plans. I got to go out for a little while," said her mom. "Be back shortly."

"If ya go, I be pissed at ya," insisted Angie. She had always believed that her mother simply abandoned her. Just like her father.

Since Angie's mother disappeared, she had sometimes heard people talking about her; calling her "the beautiful prostitute." From time to time she heard it said that Angel Hester 'serviced some of New York's richest men," which she hated to hear.

* * * * *

Millhouse Bates, at twenty-two, was a natural leader who despised immigrants. He and twenty-year-old Greg Lopat were in the backyard at the loading dock of New York's most elaborate and costly concert saloon, the Louvre. Located on Fifth Avenue, just a stone's throw from the residences of some of the city's most exalted personalities, the Louvre catered to New York's so-called *finest gentlemen.*

Millhouse Bates, better known as Batesy, had good fortune on his side; he had some important connections that destined him for *bigger things.* A close friend of his deceased father, named Bill Bailey, owned the Louvre. He was a well-known figure in the sporting world with a shady past and was also a leading member of a fire company. Most importantly, he had the support of big money. Bailey hired only native sons.

Bates started work in the Louvre as a backup bartender who also performed menial work. Thanks to his father's friend, Bailey, he had a lock on the next opening for a full-time bartender, an envied position, especially in this establishment.

He called himself Batesy because he detested his first name, Milhouse. His cohort also possessed a sore spot: an overly broad forehead that he often rammed into people's faces when they poked fun at him, especially during gang fights.

The two sweat-soaked men finally took a bit of a break. First things first, they each guzzled some water from an outside water spigot. Lopat sat his butt on a beer keg and leaned back against the brick wall and rested his feet on an old desk scheduled to be picked up by the junkman. Batesy stood in front of his *personal mirror*, acquired from the newly renovated *Gents* room, singing with rather fine tenor voice, "Batesy is my name. Looking good is my game," as he made several runs of a comb through his thick black hair.

They had just helped off-load two dozen kegs of beer from the F & M Schaefer Brewery wagon and brought them down to the basement, then loaded a similar number of empties back onto the horse-drawn truck.

"Greg. You know that little redheaded Yimmy fuck?" asked Batesy, still staring at the mirror, messing with his hair.

"Sure, Millhouse. The one that KO'd Scafoni with the hydrant—"

Without taking his eyes off the mirror, Batesy slammed the back of his hand across Lopat's mouth.

"Wot wuz dat for?" Lopat barked, jumping to his feet with his clenched fists shaking. He felt his lips for blood.

58

Batesy replied as though nothing happened, in a serious tone: "As I said before, 'Batesy is my name. Looking good is my game. Don't ever call me that name again.'"

Lopat wanted so bad to pummel his face, but knew better. His livelihood depended on Batesy.

"Now if I may continue," said Batesy. "At that fire the other day, Chuck showed a lot of interest in that little redheaded guy. Couldn't take his eyes off him. Even knew his name. Hester, I believe."

Lopat's stomach dropped. He could feel the blood draining from his face. "There was a beautiful whore . . . a few years back by that name," Lopat said.

Batesy continued, "He swears the guy with the red hair looks just like a woman he knew. I don't know why, but he believes the redheaded prick has to be a girl, and when I asked him why he says that, he doesn't know why other than that he looks like a girl."

"That low-life fuck screwed the woman and refused to pay her," said Lopat.

"Did he finally pay 'er?" Batesy quipped.

"Yeah," lied Lopat who then asked, "Those kegs were heavy, weren't they?" hoping to change the subject.

"Then he can't be all that bad. Is she still around?"

"Oh I . . . I wouldn't know," said Lopat, no longer able to look Batesy in the eye.

Batesy wondered what made Lopat so edgy. But before he could go any further with his questioning, twenty-four-year-old Chuck Jansen, the gang member they were talking about, appeared. The three of them were members of a street gang, which Jansen headed up. Members had to be at least second-generation Americans.

"What am I to do?" asked Chuck in his deep voice, shifting from foot to foot.

"Don't worry about it," Batesy said. "According to Bailey, there will be no questions asked by the police. It's hands off. Besides, the O'Hara lady's just another unimportant immigrant. But you gotta disappear for a while."

Chuck grasped Batesy's hand and shook it, saying, "You saved my ass again, boss."

"And don't you forget it when your sitting on your ass out on Staten Island instead of hanging from the gallows at the Tombs," Batesy said, his cold eyes staring into Jansen's. Actually, Batesy wanted him sent to the island permanently. He feared Jansen's superior intelligence, size, and masculinity. Batesy believed he had been selected as top dog in the fire company and the gang because of his deceased father's tightness with Bailey. But that's not how his success came about at all. He'd been selected because of his leadership ability and proven persistence in achieving his goals. Perhaps if he believed in himself, he would not be constantly worrying about being pushed out of the position by Jansen.

"Oh no. Back to that shitty place. Isn't there any place closer I can go?" pleaded Chuck.

"No. Orders from the top. Now about yesterday. We did a great job. No more immigrant fire company. And the word at the council and fire department is that the fire was started by none other than the Young Immigrants, who were drunk." Batesy laughed hardily.

"C'mon, boss. Can't I go to Brooklyn? At least there's life there," pleaded Jansen.

"That's where I'd like you to go," Batesy lied. "But there's just too many people out there to recognize you. You must be isolated. That's why they want you out there. Back to the Humphrey farm."

Chuck nodded. "Yeah. I got some business to take care of first."

"Fine," said Batesy. "Just make sure you're on the ferry by Thursday morning."

CHAPTER SEVEN

Johnny O'Hara was grateful for the large crowd of his mother's friends at her funeral mass. Especially for the turnout of so many of the people whose loved ones she had cared for. For the past nine years, not long after arriving in New York, she had tended to the sick and elderly of the parish. That included Fionna Brogan, mother of the Brogan brothers; and Maria Dagastino, wife of Mr. Dagastino who owned the Waterside, who she took care of for more than half a year. Many considered her a saint.

Katie's teacher, Sister Ann, stood with her, as did Johnny and Red. And just as the celebrant, Father Rafferty, had promised, a pall covered the coffin.

After the mass, Johnny and Red, wearing ill-fitting black coats, white shirts, and ties lent to them by Fr. Rafferty, and several men from the parish similarly dressed, served as pallbearers. Although short for the task, Red's strength made up the difference. With the guidance of Mr. VonSharp, they removed the casket from Holy Cross Church and placed it in the waiting hearse. Then, on VonSharp's prompting, they walked the horse-drawn wagon around the corner to the church graveyard, with Katie close behind, where they laid Mrs. O'Hara to rest.

* * * * *

"Why don't you guys and Katie go see Father Peter? He's right in there," said Father Rafferty, looking at the rectory entrance.

Johnny nodded. "Yeah. Okay."

"And Red, I hope you agree that everything was dignified. Just as you requested."

"Yeah, it wuz, fadda." Red shook his head. "I mean father." After the priest left, Red asked Johnny, "Wot he means by dat big word?"

"Dignified. Meant everything came off very respectable. The way you wanted it. And it did. Thanks to you."

"Wuz good, wuzn't it," agreed Red, stepping up to the rectory door. "Doan just stand dere. Bang da door," Red told Johnny.

"Okay. And it's knock, not bang."

Thump! Thump! Thump! Johnny knocked. *Whoosh!* The door swung open releasing a welcome gust of cool air. A tall, olive-skinned priest welcomed them.

"Hello," said the priest, speaking with a Spanish accent.

"Good morning, Father. I think Father Peter expects us," said Johnny.

"And who might I say is calling?" asked the olive-skinned priest.

"I'm Johnny. She's my sister, Katie. This is my—"

"I mean your surname."

Red gave the priest a confused look, but said nothing. All of a sudden he became conscious of not having attended school.

"O'Hara. My sister still goes to school here. And this is my best friend, Red Hester."

"Sorry. Take a seat while I fetch the good Father."

Red smiled, wondering what he meant by *fetch* and *surname.*

As soon as he left the room a bell chimed, followed shortly by the heavy thumping of the feet of the big man who descended a flight of stairs diagonally across from them.

"Welcome my friends," said the ruddy-faced priest, extending his hand to Johnny. "I am Father Peter. You must be Johnny O'Hara? And the young lady next to you must your sister be Katie?"

How does he know us, wondered Johnny. "Yes," Johnny replied.

"I'm truly sorry about your mother. Gave so much to the parish. Did so much for the elderly and the sick. She will be sorely missed. But she is in a better place. She's with your father now."

Katie smiled contentedly. "Mommy, mommy. My dear mommy," was all she said. Johnny just listened.

"Yes Katie. Mother's in heaven, with Da and we should be happy," said Johnny, again embracing her. Johnny's mind drifted to thoughts of his mother and how she delivered meals to those in need. He pictured the sweat dripping from her face as she ascended the stairs in the hot, steamy tenements during the summer months; the steam coming from her mouth and her often-shivering arms when she delivered during the bitter cold days of winter.

"And who's this young lady?" The priest asked, looking at Red, appearing a bit puzzled.

"Hay fadda," Red blurted out. "I'm a he! Da name's Red Hester."

"It's Father. Not fadda," said Johnny.

"Who cares? Why he gotta call me dat?"

"Pardon me!" Father Peter burst into laughter. "The good Lord has endowed you with gorgeous hair," the priest continued, pointing to his own identical colored hair. "And exceptional looks to go with it, if I may say so."

Poor Red didn't even know if the priest's remarks were insults or compliments.

An elderly, smiling woman entered the room with a tray of sandwiches and glasses of milk, which she placed on the glass-topped table in front of Katie. "I make just for you," she said, speaking with a German accent.

The three of them lunged for the sandwiches, right away biting into them, dropping crumbs on the hardwood floor.

"Wait!" The priest smiled. "Let us first thank God for this food," he said.

Johnny and Katie prayed with him, as Red remained silent.

After the prayer, the three of them again attacked the sandwiches, literally shoving the full of the half sandwich into their mouths.

"Mother of God. When did ye last eat?" the priest asked, a sad, surprised look registering on his face.

"Yesterday in da morning," said Red, sounding cocky.

"You're surely hungry people. It couldn't have been a good hot meal ye had?"

With devilment in his eyes, Red replied, "Nah! Wez ate a loaf a bread dat fell from da truck." He chuckled.

"Ye poor things, ye." The priest shook his head. "Fell from a bread truck is it?" He too chuckled. "I hope you don't get all your food that way." He paused, looking Red in the eye. "Well, where are ye staying now?" he asked.

Red replied, "Dey gonna stay wid my folks."

"I'm sure it's a great inconvenience for them to have to provide food and shelter for two more."

"Uh—uh," Red objected.

"Hear me out first," he said. "Especially you, Johnny. Being that your mother has done so much good for the parish, and the fact that Katie goes to school here, we thought it would be a good idea for her to stay here. To live here for a while."

"No way, fa . . . father. She stays with me, with us," said Red, at which Johnny smiled, thinking how he remembered to say father rather than fadda.

"No, no!" Katie cut in. "I wanna stay with Johnny." She became nervous, starting to cry.

"Come on, sis. Let's hear what Father has to say. You might like it."

Shaking his head appreciatively, Father Peter continued in a soft voice, "Just hear me out." He had their attention. Smiling pleasantly, Father Peter looked her right in the eye. "Your teacher, Sister Ann, will be your minder and you will live with other girls your age. Just like in school. And you'll never go hungry."

With that Sister Ann, a friendly-looking young woman, entered the room. "Katie. My dear Katie. It's so nice to see you."

To everyone's joy, Katie's face lit up. Jumping to her feet, she rushed to the nun and embraced her. "Katie's my best student."

"Johnny, would you mind if Sister Ann showed Katie where the other girls live?" asked the priest.

Johnny replied with enthusiasm, "Not at all."

"If you'll excuse us," said Sister Ann, taking Katie by the hand. "Come with me, Katie. Let's have some fun. Let me show you where Helen Murphy and Susie Smith stay. And the kitchen where there is always food."

Once they left, the priest continued. "I am sure you understand, Johnny. This is the best thing for her."

Johnny agreed, but made one stipulation: "She's free to leave if and when I'm set up to take care of her, if she wants to."

The priest simply nodded in agreement. "She'll have everything she needs here. An education. Good hygiene. A place to sleep. And she'll always have something to eat."

"When will I see her?" asked Johnny.

"Whenever. Except during school hours." Fr. Peter chuckled.

The O'Hara kids have always been close. They were a tight-knit family. Mrs. O'Hara had always preached to them to protect each other, and equally important, to respect at all times the family name. Hardly a day went by when she did not remind them: "We must love each other, help each other, and respect each other and never do anything that would disgrace ye father's name."

"Fadda, I mean Father. I gots a queskin," said Red.

"What 'tis it?"

"How ya knowd wez wuz coming?"

"It's 'we we're' not 'wez wuz,'" Johnny interjected with a smile.

"Yuz calling me stupid, hah?" Red snapped. He didn't like Johnny correcting him in front of the priest or anybody, for that matter. He didn't mind being corrected in private. "I like dat," he had told Johnny, "when yuz corrects me 'cause I is learning to speaken, I mean speak properly."

For years he had been conscious of his lack of schooling, and at times felt inferior, especially when most of his friends had a better understanding and diction of English.

"You're not stupid," Johnny shot back. "You're as smart as any of us. Maybe even smarter. And you're my best friend—tough guy."

Red's eyes lit up. He looked up to Johnny.

"Johnny's right," said the priest. "It's just unfortunate that you did not go to school. And I am sure that Johnny and Katie would be delighted to teach you. And now, to answer your question, it was Mister Mulvihey who told me to expect ye."

"Katie keeps me reading, you know," said Johnny, with a proud look about him. "She has always brought me books home from the school library. Something I never did."

Being an avid reader, Johnny kept up on current affairs, including current stories about illegal boxing matches. He read many a good book, especially about American and world history. He read inside and out every newspaper he got his hands on. And Red would demand of him that he read it aloud, which he'd be glad to do. By 15 years of age, he had already read *Moby Dick, Tale of Two Cities,* and *North and South.*

"Father Rafferty told me a great crowd attended the funeral. That says a lot for how much the community loved and respected your mom." Father Peter's cheerful look turned to one of a serious nature. "There's something else I want to talk to you about."

Johnny became suspicious. *What's this all about?*

"Mr. Mulvihey told me that you know who did it."

"Yes. And I'm going to get him."

"And I'm gonna help him get him," added Red.

"That's what I am afraid of. Listen to me, both of you. That's not God's justice. Let the police handle it. But that's not what I want to talk to you about. I think you'll like what I have to say. It's your future, and yours too, Red. They're talking real serious now about creating a paid fire department. In the near future, and I know you guys are volleys, it will be right up your alley."

"Wez doan want dat,' snapped Red, his temper being tested.

"Listen to me. It's going to happen whether we like it or not. And it would be a steady job for men of good character. I mean men without police records. You'll always work and get paid. A job you can raise a family on and provide them a decent home."

Johnny listened keenly to every word he said, being at awe with everything to do with firefighting. He'd often dreamt that he would one day be in charge of the fire department.

"Sergeant Desmond O'Connell, and your man, Mr. Mulvihey," said the priest, "were very fond of your mother and her good works. They told me they'd do whatever it takes to make sure you get the job. And as big and strong as you are, young man, you'd make a hell of a fireman."

Johnny's face beamed with pride, while Red's face flushed with anger.

"Hows 'bout me?" barked Red.

Johnny cut right in. "Red is as tough as any fireman I ever worked with. He'd have to get the job too."

"I'm sure they'd arrange that. And I can understand what you mean by him being tough. With those shoulders, he'd be darn good."

Red's taut face muscles relaxed. A hint of a smile returned.

"I think I would like that," said Johnny, "even though none of the other volleys would."

"But," continued the priest, "if you go after that man that did this terrible thing to mother, and God forbid you," he hesitated, "harmed him, you'd never get the job. Instead you'd be hanged at the Tombs."

"I don't want to hear anymore," said Johnny, getting to his feet, joined by Red. "We're outta here, Father."

"How about a hot dinner before you go?" asked the priest as he stood.

"No," said Johnny, shaking his head. "We're full. Please tell Katie I'll be by tomorrow."

"I'll do that," said the priest. "Me invitation will always be open to ye."

Red reached for some sandwiches, but did not touch them, waiting for Father Peter's nod. And when the priest nodded, saying, "That's what the bag is for," he grabbed four halves and the bag. "Tanks, fa . . . ther."

* * * * *

The *Times'* morning headline read: *Drunken Mob Kills Mother of Two.* The front page story reported: "According to police reports, yesterday's devastating fire at North River Lumber on Tenth Avenue that put more than thirty men out of work, was the result of a drunken brawl between local immigrant thugs . . . a forty-year-old woman was shot dead in an exchange of gunfire between the two mobs . . . police sources stated that they have no leads as to who started the fire or did the shooting or why. There have been no arrests as of yet . . ."

The *Times* story continued: "Firemen responding to the fire were attacked by the same drunken mob." The report did not mention that the attack took place several blocks from the fire or that the assaulted firemen were all immigrants; nor did it mention the destruction of the fire engine and the fact that the attackers were all generation Americans.

The story pointed the finger of blame, without saying it, at the well-known Young Immigrants. Another stab by the rabidly anti-Catholic establishment against the city's huge, mostly poor, uneducated, Irish-Catholic population.

The unwarranted attacks by the *Times* on the good people of the immigrant neighborhood enraged them. Some of the youngsters went into nearby upper-class neighborhoods, roughing up a few men and breaking windows; causing general mayhem. To that incident the police responded quickly, unlike their response to the fire, but not in time to catch any of the *ruffians.* Rumor had it that several youngsters came across the *Times* reporter that penned the story. According to one of the youngsters: "He run like a wee girly. Waving his hands and screaming."

When Alderman Sean Mulvihey and Sergeant Desmond O'Connell returned to the block, hoping to soothe the furor, they were greeted with boos and catcalls. A few of the more aggressive gang members even threatened the cop. Some in the community felt betrayed by the two men.

"Wait a minute now," shouted O'Connell, his Irish accent quite obvious. "What the hell ye pissed at us for? What 'tis it we've done?"

One of the youngsters shouted back, "We thoughts yuz woz gonna make dem tell the truth."

"If we could," snapped Mulvihey.

Big Mike saved the day. "Easy, boys. Alderman Mulvihey and Sergeant O'Connell are good men. Trying to do what's right. But it's not up to them. The bums with the power, hell, they're all against us. The two of them alone can't fight city hall."

"But maybe one day we'll change that. If we so-called immigrants stick together. All of us: Germans, Irish, Italians, and whoever. Vote those Catholic—haters out of office," shouted Mulvihey, sounding like the astute politician he was.

O'Connell stood by him, grinning broadly. He nodded in agreement and said, "We're Americans, too. Hell, many of us were born here. Not me, of course. And I know damn well if there's to be war, we'll be right in the middle of it."

Mulvihey and O'Connell agreed with Thomas Brogan's wish that his brother, Big Mike, should get involved in the Democratic Party and seek office.

Surprisingly, Big Mike Brogan made a good role model for the younger generation. Granted he was a two-fisted brawler, but only when necessary: like protecting the neighborhood from outside threats. And when responding to a fire in his district, he would always be ready to battle those who would try to steal his company's fire. He never took advantage of his size to intimidate people, nor did he steal another man's property, which his folks drilled into him. Of course, some of his jealous neighbors said he didn't steal only because his brother Thomas was a successful junkman, who made certain the family's needs were always met.

And, as his mother often boasted, he had attended and finished school at Holy Cross, where he was a good student. And he did not fear hard work and took any job he could get. Of course, jobs were limited for him, being the son of Irish immigrants. At least once a week he'd pick up a day's work with his brother.

"Them reporters never asked us any questions," somebody yelled.

"Dey didn't wanna knowd the truth," barked Battler.

* * * * *

In the back of Lansing's grocery on Prince Street, further south in the City, where the Patriots dominated, Batesy held court with a dozen or so members of his gang, including Chuck Jansen and Greg Lopat. They were in the backroom of the grocery, which also served as a grog shop, where one could get whiskey by the glass or by the bottle, among other things to get them high. Those who didn't hang out in the saloons could go there to catch up on the current events of the community, the political happenings, and find out whom they have to vote for on Election Day. Of course, foodstuffs including vegetables and fruits that were anything but fresh were also available in the front of the shop.

The young thugs sitting in the dingy, poorly-lit grog shop boomed with excitement as they passed around a water pipe, smoking cannabis.

"I love it. Look at these headlines! They're blaming everything on the donkeys and krauts," Batesy shouted, flinging the *Times* on the table. "Now those Yimmy fuckers will never get a charter."

Several gang mates scrambled to see the papers as others shouted for them to read the headlines.

"Here, Chuck. You read this for these dummies. You're good at that," ordered Batesy. Jansen was the most educated of them all, even more so than the boss. He finished elementary school and actually had a year of higher learning. His parents were known as "good citizens," even though his father had served time in prison back in Germany for a violent crime.

Jansen stepped under a stream of daylight shinning through the skylight. "Here you go, dummies," he said. "Here's what it says: 'Drunken Mob Kills Mother.' And right under that it says, 'And Wipes Out Many Jobs.'" He showed no remorse whatsoever for shooting Mrs. O'Hara dead the day before.

The boss, Batesy, shared his delight, for he had planned the assaults and the fire at the behest of his boss, Bill Bailey. Of course, Bailey got the *idea* from his financer, the honorable Charlton Bimsbey.

Then Batesy took the paper from Jansen. "Right now," he said, "everything's going our way with the city council. Here's the part I really like. Quote, 'There will be no charter granted to open a firehouse in that troublesome neighborhood. The people there are too irresponsible and reckless to undertake such responsibility.' I love it," he shouted with glee. "And guys, make sure you don't do anything to upset this success. Nothing."

CHAPTER EIGHT

"Wez gots ta git some money," said Red, with the devil in his eyes.

"Yeah. And what does that mean?" Johnny took a drag on a cigarette, then passed it to Red.

"Wez gots ta eat, doan wez?" Red laughed. "Dat takes money." He took two draws on the butt and gave it back.

"And how're we gonna get it? From some Protestant holy man to whom we'd have to sell our souls?"

"Nah. From some udder rich jerk. Likes dem dopes wid da watch hanging from dere pocket." Red chuckled. "Wez find dem over at da East River thermal. Soon dere be a big bunch coming from Booklyn—"

"It's Brooklyn, not Booklyn. And it's terminal not thermal."

"Yeah, I knows. Wad ya tink I say Booklyn?" Red laughed real hardy like.

"Listen, I don't like this. Especially now after what the priest said. You know if we ever get in trouble with the law, we won't get on the new fire department."

"Johnny. I'z hungry as hell. Gotta git some money so wez can eat. Dis the only way I knows how," Red came back.

"This scares me."

"Doan worry. Dey be squeezed together like beans in a can. Wez have our pick. Timepieces. Bags of all sorts. When dey puts dem down, wez picks dem up. Ha, ha, ha."

"How do we do that?"

"Ya get dem to look at ya. Den I takes the ting," said Red, still chuckling.

"Is it that easy?" Johnny asked. "You know, I haven't done this before."

"Yep. And if the man's gonna come after me, you do someting to stop him."

"Like what?" shot Johnny. He did not like this, but he knew they're going have to do such things if they want to eat.

"Askin to help 'em. Wid their bags or someting. Grab the bag. Dat make dem stop."

They were two blocks from the terminal when they heard the harsh warning blasts of the arriving ferry. They could see its image on its way to its pier.

"It's coming," said Red, stepping up the pace. "Hurry up. Gotta git a good spot. Wez meet back here."

When they got to the wharf, the captain had already began docking the vessel.

"C'mon," said Red, grabbing his hand and pulling him towards a photographer. "Jimmy, take our picture, awright?"

As the man snapped the picture, the ferry docked, sending tremors through the pier. They could hear the waves crashing beneath the pier.

"I let ya know when they're ready," the man shouted after them.

The bulk of the passengers, more than a hundred or so, were gathered at the ferry's loading gates, anxious to get off. And when the gate tenders opened them, the travelers rushed off on to the pier as if in a race to be first off. Many stopped as soon as they stepped foot on the dock, where they dropped their bags to greet someone or to light up a cigarette. Or both.

That's when Red made his move into the crowd, moving like a flash. His red hair made it easier for Johnny to know his whereabouts. He near panicked when he saw one man turn as if to go after Red, but when the man looked to his feet and saw his bag was there, he seemed satisfied. *Probably just jumpy,* thought Johnny.

"Get that little bastard," another man shouted, getting everybody's attention. Instinctively Johnny intervened, reaching for the man's bag. "Can I carry this for you, sir?"

"Keep your hands off that," the man barked, tugging his bag free of Johnny's grip. I'll carry my own bag."

"I'm sorry sir. Just wanted to help," said Johnny, turning and walking away. Again he heard the man shout, "Where did that little thief go? He got my time piece." Then he heard a woman shout, "Somebody took my bag."

That's it! I'm outta here. Johnny, his stomach in knots, decided it would be best for him to disappear. He blended into the crowd. *I'll work my way back to Red.* He felt good about himself. *Hell, I grabbed that guy's bag by instinct. Without even thinking. And that's when Red got away.*

When he didn't see Red back at the corner where they were to meet, the knots in Johnny's stomach tightened. *Did he get caught,* he wondered. But relief came quick, upon hearing his name being whispered. He followed the whisper to the lightless hallway just beyond the small entrance lobby of a tenement, where he got a glimpse of Red's face.

"Anybidy folla ya?" murmured Red.

Shrugging, Johnny glanced to his rear and seeing nobody, stepped into the doorway. "You ran away without getting anything. Why?" Johnny snapped. "Heck, you left me to be caught by the coppers."

"Oh yeah? Den wot's dis?" Red grumbled, holding up with one hand a genuine leather valise and with the other a gold pocket watch dangling on a gold chain. "Ya makes me mad. Did I ever chicken out on ya?"

Now Johnny felt guilty. How could he ever doubt Red, his best friend, who never failed him? He wrapped his powerful arm around Red's shoulders and squeezed, pulling him close. "Now I feel like shyte. I don't even know why I said that. I even heard a guy shout that somebody got his timepiece. I guess because I didn't see you near him, I didn't think it was you. Are we still friends?" He reached for Red's hand.

"Yeah. But never agin." Red snapped a straight left jab to Johnny's jaw that he stopped intentionally an inch short of his face, before he could even react. By that time, Red was returning his handshake. "I'm fast wid da hands, 'rn't I?" said Red, as he shook hands with Johnny. "Dis is all about speed. Grab da ting and run like hell . . . Come on. Now wez stuff our bellies. Dese tings gots to be worth 'bout ten dollars."

"You sell this stuff?" Johnny asked.

"Wot ya tink I duz wid it?" asked Red. He liked having the upper hand over Johnny.

CHAPTER NINE

On the way back to the neighborhood, the anxious duo hurried along Misery Row's riverfront, a dangerous place to be, but they wanted to avoid the coppers, some of who would certainly confiscate their ill-gotten goods rather than arrest them. They also wanted to avoid the possibility of being bushwhacked by other *bandits*.

It wasn't until they reached the old fire tower on 33rd Street, when they were back in their own turf, that they felt safe. Now they could think about easing their hunger. They went straight to the Waterside, a rough and tumble workingman's hangout where one could get a good hot dinner at a price a poor man could afford, as well as get into a good knock down, roll around fight, if they were looking for one. Yet the saloon had the reputation of being a friendly neighborhood place.

They arrived just before seven, just before they stopped serving dinner. The menu was limited to chuck steak, ribs of beef, or the special of the night: lamb stew, all priced at two bits.

In the Waterside, everybody knew everybody. It had two large, dingy rooms with poor lighting. One room served as the bar and the other served as a dining room/kitchen combination. The place smelled of stale beer, onions and cigarette smoke. The floors and walls were constructed of plain, unpainted wood planking. There were ten antiquated, three-foot-square wooden tables, each with four equally old and rickety chairs, set around the dining area. Also, there were benches along two of the walls, with nine-foot long bench-like tables in front of them for patrons to place their plates and drinks on. A pianist banged out *Jeannie with the Light Brown Hair*.

Mr. Dagastino, the owner, rushed to Johnny's side when he entered the shop. In a gravely Italian accent, he said, "I'm sorry about your mama, Johnny." With both hands, Mr. Dagastino held Johnny's hands and shook them. "Mrs. O'Hara was a good, good woman." He paused looking sadly at the floor. "She was so good to my Maria when she was sick. We'll miss her so." Freeing his hands, he blessed himself. "Now why don't you and Red have a big bowl of stew? You be my guests, okay? I be right back."

"Thanks, Mr. Dagastino," said Johnny.

Red smiled a big smile, nodding yes.

"Good thing it's free," said Johnny as he counted the change from the silver dollar his sister had given to him. "Don't think I got the fifty cents to pay for it," said Johnny. "And here he comes, already."

"When I say right away, I mean right away," the smiling Mr. Dagastino cut in on their conversation, plopping the two steaming bowls of stew down on the table.

The time had passed quickly while chatting with the McCarthy brothers, Battler, and friends of his mother. The daylight outside had given way to the evening shadows.

Johnny rubbed his belly. "My stomach is full."

Red snapped, "Yeah, me to," sounding like a real tough-guy.

In the background someone sang *My Old Kentucky Home* as the pianist played.

"My mother liked that song," said Johnny. His eyes moistened.

"C'mon, wez best git movin," said Red, getting to his feet. He tugged Johnny's shoulder. "Befo it's dark and da crooks are out." He laughed at himself. "Guess I can't talk."

* * * * *

It didn't take them long to get through the neighborhood. Johnny moved fast, keeping his head down with Red keeping abreast of him. He did not want to be recognized by the local women and children—the little ones rolled in the germ-infested dirt and horseshit covered earthen street—who lined the streets outside their ramshackle tenements and huts. Good-looking women they were, but everything about the paupers was unkempt. They were dressed in the worst of dresses.

He just couldn't hide from them. Like almost everybody spotted him. He and Red couldn't get to the railroad tracks and that stinking slaughterhouse fast enough. He heard many female voices shouting: "Sorry 'bout ye mommy, Johnny O'Hara," Some of the voices were just downright nosy, asking: "Where ya goin, Johnny?" or "What ya got in dat 'barrow, Johnny?"

Red was correct in his assumption that where they were heading would be empty of God-fearing people. Once they left the neighborhood and passed the train tracks, all they saw were a couple of men guarding some warehouses, who watched the two of them like hawks. If anyone did mess with them, or tried to take Johnny's belongings, they would have to get past the powerful blows from the 18" iron bar he kept at the ready in the wheelbarrow. And the six-inch knife Red carried under his belt; the blade he would not hesitate to use to protect his interests or the interests of his new *roommate*.

"Wez gotta stop here. Gotta git sum money fo dese," said Red, halting at 29th and Eleventh, right where the neighborhood ended.

"Where?" asked Johnny.

"From da boss. Brogan. Wait here. I cum right back," he said, then disappeared briefly into the dark of a tenement entryway, making Johnny nervous.

"You okay in there?" Johnny called out. When Red did not answer him, he stepped into the vestibule to investigate only to run into Red's smiling face as it reemerged from the dark.

"Wez got ten bucks. Check it out." Red counted out five one-dollar coins and handed them to Johnny. "Dat's good, hah?"

"That's a lot of money," said Johnny.

* * * * *

They just passed the new gas works plant heading, towards 25th street, not far from Eleventh Avenue, a block from the river; where there existed another pocket of hostility; another rundown district with many jerrybuilt, low-ceiling shacks slapped together with scraps of wood. Rags filled voids between the shacks' planking helping to keep out the hot rays of the sun in the summer and the cold winds during the winter when the penniless occupants would do anything for a few pieces of firewood or a bucket of coal.

A new warehouse under construction had a couple of armed security guards protecting it and the building materials stacked behind the fencing. Next to it a cellar was being dug, readying for the construction. Red couldn't help but step up to the gate to get a look in.

"Get away from there," came a shout from one of the burly guards.

"Ah, doan git all excited, will ya? I used to do dat work," he shouted, flexing his bulging shoulders and biceps. "Where ya tink I gits dems from?"

The guard laughed. "Ah, awright," said the guard. "Guess it's okay for ya ta look through the fence."

"Tink of me in there, just seven-years-old. Picking away and shovlin the whole day. Lil ole me," said Red, impressing both Johnny and the guard.

"You started young," said the security man.

"Ah, well. Wot could I do? I worked wid my fadda," he said.

"Well, it didn't do ya any harm. Made ya strong, didn't it?"

Red saluted the man, saying, "Tanks," then continued off with Johnny.

The inhabitants of the area they were in were destitute, many of them doing bad things to survive.

"Wez stay on dis street," said Red, meaning Eleventh Avenue. "Dat should be empty. Nobidy working dere by now. If we didn't have that wheelbarrow, I'd go right along the river. Id be safer dat way."

They walked on the riverside of the street in front of Macon's Beef, a one-story brick slaughterhouse that took up the whole block, stretching right down to the river. There were two large holding pens filled with sleeping cattle, one on each side of the slaughterhouse. Silence prevailed with the exception of an occasional bawl.

"You really tink getten rid of da volleys is a good ting?" asked Red.

"Yeah. And it's gonna happen, whether we like it or not. Heck, can ye imagine getting paid for doing something you like to do?"

"But dey woan take me. Can't speak right. Can't write right," said Red, sounding disappointed.

"Will you stop saying *woan* and *doan*. It's *won't* and *don't*. Heck, you know you can learn to read and write easy enough. Me and Katie," he put his hands to his chest, "will help ya. And I just know Mr. Mulvihey would help get you appointed. He seems like a good man." Johnny then put his arm around his smaller buddy. "Ya know, Red. I wouldn't want to be a fireman if you weren't with me."

* * * * *

"Chuck, look!" Greg Lopat elbowed Chuck Jansen.

"Look at what?"

"Ain't that the little red head that kicked your ass yesterday?" said the grinning Lopat, from their vantage point across the street, hidden in a dark passageway between two buildings. "The one that reminds you of you know who?"

Chuck strained to see Red as he passed under a dim streetlight. "Fuck, if it isn't him. Or should I say her? I remember those shoulders. Tried to rip my throat open." Gently, he touched the scabs on the sides of his neck. "Besides, how could I forget that ass? Just like her mother. Angel, right? I know she had a daughter whose name was Angie. Even had red hair."

"The way you talk about that kid, it better be a girl." Lopat giggled quietly. "Isn't right for a guy to be checking out another guy's ass."

"Fuck you," said Jansen, continuing to watch Red. "Let's find out. And, maybe we can use that shit they're pushing." He pulled his mask over his face. "That face reminds me so much of that Angel Hester. I hope it's her daughter. I'll stick it up her ass."

"You're joking, I hope," said Lopat, who also wore a mask. "Wasn't her mother enough?"

The two of them routinely roamed the streets at night when short of money, looking for some drunken fool that wound up where he didn't belong. Often enough they were drunken businessmen from out of town, looking for fast women and mistakenly wondered into the area. Often enough they were beaten and robbed—occasionally murdered.

Although Lopat didn't savage his victims, Jansen quite often did. He'd club a poor fool senseless. They would do their dirty work in the dark of night at locations bordering on immigrant neighborhoods to give the impression that the culprits were foreigners.

Following the dark shadows of night, the two masked men moved like cats stalking their prey, just as they did many times before. They crossed the dung-covered street, and within seconds, were upon the unsuspecting duo.

"What the fuck you people doing in my turf?" Jansen bellowed in his deep voice, startling them, and at the same time, grabbing the hair at the back of Red's head.

That voice. I know that voice. The sound of that voice stunned Johnny, cutting out all that was happening around him. All he could think of was *that's the voice of my mother's killer.* He saw her in his mind's eye, lying dead in her own blood.

With one hand, Jansen yanked Red's head back. And when Red reached for his hand, he grabbed between Red's legs feeling for a penis. "It's a fucking she," he shouted. "Got no dick!" Holding his already erect penis, he shouted, "I'm gonna fuck you Angie Hester."

"Try it ya fagot and I cut ya dick off," Red responded, reaching for her knife, at the same time shouting: "Johnny, it's him. It's him."

The much-bigger and stronger Jansen, yanked the knife from Red's hand, then slammed her down on her back, hurting her, forcing the air from her lungs. With one yank, Jansen ripped the frayed trousers and underpants from Red's body, leaving her bare from the waist down, exposing her womanhood.

"What you doing?" Lopat shouted. "Wasn't one enough?"

79

Red fought like a tiger, punching and clawing at his eyes through the cloth mask he wore. She even stuck her fingers up his nostrils through the mask openings. But Jansen, like a dog in heat, ignored her blows, moving his hand over her buttocks and forcing it between her legs.

Johnny still didn't know what was going on around him, transfixed on the guy's voice, the voice of his mother's killer. *I must kill him.* He yanked the iron bar from the wheelbarrow.

"Stop! Stop it," Red screeched just like a girl upon feeling his fingers trying to enter her. She pounded and clawed at his back.

"Spread those fucking legs," he roared. Panting like a dog, he pulled at her legs with all his might. With all her strength, she resisted.

Again Lopat shouted, "Stop! She's only a fucking kid."

"Johnny, wot ya doing? Stop him," she shouted.

"Get off her," shouted Lopat, tugging at Jansen's collar.

His mind no longer blurred, Johnny finally became aware of his best friend's horrible predicament—and that *he* was a *she. He's trying to force his dick into her. Hell, he's raping her.*

Without uttering a word, his powerful arm delivered a crushing blow of the iron bar to the side of Jansen's head, splitting his scalp. Jansen's large body turned limp and collapsed on Red, spurting blood from the wound. Red felt the warm liquid splash on her face. "Get him off me," she cried in revulsion. She then began heaving, wanting to vomit.

With his abnormal strength, the 15-year-old O'Hara yanked the monster off her, roughly ripping the mask from his head. "It's him! It's him," he roared, exhilarated, he again hit the unconscious Jansen, ripping open another long gash in his scalp.

"You killed my mother," he screamed, tears wetting his face, preparing to deliver another blow with animal force—a blow that he hoped would split his skull open and finish him. But then the barrel of a pistol, made clearly visible by the streetlamp overhead, appeared between him and Jansen's head, almost close enough to touch his face.

"Drop it or I drop you," Lopat blurted out. His voice quivered, the revolver shook in his hand, being more nervous than Johnny.

Growling like a cross dog, Johnny hesitated, the iron bar still held over his head. "You know he's no good," he shouted. "Leave him with me." Then again O'Hara remembered the priest's warning if he should harm this man. He'd have no future with the fire department.

"I'll shoot you," Lopat threatened while struggling to lift the profusely-bleeding Jansen to his feet. Lopat kept the gun trained on Johnny. "I got no beef with youse guys," he said. "Just back off."

"I kill 'em for dis," Red cried, her knife back in her hand, ready to inflict damage on Jansen.

Seeing tears glistening in her eyes angered Johnny. Not ever before having seen her cry, he knew just how much of an embarrassment it must have been for her, knowing her thinking that tough guys don't cry. Although he felt like a heel, he could not stop looking at her exposed privates, fascinated and excited by her nudity, even though there wasn't much to see in the darkness but the V-shaped patch of pubic hair. Then his gentlemanliness won out over the devil and he removed his shirt. "Here. Cover yourself. I'll get you something."

While going through his few belongings to retrieve a pair of trousers for her, he experienced a feeling he thought very awkward: Red's being a female made him happy. He even felt relief. *Why,* he wondered. Did he feel relief because he had always been too attracted to her, when he thought of her as a boy, which sometimes almost turned his stomach and made him ashamed of himself.

"Stop looking," Red snapped, in her natural voice.

"I'm sorry," he said, almost stupefied by the whole experience. *What a cute voice she's got,* he told himself. He threw her a pair of rag-tag trousers. Once she had them on, they were right back on the move. But this time she had the open knife in her trembling hand.

"Tanks," she said, without looking at him, then snapped, "Men. Youse all da same. Just like my fadda. All youse wants is sex."

"How can you say that about me?" His face a picture of hurt. "I never did anything to you. Touched you anywhere I wasn't supposed to."

"Dat 'cause ya didn't know I wuz a girl."

"I often suspected you were. I'm glad you are. Many a night I went to bed thinking about you. It made me sick. Imagine how I felt when I was thinking these thoughts about another boy. I began to think I was a queer. That scared the hell outta me."

Red remained pokerfaced. She did not respond to his affections. Instead, she pleaded, "Ya won't tell anybidy. Right, Johnny?"

"No I won't. But we should tell the coppers about this."

"No," she insisted. "Wot would dey do? And I doan wants dem knows I a girl."

"I wish you'd stop talking the way you do. "What did your father do? I mean do to you."

"He touched me. Everywhere. Ya tell them nuttin. Right, Johnny?"

"Don't you trust me? I mean, I'm your best friend," he said.

"Yeah. I don't even knowd wot I'm talking 'bout."

The two trembling, hard-nosed youngsters continued along Eleventh, Red pushing the wheelbarrow and Johnny walking beside her, this time carrying his iron club at the ready.

"I let you down," he said, gloom-faced, looking straight ahead.

"No, Johnny. Ya not ta blame. Youse wuz tinking 'bout ya mudda."

His face saddened. Not because of his mom, but because he suddenly revisited in his mind the many times he saw Red fighting, sometimes taking a bad beating. And he didn't help her because they called for a fair fight. All because she wanted to be a tough guy instead of being her beautiful self. *Oh, if I only knew.*

"If anybody ever messes with you again . . . I'll kill 'em, I swear." He wanted so bad to embrace her, to be her protector.

"Hey look, big guy. Iz kin still take care of meself," she shot back.

"Not while I'm around," he insisted. He took the wheelbarrow from her. "That's me job."

When they reached the long-neglected McAdams family property, she began whacking the overgrown brush with his iron bar, clearing a pathway to the waterfront.

"Gee. Dey gots da house all closed," she said.

"Guess they don't want anybody going in there."

The McAdams family property had once been a picturesque waterfront meadowland.

Being dark made their trek ever more difficult, a bit of a struggle to get the wheelbarrow through the thick brush, some of it over six-foot tall. They must have hit every boulder and rut on the way.

"Where da heck's da trail?" spouted the irate Red. Just then they broke out of the brush onto the trail. "Okay, least nows wez can see."

Then *thump!* The wheelbarrow hit a large stone. They froze as if expecting something to happen. But nothing did happen. That was the last stone to be hit. Things got easier from that point on. When they reached the shoreline, they were at ease. They could relax and enjoy the total peace of the river. Not even a wave sloshing against the shoreline. The only noises they heard were their footfalls swishing in the wet sand.

Shortly thereafter they reached what Red called home: an seven-foot deep by twelve-foot square hole in the ground under a wood-plank floor in a twenty-foot by thirty-foot wooden shed that she inherited from a deceased friend. A trapdoor lay hidden under a coating of hay. The shed sat about a hundred feet from the shore, in a safe area where she had many trusted friends. Yet on two occasions, people invaded her abode, but they were severely dealt with. That's why she briefly stopped and observed the surrounding area before entering the shed. She never wanted to be seen going into it. Then they entered the unstable structure, going right to the trapdoor.

CHAPTER TEN

"**I**s this your . . . your home?" he asked. His eyes were wide with surprise.

"Wot ya, a wise guy? Doan make funna me," she warned.

"Easy. You could have lived with us, for God's sake. Why didn't you say something?" It upset him to think she lived like this.

To his dismay, she took his hand and whispered. "Johnny O'Hara, I kin take care of meself. And always will." He had hoped she would welcome him as her protector.

They hid the wheelbarrow inside. They dropped his belongings through the hatch and then they dropped themselves into the musty-smelling, pitch-black opening in the ground, with its dirt floor covered with a thick layer of hay. Standing on a wooden crate, she reached up and closed the trapdoor. Producing a candle in a holder, she placed it on a box and lit it, giving off a dim light that created a cozy affect.

At one end of the room lay her bed: a pile of hay. Adjacent to the bed rested a box with the candle on it. Along the wall rested a shovel and a pitchfork. On the wall opposite the foot of her bed was a crude shelf on which sat a basin. Hanging from it were a washcloth and two well-worn towels.

"Dat ting's to wash wid," she said, pointing to the basin. "Soap's in it. Da water ya get in the river." She laughed. But her pretty smile quickly turned sour. "I feel durty as hell after dat big fuck. I going in the water."

"You mean now? In the dark?" He shook his head. "You're crazy?"

"Gotta clean myself. I feel durty. Dat bastard." She thought of Jansen's hands on her privates.

"It's dark out there."

"So what?" she said.

"Where'd you learn to swim?"

"You tink I live by da water and don't go in. On dese hot days? Ya crazy. Heck I swim to Jersey and back. And goes back sometimes agin."

"Here. You can use this." He handed her Katie's mattress.

"Dat's great," she said, pointing to the space across from where she sleeps. "Put your stuff dere and ya bed over dere." She pointed to the opposite wall. She threw Katie's mattress over her bed of hay.

Red learned to sleep anywhere, mattress or no mattress, from her hard experiences living on the streets. Many a night she slept in an alley or a field, with nothing between her and the earth she slept on. During the winters she'd sleep in basements, some of which stunk to the high heavens of human waste. Even that she got used to.

He removed three books from one of the bags, placing them on his bed. "I read a lot, you know. If you want, I'll teach you, too. And Katie. She's a good teacher."

"Ya know, me tinks I'd like dat. Is it hard?" she asked.

"Uh-uh. First you learn the letters, then the words. Then you read books. It gets easier and easier," he said.

"Den I won't be so dumb," she said.

"Will ye stop saying that," Johnny snapped. He did not like her putting herself down. "You're not dumb."

"You really mean that, Johnny?"

"Of course, I do. For Pete's sake, will ya listen to what the priest told you?"

She smiled, without responding.

"What do you do for a privy?" he asked.

"Go out back by da big tree. Make sure you dig a hole if ya gonna dump. And bury da stuff soes mys frens doan smell it. Or step in it. Ha, ha, ha. C'mon. Let's go swimin."

"I'll just watch."

"Go ahead. I gotta change," she said.

A few minutes later he heard her voice from a good distance out, challenging him to join her.

"Nah. Another time," he said, standing at the shoreline, shaking his head. All though he pretended to be calm, he feared the water and didn't know why. Not once since he lived in the area did he go into the North River. "You're crazy," he continued, whispering forcefully. "You don't even know what's out there." In the light of the moon reflecting on the placid water, he could see her head bobbing peacefully, her arm motioning him in. Then she swam off, going further out.

"Please don't go out there," he shouted, again a forceful whisper. He could feel the bottom of his gut getting all knotted up. *Where is she,* he wondered when he could no longer see her head or hear her strokes cutting the water. He scurried back and forth along the beach-like waterfront, his eyes darting wildly out at the water.

"Red . . . Red Hester! Where the hell are ya?" he shouted, no longer concerned about being heard. "Don't do this. You're scaring me. Come out, will ya? Come back here." Not until the water reached his waist did he realize he had stepped into the river. "What am I doing," he shouted, then hurried to get out of the water.

The distraught young man's eyes continued darting all over the water's surface, looking for her bobbing head or her arms stroking the water. "Not Red too. Please." He sighed with emotion.

"Ey, look up 'ere," he heard her scream from high above. Turning, he gasped, almost shitting himself as he watched her let go of a rope attached to the top of a listing, scuttled schooner's mast and drop a great distance into the water. His legs almost gave out on him.

As she swam to shore, she shouted, "You don't gotta worry about me. Iz the Crazy Mermaid. Da best swimmer ever."

"I could give you this," he shouted, cocking his fist. "This ain't funny. You scared the hell out of me."

When she saw the terror in his eyes, she suddenly realized she went too far with her joke. "Sorry, Johnny. I shudda knowd it's no time for joking." How he worried about her gave her great surprise.

Little did Johnny know, but he had nothing to fear. When it came to swimming, nobody could top Red. At least not from the neighborhood. Her work as a digger gave her great strength throughout her body, with exceptional shoulder strength that greatly enhanced her ability to swim. And she had ample opportunity to swim while living along the North River. Not a summer's day passed that she didn't get in at least one complete lap back and forth across the river, fighting the current each time. Day or night, it didn't matter.

And in quick order, she put her swimming skills to work for herself. From her riverfront *hole in the ground* she would often swim out to a passing vessel. "Trow a coin and I git it befo it hit da boddom," she would shout to her audience. Hardly a vessel would pass where at least a couple of people would throw her a coin, and most times she would recover them. Or at least she'd come up from down under, waving coins between her fingers.

"She was fascinating to watch as she surfaced and dived like a Dolphin," a *Herald* reporter on board one of the vessels had once written about her. "They loved her, that little redheaded powerhouse. They oooohed and ahhhhed, cheered and applauded, as she swung through the air high above the water. They gasped when she let go and went into a dive of more than fifty feet. We never got to know that little gal, *The Crazy Mermaid of the North River . . .*"

Ships' officers would routinely stop their vessels for a few moments to enable the passengers to enjoy Red's antics and swimming prowess, and to throw her coins, sometimes even silver dollars. She was such a strong swimmer that when these opportunities arose, she would often dive after the coins and then reemerge with such force she would break through the water's surface, sometimes rising a few feet into the air, just like a fish. Sometimes she'd rise with a silver dollar between her teeth, thrilling her audience.

"Ya knows dey called me da Crazy Mermaid? I wuz in da paper."

"Holy crap. And to think that was you. My friend. The Crazy Mermaid of the North River."

"As youse guys would say, 'I wapped dem awound mys finger.' I knows how to. At times I fooled dem. You know, with the coins. One time tree guys dropped tree coins at the same time. Dey said I wouldn't be able to git dem. I duckdid under and came right back up with tree of dem. And when they clapped at me, I show dem anudda coin and I start laughing. Ya shudda seened dere faces. Did I gets dem or wot?" She laughed again.

Her North River antics didn't stop with her swimming and high diving. She also excelled at rope climbing, hand over hand style, pulling herself up to the top of the fifty-foot high mast of the scuttled schooner that sat rotting beside the abandoned pier.

"Let's go back. I did wot I had to do," she said.

"You know, I'm glad you're a girl," said Johnny, looking relieved. As though getting a load off his mind.

"Why?" she asked.

"Because I like you." He watched closely her reaction.

"Yeah. I like you too. You're my best friend," she responded.

"That's it. A best friend?" he asked, his face giving away his hurt.

She turned her back to him, hiding her surprise, and the fact that she didn't know how to react to him. She had never before thought about being somebody's girlfriend. After all, she had always played the role of a boy, a tough boy at that, and portrayed herself in every way as one. "Ya means boyfriend and girlfriend?" She still didn't look at him.

"Yeah. What's wrong with that?" he asked, getting to his feet. Again he watched her every move.

Then she faced him. "But I *wanna* be a guy. Not a dame. I'm one of the boys. Wot would dey tink? Right? Ya'd spoil mys repatation."

"Its reputation . . . not repatation . . . Do you like girls then?" he asked, blushing. He sensed her embarrassment. But he didn't care. He was angry with her.

"Wot you tink? I'm one a dem?" she said, again avoiding eye contact.

"You certainly sound like one," he answered, unable to hide his upset.

Red remained standing, flushed with anger and embarrassment.

"I want to kiss you," he continued, grabbing her arm.

"Why? So ya can try what dat Chuck guy did?" she flared up, yanking her arm free then pounding on his chest the way a woman would, not like a street fighter. "Like all dose udder horny bastards. Dat's all youse tink about."

Shocked by her outburst, he lunged at her, grabbing her shoulders and shaking her. "Whadda you talking about? Hell, I love you, Red. That's all," he said.

She closed her eyes and covered them with her hands. "Stop it," she sobbed, turning away, not wanting him to see her crying.

"You're crying. Why? What have I done?" He tried to hug her, but she pushed him away. "Red! I've never seen you like this."

She faced him, tears streaming from her eyes. "It's not you. I just can't get close to men. It's what they've done to me."

"Then why make believe you're one of us?"

"For protection."

"From what?

"From men," she snapped. "When dey tink I'm a man, dey don't bodda me. Dat's wot. And ya'll keep my secret, right? Right, Johnny?" she insisted, nodding her head.

"You don't even have to ask that." He plopped down on his bedding, staring her in the eye and after a brief pause, asked, "Will ya tell me what they did to you?"

"Everyting. Ever since me wuz a liddle gurl. First my *fadda*. He made me do things to him. Touch him you know where."

"Where is your father? I'd like to—"

Johnny didn't get to make his point. She stopped him short, saying with emotion, "He's dead. Drink'd too much."

At a very young age, Red had a body that turned men on. Just like her mother. Boys would grope her. Vagrants molested her, especially when she lived on the streets. That's how she learned to defend herself with a knife. On two occasions, her skill handling a blade saved her from being raped. She even *carved up* one of her attackers, slicing his penis.

That night Red slept with her knife at her side while Johnny slept across the room.

* * * * *

"My head's sore as hell," said Jansen, holding the sides of his bandaged head, staring at the ceiling from his resting place. He was flat on his back on a tenement cellar floor. Lopat didn't bring him home because of his messed up condition. His landlady wouldn't tolerate his condition and would question him. "What the fuck happened?" he asked.

"The woman you shot. Her son got you good. He'd a killed you if I didn't put my piece in his face," said Lopat. He tapped the revolver he had tucked under his belt.

"Why didn't ya shoot him?" barked Jansen. He gave Lopat an angry look.

"I'm no killer. I'll leave that shit to you," Lopat shot back, returning the angry look.

"I'll get him. But first I wanna fuck that bitch Hester."

"How you know she's who you think she is?" asked Lopat.

"That Red hair. The face. She looks exactly like her dead mother, Angel Hester. Exactly like her," said Jansen, with no emotion. "Who else could it be?"

"Oh God. Don't even remind me," said Lopat, closing his eyes for a moment, wishing to forget.

"I *gotta* do it before Friday."

"Why did you have to kill her mother?" asked Lopat. "I was there when he told you just to beat her. Give her a good scare."

"That's right," said Jansen. "But accidents happen." He glared at Lopat.

"If I'd of known that would happen, I would never have gone with you," insisted Lopat. "What did she do to that rich guy, anyway?"

"He got her pregnant then insisted she get rid of it, which she wouldn't. She wanted him to marry her."

Again Lopat insisted he would have had nothing to do with it if he knew what the outcome would have been. "You. And that banker. Youse got my mind all fucked up with this thing. He's a weirdo. Him and his long hair. I mean like down to here." Lopat tapped his elbow. "Wonder if he still wears it like a horse's tail?"

"Don't know anything about him, except that when he goes whoring, he lets it hang. To cover his face. Now I got a question. Where did the redhead and her boyfriend go?" Jansen stuck his face close to Lopat's, to scare him, to pressure him to tell him.

Lopat didn't want to tell him where they were, but knew that if he didn't, he would turn on him. With a sense of guilt, he answered, "By the river. Think they're staying in the old shed."

"Where we buried the redhead's mother?" Jansen grinned.

"Yeah. But you got to leave the redhead alone," he insisted. "For Pete's sake, she's only a kid."

"Sure. Just for you, Greg. Just want to tell her I'm sorry," said Jansen.

* * * * *

Johnny awoke to a dark room with a couple of slivers of sunlight shining through straw-covered seams in the flooring above. Coming from somewhere outside, from a distance away, he could hear the muted hollers and cheers of men. What the hell is that, he wondered. "Red, Red," he muttered. When he got no reply, he sprang to his feet. In the dark he saw on the floor the outline of the wooden crate, over which he knew the trapdoor was located. With a push of his hand he opened the trapdoor. Then standing on the crate, the six-footer easily pulled himself up. The cheering and hollering died down, but still he could hear the voices of people talking excitedly—some of them foreigners. Had to be the slaughterhouse. But he could not make out what they were saying. Slowly, he stuck his head out of the shed. Again he heard the sounds of cheering men growing louder and louder.

With caution, Johnny worked his way towards the shoreline, where the sounds were coming from. He hid behind anything that provided concealment. Then, right before his eyes, he saw Red doing her thing, swinging wildly from the rope at the top of the mast. "Oh my God," he muttered. "She's crazy!"

Listening to the cheers and applause getting louder and louder and watching her swinging back and forth going higher and higher, once again scared the hell out of him. And when she let go of the rope and soared even higher into the air, he covered his eyes with his hands. "Oh God," he groaned. "I don't want to see this." Seconds later he heard sustained applause. He opened his eyes to see Red's smiling face in the water; watching her waving to her audience.

Johnny started for the shoreline, his angry eyes stuck on Red. He wanted to scream at her for scaring the shit out of him. But he wouldn't get the chance.

"Who you be? Wot ya doing here?" a manly voice shouted, coming from nearby.

"Who wants to know?" he shouted back. He spotted a group of vagrants standing by a fire in the center of a mini-forest not far from the water. He traced the voice to a monster of a woman who challenged, "Ole Battle Axe here wants ta know. I tells ya, big guy, if it's trouble you want, ya gonna git it."

Johnny did not appreciate the threat. He wanted to lash out, but held back, assuming her to be a friend of Red's. "I'm Johnny O'Hara," he shouted back. "I'm with her, that crazy—"

"Sure. It's Red's pal. You okay den." Battle Axe smiled approvingly. The others followed suit, smiling and shaking their heads in approval. "Hows 'bout some tea?"

"Not now," said Johnny, anxious to get to Red. "Gotta make sure she's okay."

"Ya ain't got nuttin to worry 'bout. She be okay. Heck, shes be halfway across the river bys now."

Sure enough, by the time he got down to the water, Red was already midway to the other side.

So happened the middle-aged woman, Battle Axe, cared for and protected Red until she could protect herself.

In her earlier years, Battle Axe also belonged to a gang, just like Red. She fought side by side with the boys. And she cracked many a head and ripped a lot of flesh with her weapon of choice, a wooden club with two spikes. Eventually she retired from gang life. It just wasn't worth it, having spent much too much time incarcerated on Blackwell Island.

Battle Axe weighed 180 pounds and stood six-foot tall in her prime. These days she was pushing over 200 pounds and remained a ruthless brawler who still administered a terrible beating, when necessary. And if what her homeless mates said was true, at least two of her opponents never again saw the light of day. Needless to say, her riverside settlement became a *no-go* area for unwelcome visitors.

Just like every morning, this morning they had tea and coffee working, but this day they also had a loaf of bread. Red and Johnny stood there eying the two thin cuts of bread that remained on the bench.

"So dis ya fren, hah Red? The one ya been telling us about," Battle Axe asked, speaking in her normal, gravelly voice. With her hand, she signaled them to take the bread.

"Yep. Dat's him. Johnny. My best fren." She smiled at him, then introduced him to the others. "Battle Axe wuz like me mudda. Took care of me 'til me gots old enough to take care of meself." Red looked fondly at Battle Axe. "For dat I always be tanksf . . . thankful." She laughed. "Dats right Johnny, right? Thankful."

Johnny smiled, being a little taken aback when she corrected herself. "That's great!" he said.

"And he's as big as ya said. Dat's good. Now he kin do the brawling instead of me. Ims too old fa dat shit," said Battle Axe with a gruff laugh. Her smile revealed numerous facial scars and several missing teeth.

Just as they did every morning, they hung out among the trees, speaking softly, keeping out of sight until after 7 AM. That's when the workers at the nearby slaughterhouse, who were well aware of their presence, were all indoors or on the north side of the building shooing in the beef stock. They did not want to attract the attention of any young ones that might look to cause them havoc. While the vast majority of the workers knew enough to stay away, there were on occasion a few who didn't know better. Besides, Battle Axe really didn't look forward to any more violent confrontations.

And as soon as the meat handlers were inside, starting their day's work, Red elbowed Johnny. "Let's go," she said.

"Where ye goin so fast?" asked Battle Axe.

"Gotta make some silver." Red knew every nook and cranny along the shoreline, exactly how to stay out of sight. On occasion she went via the river's edge to get to South Ferry, a good distance to the south, but usually once outside of her own turf, she used Eleventh Avenue.

"Wot dem people don't knows won't make dem sick," she said. "Nobiddy has to knows where wez live."

They passed under the dock, where the slaughterhouse workers had just begun unloading cattle by the scores. There was much noise between the cattle bawling and the men shouting above. And there was reason for caution to avoid the cow dung and urine droppings that seeped through the cracks of the pier's planking. Proceeding this way for more than ten minutes along the riverfront, they reached a clearing between two warehouses then cut out onto Eleventh.

"It's awright now. Wez can walk reg'lar agin."

"Damn Hester! Your English is a pisser. We have to work on it."

Little did they know that Jansen had been watching them from the south side of the slaughterhouse dock. He had watched them with great interest, including Red's diving exhibition, which he actually enjoyed.

Eleventh Avenue was alive with people and noise: the clip-clop of horseshoes on the cobblestones, the groaning of wagons and their wheels, the neighing of the horses, and the arguing and laughter of the workers.

Wherever one looked, there were horses and wagons and horse droppings. Wagons were backed against the loading docks of the different warehouses and depots and slaughterhouses, being loaded up with the day's supplies. The wagons waiting to be loaded were lined up, waiting along the sidewalk. The loaded wagons could be seen heading off in all directions. Then came the trucks carrying the late day supply of meat and fish to the restaurants and hotels.

So too were the 'dung wagons' on the move. Their crews of men with Irish accents shoveling the overwhelming amount of horse manure that covered the streets onto their wagons that they would eventually dump in the nearby North River. One crew hoisted the bloated carcass of a large hog onto its bed while just a few feet from them, several swine were devouring the cattle innards that had been inadvertently dropped on the street.

Hammers banged driving nails as saws scraped back and forth ripping wood at the site of a large one-story structure under construction. Lopat was one of the workers swinging a hammer. He spotted the flaming redhead with her hair cut short like a boy, with her comrade Johnny, sloshing through the muck and mire covered street. "Hey you, Red," he shouted, running after her.

Johnny and Red turned at the same time to see Lopat running, closing in on them with the hammer in his hand.

"What the fuck," shouted Red, turning to face him. She flashed her knife.

Johnny stepped in front of her to cut him off. "Drop that fucking hammer or I drop you," he commanded, raising the iron bar over his head.

"Hold it. I'm not after youse," yelled Lopat, making a dead stop, securing the hammer on his belt. He saw Red's knife at the ready. "No trouble, I promise."

"Whadda you want?" shouted Johnny, the bar still at the ready.

"Easy, boss. Just wanna tell her something."

"Yeah, what?" snapped Red, her hand now in her pocket, still gripping the knife. She looked around, obviously nervous that someone would hear him refer to her as *her*. There were no familiar faces about.

"I was with that guy that . . . that jumped you last night."

Anger flashed across her face. She again drew the knife.

"Wait! Wait a minute," he shouted, jumping back. "You crazy or something?"

"Let him talk," said Johnny, again stepping between them.

"I'm really sorry about last night. And I had nothing to do with it. I swear," he said.

"I remember your voice," she snapped.

Lopat continued, "There's something else, too."

"Yeah, what?" she asked, sarcastically.

"Hey don't be a wise guy. I don't have to tell you anything. So back off. Okay?"

"Well fuck ya, den. Put up ya dukes," she barked, putting up her fists.

"Wait a minute! Will ya?" Johnny wrapped his arms around her, shouting, "Hear what he's got to say. Say your piece, will ye?"

Lopat spoke haltingly. He felt like a traitor telling on Jansen. "He said he's gonna kill you. And he'll do it. He's a killer."

"I'll be waiting," said Johnny, choking up thinking of his mother.

Red chimed in, whipping out her six-inch blade not as a threat to Lopat. "And if he doan git him, I will."

"I know. I mean, we know he's no good. One more thing. If you don't see him by tomorrow, then you won't see him. He has to disappear for a while," said Lopat.

"To where?" snapped Johnny.

"That I don't know," Lopat lied. "I gotta get back to work." He turned to leave.

"Hey! How do he knows me anyway?" asked Red.

"You won't like the answer," said Lopat. Again he turned to leave.

Red's expression hardened. "Hey, tell me, will ya? I wanna knows, okay?"

"You're Angel Hester's daughter? Is that right?"

The question shocked her.

"She … she was," Lopat paused, "a prostitute."

"No! No! Ya fucking liar," she cried out in a whisper.

"I told you ya wouldn't like it. I better go," he said. He retrieved his hammer and left.

"Doan believe him, Johnny. He lies. He wanna make me mad. Dat's all." She became silent.

"Say something, will ye?" said Johnny. "What's the puss for?"

She nodded. "Why I had to askin him?"

"Tell me what's wrong," Johnny insisted.

"My mudda—she always go'd out at night. And she always come back late. And sometimes she dressed weal fancy like. From the window I sees her getting into dem fancy wagons. A lot of times she git into a weal big white one. Iz always remember da big black horse dat pulled it. Musta been a weal rich guy."

"C'mon," said Johnny, reaching his strong arm around her broad shoulders, giving her an instant sense of security. "Forget that shit. You have to teach me how to pick pockets. Or whatever it is that we will be doing."

"Yeah. Ya right. Let's git to work. Make sum money," she said.

"Yeah. And ye know, I don't like to do this," said Johnny.

"Neither does I. But if wez wants ta eat, wez gots to," she said. Then stepping out briskly, she looked like the orphan she was, wearing Johnny's tattered trousers, the cuffs too high and rolled too many times; the waist much too big. And her feet were bare, which he hated.

* * * * *

With the completion of the railroad along the west side came an industrial boom: factories, breweries, slaughterhouses, warehouses, and lumber and brick yards. And with all the industry came jobs and of course, more competition for them. The boom also brought about the hasty construction of flimsy tenements to house the workers and their families. By the end of the Civil War, over three hundred and fifty thousand people were packed into the city's west side.

Right in the heart of all those new structures, north of 20th Street, stood a burned out, one block square three-story warehouse. The fire had so thoroughly burned away all of its siding and roofing that only a skeleton of charred beams and studs remained.

"Dat wuz a tough one, ah Johnny?" she asked, looking at the blackened remains. "We woz dere almost a whole day putting it out. Remember Johnny?"

"Damn, you have to learn how to talk right. Promise me, you will."

She nodded. "Yeah, okay."

"Now, how we gonna … ha," he laughed. "Now you got me talking that way. How are we going to make this money?" he asked.

"Dis time the South Ferry thermal."

"Stop," he gestured with his hand. "Remember what I told you. It's *terminal,* not *thermal.*"

"Awright. This one's not as crowded, but da people are more stupider. Dey leave dere bags down den take off. Dat—that's when we walk in and take off." She laughed. "Wid the bags. Easier than da udder place."

"It's *more stupid*, not *stupider*. How many times I gotta tell you."

"But I'm doing better. Now I say that. Not dat. And them not dem. So don't talk. Okay?"

Johnny chuckled. "By the way. What's with the bags?"

"Hide da loot. Dis, I mean this ragamuffin would look funny wid a fancy suitcase."

A familiar voice called out, "Johnny O'Hara."

Handsome Sergeant Desmond O'Connell headed their way. "Good morning to you, Johnny. And to you, young Hester," he said, cracking a smile. As always, O'Connell looked very smart in his well-maintained and fitted uniform. His shoes, cap, and buttons were highly polished.

Red nodded in return, but said nothing.

"Have ye heard anything I should know?" he asked, staring at the burlap bags. They simply shook their heads. O'Connell continued, watching their body language. "Somebody assaulted a man fitting the description of your mother's killer down by Macon's last night. You wouldn't happen to know anything about it, would you?"

"Nuttin," shot Red.

"Baloney," Johnny cut in. "You're right, Sergeant. The guy who shot me mother. And last night he—"

Red swung around in front of Johnny, grabbing his shirt. "Shut ya mouth," she shouted, several times. But to no avail.

"Not this time," Johnny replied, grabbing her wrists and pulling her to him. "We gotta tell. He tried to fu... fu... screw her. Ripped her clothes off."

O'Connell went out of his way to make sure he showed no reaction to learning that Red was a girl. Still the red-faced gal could not look him in the eye.

"That's when I clocked him with this," said Johnny, waving the weapon in front of O'Connell. "I wanted to kill him! But his friend put a gun to me head."

O'Connell exclaimed, "Bejasus, I'm glad he did—"

"What?" snapped the startled Johnny.

"That's not what I mean. Let me finish. The last thing I'd want to see is ye go to jail for that piece of trash. You have to promise me you'll not take the law into your own hands. Please."

Johnny looked O'Connell in the eye. He wanted to believe him.

"No jury," O'Connell continued, "would let him off. Especially with what he did to you, Miss Hester. There'd be a hanging at the Tombs."

When she realized O'Connell didn't react to her femininity, she gradually made eye contact with him.

"What makes you think you'd catch him? Would those Metropolitans even look for him?" asked Johnny.

The sergeant made sure he had their attention. "Look in me eye and listen to what I have to say. Not all the coppers despise us, Johnny. But

99

that's not my concern. It's you. Johnny O'Hara. We want you on the straight and arrow. You're a good person from good stock. You're a good example for the young ones around here, including this young lady here. We need you. For them!"

Johnny had calmed, impressed with what the sergeant had said.

"Enough of that. Think I got some good news that might interest you," O'Connell said, getting their undivided attention. "The City Council's talking about creating a paid fire department."

"Heck no," barked Red. "Hows 'bout da volleys? Wot happens to us?"

"You'll probably get first crack at it."

"But why?" asked Johnny.

"They're under a lot of pressure from Albany and the insurance underwriters. They want an end to the reckless volunteers. As you know, the volleys spend too much time fighting each other instead of putting the fires out. Cause too much damage. And besides, the city's too big to be served by volunteers. It'd be a good job for you, Johnny. A career. Just like the Metropolitans are for me. You won't have to worry about being let go. And there'd be no limit on how far you can go in the ranks. Even the top spot. The chief engineer."

"You really think so?" asked the blushing youth, scratching his head with both hands, shifting from foot to foot. I am so embarrassed.

"Holy cows. My fren Johnny, a hot shot. Ya be Assistant Engineer John O'Hara. Holy cows," she said, chuckling.

"Yes. And I'm sure we can get at job at Holy Cross for Miss Hester."

"Baloney! Me a fireman. Ain't gonna work at no church. And doan call me miss. Call me Red," she insisted.

"Why in God's name do you want people to think you're a boy?" O'Connell asked, a bit perplexed.

Johnny cut in. "She was attacked once too often by men. When they think she's a boy, they don't bother her."

"Guess that makes sense, now doesn't it?" said O'Connell. "With those looks and that red hair. But you won't get away with that forever, you know."

"Tanks, Sergeant." Red sighed, her eyes rolling back in her head.

"Well, have a good day," said O'Connell. "And please don't make any mistakes, Johnny." Again he looked at the burlap bag under Red's arm. "You come from good stock. And you're friend there, I don't know much about you. But if you're his friend, I'm sure you're okay." The Sergeant started to leave, then turned. "Miss, I mean Red. Was your mother Angel Hester?"

"Why you askin?"

"No reason. Just curious."

"You knowd her?" she asked.

"I knew of her. Good day." He continued on his way.

"Why he ask'd 'bout me mudda? He knows someting I doan?"

"I don't know. Maybe he liked her. Who knows?" said Johnny. "He scared me, saying I'd hang if I'd killed that guy. What am I to do?"

"Den I'll do it," insisted Red.

"Yeah, sure. Get yourself hung. Then I won't have a best friend." He grabbed her by the shoulders. "What would I do without my best friend . . . covering my back. Ah hell! You know what I mean. Like you mean a lot to me, Red."

"Ey doan talk dat boy-girl shit wid me."

"Well, what are ye?" he snapped, shaking his head.

CHAPTER ELEVEN

On her thirteenth birthday, Red got caught in the act of picking a pocket watch from a doting visitor who had just stepped off a streetcar. As soon as she completed her act, unknown to the visitor, she turned to run only to slam into a big Irish copper, her eyes staring at his broad chest.

"And what might ye be doing?" he barked, scaring the hell out of her. He gripped her under the armpits, lifted her off the ground, and walked her back to the grateful gentleman. "Now give the good man his time piece," he said, winking at the man. "And tell him ya sorry," which she did. Fortunately for Red, the man looked sympathetically at her. Seeing the gentleman's expression, the copper said, "My good man, would you mind if I handle this my way?" He winked at the gentleman.

"Please do, officer." The man nodded and walked off.

"Why 'tis a little ting like yeself doing such a bad ting?" he asked. Obviously he felt for Red's plight. Not because he never saw a destitute child, but because this young Irish gal struck a chord with him, he being a survivor of the Irish hunger. "Ye know it's wrong, what ya did, don't ye?"

With puckered lips and drooping eyes, she nodded, then whispered in a most effective *little boy's voice*, "Yes."

"C'mon now. I be taken ye to ya folks. I'll have to tell them what ye did. They can do the hammering."

Still sad-faced, she looked him in the eye and with her *sweet little voice*, muttered "I ain't gotten no mudda or fadda. Dey gone."

"Then who . . . where do ye live?"

"Nobody."

"Ya codding me," he said. For some reason he believed her.

"I not foolin ya. I live by meself down by the river. By Macon's."

Then it donned on him. A little red-head with broad shoulders. The one that puts on the swimming show and the rope tricks. "Bejasus. You're the swimmer?"

She nodded.

"The Crazy Mermaid?"

She smiled. "Yes, I am."

The copper, who never gave his name nor asked for hers, gave her five pennies then let her go with a warning: "Next time I won't be so easy on ye." Red hoped to see him again, but never did.

* * * * *

Wednesday's downpour had turned the streets into the usual wet-weather mucky mess. Horse dung, pig shit, and rotting animal carcasses in the tenement districts were all mashed into one grimy mush. It wasn't fun for Red with her feet wrapped in rags, to pass through the mess. Everything seemed to cling to the rags and squeak with the muck juice. But they had to *get to work*. And besides, there were many mild days when she wore nothing on her feet, which she preferred. Hell, she often walked to Whitehall barefooted, to await the ferry when operating on her own.

"With whatever we get today, we're gonna get you some brogues and decent pants," insisted Johnny. "Even if it means I get nothing. We'll stop at Brogan's Junk. For sure he'll have everything," he continued.

"Dems a waste of silver," said Red, quickly correcting herself. "I mean thems. "

Johnny shook his head at her poor choice of words. "It's *they are* and not *dems* or *thems*. And you got to get shoes. You owe that to me," he insisted.

"Wot ya mean?" she shot back.

"Your feet. The rags on your feet. They stink like shit," he shouted, laughing at the same time. "They stink all the time. With shoes there will be no smell."

"Oh shyte. I—I never tought of dat, I means that," she said. "Stop. I gotta gits me a whiff. She sat on the steps of a loading dock. Leaning forward, she lifted her foot across her knee and sniffed. "Eeegad. You're right. Okay."

* * * * *

They timed it perfectly, arriving at the busy Whitehall Street terminal as the ferry pulled in. On South Street, the common folk waited for friends or family to depart the steam-powered vessel. Behind them waited the hacks with their livery coaches, looking for a fare, and the chauffeurs with their carriages, waiting to pick up the bigwigs they worked for.

The two hungry would-be thieves separated, with Johnny taking a position as blocker. The ship had an unusually large crowd of passengers that day. They brought with them considerable luggage, much of which looked expensive, especially the fancy leather cases in the hands of well-to-do looking individuals. Those individuals were probably the company executives that would be chauffeured away in the waiting carriages.

"I wants ta git ona dose big shytes," said Red, nodding at the company people. Then she warned Johnny, "Watch for da booly-dogs."

They perused the crowd, looking for the coppers who were easily detected by their gray-domed helmets.

"Fo now on, me tinks me cover me hair anymore. Here." She pulled a black cloth hood over her short red hair, looking a bit odd for that time of the year. "Dey'll be looking for a tough guy wid a black hood. Not a redhead," she said.

"Tough guy? You mean a good-looking girl with flaming red hair," he insisted.

"There's the one," she said, discreetly pointing to an obvious man of wealth. Stay just behind him and block him when he turns," she directed.

The man grounded his expensive luggage and rushed forward to scoop up a cheery-faced little girl. Johnny stepped right behind him to block his view, and when the man turned to get his bags, he collided with Johnny. He pretended to stumble and grabbed onto the man as though trying to prevent himself from falling.

"Oh sorry. Sorry," said the man as he turned to Johnny. But when he saw Johnny's pauper-like status, the man waved him off shouting, with a nip of arrogance, "What are you doing?"

"Pardon me, old boy," said Johnny in his finest take-off of an English accent, while losing himself in the crowd.

And while the man displayed his revulsion against Johnny, Red had already reached the shed at the southern end of the pier, where she started jamming the contents of the man's suitcase into a couple of burlap bags.

She then dropped the bags and herself to the beach-like surface beneath the pier and moved unnoticed on her way to meet up with Johnny.

By the time the man shouted that someone had snatched his luggage, the two of them were nowhere to be seen. Once Red emerged from the underside of the pier, she started her trek around the tip of Manhattan Island to get to Murray Street. Johnny cut through an unused lot to meet up with her. He saw her hurrying along by the riverfront. He also saw two men step out of the brush from behind her and start after her. He quickened his pace to a run with his eyes glued on the two men.

"Hey kid! Gimmie dat stuff or I take it," one of them yelled.

Dropping the burlap sacks, Red turned on a dime, whipping out her trusty blade. "Just try and ya bees eaten me shive," she said, waving the knife, as fear gripped her innards.

She heard a voice from a passing schooner shouting, "Look, he's got a knife."

"Oh, the little one wants a fight, does she?" said one of the assailants. They started to encircle her, each holding a club. "Make it easy on yaself. Drop the bags. Step away from the bags or we beat da shit outta ya and take the stuff anyway."

Red stood her ground hoping that Johnny would arrive on the scene. "Oh yeah, ya big jerk! Not before ya feels dis," she growled in the best of her manly voices while jabbing the knife at them. *If they find out I'm a girl, I'll be fucked.* A chill ran up her spine.

"Tough guy, ha," one of them roared as he charged at her with the club raised over his head. That's when a rock the size of a cobblestone thumped the back of his head, dropping him like a ton of bricks, with his nose and mouth submerged in the water. Red ran at him to stick him with the knife, but stopped short when Johnny shouted, "No! No! The Tombs! The Tombs!"

As the fallen man's mate turned on Johnny, Red clocked him with a straight right. The man's eyes bulged with shock as he staggered sideways, stunned not only from the punch, but from the power of the punch delivered by this little girl.

"Why, ya little shit," the dazed assailant muttered. At the same time Johnny shouted, "What was that?" The man stumbled off, abandoning his mate.

"I wouldn't want you doing that to me," said Johnny.

"Keep messing wid me," she said with a chuckle, her fist cocked as if ready to throw a punch at him.

With one of his giant hands, Johnny grabbed the man by the hair and pulled him from in the water just far enough to prevent him from drowning. "I should let ye drown ya bum, ya," he said.

"Why da hell ya do dat?" Red snapped. "He'd a let us drown."

"The Tombs. Remember, we don't want to be hung in the Tombs. And it's *that* not *dat*." He picked up the bags. "Let's get the heck outta here." As soon as he started walking away, he heard the sound of water splashing from behind him. Spinning around, he saw Red in the water, holding the unconscious man's club in both hands, with both hands, readying to smash his head.

"No," Johnny shouted. "You'll kill him, for God's sake. Stop!" Dropping the bags, he ran back and grabbed her arms. "What did I just tell ya? You'll kill him." He threw the piece of wood into the water, then took her by the arm and pulled her along. "Let's get out of here before somebody sees us and gets the coppers."

"Fuck him. He deserves to die." In her fit she didn't give a damn what he had to say. And for the moment, he didn't give a damn either.

"Listen," he said. "Maybe you don't care about being hung. But I do. And if you kill someone like you wanted to do that guy, I'd be hung too."

"Why?" She snapped at him.

"Because I'll be what's called an accomplice. That means I had something to do with the killings. And being an accomplice, I'd probably be hung with you."

"Well ha, ha, ha. Ain'ts dat too bad?"

Here they split up, according to plans. Each would take one of the bags and head to Brogans.

"Don't let dems booly dogs see ya with da bag," she warned.

* * * * *

Thirty minutes later they were standing by Brogan's Junkyard, in front of the gate that led to his property. A nine-foot high wooden fence, topped off with barbed wire, surrounded the property. Signs on the fence warned: MAN EATING DOGS. When closed for business, hungry dogs roamed the yard. The entry gate led to a 30'x50' wooden clapboard structure that had a typical A-frame roof. The building had but three windows, two of which faced the street. They were filthy and covered with iron bars to prevent break-ins. The third window was boarded up. Passersby had to go inside to see the contents of the structure, which they wouldn't hesitate to do. Curiosity killed the cat. The large interior contained a little of everything and anything.

"Ya still mad at me?" he asked.

"Nah. Ya right. I gots to use me head." To his relief, she gave him a big smile.

They could see heaps of used clothing: shirts, trousers, dresses and plenty of shoes and brogues for men and women. There were armchairs, different sized tables, hot irons, window curtains, wall clocks, hand drills and bits, hammers, sledgehammers, pick-axes, and wagon wheels. They followed a muddy footpath to the rear yard, avoiding many stacks and piles of valuable clutter: bricks, lumber of all sorts and sizes, and tightly secured lengths of piping. A dozen or more old but serviceable wagons sat in the open lot.

Thomas Brogan handled stolen property at the rear of the building, which sat about fifty feet inland from the river's edge. His rule for doing business was simple: *make sure there are no coppers or suspicious looking people around when you bring your takings on this property.* One always did what Thomas said. He had a solid-wooden, nine-foot high privacy fence erected a few feet from the shoreline that was also topped with barbed wire. That way he was assured his *business* transactions weren't observed from passing water-borne vessels or the police boats that patrolled the river. Not that being spotted was his biggest fear. He had important friends. Their influence reached everywhere. His rules were more about respect.

Brogan was a survivalist. He did what he had to do to protect his interests. He routinely paid off the appropriate members of the police department and in exchange, they didn't bother him. What the coppers did ask of him was that neither he nor his clientele flaunt what they were doing. There was a positive side to his business. He kept several men working full time, enabling them to feed and house their families. Brogan had no family of his own; only his younger brother Big Mike.

Just inside the solid steel rear door of Brogan's building stood a large bench-type table next to which Brogan himself stood.

"Dump your swag," he growled, pounding the bench. "I like the company you keep," he said to Red, as he reached out and shook Johnny's hand. "I'm truly sorry about your mom. She was a fine woman. None better. And I will never forget what she did for me mom, especially when she was ill. Before her passing."

Johnny returned the handshake, saying only, "Thank you, sir."

"Call me Thomas or Brogan . . . I like the luggage. And look at the contents. Made a killing, I see. That's quality stuff." He removed from the bag a soft-blue shirt with white pin-stripes. "Silk," he said. He then lifted a similar shirt. This one's white with blue pin-striping. Also silk. "I know exactly who'd want these. Tell me, Johnny," he placed his large hand on Johnny's shoulder, "is this what you're going to do with your life?"

Taken aback somewhat, Johnny replied, "With mom gone, there's no more money. No place to live. Gotta do this. I got to." He stopped what he was saying and looked at Red. "We have to eat, Mr. Brogan."

Thomas shook his head. "I know the feeling, lad." He turned to Red. "Give ye twenty-five." Her eyes lit up, "If ye promise me you won't do any more misappropriating for the rest of the week. Them Tombs is not a nice place to be, you know."

"Sure," said Red, with a big smile.

"Besides, this is good stuff. Three brand-spanking new Brookes Brothers slacks to go with the shirts. These shoes. Imported. Costly as hell, you know. And don't tell anyone of my generosity," he said, counting out five five-dollar bills. "That should hold ye for a while, don't ya think?"

Brogan noticed Johnny staring into an open desk draw in which the handle of a pistol revealed itself from under a stack of papers. When Johnny looked up, Brogan remarked, "On occasion, bad people visit me. It's good to be ready for them." He closed the draw.

"I wish we had our own firehouse," Brogan continued. "I'd put you guys to work in it. So you'd never have to do this shit again. Just so you can eat. One day, God willing, we'll have that firehouse. And our own saloon too, to do our politicking. And we'll get you, Johnny, elected as our alderman. Yeah. That's what we'll do."

"You serious, Mr. Brogan?" asked Johnny. "Me. A politician. I don't know. Think I'd rather be in charge of the fire department. Oh! We almost forgot. Red needs shoes and a pair of pants."

"I'll throw them in, too," said Brogan. He directed them through a door to the front of the shop, where he kept the apparel and footwear. "There's a pair of women's boots with a pocket for a knife. Take them, sweetheart. Me tinks I never saw you wearing shoes."

Red looked at him, her face flushed with embarrassment.

"You didn't think I knew? With a sweet face like that, what else could ye be but a young lady?" said Brogan. "And if ye don't have a knife, you should. For your own good."

With that, she flashed her blade.

"Johnny. If you're available later, meet me at the Shamrock. I want to talk to you about something real important. In private." He winked at Red.

"Dat's okay, Johnny. Jus git me dat hot meal ya promised me, furst," she insisted.

"Sure," said Brogan. "I'll be in there for much of the evening."

* * * * *

Ham and pea soup or boiled beef were the specials of the day at the Waterside, where a large, round woman, with a large, round happy face, played the piano, banging out her version of *Dixie*. She sang along with her powerful voice that forced itself on everyone in the smoke-filled room, where feet stomped on the floor and people joined in the singing. There was

109

a loud, steady hum of people noise, loud enough to allow Red and Johnny to speak freely.

It was after six when they got their glasses of ale and steaming bowls of soup with chunks of ham, potatoes, and carrots.

"Damn, dis good," she said, withdrawing the spoon from her mouth then washing it down with a slug of ale. "Dis . . . this taste good, too," she smiled.

"I feel rich with all this money," he said. "Thanks to you." He gave Red a warm affectionate look. Wanted to reach over and just hold her in his arms. But that just couldn't be. He didn't know how to handle those feelings he'd been experiencing since confirming her womanhood. Johnny always had special feelings for her, but now they were different. Now he was in love with the *guy* who often covered his back in gang fights. That tough little son-of-a-bitch that kicked many an ass is really a beautiful, sweet little thing. Well . . . maybe not a *sweet* little thing. How would that tough little redhead feel if she knew he had a hard-on for her?

"We'd a lost everyting only for ya beaned dat guy. Dey woudda tooken all the stuff," she said.

Still with that warm, affectionate look that made Red uneasy, he asked, "You know. I only know you as Red. What's your real name?"

"Angela. Angela Hester. Dat woz me mudda's name, too. Dey . . . they called her Angel."

"Angela. Angel. Sounds nice. Can't wait to tell everybody."

"What!" She glared at him through furrowed eyebrows. "Doan ya dare," she growled, getting to her feet with clenched fists as if ready to pounce on him.

"Sit down," he said. "I'm only kidding ya. When are you going to trust me?"

"Why ya gotta tease me? Hah, wise guy?" she said, finishing her glass. She called out to the waiter. "Two more, Dominick."

"Not for me," he said. "I got to go. Can't keep Brogan waiting. What'll you do?"

"Make dat one, Dominick," she shouted. "I meet ya back at da place," she slurred a bit, with a smile.

* * * * *

Brogan's shouts could be heard over the roars of the Shamrock's raucous crowd, "Over here, Johnny boy," a real confidant air to his voice. O'Hara had no difficulty spotting him, his arm waving over the many heads in the dining room, sitting at a corner table.

"Have a seat," said Brogan, welcoming him in his gravelly voice and directing him to sit at the chair opposite him. With his hand in the air, he got the waiter's attention, "A beer. And a sasperilla. As I said, your mother was a godsend for me mom. I won't forget that. That brings me to why I asked you here."

Johnny's eyes darted back and forth from Brogan's eyes to the pack of cigarettes on the table.

"Help yourself." He waited for Johnny to light up. "I was surprised to see you working with that gal Red. You're bound to get caught, bucko."

"But it's so easy to do," said Johnny. He dragged on the cigarette, its tip glowing.

"Sure. Until you get caught," Brogan warned. "And that would mean doing time on the island and slandering the proud and honorable O'Hara name that your mother worked so hard to protect."

The barman delivered the drinks.

"I wanna make a toast. Raise your glass, me boy. Tap it against mine," said Brogan. "Here's to Johnny O'Hara, the man of the family, who, from this day forward, is entirely responsible for his family. That means your wee sister. May he always do the right thing and make her proud."

Johnny's flushed with confusion. "Wha . . . wha," he uttered. "What do ya mean?"

"You got the makings of a real success story. Something big that'll make us all proud. A big time politician, perhaps. Maybe a commissioner of some kind."

"Why do you say that?" asked Johnny.

"The way you handle yourself. You've got it all. Self-assured. Smart. With an education. And you're a natural leader." Brogan spoke with conviction, impressing Johnny. "Now back to what I was saying. For you to get in trouble with the law would finish any chances you'd have of getting a *good* position. Like being the head of the New York City Fire Department. You would never even get on the professional department they're planning, when it comes to be."

"Yeah, Sergeant O'Connell agrees with ya. You expect a professional fire department?"

"Let's face it. This is a big city and it's growing in leaps and bounds. It needs a disciplined service. Something the volunteers just can't provide. Besides, it's what the underwriters want. And they have the money to buy the necessary influence."

"But what am I to do in the interim?"

"Work for me. Two dollars a day with lunch. You'll be rich," Brogan laughed.

"Twelve dollars a week. Gees! With that we can move out of that hole in the ground. And even better, we won't have to go down to the terminals anymore. And risk getting thrown in jail."

"All you gotta do is run the front shop. You'd have nothing to do with the back," he paused, watching Johnny's reaction. "Big Mike will take care of that and all the loading and unloading of the wagons. Once in a while, he'll need your muscle. And a fine strapping lad like you will have no problem with that."

Johnny liked what he heard. He pictured himself well dressed, just like Brogan's brother, Big Mike. If Mike could afford all the fancy clothes, why couldn't he with twelve bucks a week? And free lunch? Hell, he'd even be able to buy clothes for Red. Girl's clothes at that.

"But how about my buddy Red?"

"She'll do okay. She always does."

"I can't do that. She's my friend. She covers my back."

"You're loyal too. Another asset," said Brogan. Reluctantly, he agreed to Johnny maintaining his friendship with Red.

"But what you just said. You knew she had no folks?" asked Johnny.

"Yep."

"Did you know them?"

"Yep. When they were still in the land of the living," Brogan answered. He removed a cigarette from the pack and lit it, dropping the match on the floor.

"Does that mean her mother is definitely dead?" Johnny asked, dreading his answer.

"Long presumed dead. A good looker and a prostitute. Her daughter's the image of her. Why are you asking me about this?"

"We heard the same thing yesterday," said Johnny. "And didn't want to believe it."

"You mean her being a prostitute. Everybody knew that," Brogan assured him. "Rumor had it at the time that she tried to blackmail one of her *clients,* a big banker who made her pregnant. That's when she disappeared. Presumably, but never proven, he was behind her killing. But they never found a body."

"Who was the banker?" Johnny pushed.

"Nothing ever came of it. The newspapers never touched it; never mentioned any suspects. She quickly became a statistic. Just another missing person," Brogan continued. "A cover up, friends in the police department said. She disappeared on a Sunday night. A silent investigation revealed the banker picked her up at her place every Sunday night. But that info was suppressed. You understand all this?"

"Yes." Johnny was dejected. *Poor Red. How's she gonna feel?"*

"Johnny. Now back to the business at hand. I've big plans for the future. They include you in a big way. You're the smartest of all the gang. Don't waste those smarts. And ya got the brawn and guts to back it up." Brogan hesitated, looked around the room then back at Johnny. "And I know you can read and write. Ya read all that fire department stuff, like meself. Ya good with figures, which I'm not. You'll be a great asset to me, bucko, when the time comes. So. Will ya be part of my organization?"

"Yes. Yes. How can I say no?"

"You know, I am a wealthy man. That I get away with a lot of things because of that wealth. I buy influence. Big influence," said Brogan, before being stopped by Johnny.

"But you're one of us. Why would the Prods listen to you? Don't they hate you, just like the rest of us?"

"Of course they do. But they love my money. Especially here in New York where everything is about money. So they take it and I get away with the things I do that would put others in prison for a long time. And in the process, I accumulate more and more wealth to buy more and more influence. I have access to the mayor.

"Now back to what I was saying. I intend to be a big man in the paid fire department. I've already been talking to the right people about that and have made my intentions known. The only thing that would stop me would be if I'm gone off on a gold rush somewhere. In that case, Big Mike would take me place. As you know, like yourself, Mike is one hell of a fireman with a good head on his shoulders, which even the Americans acknowledge. Just like you, Johnny. You will always be part of my scheme of things."

Then a puzzled look came to Brogan's face. "I know you like Red. That *ye* are good friends. How come you guys are not an item? Hope she's not one of those homosexual women that prefer women over men." He chuckled.

Johnny smarted keeping a smile on his face, but under the table he squeezed his knees to ease his anger. "I honestly don't know. What I do know is that she hates men."

"Why?" Brogan asked, as he took a last puff on his cigarette before squashing it out with his shoe.

"Too often they did bad things to her. Only last night somebody tried to rape her. But please, don't say anything to anybody."

With a flick of the hand, Brogan dismissed his concern. "I'm not a rat bastard," he said, shaking his head. He looked at Johnny and smiled approvingly. "When I talk to you, kid, I think," he scratched the side of his head, "I think I'm talking to meself. I, too, was the man of the family at a very young age, when Da died. Me mom died when I was just sixteen. Had to grow up fast. But at least I had Mike with me to share the load. That's why when I talk to you I feel like I'm talking to a man."

"Never thought of it that way," said Johnny, shaking his head.

"Ah well. But I got a secret for you. As soon as the next gold strike is confirmed, I'll be on me way. That's when I'll build my empire." He stood and then walked to the window, signaling Johnny to follow. "That's where I'll build our own firehouse. Right there," he pointed, "in that empty lot on 33rd. I own that too, bucko." He sipped his beer and Johnny finished his sasperilla.

"I must go," said Johnny. "And thanks for the job. And the sass." He plopped his empty glass down on the table.

He'd been with Brogan longer than he had anticipated, which caused him concern about Red's safety. Didn't like her heading home alone after what had happened the night before. He ran back to the Waterside. She was gone.

* * * * *

Chuck Jansen spent the day watching the shed from a hollow in a clump of bushes at the base of a dying weeping willow, carefully avoiding Red's vagrant neighbors, determined to get her and Johnny before the next morning; before he would disappear to Staten Island. When the dark had set in, he decided to move inside the shed. He stopped just outside of the shed, a place he knew well, where he used to make out with girlfriends. And on occasion, a place he used to rape a few women friends.

He entered with caution, moving slowly across the floor, shoeing clumps of hay, looking for evidence of recent human activity. His hand kept feeling the pistol tucked inside his belt hidden under his shirt.

He looked to the rear of the shed with the most evil of looks, his eyes stuck on an 8 x 8 wooden post. He sighed, then approached the post. He felt the crude carving of a cross.

Jansen stood on Angel Hester's burial site, looking for evidence of his dastardly act. He saw nothing. If he completed today's mission, he'd have two more bodies to bury and two more crosses to carve.

Where the hell do they sleep, he wondered. Like an athlete doing a pull-up, he hoisted himself up on the empty loft, displaying great strength and agility. *Nothing up here but hay,* he concluded, as he kicked hay around. *Where the hell can it be?* In another athletic display, he swung himself to the floor below, landing right on the concealed hatch. It rattled.

What have we here? He brushed aside the loose hay, enabling him to make out the outline of the straw-covered hatch, which he studied momentarily, then removed. He grinned. *There it is. Their palace.* The twilight provided him ample lighting for a glimpse of the pit. He did not go down. Instead, he again pulled himself up on to the loft taking a position by the outside lift opening, where he could watch the pathway he assumed Red and Johnny would be using.

How will I handle this? I'll shoot the guy, fuck her, then shoot her and bury her right on top of her mother. He smiled. *And tomorrow I'll be gone.*

CHAPTER TWELVE

By 8:15, after night had settled in, Jansen heard humming off in the distance. Soon after an image appeared in the distant dark, an image he knew to be hers, one he thought about many times since first seeing her. *She's alone.*

Grabbing his penis, he thought about what he would do to her. *With this,* he felt his pistol, *I can get her to do anything.*

From the loft, Jansen watched her enter the barn and descend into her hole-in-the-ground abode.

Jansen returned to the lift doorway, for another look at the pathway from the river and the tree line, not wanting any surprises. For a big man, he moved with the silence of a serpent. He changed plans. No, he'd rape her on the main floor, then at gunpoint, force her to dig her own grave over her mother's. When ready to lower himself to the main floor, the hatch door opened. Freezing in place, he watched her reach up with the basin, then pull herself up with the greatest of ease and head off to the river.

She's going to be nice and clean. Just for me. He laughed softly while again stroking his manhood, waiting for her to return so he could strike. Again he returned to the lift opening to watch for her. When she reappeared, he crawled to the loft's edge and leaped down to the main floor. There he lurked in the dark, several feet from the floor opening. He was half-crazed when she entered the shed. He watched her body movements as she bent over to open the hatch, next to which she placed the towel covered basin. Unable to resist any longer, he lunged for her and grabbed her from behind. Holding her around the waist with one arm and lifting her, he jammed the gun into her ribs and whispered, "Don't make a sound and you'll live for another day."

Recognizing the voice, Red pleaded, "Don't hurt me. Don't hurt me." She shook from head to toe.

"Just do as I tell you," he said, breathing heavily and trembling with desire. Take off those fucking pants," he growled, tearing at them at the same time. He ripped the threadbare trousers from her, ignoring her boots. He hurt her with his enormous strength, pushing and pulling at her legs. She didn't fight him, wanting to stay alive. She gagged loudly as he entered her.

"Be quiet, I told you," he grunted. Twice he butted her face with his pistol, bloodying her nose and mouth. Again she moaned with pain as she slowly reached down to her boot for her knife.

"When I'm finished with you, I'm gonna stick this up your ass and blow your brains out," he said, panting like a wild dog.

With that said, she slashed her razor-sharp blade across his throat, cutting hard and deep, before he knew what happened. Death came swiftly. His body jerked and bolted upright; his penis fell limp and withdrew from inside her. Blood spurted from severed arteries. The pistol dropped from his trembling hand, just missing her face. Jansen gasped his last breath and then his massive frame collapsed on top of her.

Still in her fear-driven blackout, her body convulsed, rebelling against the feel of his warm blood spilling over her. "Get off! Get off me," she screamed, rolling his half-naked body off hers. Getting to her feet, she didn't look down at him, but vomited almost on top of him. "Ya dog! Ya bastard!" she shouted. "Fucking men!"

Somehow, in her state of sub-consciousness, she descended to her den and staggered to her bed. She curled up into a fetal position and began to sob.

* * * * *

With his weapon in hand, Johnny jogged along, slashing his way through the field adjacent to the McAdams property, heading to the shed while humming *Dixie*. At the shoreline he admired the darkened images of the few vessels anchored nearby, but kept moving, hurrying through the dark, his way lighted by the moonlight. Soon he saw the outline of the shed. *God it's peaceful here,* he thought.

Johnny enjoyed living with Red, just like they were family. He couldn't wait to tell her about Brogan's offer and that they could now live well on the money he would earn at the junk shop. That they wouldn't have to pick pockets anymore.

With the reflection of the moon illuminating the area in front of him, he stepped into the shed. *Something is amiss,* the thought flashed through his mind. *Yes. The layout of the floor, the hatchway to the den.* He froze and listened. *Somebody's sobbing. Down in the pit. Shit! Red! What's wrong?* Raising his club, ready to use it, he moved towards the floor opening, his foot slipping on something wet. *What's that?* Dropping to his knees, he saw the body. Touching it, he felt something wet. He pulled away, repulsed by what he suspected. Images of Red's face flashed through his mind. Raising his wet hand he saw blood; his stomach churned.

The sobbing from the den grew louder and more frequent. *That's Red.* He felt a sense of relief.

"Red," he shouted, dropping down into the den, iron bar at the ready.

"Johnny," she cried, her voice weak and shaky.

His heart sank, dreading something had happened to her. "You okay! Are you okay!" he repeated, talking real fast. He felt his way over to her.

"Help me, Johnny," she called out, sobbing.

He exhaled, his stomach finally relaxed.

"He's dead. Tell me he's dead," she whispered.

"Who?" he asked. "Who is that?" His bowels roared, feeling he had to go.

"The big guy. Is he dead? He shot your mom. Is he dead? He did it again," she cried aloud, shouting, "The *durty* bastard."

"What happened?" he whispered with force, trying to snap her out of her mild shock. When he saw her nakedness, he grabbed his blanket and covered her, then wrapped his arms around her and held her. "You're okay now. Your protector's here." Himself shaking, he rocked her to and fro. "Everything's gonna be okay. Johnny will take care of everything."

When her sobbing stopped, she asked, "Wot wez do wid him? The coppers. I'm afraid."

"Nobody knows anything, right? Nobody came here, right?"

She agreed, shaking her head.

"Just don't worry. He deserved it . . . I'll bury him." He stood and fetched the shovel. He threw it up through the opening in the floor where it made a dull thud, sounding like it landed on Jansen's corpse? Then he pulled himself up and out of the den.

"I—I—I so a scared, Johnny." Every inch of her body trembled.

"Does anybody ever come here?" he asked as he reached down for her hands with his tree-trunk like arm, lifting her up and out, every muscle in his arm bulging.

"Damn, ya strong," she said, suddenly feeling safe again. "No. Nobody." She struggled into her trousers.

"Then I'll bury him in the shed back there." He grabbed the big man's arm and Red grabbed the other. Together they dragged him to the back. He drove the tip of the shovel into the soft earth. He worked fast. Shovelfuls of earth and straw flew. "Maybe you better keep an eye out the door. Don't want anybody sneaking up on us." She glanced outside— listening to the quick succession of the shovel thrusts penetrating the earth—and saw no one. Being confidant from experience that nobody would appear, she returned to help Johnny, who had already dug down a couple of feet. He didn't want a break, but Red insisted on digging. She wouldn't have it any other way. After all, as a child she spent many a day digging.

She yanked the shovel from his hand. "I need dis to calm meself."

They changed positions. Johnny watched for intruders as Red dug with vigor, tossing shovel after shovel of earth into the air, not to be outdone by Johnny. She felt better about what had happened, realizing she did what she had to do to protect herself. She hadn't killed him to revenge Johnny's mom's death or because of his previous attempt to rape her, but to stop him from raping her.

Johnny returned to her side. "We got to clean that," he said, motioning towards the bloody mess on the floor. As Johnny finished digging out Jansen's final resting place, Red cleaned up what she saw of the bloody mess and threw it into the hole. Then, when Red left to take a swim to clean herself, Johnny, who was filled with rage, gripped and twisted Jansen's collar with such force that he heard a cracking sound from his neck. With brute strength, he rolled the large, dead-weighted body to the edge of the hole and pushed it in. He dropped the pistol where he thought Jansen's face would be. *I wish it were I that slit your throat.*

Quickly, he worked the earth back into the hole, filling it to within a foot of ground level. Figured he'd finish it at morning's first light after he checked to make sure no evidence of what happened had remained above ground.

Red returned soaked, her skimpy clothes clinging to her perfect body; a body she didn't even appreciate. But Johnny did. Again he was aroused by her. If she knew what he felt, she'd clock him. Red the tough *guy* would not be able to handle the idea of her buddy thinking of her that way.

"Took a swim, did ya?"

"Felt *durty* after wot dat creep did," she answered. "I left some water outside for ya."

"Good idea," he said and went outside."

* * * * *

"Let's hit the sack. We got things to talk about," he said, after returning from his quick wash-up. He looked everything over, making sure things were in order, gave a quick look outside, then followed her into the *den*. She lit a candle that sat in a dugout in the wall.

"Does anybody ever come here?" He removed his shirt and dropped it on the burlap sack filled with his belongings.

"No. Only if I askin dem," she replied.

Johnny then plopped himself down on his sack, flat on his back with his arms crossed under his head. "Then ya got nothing to worry about. And don't forget, nobody will be looking for him. Remember what his friend said. He'd be disappearing tomorrow morning. Won't even be missed."

"Wot I did wuz right. Right Johnny?"

He stood up and grabbed her by her shoulders. "Of course you were right. If you didn't get him, he'd a got you. He told you he'd kill ya."

"I sees meself hanging in dem tombs," she said, her voice quivering.

"What the hell's that?" he shouted as something brushed against his bare foot.

That got a smile from Red. "Dats me fren."

"That's a rat, isn't it?" he snapped, with fear in his voice.

"Yeah, but he woan hurts ya." Her smile disappeared. "Now ya see why I hates men?" She watched his reaction.

"Does that mean you hate me?" he questioned.

"Youse different. But ya still one a dem," she said. She saw the hurt in his eyes. "I just can't trust youse. Like ya all preverts."

"You gotta be kidding," he snapped. "Ye mean you still don't trust me? Hell, twice I was with you when you were butt-ass naked. Did I touch you? No-o-o."

"Yeah. I trust ya," she said. "And I didn't mind ya seeing me, eider. Can't wez talk about someting else?"

He smarted and wanted to hurt her back. "Are ye a queer girl?"

"Wot ya mean?" She sat up in her bedding.

"Do you like girls . . . instead of boys? That's what I mean." Now he regretted what he said and wanted to take it back, but remained silent and stunned while she responded, looking him right in the eye. "I don't know. I just knows I hate men."

* * * * *

Charlton Bimsbey functioned best when addressing his peers about actions underway to keep the working classes feuding. He enjoyed choosing the tactics to be used and selecting the antagonists to carry them out—with the help of his minions—and then see the end result. He played it like a game. Did his tactics always workout the way he wanted them to? Most often they did.

"Since the attack by *our boys* against the Yimmies," he laughed, "and the burning of the new firehouse and lumberyard, there have been three more like riots." He sat on the edge of the conference table as he spoke.

Bimsbey had no favorites. Didn't give a damn about who won the battles as long as the Yimmies and the Yanks kept fighting each other.

"Also," he continued while staring out the large front windows, "I am glad to say, the Bowery Boys and many of the volunteers are now getting involved in the fighting." Then he shouted like a preacher on a high with himself, "Which I am sure will keep the *working classes at each other's throats*." Again he laughed. "At the same time, I am worried that the Bowery Boys, many of who work at the gas works, will start organizing for better wages and conditions. Organize a union, that is. We must keep the fighting going."

"They'll be overly busy spying on each other and blaming each other for their woes," said Prago, smiling as he spoke. "And we'll be unseen, unheard, and unknown. I love it."

Jules Rothchilder was beside himself. "Charlton, my friend. I must admit you are good. Real good." Rothchilder had plenty of money and the finest of clothes, but he lacked good looks.

"And what might I ask provoked such a compliment from you?" Bimsbey asked of Jules.

"Your solution to our *workers'* problem. I've given it a lot a thought. I like it and I appreciate its potential for huge financial benefits," Jules replied.

"Yes. Yes," said Prago Santan, clapping his hands. "You are to be commended."

Leonard Morgan shared their enthusiasm.

"How about you, Jacob?" asked Bimsbey. "Are you with us?"

"Of course," said Jacob. His upbeat response surprised the others.

"Well, Jacob. You reversed yourself? Don't you care anymore about your poor workingman friends?" asked Bimsbey.

"I guess you can say I see the writing on the wall." Jacob Bosh hadn't changed his mind; rather he would not give himself away and find himself excluded from the group.

Rothchilder continued: "I would never go blindly into something with such powerful ramifications without first knowing the matter utterly. I've checked thoroughly with the council and police department, even some colleagues in Washington."

Jacob Bosh couldn't refuse cutting in. "You mean 'the money-hungry vultures' in Washington. The kind that would sell out his people for the almighty dollar."

"Isn't that what politics is all about?" said the grinning Rothchilder. "It's Washington's greed that will eventually enable us to run this nation."

"Yes, it is. But is that the way it is supposed to be?" challenged Bosh.

"Now let me finish," said Rothchilder. "I've even queried friends in the newspapers and they, too, see it our way: Americans and immigrants fighting over jobs. Although the reporters haven't a clue of who's instigating it all."

Bimsbey sprang to his feet, at the same time pounding his desk that cost him more than two months of salary for ten workingmen. Again the firebrand preacher in him surfaced. "Just as Jules said, in another hundred years our people will run the entire country—its wealth—no matter what the economic situation. We will control the workingman and their unions, which, I assure you, has already started. The same with our politicians. They're for sale." Then he laughed. "There should be *Influence for Sale* signs wherever they gather. But not yet the newspaper people. Not all of them that is. But that too will come, even if we have to buy them up. Must make sure nobody will hinder progress." He made eye contact with each of them as he spoke. "We will be the center of economics, no matter what's transpiring in the nation. We will prosper in war and in peace. And we, our future generations that is, will never have to fight its wars . . . if that's their wish. We'll leave that for the working classes, *our boys,* and the *Yimmies.*"

His colleagues were jubilant. They had hung on every word he said. These ultra-rich individuals were behaving like children.

He continued, "And we must be part of the political machine. That's right. We must run candidates for local and citywide office. Not directly, of course."

He paused to observe their reactions. "You probably want to know who's going to do the organizing. There are a few dozen young men, some of who are immigrants, who are presently organizing the volunteer firemen and gangs throughout the city and Brooklyn for the purpose of causing confrontations such as we have recently witnessed between the workers. On the one side, we also have people pressuring places of business to hire only immigrants. On the other side, we have people compelling the bosses to hire only Americans. The next time you are out strolling, check the windows of the shops. You will see *No Irish Need Apply* signs hanging on some of the windows. And, of course, we have those individuals whose function it is to stir the pot. What do the workers call them? Shit stirrers." He laughed.

Bosh cut in, "If the war breaks out between the north and the south, do you think the *No Irish Need Apply* will apply?"

"I want to make a point," Leonard Morgan said, raising his voice, only to be cut off by Bimsbey. "Let me finish," insisted Bimsbey. He smiled at Morgan. "We will also run candidates in the fast approaching council elections. It's time to take the council back from those uncouth immigrant hoards." He then nodded to Morgan, motioning him to speak his piece.

"Are you saying you're directly involved with this trash?" shot a startled Morgan.

"Indirectly, Leonard. We are so far removed. Subordinates who know just what we want will handle these matters. Some of these people we all deal with from time to time, rarely though, but only for business reasons. At the end of the day, if people are to go to prison for *their crimes*, it will in no way affect us."

PART II

CHAPTER THIRTEEN

MARCH 1859 – When Thomas Brogan got word of the discovery of large lodes of gold in the Kansas Territory, near what would soon become the city of Denver in Colorado, he was on his way out west like a *fly on shit*, to fulfill his life-long dream, to strike it rich in a gold rush. He had sworn to himself a decade earlier, at the time of the California Gold Rush when he was too young, that he'd not miss the next one. And besides, he now had the capital he needed to give him the edge over his competition.

The major gold finds, according to his financial advisors in a Wall Street firm owned by none other than Charlton Bimsbey, were concentrated at the South Platte River, the Clear Creek canyon and South Park. They advised him to go immediately to the area of the South Platte River.

Two days later he boarded a train at Thirtieth Street to begin his long journey west to stake his claim, well ahead of some 100,000 prospectors that would be joining him throughout the year. The railroad took him to Missouri, as far west as it went. There he joined a wagon train that traveled to Denver, along the South Platte Trail, following the old Oregon Trail.

In his absence, Big Mike took over running the junkyard, with Johnny moving up the ladder, taking over Big Mike's position. Thanks to Johnny's persistence, Red took over his position. It was a tough battle, but Brogan finally relented, just one hour before he departed, with the stipulation that Red kept her secret; that she continue to pass herself off as a young man. "There'd be no women doing a man's work around my place. At least not to be seen," he warned Johnny.

Brogan had one question for Johnny: "Does she have tits? Don't see any bulges."

"I hope so." He blushed.

One of Johnny's responsibilities would be keeping the books. Being a learned individual, he'd have no problem learning bookkeeping. He possessed a talent for comprehending and remembering what he read.

Brogan's last words to him were: "I will build the Young Immigrants a firehouse. And I will provide all the necessary equipment, including one of those new steam pumpers, to protect our neighborhood from that red devil. For that purpose, I'll set up an account in the Bank of New York."

Johnny stood frozen, his mouth agape. "I—I—I."

"Say no more," said Brogan, silencing him. He turned and departed.

"Thhhh-thank you, Thomas," he shouted. "For everything."

"Just keep that redhead in line." Brogan yelled over his shoulder, smiling.

* * * * *

APRIL 1861 - At the outbreak of the Civil War, two dozen of the eighty-nine members of the Young Immigrant Engine Company joined the New York Militia's 2nd Regiment of Irish Volunteers, the Fighting 69th, for a 90-day hitch to fight the war against the Confederacy. They did not enjoy the support or blessing of all the members. Some questioned why they would fight for a nation that discriminated against them; that treated them as second-class citizens.

Unknown to everyone, Big Mike had signed up and did not tell Johnny until after the bunch of recruits were about to depart for training. It did not sit well with O'Hara, for he also planned to join the fight. But with Big Mike gone, running the expanding junk/building supply business became Johnny's responsibility, which he felt he owed Thomas Brogan. Even Red hinted at joining up with the Union Army, but Johnny insisted she not go, telling her he would not be able to run the place without her, a simple truth she knew to be true. He even posed the question to her, "Would you be safe among so many men? They're bound to find out." She knew he meant it.

On April 23, 1861 the citizens of New York gave the 69th a rousing send off as they marched from Great James Street down Broadway to Pier #4. Johnny, Red, and every member of the Young Immigrants, including those who disagreed with them joining the fight, were there for the sendoff, along with thousands more grateful New Yorkers. They hooted and cheered as Big Mike and the other gang members marched by in their uniforms with their shiny gold buttons. Johnny would never forget the pride he saw in Mike's eyes that day.

Several months later, just a few days before their three month hitches were to expire on July 21, 1861, Big Mike lost his life during a major rout of the Union Army at the first battle of Bull Run. Thousands of northern troops fled in disarray from that fight. Many of the poorly trained soldiers dropped their weapons and backpacks. Still there were men of the 69th that didn't run, who were prepared to stand and fight under the leadership of Colonel Michael Corcoran, only to be ordered to flee by the Brigade Commander General William T. Sherman. One of the few heroes of that battle was Big Mike Brogan. The news of his death shocked and saddened the neighborhood. Yet, at the same time the community felt a great pride for their hero Big Mike, an immigrant son. His name appeared in the *Herald* along with thirty seven other members of the 69th killed that day. Right below the casualty list was a prominent story of how several of the soldiers died, captioned: *Fighting Irish Save Colors.*

According to the report, "*. . . At one point during the fighting at Bull Run, the Irish Brigade's color bearers were ripped apart by canon fire. The shredded Colors fell beside them. A thinking Reb snatched them up, gave out with a victory cry, but before he could get far, was taken down by 'an Irishman from the 69th', Private Michael Brogan of Ninth Avenue. Just before the big man pounced on the Reb, he was heard shouting, 'Over me dead body will you get them, Reb." In the ensuing skirmishing between Brogan and his squad and the advancing Rebs, Pvt. Brogan, who at one point single-handedly fought four Reb soldiers, was cut down. Brogan's heroic actions resulted in the 69th recapturing its Colors.*"

On that day Big Mike became a bigger than life hero. He was talked about with admiration everywhere, by immigrant and native alike, even in the Louvre. Sergeant Desmond O'Connell told Sean Mulvihey that the police estimated more than two thousand people walked behind his hearse all the way to Holy Cross Church for the mass and burial.

Now there would be no war for Johnny. Thomas Brogan telegraphed the twenty-one-year-old, imploring him not to join the army, but to stay on to take over for his deceased brother. He was to run the business, take charge of setting up the new firehouse and equipping the company, and take over the Young Immigrants. That would be the gang manning the fire company. Johnny agreed, with the stipulation that he have certain freedoms in running the business, including adding building supplies—which he had already started doing—and to change the company name from Brogan's Junk to Brogan's Building Supplies. Johnny had worked out a good deal on building bricks from VerVallen out of Haverstraw, New York, about 30 miles up the North River. Bricks and lumber were in big demand in the growing city.

"You're in charge. You make the decisions," was Brogan's telegraphed response. And to Johnny's great pleasure, Brogan said, "I'd be delighted to give up fencing," which Johnny had urged him to do. Brogan also informed him that he had wired fifty thousand dollars to the bank.

While Johnny's economic and political prospects looked real promising, his future with Red, whom he loved dearly, wasn't so promising. Seemed the more he pursued her, the more she avoided him. Red had become consumed with great internal turmoil over her identity. Even though her fellow gang members and firefighters respected her as a gutsy, two-fisted brawler, they began treating her like a lady, which she resented utterly.

"Treat me like one of the boys, will ya," she one day exploded, demanding of one of the McCarthy brothers, who only wanted to help her pull a length of hose at a fire. And her gang mates no longer wanted her involved in the battles. They did not want her to get hurt. And making it worse for Johnny's sake, some guys kept coming on to her. And why not? Now twenty, she possessed exceptional beauty.

She began withdrawing from the gang. No longer did she dine with Johnny after work, which broke his heart. Nor did she hangout with him and the others. She went straight home and stayed to herself. At work she limited her dealings with him to the business. He gave up trying to talk to her.

For the longest time, she could not understand or control her behavior. She hated herself for it, for treating her best friend this way.

And her attraction to women became stronger than ever. But she never thought of having sex with a female. To her, women represented companionship and safety. And when she thought of sex, which she perceived as repugnant, she always envisioned doing it with a man, and that man would always be Johnny. Never having a romance left her totally naive about the matter, clouding her thinking.

It all came to a head early one morning in late August of '61. Unable to sleep, she lay with closed eyes, facing the wall and thinking about when Johnny had told her how he loved her. *I never did anyting to make him tink I love him. He knowd how I feel about men.* The guilt she felt about not being able to return her best friend's affections upset her so. Yet she always sensed a special feeling for him. But what that feeling was, she did not know.

Without making a sound, she rolled out of her bed and then tiptoed into the kitchen, where she dressed in almost total darkness. Hanging her head over a galvanized basin, she poured a cup of water over the back of her head. The cool, refreshing feel of the water wrapping around her head and face invigorated her. Woke her up. She dried herself, rinsed her mouth, and brushed her hair in the dark. Then thinking Johnny was asleep, she went to his bedside and knelt beside him.

But Johnny wasn't sleeping. How could he? His stomach was a ball of nerves just as it had been for weeks now, waiting for something to give with her ever since she began isolating herself. And tonight's the night, he gathered. *Why else would she have that bag by the door, all packed and ready to go? Why else would she get up this early?* His heart weighed heavily. So when she knelt down, he lit his reading candle and faced her. On seeing tears in her eyes, which she did not try to hide, he grabbed her hands and kissed them. "What's wrong? Why are you crying?" he asked with emotion.

The feel of his lips kissing her hands sent a strange feeling through her, right down to her privates. "Johnny . . . Johnny, say nuttin, awright. Just lissen."

"You're leaving."

By the light of the candle, she saw tears welling in his eyes. It tore at her heart, the sight of the big man teary eyed. But she wouldn't let it stop her from doing what she had to do. "Sorry I can't give ya wot ya want," she continued. "I really ams. I gotta find meself. Like ya tell'd me before, I gotta find out if I a homo woman." She grasped his hand. "So don't cum after me. I doan wanna break ya heart agin. If I wants, Iz find ya."

She pecked him on the lips, then went to get up, but he yanked her down on her back. He rolled over on top of her, pressing his lips firmly against hers. At first she returned his kiss, but then twisted herself free.

"Please Johnny," she said, gently. "Maybe anodder time."

"What am I going to do without you?" he shouted. "Will I ever see your face again . . . your hair

. . . your eyes."

Again she took his hand in hers. "Sorry I can't give ya wot ya want. I mean dat. I hopes wez still be best frens."

He replied, "'until the day I die."

Red turned and walked toward the door.

"Wait," he shouted. He retrieved from under her pillow her copy of *Reading & Writing*. Handing it to her he said, "Don't give up on this."

* * * * *

Johnny easily coaxed fellow gang member, Battler Quinn, to take Red's place at Brogan's, offering him a good wage. Battler was an excellent worker and delighted with the opportunity to make an honest living, especially with such a responsible position; such an opportunity he would never get at a WASP-run firm where the policy of "No Irish Need Apply" prevailed.

Battler supervised well. He kept his men working, kept the supplies moving, and delivered to the job sites on time. He also shared oversight with Johnny in the construction of a pier for receiving the barge loads of bricks coming down the river from Haverstraw. They arranged the dock so that the bricks could be mechanically unloaded from the barges and loaded directly onto flatbed wagons for delivery to job sites, saving their customers the time and expense of handling them twice.

As directed by Brogan, Johnny hired two more gang members to assist Battler in running the ever expanding operation. They were the McCarthy brothers, Francis and Timothy, who had fought alongside Big Mike Brogan at Bull Run. Quickly, Johnny had the three of them running a smooth day-to-day operation, which freed him to concentrate on carrying out the completion of the firehouse and organizing the company of firemen, another of Brogan's goals. In getting on with the firehouse construction, he had to first finish its design. This he did, based on the floor plans of several recently built fire stations and input from Battler and the McCarthy brothers. Once the plans and security features were approved by Brogan, and the proper permits secured, Johnny hired a crew from the neighborhood's pool of unemployed laborers as well as skilled carpenters and bricklayers who would all go to work as soon as the diggers finished their job.

With swinging pickaxes breaking up the earth and pointed shovels lifting the soil, the diggers cleared the lot then dug out the cellar, getting the foundation ready for the placement of the cement.

The main floor would be the garage area for the fire pumper and hose tender and stable area for the horses, including a bin to store their hay. A direct connection from the coal furnace in the basement would be mounted by the steam engine for a quick hook up to keep the pumper always ready to pump water at a fire. In addition, the plans showed an enclosed kitchen-meeting room combination and a separate bathroom to be constructed at the rear of the main room. A spiral staircase would be installed instead of a conventional flight of stairs that would prevent a loose horse from attempting to wander up the stairs.

At the right side center of the building, a twelve-foot wide by three-foot deep brick shaft would extend from the cellar right up to nine feet above roof level. This shaft was to serve as a hose drying tower.

He startled Battler and the McCarthys when he told them he wanted to set up the old warehouse as a temporary firehouse.

"How ya gonna do dat?" questioned Battler. "We still ain't got no charter. Right, Johnny?"

"That's the least of our concerns," he replied. "We got to worry about being burned down. Some of the volunteers don't want us *immigrant scum* to have our own firehouse. They'll do again what they did in '55. If we let them."

"Not this time," said Battler. "We be waiting for dem. But wot will they burn. We've no pumper or tender."

"They're on the way," said Johnny. "Thanks to Brogan, we're getting a LaFrance Piston Steam Engine, hose tender and 50 helmets. With 50 red shirts, to boot. And," he shouted, waving his finger, "he's also sending a couple dozen full-size rubber coats to enable us to get closer to the fire. He says we'll be the first in the city so equipped."

"He must be real rich," said Battler.

"Yeah. Eighty-five hundred just for the engine," said Johnny.

"Eeegads! By da way, why'd Red take off?" Battler asked.

"Don't know. Think she just couldn't take being found out. You know she wanted to be a tough guy. Not a tough girl."

"Heck, I miss her already. She was one of us," said Battler.

"Did she ever go out with a guy?" asked Timothy.

Johnny shrugged his shoulders. "Oh, I'm sure she did one time or another." He knew better.

"Don't tell me she likes girls," Timothy continued.

"Give her a break, will *ya*," said Johnny. He rolled his eyes then snapped; "Don't be talking about her behind her back."

CHAPTER FOURTEEN

SEPTEMBER 1862, IRELAND – "I have given you everything a young man could want. The best of schools. Trips abroad, away from this papist scum you call your friends. In return, I've gotten from you nothing but defiance and insubordination. You have shamed me once too often," Lord Hennington Bosh roared in his most arrogant English accent, trembling with anger. *Crrrack!* His slammed his thorn stick down on the dining room table making a loud cracking sound that resounded throughout his Skibereen mansion, sending tremors across the table's surface and rattling his finest Wedgewood teacups and saucers.

But the equally angry twenty-two-year-old, Tony Bosh, cared less about his father's ranting. He gave out with his own tirade. "You said it pleased God to let our tenants starve to death that it was His way of clearing the land of heathens. They died on the land we stole from them. You said they had no food," he shouted at the top of his lungs, "but there was plenty of food. Food *they* produced. The barley, the wheat . . . the oats. You took it all and shipped it out for your bloody profits, letting them starve. That wasn't God's doing!"

Shaking with rage, his father raised the thorn stick over his head.

"Go ahead. Kill me too," Tony shouted. "You killed everything I ever loved. You bastard, you. And you called it 'Devine Intervention.'"

Instead, Lord Bosh crashed the stick down on the table again, this time shattering two of the cups and driving others to the floor.

"What you have done! What our people have done is genocide; murder." Tony pounded his chest. "You're ashamed of me?" he laughed angrily. "Bloody Hell! I'm the one that's ashamed. Ashamed of you. Ashamed to be English. I hate you! I hate you!"

"Shut up, shut up!" shouted the Lord, now covering his ears with his trembling hands.

Tony shouted even louder. "Why couldn't you be like Barclay? He treated his tenants like humans."

"He was a fool," shouted Lord Bosh. "An even bigger fool to pay their passage to America. What did it get him? And I know you used my money to pay the O'Hara's passage. Money you stole from me."

"Yes, I did pay their way. And I am forever grateful for that."

Pointing his finger at Tony, Lord Bosh calmed himself then said, "You are no longer my son. I want you off my property by week's end."

"Finally we agree on something . . . Mr. Bosh," snapped Tony.

"And I'll give you nothing. What your mother left you up in Dublin is all you'll get. When that's gone, you're on your own. If you wish to survive I advise you to leave Ireland. To go to that fool uncle of yours in New York. He'd be inclined to support your foolishness."

Tony Bosh and his father, who had turned to drinking heavily since the Great Hunger, had many bitter arguments. Tony never forgave his father for the deaths of the O'Hara children, a family he loved dearly, and then their transportation to America. Tony had been very fond of one of the O'Hara girls.

Lord Bosh repeatedly accused Tony of being a traitor because he took the Irish side. And young Bosh always responded, "If feeling compassion for the tenants *you killed* be traitorous, then a traitor I be." Often too, he told his father that when he's on his own, he would pass himself off as an Irishman.

Two days later Tony Bosh left his father, disavowing him and everything he stood for, seeking a better life in Dublin. As much as he wanted to forget the past, he could not leave behind the memories of the starvation and the guilt he felt for being his father's son. He bounced around aimlessly, trying his hand at different jobs: accounting, banking, even importing and exporting. But nothing he tried fulfilled his needs. He found solace in alcohol to the point that he could not hold onto employment of any kind. With the small fortune his mother had left him running out, he knew he had to do something drastic. But what?

Then one morning he awoke to the realization the he must travel to America to work for his uncle and to find the O'Hara's. He remembered his father's driver telling him the O'Hara's were going to *"Westside thirty-third."*

Even if he did not find them, there would be great opportunities for him in New York, guaranteed by his uncle, Jacob Bosh, a very successful textile manufacturer and distributor of mining supplies. His uncle was an equally successful importer. He would never have to worry about earning a living.

* * * * *

DECEMBER 1862 -- "Watch that bag you little jerk, ya," somebody shouted as Red shouldered her way through the crowded omnibus, pushing her suitcase before her. Aggravated, she ignored the voice. But when she heard the voice again say, "You hear what I said, jerk? Watch the bag," she responded, "Sumbiddy lookin fo a punch in da mouth?"

"I'll have none of that on my bus," ordered the driver.

As the bus stopped, she shouted, "Well I gitten off. Ya woan have no tru'ble from me. But if dat jurk wants a bunch of bumps all over his face, he kin joins me." Nobody did.

She had arrived on Bleeker Street, exhilarated by what she saw. *But should I be*, she wondered. She heard good things about the Village. Plenty of artists and eccentrics of all kinds. And women who liked women. But she knew nobody there, nobody to say hello to. The few that did greet her, hell, she didn't like their looks. From the start, she missed the old neighborhood and the camaraderie of the gang. But there'd be no going back. To do so would mean she failed. Her pride wouldn't permit it.

So she set out on her search for a job. Instinctively, she sought to work in the building trades, preferably in building supplies where she had so much experience—of course she was dressed like a young man—and when she located a building supply company, the only one in the area, she felt upbeat and confidant. The management liked the fact that she had kept books and that she had performed many of the business' functions. But when she told them where she lived they said no. "We only hire Americans," one of the owners responded. A paint shop owner accused her of being a girl. "Hey, you're a woman," he said, pointing at her chest.

She knew she could get work serving drinks in a local dive, but that didn't appeal to her. So for several weeks she continued checking out the many shops throughout the Village and surrounding areas, with no luck. In some of the shops where she applied she saw *No Irish Need Apply* signs. In the first few places, she called the owners *jurks* and threatened to "*put liddle bumps on dere faces.* Eventually she ignored those shops.

Finally, with her savings exhausted, she made the choice to do what she said she would never do, turn to the dives, to be a drink server. With her good looks, she got a job in the first place she applied, with the same promises the owners made to every young gal they hired: fair wages with free room and board. In short order, with the cold winter on its way and the threat of starvation a real possibility, the dive owner put it to her bluntly. *Put out or get out.* She was to sell her body for sex. The owners and their bouncers were not above beating the girl servers senseless if they did not comply. But these men were barking up the wrong tree with Red, the street fighter.

For many months she went from working in one dive to another. It never failed that her employers had promised that she'd not have to prostitute herself, yet each time, after a month or two, they compelled her to *put out or get out.* On two occasions she had *fistfights* and wound up clubbing the owners with full whiskey bottles. And both times, she whipped out her trusty blade and placed it at their throats, threatening: "If anybidy cum after me, I use dis on dem. And I tell me big shot copper frens 'bouts dis place." But that wasn't the end of it. One night, shortly after the second incident, a hooded man stepped out of a dark alley and attacked her. He grabbed her throat with a large hand and slammed her head against the wall, which knocked her silly. He began choking her, and at the same time, punching her face repeatedly with great force. This time, before she could pull her trusty knife, she collapsed unconscious. He left her body on the pavement. Her face badly beaten. Both of her lips busted and bleeding, her nose bled, and her right eyebrow split and bleeding. There was also a bleeding three quarter inch gash on her chin. With teary eyes, she made her way home, vowing to herself, never to let that happen again.

Although for the most part her street smarts protected her from the dive owners, they also kept her out of work. None of the owners wanted to have to deal with her or find out if her *big shot* copper friends were for real or fabricated. But the "tough little redhead," as she became known, did not starve. She reverted back to her old ways: stealing, which she genuinely resented, but only enough to keep her in food and a roof over her head.

In her dreams she envisioned images of dollars. She saw herself as a pauper with her face in the same gaunt condition that Johnny had described of how his brother and sister looked before they fell victim to the Hunger.

The more she stole the more frequently she suffered bouts of depression, often caused by the very fact that she could easily be at Brogan's doing an honest day's work and earning good money. And she missed the gang. But just when she felt utterly hopeless, she ran into a recent acquaintance who informed her that the owner of the *Love Nest* wanted her to work for him. Two nights later, she began her new job serving drinks to a large crowd of lesbian women and homosexual men. It wasn't her favorite kind of work, but it beat stealing. Things went well enough for the first several weeks, but she always felt uneasy. Too many of the lesbian women found her attractive, And not all of them kept their feelings to themselves.

"Hey you, good looking?" a big, wine-drinking gal shouted at Red as she passed her table. Red gave her a "get lost" look. "I love your hair and those green eyes," the gal continued. She even reached up to touch Red's close cropped hair, while saying, "You excite me, good looking one."

Red slapped her arm then pointed in her face. "Doan ya touch mees agin," she snapped and at the same time picked up an empty wine bottle.

The big woman got to her feet, staggering. "I'll touch whatever I want," she jabbed her finger at Red, "you bitch you," then grabbed her breast.

In a flash, she had the wine bottle in the air, heading for the side of the big one's face. Instantly the bottle was blocked by the feminine arms of screaming Moe Jammer, the six-foot-two owner of the Love Nest—wearing red lipstick and red rouge. Red always thought he looked like a clown.

"Now, now, Helen," he said in a girlish voice. "You have to pay to touch my Red. Nothing for nothing, you know the rules."

"I want that red-headed bitch in my bed. Tell her she's mine," she shouted, hardly noticed by a loud, heavy drinking group of boisterous females. They were celebrating two of their own, announcing their becoming *lovers for life,* a not uncommon occurrence at the Love Nest, a concealed cellar dive in the rear of a tenement deep in the heart of Greenwich Village.

Moe Jammer called Red aside. "It's time you do our customers some sexual favors. Take her upstairs and satisfy her. I'll make it worth your while, sweetie," he said, shifting his hips.

"I serve da drinks," she snapped. "Dat's all. Nuttin else—"

"Yes, but it's time for you to do other things for the girls. Many of them come here because of you. They love your looks and want sex with you. You'll get paid to make them happy."

Red glared at Jammer. "Ya didn't tell mees dat . . . when I started," she snapped.

"I know. But you're so popular. They want your body. So would I if I were one of them," Jammer continued in his girly voice.

* * * * *

During the sixteen months Red had resided in the Village, she lived by herself, once again in a cellar flat with an earthen floor. She had spent most of her off time struggling to learn proper English. Rarely did she have a night off. She worked into the wee hours of the morning as a waitress, wearing the required tight, skimpy attire from which she scraped out a fair income; with tips of course. She found the women to be no better than men, just as horny and aggressive. They too had molested her, but the offenders usually paid a price.

On one occasion, late at night, she waited in the shadows of an alleyway where she knew one of her wrongdoers would pass. She grabbed the half-drunk woman by the hair, dragged her into the alley, and rammed her head against a brick wall, knocking her to the ground.

Moe Jammer had suspected Red as the culprit, but could never prove it.

Eventually, her day-to-day experiences with lesbian women cleared up her confused thinking about men. She just could not accept the idea of having sex with another woman. That's when she realized that she didn't hate men, rather she distrusted them. So, too, she began to appreciate her own beauty and exceptional body. It was that beauty and body that caused men to behave the way they did around her; the price she paid for her exceptional beauty.

She also missed Johnny's company, and found herself becoming sexually aroused when thinking of him. *I tinks—I think I'd pull him into me, my bed, she often told herself.* But at the same time, she doubted Johnny would have anything to do with the *lowlife* she considered herself to be.

Yet her pride and the idea of her old friends seeing her wearing a dress rather than a man's outfit stopped her from returning to the old neighborhood to look for him. *Dere—there, that is,* she corrected herself, *ain't no way in hell I'd let them see me like dat—that.* She continued improving her English, mostly through the people she worked with. She also improved her reading and writing by using the book Johnny gave her.

Red's popularity with the queer women continued to soar. She learned how to charm them and at the same time keep them at a safe distance. She doubled the Love Nest's business. Moe Jammer continued to push her to prostitute herself. And every so often, he'd step up the pressure. On the coldest night of the winter he decided to gamble, to threaten to fire her if she didn't put out. Of course, Jammer had no intention of terminating her employment, for he knew he'd lose half his trade.

"You're not nice to the ladies," he said in his well-practiced girly voice. "And you never do them sexual favors. Maybe you don't like working here. Maybe you should go somewhere else. But who'd have you?"

"The only ting—thing," she corrected herself, "I'd let them do is kiss me asshole," she said, showing no emotion.

"I'm sure some of them would be happy to do that," he said.

"I doan—don't mean that, dumdum," she barked at him. He got her at the wrong time. "As a matter of fact, you can shove this job up your sissy ass . . . hole."

His eyes exploded with shock. "You can't talk to me like that." He grabbed for her hair, but she saw it coming. Her open right hand slammed his face, making a loud walloping noise that filled the room—everybody turned, frozen in place. Moe's eyes were wide with shock. He raised his open hand real feminine like to slap at her, but Red's knee drove up into his testicles. He screamed and as he bent over from the pain, Red followed through with a lightning-fast *boxer's* left hook that landed flush on his mouth and nose, accompanied by a thumping sound and a splatter of blood from a busted lip and a bloody nose. By then the big lug of a bartender had lunged over the bar coming to Jammer's aide. Jammer's eyes rolled upwards as his frame stumbled backwards. He then fell, hitting his head against the wall, making another loud thud.

Red saw the barman coming. She must have felt like David when he confronted the giant Goliath. No, Red didn't have a slingshot, but she did have her favorite bar weapon in her hand, an empty wine bottle made of thick glass. As he grabbed for her, she swung it toward his not-to-healthy looking front teeth. as he grabbed for her. He never saw the bottle coming, nor did he see his few remaining front teeth hitting the floor as he collapsed on top of Jammer.

One by one, Jammer's customers turned away as Red sought eye contact with any of them who might want to brawl. She shouted, taking the time to properly pronounce her words, "That's what happens when you mess with a Young Immigrant."

Cockily, she strutted to the cash register behind the bar and removed some cash. "Listen to me," she said. "This is my day's pay. And tell him," she pointed at Jammer's motionless body, "if I catch any flack over this shit, I will go to my copper frens, oh hell—friends, and tell them about this house of fruitcakes." On the way out the door the thought passed through her mind, *Now what do I do for money?*

* * * * *

For several nights since her forced retirement, she'd been doing a lot of shivering and soul searching. She sat on a hardwood chair at her crude kitchen table, furniture that several times she contemplated using as firewood. *God it's cold,* she kept telling herself.

Her mind had been digging into her past and projecting scary thoughts of her future. All very depressing as were the sounds of the frigid winds that had howled for the past three nights. Sometimes, just to kill time, she would count the paint chips hanging from the ceiling or listen to the *clippidy clop* of horses passing by outside. And wisely enough, she spent a lot of time reading her *Reading & Writing* with which she had made considerable progress.

And much of the progress resulted from her chance meeting with an old neighborhood friend, a prostitute named Anna Flipit. This kind courtesan spent many an hour teaching her the ABCs. It all came about because Anna brought up to her, as a joke, how Johnny used to correct the way she spoke. And when Red told her how he kept pushing her to learn to speak *the right way* but she didn't see him any more, Flipit made her an offer: I'll teach you if you provide me supper. So a couple of times a week, Anna visited Red for dinner and taught her the ABCs.

On the second morning of her forced sabbatical, Red Hester began roaming the streets, bright and early, scrounging whatever she could. Stole a bottle of milk and two loaves of bread from the stoop of a rich man's grand home: a three-story brownstone with brown granite pillars that sparkled like glass, topped with gargoyles on each side of the sandstone stoop. And for once, she even buried her pride and took Father Peter up on the free lunch offer he had made to her in the past. Her pretty face got her a couple of apples from a street vendor. And she ran into a bit more luck: Sergeant O'Connell who got her several days' supply of coal, no questions asked.

Finally, she had spent all of her rainy day reserve. She would no longer be able to purchase any more coal or wood. How the hell would she keep from freezing? The blankets she kept wrapped around her feet, legs, and torso hardly did the job. Her knees knocked endlessly.

From the table, she stared into her open food pantry, where she saw very little sustenance: a near empty jar of strawberry preserves and the remainder of a loaf of bread wrapped in a damp, near frozen towel. A sole overly ripe apple sat behind the bread. And in the food box sitting on the sill outside the closed window, she saw two eggs that were probably as solid as ice.

When about to ask herself *What am I gonna do*, she saw the bottle of Paddy's Irish Whiskey sitting on the nearby windowsill, which brought a smile to her face. *That's what I need. A warmer upper.* She grabbed the half full bottle, which was a gift from a customer, pulled the cork and put it to her mouth. She took a generous swig. In an instant, her burdens were lightened. Her body enjoyed the warm rush. But that warmth faded a bit when she glimpsed at the coal bucket. She saw just enough for tonight and maybe tomorrow night if she included the six pieces of wood stacked by the fireplace. *If only I could run into that O'Connell again.*

Out of the blue, she muttered, "Oh momma, I miss ya." Her eyes began to tear. "Help me, woan ya? " She saw her mother's face plain as day, deep in the recesses of her mind, bringing with it a sudden surge. *I know you didn't leave me, but I just couldn't deal with it, mother dear.*

Of late, she'd been thinking more and more of her mother; her bitterness toward her lessening. And she'd also been thinking a lot about Johnny. She told herself just how dumb she had been to think she couldn't love a man.

She half-filled a small jar that served as her drinking glass, with Paddy's. She right away sipped the whiskey, washing it down with a couple of swallows of water from a jam jar that also sat on the table.

Mixed thoughts of her father also emerged: *That no good sonofabitch.* She stared over at the Ulliean Pipes. The cold wind rattled her window, some of it forcing its way in through the loose fitting frame.

Most of what she remembered about him had to do with the two of them working together as diggers, and his many bouts with alcohol. She started working with him on her seventh birthday. He dressed her like a boy and kept her hair cut short. It wasn't long before he had her digging and pushing the wheelbarrow. Some of the men complained to him, without affect, about how hard he worked her. Little did they know her gender.

She shut out all thoughts of the sexual abuse he inflicted on her. But she rationalized for the first time that Johnny treated her with respect and that he could be trusted; that he had never come close to abusing her, sexually that is. And for the first time she understood that he respected her and that he had loved her for who she was.

Hardly did she miss her father when he vanished. Nor did she hold him in high regard, but she did admire his fighting prowess and attributed her fighting skills to him. And she would be forever thankful for the Ulliean Pipes he left her.

By her ninth birthday, the digging and pushing of the wheelbarrow had lined her body with hard muscle and broadened her shoulders. Many of the local boys feared her and even backed down from a fight with her. And the ones that didn't back down had a tough fight when they fought. She chuckled, thinking about how many times she came home with a swollen lip or a black eye or both.

Grabbing her pipes, she pumped air into its bag and pressed it against her side with her elbow, making it give off a drone. Then she played its chanter that made a soft high-pitched sound. She played a lament. In short order, tears again filled her eyes. She was thinking about Johnny, wishing he was there with her. Then she heard pounding on the ceiling and muffled shouting. With narrowed eyes and puckered lips, she glared at the ceiling. She opened her mouth to shout, but then smiled and put down her pipes. "Ah, go ta sleep ya grouch," she muttered.

In childhood, Red often found herself protecting her mother, Angel Hester, who often found herself the victim of unwanted advances by men. From all the abuse, Red learned that it would be to her benefit to dress like a boy.

When she asked herself how she would earn money, prostitution came to mind, but that wasn't an option.

She took another sip of Paddy's, again washing it down with water.

Yet the word prostitution forced her to think about something she still refused to deal with, and that was what Lopat had said about her mom. He said that Angel Hester had been a prostitute. She began opening her mind to memories she had shut out, about the many men who came by the house in their fancy coaches. And how often she begged her mother, *"Stay wid me and learns me ta read,"* to which her mom would always respond, "Gotta work. Mommy has to make money. Gotta be able to feed my beautiful daughter and pay the rent."

The memory that haunted her most was when she last saw her mother. That was the night the big black stallion with the white diamond on its forehead pulled its big white carriage up in front of her house to await her mother. But the people in the carriage were different. That night the well-dressed man that stepped out of the coach wore his hair in a wild manner, just about covering the whole of his face. He did not have his normal ponytail.

Staring at the bottle of Paddy's, she envisioned her mother's beautiful face. Could see her like it just happened: mom applying her makeup, standing in front of the small mirror with the crack running through it that hung on the similarly cracked kitchen wall. She could still hear her clearly, asking, "How do I look, my redheaded beauty?"

And her answer to her mom came right back to her: *"Weal good. Like always, Mommy. Ya gonna learn me to read damorra? Will ya?"*

"I'll be leaving now. Be home in the morning," she remembered word for word what her mother had said that night as they kissed and hugged, cheek to cheek. "Mommy loves you," she said stepping out the door.

By now she bawled, sobbing heavily and heaving like never before, helped on by the whiskey, of course. Again she put the bottle to her mouth, her face cringing as the alcohol burned its way down.

Then, for the first time since that fatal day, she opened her mind to what she saw from the window when she went to give one more wave to her mom. Suddenly it became crystal-clear to her. The well-dressed man—his hair down around his head like a weirdo—had slapped her mother repeatedly across the face. And she saw clearly the face of the chauffeur, who was not the regular driver. This one was a tall, burly young man with blond hair. Damn, damn, she cursed herself. It's him. She made out the face of Chuck Jansen, the person who had jumped down to the street and manhandled her mother into the coach. She remembered now the well-dressed man shouting, "I'll teach you. I'll teach you." The two of them punched away at her body. And she remembered, too, that her mom's screams were muffled, as if another person already inside the carriage had her mouth covered. She remembered the coach rocking under the pounding as the horse neighed and shifted about nervously.

Red squeezed her tear-filled eyes shut and covered her ears, trying to shut out the sound of the punches raining down on her mother.

And she remembered that when they were ready to leave, the man with all the hair whispered, "Go, go, go."

The coach bolted forward behind the galloping stallion. Deep in her mind she could still hear the hoof beats as they diminished.

Wotever—whatever—the hell made me think I wanted a woman? She massaged her breasts. *Hell, these things are for Johnny. If he still wants 'em. But right now I needs money. What I—am I gonna do?* She thought of what she did best, when she needed money. Rob a joint. But where? Staring at the wall, her mind raced, thinking of targets. Very few popped up. Then the *brilliant* alcohol-induced idea came to her . . . *rob Moe Jammer's house. Be a cinch.*

* * * * *

Red had carried out more than a dozen burglaries since leaving the neighborhood. And she stole not for the sake of robbing but out of desperation to feed herself and to keep a roof over her head. Some of these burglaries were acrobatic spectaculars, like her North River antics when she was known as *The Crazy Mermaid*, flying through the air at the end of a piece of rope. Her continued swimming in the river, and rope climbing paid off for her. They enabled her to scale the sides of buildings both up and down.

An art dealer had recently made her an offer she could not refuse: $150 plus $10 for the cost of a hundred feet of rope, if she would snatch a painting. There were no other moneymaking opportunities for her outside of prostitution.

The painting hung somewhere in the offices of a securities firm named Bartland & Bates, on the top floor of 511 Barclay Street, a newly constructed seven-story edifice just off Broadway.

Riding a borrowed bicycle, Red pulled up in front of 511 and placed it in the bike rack. Disguised as a delivery boy carrying a package, she hurried inside shouting "good morning" to no one in particular, then ran up the stairs before being challenged.

"Package for Milton Roebles," he shouted behind her bright-eyed smile, bolting through the office entry door right past the receptionist, who she pretended not to see. The receptionist leapt to her feet shouting after her, "You can't go in there," but by then Red had reached the hallway, moving fast and looking into the different offices until she found the picture. Mission accomplished.

"Oh I'm so sorry," Red shouted, responding to the receptionist.

"There's no Mister Roebles here," snapped the stern-faced secretary who had chased after her. "What company's he with?" The secretary glanced at the *Downtown Delivery* tab affixed to Red's leather-peaked cap, also borrowed.

"Great American," Red answered, still smiling.

"That's two floors down."

Red smiled. "Thank you," she said, pleased with the knowledge of the painting's location and what window she'd have to use to get in. This should be a cinch for her, well worth $150. And she didn't even have to carry it out, just cut out the canvass and bring it to the shady character that hired her.

The artwork was a large life-like depiction, about six-feet wide by three to four feet in height, of an enormous black stallion with a white diamond on its forehead. The stallion was harnessed to an unusually large, one-of-a-kind, white Brougham Carriage. That was completely enclosed, with *Blackie* painted on the door panel.

The painting itself was an *illegal* reproduction of a commissioned painting of the unique carriage built in England by the Robinson Carriage Company for a wealthy New York businessman. Although the forgery had no monetary value, the New York businessman simply resented there being an imitation.

That giant of a horse. I've seen it before. But where? In a flash she felt disturbed, shaking her head as she hurried down the stairs. She felt the nerve endings in her gut tighten. *Something's wrong with that picture. What is it?*

CHAPTER FIFTEEN

At 3 AM the next morning, Red scurried along the deserted streets, heading to 511 Barclay while keeping herself as near to invisible as possible. Strapped to her was a canvass backpack containing a hundred feet of fireman's rescue rope. Her physical strength overcame the rope's heaviness. Little did she know, but a lone copper standing at the corner of Church and Barclay had already spotted her. He, too, kept himself out of sight.

On one of her earlier observations of the building, she had detected how easy it would be to scale its face. All she'd have to do is shimmy up one of the four ridge-covered concrete columns that stood at the front of the building. They were standing some fifteen feet in height and topped off by a large overhang. The fancy stone and brickwork and the many ornate gargoyles projecting from the façade, coupled with the floor to ceiling windows that lined the face of the structure, created many ledges for her to step on. The ordeal would not be too risky for her being such a fearless and experienced rope climber in her physical condition. This attribute she gained from years of climbing and diving from heights of up to fifty feet when she lived by the river.

She stood in front of the building, dressed for the occasion in tight trousers and soft, snug rubber shoes. She sized up the building front one last time and checked the street for possible witnesses. Nobody. Up she went, moving with caution and grace. She stepped from ledge to ledge—little spaces that were perfectly sized for her small feet and her strong hands to grip. She stopped at the second floor and again looked up and down the block. *Don't look down*, she reminded herself. Not a soul. Hand over hand, foot over foot, she continued up the wall, stepping on small ledges, on the heads of gargoyles, and on more ledges. The challenge exhilarated her. She hardly felt the weight of the rope.

Unnoticed by Red, the copper had moved closer, still keeping out of sight. He too, sized up the situation. It's a little red-headed guy, he determined. And the sight of the thief scaling the wall, getting higher and higher, scared him.

Her innards rose to her throat—she almost screamed—as her foot slipped from a narrow fifth-floor ledge, sending a tremor of fear rocketing through her. Luckily, she maintained tight grips with her strong hands as her foot regained its footing.

On the street the copper saw climber's foot give way. He jumped, almost wanting to run under this little guy and catch him should he fall. But he watched with admiration as the thief maintained his grip, paused, then continued on. *My God what nerve,* thought the police officer.

When Red got to the sixth floor, she stopped to take a break. A minute later she was on the move again, this time moving with a little more caution. Finally, she reached the sill of the top-floor corner window. To the copper's amazement, she had the window open and was inside, all in a flash. *Thank God,* thought the copper, feeling relieved. Then he wondered why he cared about what happened to this little thief?

Didn't take her long to locate the picture. A beam of moonlight shining through the skylight lit up the large painting. She had her blade out and with a few quick strokes had the canvass removed. She folded it as compact as she could, shoving it under her belt flat, against her back. As she removed the rope from the backpack, she remembered the one thing she forgot earlier when casing the place; a secure object around which to fasten the rope. No problem! A few feet from the window sat an enormous American Bank Lock safe solidly anchored to the floor, around which she tied the rope. She tugged it real hard, several times. *This won't move,* she assured herself. She again put on her padded gloves.

She went back to the windowsill and took another look for unwanted guests. She let the rope drop. Gave it one more good hard yank. *Let's go,* she told herself. With one movement, she straddled the window, pulled at her padded gloves one more time, then gripped the rope and swung her body outside against the building. Down she went, twice springing off the building as she repelled. In a matter of seconds, she had passed the second floor. She felt great about her accomplishment, that is, until she saw that familiar face running towards her. *No, not him.* Abruptly, she stopped her descent some 10 feet above. Instinctively, she started pulling herself back up the rope.

"C'mon now, Red," said an astonished Sergeant O'Connell. His hands reached up as if trying to grab her feet. "I can't believe it. Tis this the appreciation I get for the bag of coal. Sure you've let me down. And ye scared the living hell out of me, to boot. Me heart was in me mouth."

"So sorry, Sergeant O'Connell," she said, dropping to the street. "It was either this or ta be a whore."

He didn't make a move to apprehend her. "Let's step in here. Best not to be seen," he said, cupping her elbow as though escorting her. He guided her into a doorway. "You're crazy, young Hester. That's the craziest ting I've ever seen in me years as a policeman. Now what were you doing up there? And don't feed me any blarney."

She removed the canvas from her trousers and handed it to him. "This," she said. She watched his reaction as he opened it up. His eyes widened. "I've seen this coach before. The huge horse. God knows I've seen it."

"Sergeant, I knows I'm wrong, but I needs—need the money. And I doan wanna to be a prostitute. For God's sakes, doan . . . don't put me in jail."

"Ye put me in an awful predicament. I tink the world of you and that Johnny lad. I don't want to see ye in trouble." He looked up at the dangling rope. "Can ye get that down?"

"No."

"If you promise you'll not be doing this again, I'll let you go."

"I promise," she said with sincerity in her eyes.

"Then leave the rope and go. You'll not hear another word from me."

* * * * *

Yep. Moe Jammer's it is. She was alive again. Excited. Her promise to Sergeant O'Connell that she'd never burgle again never even entered her groggy mind. Getting to her feet, she checked her timepiece. Ten o'clock. He'll be at work.

After slipping on her tight trousers and soft, snug rubber shoes, she bundled up in a sweater and an old sailor's pea coat, topping it all off with a black woolen cap that she pulled down over her ears. Being used to wearing woman's clothing, she enjoyed the feel of the clothes she used to wear. *Better bring some rope, just in case.*

Out the door she went, collar up, gloved hands in her pea coat pockets. She leaned into the wind that chilled her legs through her threadbare pants as she hurried to West 10th.

Not a soul in sight. She'd been to Jammer's place often enough to know her way around. He kept his valuables on the second floor of his three-story brick home that stood in the rear yard of a row of brownstones. Jammer's residence stood adjacent to a similar building used as a printing shop, separated from it by a five-foot wide alley.

How do I get in? she wondered. Access could not be made through the front door. A renter lived on the first floor through which the stairs to Moe's pad passed. Still, the front entrance provided the only *safe* means of entry unless she wanted to use the rope and swing from the roof next door. But that risk would be unnecessary. Moe's entranceway consisted of a slate stoop with four wooden columns that supported a six-foot square, slightly pitched wooden crown, over which sat a window. That will be her way in. She wouldn't need to use the rope.

She moved in silence through the dark passageway between two of the brownstones on her way to the rear yard. But she didn't go unnoticed. A dog in one of the brownstones began yelping, getting the attention of its master who opened his window and reached out with a lantern. "Who's out there?" he called out. "Is anybody out there?" Red froze in a dark corner right in front of Moe's place. After another minute, the barking ceased and the head withdrew back inside the window.

She gave the windows one more check for the all clear. Instead, she got the shock of her life. She saw two naked men getting into bed with each other. She could not look. With that, the lamp went out.

What's next, she wondered. In her time in the Village community, she never did have a sexual relationship with a woman. And she never witnessed men making love with each other than cheap feels and kisses. Of course, she did hear a lot of fag talk.

151

Like a monkey, she shimmied up the column. Once on the crown, she crouched and pulled out her trusty blade to pry open the window, but it wasn't locked. *What a fool*, she thought. When she opened the window, she listened for movement inside. Nothing. It was safe to go in. Snakelike, she slithered through the window—without closing it—down to the floor on her belly then across to the bed, flipping aside a large floor mat that covered the floor area adjacent to his bed. In the dark, she felt the wooden floor for a perpendicular seam and found it. As a fireman she learned to operate in the dark. With the blade of her knife, she lifted several short strips of flooring, exposing a hidden compartment in which she felt a metal box. She grinned as she removed the weighty box and opened it. On feeling several thick rolls of what she knew were bills, she muted a hardy laugh. Into her pockets the money went. After replacing the flooring, she slithered back to the window.

On the way home the bitter cold winds hardly fazed her.

* * * * *

The next day just before noon, she awoke, still feeling the effects of Paddy. After returning home from hitting Moe's, she had a few more drinks to celebrate. The metal box contained over $300. Much more than she needed. She rolled out of her sack, a mattress lying on the floor, and dropped her head into the basin of cold water. She washed her teeth and rinsed her mouth, instantly clearing the cobwebs.

With the clear head came a sense of guilt. Not because she burglarized Jammer's place, but because she broke her promise to O'Connell. In an effort to make it up to him, she'd go to the priest and try to get a job. Whether or not they had a job for her, she'd leave a sizable donation in the church poor box.

Attired in her most modest dress, looking real lady-like, she took off for Holy Cross. *Maybe Father Peter would 'memba' me. It's remember, stupid*, she chided herself. She had improved immensely her use of the English language since leaving the neighborhood, thanks to help from friends and the fact that she practiced reading and writing as often as possible.

Father Peter, wearing his cassock, with a cigarette in hand, answered the door. "How can I help you, young lady?" he said, his eyes glued to her red hair. *I've seen this person before*, he ascertained.

"I'm looking for work, Father," she said.

"Won't ye step in out of the cold?" he said, his Irish accent prominent. *God I know this woman.* They stepped into a small foyer. "I wish I could say yes. But that's not the case. And I know there's nobody in the area with work for a young lady. Let me put this out." He squashed the life out of his cigarette in a standing ashtray. "It's hard enough to get work for the men and much of that is day work like digging and cleaning."

"I can do a man's work, Father. I was a digger as a child," she said, displaying her desperation.

"I can see that in ye shoulders. But even if there should be a man's job available, we couldn't give it to a woman. It would have to go to a man with a family. You do understand that, my child."

The letdown showed on her face.

"How could I forget you with that beautiful hair and those green eyes," he said, pointing to his own hair then eyes, "and lovely face."

"Angela Hester, I am. Johnny O'Hara's friend."

"There's the answer, my child. Surely Johnny can get you a job over in the yard. He's doing very well . . . since he took over for Mr. Brogan.

"Nah. There's no work there, either," she lied.

"I'm so sorry, Miss Hester."

Now what to do, she wondered, turning to leave.

"Young lady," he called to her. "We do serve lunch here every day. You're more than welcome to join us."

"That's a good idea."

* * * * *

JUNE 1863 – Graduation Day at Holy Cross, a big day for Johnny. His sister Katie, now fifteen, would be graduating in a few hours. Like an excited child, he boasted about her graduation to everybody in and out of

Brogan's Building Supplies. He even invited some of the contractors to the celebration he had planned for the graduating class and their parents.

Johnny wanted a big party for the occasion; something his sister would always remember. Although he would be picking up the tab, he would sponsor it in Brogan's name. A couple of weeks prior to the graduation, he had the following message circulated at the school: *On behalf of Thomas Brogan, proprietor of Brogan Building Supply Company, we invite the graduates and their families to a gala celebration at the Pvt. Michael Brogan Engine Company Firehouse. We are proud of the young men and women who have successfully completed their education at Holy Cross. There will be good music and good chowder. Starting time 4 PM.*

At the beginning of the celebration, while tea and sandwiches were being served, Johnny stood on a step stool and welcomed everybody in their languages: Italian, Irish, German—he struggled with each word—and English, and heaped praise on the graduates.

"This is the only way," he said, "that we people of the *ole* country are going to make it in this great country of ours, this land of opportunity. Education, education, education." He glanced from face to face. "Without schooling we will always be greeted with the *No Irish Need Apply* sign. And please pardon me if I sound like a braggart, which I am not," he said loud and clear making sure everybody understood him, "but I know the value of an education. Thanks to Thomas Brogan's faith in me and the education he knew I received in my few years at Holy Cross, and from my sister Katie, I have been very fortunate. And I attribute my success to that knowledge," his proud eyes beaming on Katie, "my sister bestowed upon me, whether she knows it or not. It is exactly that book learning she gave me on math and the proper use of the English language that has enabled me to achieve for Mr. Brogan and myself, of course, what I have achieved."

At that moment somebody shouted, "We love ya Johnny," followed by an enthusiastic round of applause from the crowd that thronged the recently finished firehouse, all dressed in their Sunday best, which for many of them was their work clothes.

"If I can say something, please," shouted Alderman Sean Mulvihey, who attended with several other councilmen and Tammany politicians. The audience turned with curious eyes to see who was shouting.

"Yes, of course," said Johnny. "Friends, our alderman—"

"No, no, no," Mulvihey stopped him while removing his Fedora. "I just want to say thank you and let you know that we are very proud of you, Johnny O'Hara, and what you have done for this community. The jobs you have created. The example you have set for the young ones." Mulvihey sparked another enthusiastic round of applause and cheering that ricocheted around the garage area.

All the attention mortified Johnny, yet at the same time delighted him. He saw genuine appreciation on many of the faces in the crowd, including Sergeant Desmond O'Connell and Father Brian Rafferty.

"Th—th—thank you . . . ye are embarrassing me," he said, with a cocky tone. He glanced around the room, looking at the smiling faces. "I would be remiss if I did not acknowledge the man himself who made this gala possible, the man who made this thoroughly modern and fully equipped firehouse available to us; the man who created so many important jobs for us. The boss himself, Thomas Brogan. And, of course, we must remember his brother Michael Brogan for whom this firehouse is dedicated, and all the other members who gave their lives for this nation."

As the crowd expressed this solemn recognition and appreciation, a hunger producing aroma began wafting through the garage area. Before Johnny continued his talk, his nose began quivering.

"Oh God. That mouth-watering smell," he said, closing his eyes, taking in a long, deep breath and exhaling. "Yes. There is one other thing Thomas gave us," he shouted. The crowd became silent with curiosity. "He gave us a kitchen with a gas stove. And right now, on that stove sits two big pots that are cooking up great chicken-oyster chowder."

The crowd broke into laughter, with a few individuals calling for the chowder to be brought out.

Johnny continued, "I know that everyone here today, whether or not you are a member of the Young Immigrants or the Young Immigrant Engine Company, you've got to be proud of this beautiful firehouse that belongs to our community. The first one-hundred percent immigrant-run firehouse in the city."

A thunderous applause followed. The horses neighed with fear, rising up on their hindquarters, scaring many children.

"Even the horses are excited," he said, pointing at the new fire engine. "And from this day forward, our fire company will be known as the Pvt. Michael Brogan Engine Company," sparking more clapping, which he shouted over, "hero of Bull Run and who was also the former president of the Young Immigrants."

When the clapping and cheering subsided, Johnny closed with an announcement: "As a personal gift from Mr. Brogan to all the graduates, he is presenting each of you a paid-in-full voucher from Skoven's for a pair of shoes for your graduating child."

Sighs of appreciation emanated from the parents.

"God bless Mr. Brogan," a woman shouted. The same voice called out to the step dancers, "Step dancers, please take your places."

"The bar is open," shouted Vinnie McCarthy, one of the bartenders for the evening.

"You gotta vino?" an Italian voice shouted, sparking laughter.

"Yes we do, Mr. Tiso," Vinnie shouted back.

Vinnie's announcement was the prearranged cue for the band. They started with a waltz version of Beautiful Dreamer. Johnny and Katie broke the ice, the first couple on the floor. Several other couples joined in.

The muffled tapping of the stocking feet of twelve Irish step-dancers upon the sawdust-covered floor could be heard. They were loosening up to the faint sound of a fiddle while waiting their turn to dance, waiting for their moment of glory. And as soon as Jimmy Crum's Band finished their thirty-minute set of slow American standards that somebody with an Irish accent described as *uninspiring music*, the banjos, fiddles and flutes of the local Irish ceili band started with the music for the young step-dancers. The Irish in the place went wild when the step-dancers began dancing. Loud cheering filled the firehouse and drifted out onto the street through the fully-open garage door, as did the smells of the chowder.

"Mama mia! Whya we gotta heara this againa?" an Italian accented man complained, followed immediately by a couple of his comrades mouthing, "Shhh! Shhh! Shudda you moutha, Nicola."

It wasn't long before neighbors were pouring into the firehouse, grabbing bowls of chowder and filling glasses with draft beer from either of two tapped kegs.

Greg Lopat also entered the firehouse. Lopat still maintained a close relationship with Batesy, the current leader of the Know Nothings in the city, who sent him to the firehouse. His mission: to determine if the station is complete and to verify if it is an *immigrant only* operation.

Lopat hardly recognized the area. In the six months since he'd last been there a lot of changes had been made. Ramshackled huts that now dotted the area's many once lush fields—some of them abutting the river— had been erected to house the dramatic increase in the population of the neighborhood. Many tenement houses had also been erected, including new multi-story brick tenements currently under construction across the street from the firehouse. He saw, too, that many of the streets were now covered with cobblestone and others were being sanded for the laying of cobblestones, thanks to Sean Mulvihey, who had to *fight like hell* for it at the council.

"Johnny," Mulvihey called out in his distinct voice. "Can you give us a moment of your time?" The alderman stood with a group of community leaders: Karl Ovalmyer and Michael Carlucci, official representatives for the German and Italian communities; Father Brian Rafferty, representing Holy Cross parish; and Sgt. Desmond O'Connell, just appointed to represent the local Irish. O'Connell enjoyed the respect of all the ethnic groups that considered him a fair man.

"Always got time for you good folks," Johnny answered—smiling broadly—in a way that a seasoned politician would. He grabbed their hands one at a time and shook them. "Glad that you came. It is important for the children that you did. Lets them know how important people like yourselves appreciate them going to school. Very important."

"I couldn't have said it better meself," said the sergeant. He looked admiringly at the step-dancers dancing, keeping time with his foot.

"You know, Johnny, next year I'll be running for higher office," said Mulvihey. "When I do, we'll need a good man to take my place in the council." Many in the council respected Mulvihey's honesty and bluntness, even those who were not Democrats.

"I'll certainly help in any way I can. Whom do you have in mind?" he asked.

"We've thought hard and long about this. And as you can see by the representation here today, just about the whole community supports our decision," Mulvihey continued.

"Surely, I'll support your choice. Obviously he is the people's choice. Just tell me who?" Johnny's eyes darted from face to face, anxious to know their choice.

"You, Johnny O"Hara," said Mr. Calucci, his Italian accent hardly noticeable. "In my community there is a lot of support for you."

"You gotta be—," was all Johnny got to say before Father Rafferty cut him off. "Hold it, Johnny. Let me have my say first," he insisted. "We at the parish, after lengthy discussions, fully support you as the choice."

Karl Ovalmyer cut right in, speaking in broken English: "Our leaders, too, want you. So you have no choice." He chuckled. The others laughed.

"And so does the Party. And please," Mulvihey looked hard at Johnny, "do not discuss this with anyone. This conversation never took place. Alright, Johnny?" insisted Mulvihey. He sought acknowledgement from the others.

"So, as Karl said, 'you have no choice.' Your opponent will be a Know Nothing man. You are the only one that can beat him."

"And you know Brogan wants you involved in politics," said Sergeant O'Connell. "And we've been in touch with him on this."

"But—," said Johnny, only to be cut off again. Oddly enough, he did not show any emotion.

"Let me finish," said O'Connell. "You spoke today about the important role of education in the advancement of the immigrant population. But there's another equally important facet; we need good political leaders. Men we can trust. So you cannot turn us down. The community, all of us, needs you, Johnny."

Smiling, Johnny raised his hands and softly said, "Gentlemen, if you would let me respond . . . yes! My answer is yes. And I, too, have already spoken to Brogan on this matter. Or should I say, he has spoken to me telling me, he thought I would make a good candidate."

Mulvihey remained after the others rejoined the festivities.

"Johnny," he said, placing his arm around O'Hara's shoulders. "You know, Brogan's a wealthy man. That means he is very influential. By the time we have a paid fire department, he will have a lot to say about who'll lead that department. And he has told me that man will probably be you."

"Will *ya* give the old folks a chance to dance," somebody shouted to the ceili band. "Give us some music," he continued.

The tapping of the feet became louder and more organized; two rows of four couples, all adults, began dancing just like the young Irish step-dancers had. Spontaneously, a great cheer went up. And when the musicians from Jimmy Crums Band joined in, seemed like everybody started trying to do the dance that they called *Clogging*. Even Lopat started kicking his feet and moving his arms, not that he knew what he was doing. He even smiled.

So mesmerized and into this strange but great style of dancing were the people that they ignored the loud banging coming from the bar. Some crude individual kept time with the music by pounding a crowbar on the bar's brand-spanking new countertop.

"*Bejasus*, will ye stop that," shouted Vinnie McCarthy, suddenly coming to his senses. "Sure *ye'll* ruin our new bar if *ye* haven't already done so." So the big German man laid the crowbar on its side and began pounding with the side of his giant fist.

Lopat stayed in the back of the crowd not wanting to be noticed. He even wore a cap with its peak down, hiding his face and broad forehead. He didn't want his past enemies recognizing him. In bygone days he'd fought many a pitched street battle with some of these guys who just might want to accuse him of spying, which, of course, he was doing. Even though his dapper style of dress, a striped, bright gray suit, white bowler hat, and highly polished gray shoes, did draw some attention.

The sight of the new steam pump fire engine fascinated him. And if that wasn't enough, he felt a twinge of jealousy when he saw the latest system of harnessing for the horses, hanging from the ceiling and ready to drop on them when called out. He was moved by the *temporary* sign hanging out front that spelled out, *Pvt. Michael Brogan Engine Company*. Lopat had read all that had been written about Big Mike Brogan dying the hero at Bull Run. What he didn't know was that nine other members of the fire company had also been killed in battle. At the house-watch he read, with sad eyes, the *Killed in Action* plaque listing the name and date of death of the Young Immigrant Fire Company members killed in action: *John Barry, Daithe Hughes, Myer Thormanson, Danny Dagastino, Mario O'Brien, Ralph Hauser, Dominick Murphy, Stan Jensen, Michael Hernon.* Some of these men he had fought against on these Westside streets. Couldn't help but feel he'd like to see their faces one more time.

Then from behind him a booming voice queried, "Don't I know you?" startling him. In a flash, he turned around and stood face to face with Johnny O'Hara.

"Wa—wa—wait a minute," said the ashen-faced Lopat, stepping back to put a safe distance between him and Johnny. "Who are you?" He looked around to see if anybody else was listening. But that wasn't possible with all the shouting and music.

"Johnny O'Hara's the name. You're a friend of the guy that killed my mother? The fucker who attacked my best friend."

"Wha—wha—what do you mean?" Lopat stuttered, lifting his hands in preparation to defend himself.

"Tried to rape my friend Red Hester. I was gonna kick your ass but you pulled a gun on me," said Johnny, maintaining his cool. "I never forgot that gun in my face."

"Hey, take it easy. Just remember, I tried to stop him." Lopat studied Johnny's eyes looking for weakness, which he did not find.

"Yes," said Johnny. "And that's exactly why I''m not breaking your head right now."

Johnny had challenged Lopat's macho, making him hard-pressed to do something about it, but he knew he'd be on the losing end. *Keep ya mouth shut*, he told himself.

"Why are you so afraid, if you meant no evil that day?" Johnny looked hard at him.

"Because I'm on your turf. How do I know your guys won't jump me?"

"You're here spying for Batesy. Right?" asked Johnny.

"Yeah, that's right," said Lopat, starting to get peeved.

"You guys still don't think we're worthy of being Americans. Right? Even though we, too, fight and die for *our* country. But that means nothing to—"

"Well, to be honest there big fellow, when I saw the names," he looked in the direction of the plaque listing those killed in action, "of all those guys who were killed, some of who I respected, I gotta admit it makes things different. And the guy with no legs. I remember when he was one of your toughest.

"Ya just saying that to save yourself from a good beating?"

"Listen to me, O'Hara," Lopat said, his voice a bit shaky, but getting hot under the collar. He wasn't a coward. He'd fought bigger men than Johnny and won some of those battles. "My brother, who has nothing to do with us, fought at Bull Run. Alongside the 69th. He watched a handful of them fighting the Rebs to take back their colors that the Rebs had taken. 'Never saw such courage,' he said. He called them Americans. Brave Americans." Lopat shook his head with genuine remorse. Turning again to the plague, he pointed out the names of Danny Dagastino and Dominick Murphy. "They were the two men who fought alongside Brogan. They were my brother's friends."

"I still *wanna* get your friend for what he did," insisted Johnny, putting his finger to the side of his head like a pistol. "Where is he?"

"You mean Jansen, don't you? Well, I haven't seen him since the last time I saw you. I thought you guys would know the answer to that," said Lopat, his eyes glued to Johnny's, watching his reaction.

"Oh yeah. Why would ye think that," asked Johnny, surprised by Lopat's challenge.

The constant hooting and hollering of the partygoers and the music of the musicians hid the intensity of their *discussion.* Everybody was into the festivities made even livelier by the added rhythm of the metal taps on the soles of the dancers' shoes as they hit the floor.

"That morning I met *youse,* I met Jansen too. Told me he wanted to find your friend and apologize before he left for Staten Island where he'd get lost 'til things blew over. For a year or so."

Johnny's stomach knotted. He felt both angry and uneasy. He groaned. "*Ye* gotta be shitting. You telling me *ye* believed everything that fucker told you?"

"Wha—wha—wha," Lopat stammered; his eyes darting at the faces of men nearby, some of who appeared to be watching him. *I don't like this,* he told himself.

"Wha-wha, your ass. *Ya* fucking buddy raped me best friend then. Whadda ye think of that?" Johnny growled.

"But he promised," muttered Lopat, his voice wavering, unable to look Johnny in the eye, "not to hurt her."

"If I gotten him, I'd of done him."

Then in an angry outburst, Lopat muttered, "Just like he promised with her mother, Angel. The prostitute. Said he wouldn't hurt her, either."

Johnny moved in on Lopat, his glare terrifying. "What? What did you say? What did he do?" he growled, raising his clenched fists as if to hit him, but then opened them. He didn't want to use violence to get the answers, but one way or the other, he would get the answers.

"That night he lied to me," said Lopat, who became very uneasy, even remorseful. "He ruined my life."

Johnny thought he was going to get emotional. "What did he do to her? Don't protect him."

Staring at the wooden plank floor, Lopat mumbled, "Fuck him. The liar. He's a killer." Then he looked Johnny square in the eye as though challenging him to hit him. "Raped her. Then killed her," said Lopat, his eyes moistened. He walked outside, Johnny following closely.

"But why? Why'd he have to kill her?" asked Johnny.

"Don't know. After he dropped the banker off, he—" Johnny just about shoved his hand in his face, cutting him short. "What banker?" he barked.

"Don't know his name. We picked him up outside the Louvre. He looked like a madman, the way he kept his hair hanging down. All over his face. A real weirdo."

"Why'd your friend kill her?"

"All I know is what I know. Before he came to get me, he and the banker had picked up Angel. The prostitute. They roughed her up pretty good, they did. Then he dropped the banker off, then picked me up. Jansen that is. He wore a coachman's suit with a hat and all. Said the banker wanted us to slap her around; scare her. When I got in the carriage I saw the woman. They had her tied up, scared shitless. Her face all beaten and bloody. I didn't like it. Never expected her to be that bad. Next thing I know, we were heading fast over to the river. He told me she threatened to blackmail the banker. That's why they beat her. And that we're to take her to the river and beat her again. Then dump her there."

"Jansen said nothing about killing her. If he did, I'd a tried to stop him. I swear. But when we got there, he dragged her out and dropped her on her back. Spread her legs and tore off her draws. She kicked at him but that didn't stop him. He rammed himself into her. Things got out of hand. He mustta broke her neck. Whatever. She was dead. I'm so sorry."

"Where *ye* bury her?"

"Where your friend lived."

Johnny gagged. His hand flew to his face, covering it. He turned away from Lopat, breaking into a fit a feigned coughing, hiding his shock. "The shed?"

"Yeah. Why? What's wrong with you?"

"No, nuttin." Again he coughed as pictures of himself kicking and shoving Jansen's remains into his final resting place, also in the shed.

When Katie shouldered her way between Johnny and Lopat—to Johnny's relief—their conversation stopped abruptly, with their attention turning to her.

"Johnny," Katie called, tugging on his sleeve. "Somebody wants to tell you something." Two of Katie's classmates stepped forward—heads bowed shyly—looking so neatly dressed in their school uniforms: a simple white shirt and blue tie with a long blue skirt.

Johnny smiled. "Good afternoon, young ladies," he said. "And congratulations. You and your fellow graduates are the pride of the neighborhood. We're proud of you."

By then their faces were beat-red with mortification. They could hardly look him in the eye. And when they did, they had to look up through raised eyebrows.

"What can I do for ye?"

"Thank you very much, Mr. O'Hara," they said, speaking in unison. One of them continued, "We are very grateful for everything. Our parents also say thank you." They looked at each other, then on cue, curtsied.

"For what, my young friends? It is we that should be thanking you for finishing your schooling. And tell your folks they are very welcome."

"Goodbye, Mr. O'Hara," they shouted, running off.

"You sounded genuine," said Lopat, even though he looked like he didn't believe him. "I'd almost believe you meant what you said."

"That's the difference between you and me. I love these people. My goal in life is to make things better for them. Not just for meself." Johnny smiled.

With Katie and her friends gone, Lopat continued, shifting uneasily from foot to foot. Johnny believed what Lopat had told him. At least most of it.

Lopat continued, "For years I carried this terrible guilt. I have to get it off my chest. I tried to tell youse years ago by Macon's on Eleventh. You remember that?"

"Yes." Johnny nodded. "I do. Let's get a drink."

"Two drafts, Vinnie," shouted Johnny, stepping off towards the bar, his hand over his head with two fingers held up.

"Coming up," said Vinnie, at the same time staring hard at Lopat's face. He knew the face but could not put a name on it.

"But I lost my nerve," Lopat continued. "I've been carrying this guilt all this time."

"Would you tell my friend this?" asked Johnny. He walked him to the firehouse entryway.

"Yeah," he said, nodding his head vigorously.

"If you're telling me the truth, you didn't do—"

"Vaboom!" The loud noise of an explosion whooshed through the building, shaking the floor and the walls, startling everyone, sending a tremor up their legs. The garage doors and windows rattled.

Just up the block, on the other side of the street, balls of fire exploded from several windows on the third floor of a tenement, sending brickwork, wood, and glass to the sidewalk below.

No sooner had they got outside, than a large section of the side of the four-story building collapsed onto the roof of an adjacent two-story wooden house, almost completely flattening it and creating a huge cloud of dust. The thunderous roar of the collapsing brickwork followed them into the firehouse.

CHAPTER SIXTEEN

"Let's go, let's go," Johnny shouted to alert the firemen, most of whom were already preparing. "Right down the block. It's bad. Real bad."

Having heard the terrifying sounds, the people ran out to the street to witness the flames and smoke. There were a few exceptions. Some people marveled at the horses shuffling in their stalls, waiting to be fitted to the fire engine. They watched the red shirted volunteers don their new, full-size rubber-coated Great Coats, helmets, and shin-high leather fire boots. Today the firemen would be testing those new coats for the first time.

Hopefully the *Great Coats* (rubber coated, heavy wool coats) would enable them to go inside the burning building and attack the fire directly, just as Brogan's *homemade* coats did. These coats, they hoped, would enable the firemen to get to trapped people quicker than in the past and, likewise, to extinguish the fire more rapidly.

Johnny ran for his fire gear, kicking off his shoes and stepping into his boots. He donned his Great Coat and helmet, all the time giving Lopat a curious look. Reaching for another coat, he shouted at him, "Well, don't just stand there." He threw him a coat. "Put it on. Come with us."

"Fuck yeah!" Lopat shouted, snatching the coat out of the air.

"Make way," shouted Johnny. The guests in the building backed against the wall, clearing the floor for the firemen and their horses. Once clear, the house-watch man opened the horse stalls. And to everyone's delight, the anxious horses took their positions beneath the harnesses that were suspended in midair from the ceiling. The harnesses were then dropped on the horses and adjusted.

"Bejasus! The bloody tings know what to do," shouted a mother, who held a firm grip on the hands of her two young ones.

Even with the horror show going on up the block, the people still beamed with pride as they watched their immigrant brethren prepare to respond to the fire. With Battler at the reigns and Hans, the assistant foreman, at his side, they cheered as the horses pulled the new steam engine—the first in New York City—out to the street then galloped several hundred feet to the fire.

"God I hope there's nobody inside there," the ashen-faced O'Hara uttered. Images of the Perry Street explosion, which he responded to as a young recruit, flashed through his mind. That explosion was a horrible one, killing and injuring hundreds of workers. Never would he forget the sight of the body parts and torsos protruding from the rubble. Nor would he forget the cries of the injured, human and animal alike. And he would not forget the cool-headed leadership displayed by the department's chief engineer,

Alfred Carson. A man who reinforced Johnny's determination to one day be the department's chief engineer.

Much of the tiny, two-story wood-frame structure lay flattened under tons of bricks. With most of the tenement's upper side wall gone, the fire on the third floor quickly spread upward, engulfing the top floor and releasing a huge column of smoke that quickly darkened the sky above. His immediate concern: *how many people are in there?*

He hurried to the sight, remembering the lesson he learned from Carson: keep a cool head, which wasn't easy. What greeted him on arriving at the debris pile were the pained screams of a child and the horrifying whales of a young girl that suddenly ceased as the flames consumed the very spot from where he heard the shouts.

"Find the kid," he commanded.

Like bees on honey, the volleys poured onto the pile, bringing with them a hose line. Hans directed two of the firemen to connect the new steam pumper to the water hydrant.

"Get off. Get off," O'Hara shouted while pointing up at the remaining wall. "Look above ye," he roared. "That too might come down."

"Back off," he shouted. "Everybody off. You two keep that water flowing." He directed the hose men to keep the fire back from where the child was. Then, with great calm, he designated a group from the company to start removing the brick and timber, at the same time assigning the others to watch for further collapse.

Battler and the others, who wore the rubber coats, were already stretching the hose line and were on their way into the building to attack the fire.

The men on the pile went right to work, removing the red-hot bricks, not without grunts and groans. Their scarred, leathery hands weren't tough enough for them to not feel the extreme heat of the hot bricks. In short order their hands were blistered and bleeding.

Then came the shouts, "The wall! The wall!" And down it came, bringing with it a thunderous crash and another huge cloud of dust. Luckily, the remaining debris landed towards the rear of the pile. The men kept digging and calling to the child.

"More than likely, we'll once again have water on the fire before your guys get here," said Johnny, forcing a smile at Lopat. "Matter of fact, if these coats are as good as they say, hell, we'll have it out by then."

"Yeah. Sure. But they won't be happy. That new fire station – and, oh boy," Lopat chuckled knowing how pissed Batesy would be, "and wait 'til they see the new steam engine." Lopat failed in his attempt to sidestep a fresh mound of horse droppings, almost losing his footing, probably forgetting he had changed to the fire boots.

Another chilling scream came from the burning floors above, exactly from where was hard to tell.

"Shit! We gotta go through this shit all the time with you guys. Where is your Hook and Ladder when we need it?"

Lopat felt uneasy, knowing full well that the nearest hook and ladder company, which his boss controlled, should have already been at the fire. But Batesy and his crew always responded slowly when turning out to a fire call from Yimmie country.

"Whadda we gonna do?" asked Lopat.

"We don't have much of a choice." Johnny wasn't going to wait for Batesy's crew. His own neighbors were trapped. "I'll be upstairs," he shouted to Battler. "Get that line up as soon as you can."

By the time he reached the third floor, where the fire raged, the smoke was so thick it was *like soup*. It choked him, forcing him to crawl blindly with his nose almost rubbing the floor, hoping to find pockets of breathable air. If that wasn't bad enough, the fire in the burning apartment was already starting to burn the inside of the apartment's flimsy front door. In short order, the door would be burned through with fire blowing through it, rolling up the stairs and cutting off his escape route. *Better move me ass or I'll be roasted,* he warned himself.

Likewise, Battler and his men were moving fast, knowing full well Johnny's predicament.

"C'mon, c'mon," he shouted. With his arm through several folds of the hose and the pipe in his other hand, he charged into the hallway towards the stairwell, yanking the hose after him. Vinnie McCarthy rushed in right behind him, yanking his hose. They knew it wouldn't be long before the red devil, with its searing heat and choking gases, would be consuming everything in its path, right up through the roof, if they didn't get water on the fire.

"Who's with Johnny?" shouted Battler.

"Think he's by himself," Vinnie answered.

"I'll cover him," said Lopat, rushing past Battler.

"Who, who the hell are you?" shouted Battler.

Lopat disappeared up the stairs with a shout, "Just another fireman."

Johnny was now in the apartment above the fire, beginning his belly-crawling search for the trapped victim. Blindly, he scurried from room to room hardly noticing the loud roaring, crackling noises of the inferno below. *I wish they'd get up here.* It scared the hell out of him being all alone and choking in such a pitch-black, over-heated environment. He had one consolation; the muffled but discernible voice of Battler below shouting commands.

I don't belong here, he told himself. As he turned to leave, he heard somewhere to his front what sounded like whimpering. With one last burst of strength, he got up on all fours and pushed through the wall of smoke. Then he felt something soft. He knew it was a body. He grabbed at it, feeling for the armpits. Rising to a crouching position, he lifted the body. In his dizzy weakened state, he started to back out of the flat. His grip on the body began to loosen; his lungs wanted to explode for the want of air. His instinct told him to stop, to rest his body, but that he knew would be his demise. Simultaneously, he was sucking in smoke and gagging.

Gotta get some air, the doting rescuer told himself. No longer could he hold the body he was pulling; he let go. *You can't leave it here,* he told himself. Just then he let his head drop for a moment's rest, but the helmet's thud against the floor, briefly jerked him back to his senses. In his listless state, he swore he heard a voice calling his name.

CHAPTER SEVENTEEN

When Battler turned the bend of the stairwell, he saw the flames shooting from the apartment. He shouted Johnny's name several times. There was no response. The folds of hose line he'd been pulling up the stairs began filling with water: popping, snapping like a whip, almost sending him backward down the stairs.

"Steady that damned hose," he shouted, continuing up the stairs towards the fire. "Let's go! Let's go! Johnny's gots ta be up dere."

As the thick smoke pushed down the stairs, it engulfed him and the crew. With the door to the roof still closed preventing the smoke from venting to the outside, the smoke began banking down the stairwell.

From where they were they could see the inferno starting to consume the stairwell. Fire had burned its way through the apartment door and set alight the landing walls and ceilings and was rolling up the wooden stairwell. The red devil would soon find Johnny and his rescuer.

Johnny heard a voice shouting, "Where are you, O'Hara?"

"Who's that?" he asked, just above a whisper.

"Me," said Lopat, who reached out with both hands and grabbed the big man's collar, giving it a tug and dragging him hurriedly out across the landing into another flat, the door of which he had left slightly ajar. Lopat, himself also choking and gasping for air, then ran back after the victim, a small woman. He picked her up and brought her into the same flat.

"You're lucky," shouted Lopat. "Those new coats are saving your ass." He paused. "Our asses, I mean."

From their prone positions in the apartment hallway, the two of them watched helplessly through the thick smoke, the flames rolling up the stairwell that were beginning to reach into the flat where they were.

"Did you ever think you'd wind up like this with your avowed enemy," asked Johnny, in a calm tone that Lopat assumed was a bit of a put on.

"I can't believe this," Lopat answered haltingly, not trying to hide his fear. "I hope your guys got balls."

Then, from out on the landing came the sound they were praying for, a strong stream of water pounding the ceiling and walls; turning the killer flames into white-hot steam. It was music to their *burning* ears.

"Have faith in your immigrant neighbors," shouted Johnny, sounding fearless, but not fooling Lopat. They heard a shower of glass raining down on the stairwell. They watched the smoke begin to lift upwards and out through the now open bulk head door and skylight.

They could hear the water stream getting louder, getting closer. They could even hear Battler and his men down below, cursing the scorching steam that engulfed them upon hitting the fire with the water stream.

"Bejasus, that *whatter* is hot," shouted Vinnie. "Even with these *cursid* coats."

"Well, it's a lot hotter up above where Johnny is. Let's get this fucking thing out," shouted Battler.

As soon as he positioned himself in the doorway of the burning apartment and started the water stream again, Battler and Timothy McCarthy dashed up the stairs.

"It's like passing through a furnace," shouted McCarthy. "Let's get Johnny and get out."

By now they were all calling for Johnny. In the midst of all the shouting, they heard the strange voice of Lopat shouting, "In here."

"Who dat?" asked Battler.

They got to their feet and stumbled through the smoke, following the shouts of the strange voice.

"Ahhh, *ya* stepping on me," Johnny shouted. "Get us out of here."

* * * * *

"Yohnny, you not look good. You okay?" shouted Hans from the top of the pile, where he directed the rescue of the buried child while being drenched by a constant shower of water.

"Don't worry about me." Blisters covered O'Hara's face; his sideburns and eyebrows were severely singed.

Heavy fire continued lapping violently from the apartments left exposed after the exterior wall collapsed. The whole upper portion of the building blazed away. But it wouldn't be long before they had that fire extinguished. Hans had another pipe playing a powerful stream on that fire from the outside.

This was the first time they were operating their new steam engine at a working fire and already they realized its full worth. They had two powerful streams operating and both of them were being supplied water under great pressure from the same engine. Most importantly, it required minimal manning to operate it. They did not need large numbers of men to work the pumps and brakes of an old-style engine. And since no other fire companies had yet arrived, they needed every man available to fight this fire and dig out the child.

"How's the kid?" Johnny asked, carefully stepping up on the mountain of rubble careful not to undermine the tunneling already done. Hot water rained down on the men who continued to work without letup. "Why isn't he gone to the hospital?" he shouted, pointing to a body at the base of the pile. "Take him right now with the old gal!"

"Too late fur dat, Yohnny! Too late!" Hans shouted back. "Ve not know who it is!" he continued. Then he shouted with emotion, "No head. He having no head!"

The volleys swarmed over the rubble pile, like flies on a mound of dung, flinging pieces of wood and brick onto the street. As much as Lopat wanted to help on the pile, he knew he had to hightail it before Batesy saw him, and Batesy and his fire truck, with its bells clanging furiously, were already racing into the block from other end. *Time to disappear,* he told himself.

Even with their blood-covered hands all splintered and cut by the shattered wood, the men continued to dig. The weakening screams of the child drove them to work faster and harder, at times throwing all caution to the wind. One mistake and the rubble could fall back into the hole they had cleared, a likelihood Johnny quickly recognized. "Easy men," he shouted. "Slow it down or we'll have to start from scratch. We don't know if that child can hold out much longer."

The water spray continued to shower down on them, sometimes like a drenching downpour, but with good reason. The two streams of water hitting the fire, the one Battler and his crew were operating inside the building and the line Hans had operating from the street, had knocked down most of the fire upstairs. The next time Johnny looked up, he saw steam pushing from the windows, meaning most of the fire was extinguished.

Standing at the edge of the exposed flooring of the third floor from where the brick wall had fallen, the smiling Battler signaled they'd put the fire out, prompting a great cheer from the firefighters and crowd on the street. Then a second round of cheering erupted, even more enthusiastic: at that moment they freed the child from its would-be grave.

"Where is that fella, Lopat? I owe him a big thank you," said Johnny. "Hell, he saved me ass."

"Think that's him," said Timothy McCarthy, pointing to a figure of a man in extremely soiled clothing, ducking into the side street.

Johnny nodded. "Yeah that's him alright and I know why he's hightailing it." He looked over at Batesy.

At the other end of the block, Batesy, with his fists clenched, stood frozen atop of his fire engine. "I don't fucking believe this," he shouted to his men and the men of the fire company that had pulled in behind them. Must have been fifteen firemen with him, all dumbfounded, shaking their heads in disbelief, looking back and forth from the *new* steam engine to the *new* firehouse. "Where the hell they get the money?" His eyes rolled in his head.

Another fireman shouted, "You believe that? They already got it out." All heads turned to the burned-out third and fourth floors. They didn't like what they saw. The Yimmies had already extinguished what had obviously been a large fire, without their assistance. They could hardly restrain their fury. Curse words filled the air about them.

"Something's gotta be done about this," Batesy shouted, eying his men.

* * * * *

"Why'd we have to leave so soon?" asked Katie. Under her arm she carried her graduation certificate—the first in the O'Hara family—that she held on to for dear life.

"It is time for the young people to be getting home," said Johnny with a big smile. "Besides, I gotta get out of these wet clothes."

"But I was having so much fun," she objected. "And why are we going this way?" She nodded in the direction of Tenth Avenue.

"Cause I have a surprise for you."

She gripped his arm and tugged at it. "What? What is it, Johnny?"

"First things first," he said, with a hardy laugh. "When you're finished with your voluntary service at the parish, there's a job waiting for you at Brogan's."

"A real job?" she said, her jaw dropping. She stopped in her tracks. "Doing what?"

"Shhhhhh," he said, his finger to his lips. "Not so loud. Don't want the whole world to know. Bookkeeping. What do you think?"

"My own job? And I'll get paid?"

"Of course. And your own desk to work at."

"I'm so happy. Mom would be real proud, wouldn't she?" she said. "Where we going?"

"To show you another surprise. Our new home," he said.

"A new home. You're kidding. Aren't you?"

"Nope. Wait and see," he said. It made Johnny proud of himself to be able to do so much for her.

"I can't believe this. It's all like a dream," she said.

Darkness had already set, but the streets were still teeming with people, too hot to be inside in the oven-like flats that lacked sufficient ventilation. Along the streets, people continuously acknowledged Johnny with a kind word or a wave, which he returned enthusiastically. The stink of the ever-present piles of rotting garbage littering the streets and the sight of hogs feeding on it, angered him. *One day I will change all of this,* he told himself.

As part of their final year's curriculum, Katie and her female schoolmates had to deliver food to the parishes' elderly and sick; a necessary volunteer service that sometimes was wrought with danger for these young girls, especially the more shapely ones, such as Katie.

Even though he'd been doing very well financially, he had never bothered to give up living in his pitch-black, two-room, earthen floored, cellar flat that he once shared with Red; where he still ate and did his reading on the table he made with wood scraps he had procured from the North River Lumber Yard; where for light he used two candles set in the mouths of Paddys whiskey bottles.

"This is the building," he said, as they walked into 601 West 33rd Street, a corner building on 33rd & Ninth Avenue. The newly constructed five-story tenant house had electric lights at the entrance and throughout the public hallways.

"This is our new home," he said, slipping a skeleton key into the door lock, making a clicking metallic sound. Their apartment had two bedrooms and its own bathroom, and being on the first floor, it also had steam heat and a gas stove. An electric light bulb hung from the ceiling of each freshly-painted room.

"No more candles, sis," he said, showing her to the all-white kitchen, where a light bulb hung. "Now you can read under the electric light." He showed her the bathroom at which she marveled, seeing the toilet with its water tank up by the ceiling, and a large white, cast-iron tub sitting on a floor tiled with a thousand or more tiny, white octagons. Then he showed his sister to *her* bedroom in which there was a chest of draws. "This is all yours. Even a wardrobe for you to hang your clothes. And look. Another light for you to read by."

"And a new bed on legs," she screamed with joy.

"And you will sleep the night through in peace and quiet," he said, just as screaming erupted between a man and a woman, their loud voices reverberating throughout the adjacent alleyway.

"I'm sure we won't have to put up with that all the time," he said.

She sat on the bed, bouncing up and down. Looking out the window, she thought of how the sun would shine on her as she lay in bed.

Her delight pleased him very much. Then, in a sullen tone he said, "Oh, I miss Red. I wish she could be here with us."

"I miss her too, Johnny. Where is she, anyways?"

"I don't know. Sometimes I wonder if I'll ever see her again." He opened her wardrobe. "Look."

"My lord. Books and books and books," she uttered. "Where did you get them?"

"Let's just say, from a friend. And they're all yours."

"I wonder if Red reads the book we gave her?" she asked. "Hope so."

"I think of that, too," he said. "Come. Let's have a piece of your favorite cake."

"Chocolate! You have chocolate cake?"

"Yes I do." They entered the kitchen where there was a brand new white enamel table with four matching chairs, directly under the light bulb. "Have a seat," he said. He opened the window and took a cake box from the food box sitting on the sill. "This would be a proud day for Mom. Her daughter graduated from school." He cut two large pieces of the cake, placing them on two proper china cake dishes.

"And her son Johnny's a big shot at Brogan's. She'd be proud of that too, she would," Katie added. "Wouldn't it be nice, Johnny, if she were here with us?"

"And Da," added Johnny, a touch of sadness in his voice. "Poor Da . . . he never got to see you."

"Yes. Poor Da," she said. Her elation vanished, replaced by an utter sadness. "What kind of a man was he? Did he look like you, Johnny?" Katie spoke with a touch of an Irish ghetto accent that she picked up living with so many Irish-born people. Her mother gave birth to her shortly after the O'Hara's arrived in New York in 1847.

"Da was a good man. Just like mom. And an important man, the chief in charge of Lord Bosh's Skibereen Fire Brigade back home," he said, making it sound like a full-blown fire company when in fact it was a bucket brigade; a collection of buckets they would use to put water on a fire. Johnny did not remember there ever being a sizable fire.

"You're a fine young lady, Katie O'Hara," he said.

She smiled, her face turning red, but said nothing. She stood, then walked to the stove as Johnny followed. "How does this work?" she asked. He showed her how to operate the two burners.

She had good looks and a mature womanly shape, which worried him. He couldn't help but think of the abuse Red had suffered at the hands of men. *Would the same happen to Katie?* He knew she would be a proper example of a good Irish Catholic girl, with her religious training at Holy Cross, and would be worried about the young men from the neighborhood. That's why he put the word out through the gang that anyone who messed with her would answer to him.

At twenty-two, Johnny stood out in the neighborhood, not only as an honest man, but a fine figure of a man: tall, strapping, with broad shoulders, and arms as thick as many an average man's thighs.

On the table sat three books about fires and their extinguishment, gifts from Thomas Brogan.

"You said Lord Bosh. Who was he?" she asked.

"Lord Hennington Bosh. He owned all the land around Skibereen for what seemed like miles around. Sure he must have owned Skibereen."

"Do you look like Da?" she asked, again.

"Mom often said I did," he replied with a smile, looking at a mirror affixed to the wall. "Yet, others said I looked like mom."

"He must have been a handsome man, then," she said.

Johnny smiled. "Well, thank you, sis."

"I know Da died on the ship coming over. But didn't we also have two brothers and a sister?"

"Yes," he replied. He couldn't hide his pain. "Beautiful Roisin was the oldest. She'd have been twenty-five now. Then there were Danny and Sean." He sobbed. "One morning she didn't awake. God bless her soul. Mom told me how she often went without food, just to make sure I had some. I remember her bony face from the want of food. Covered with sores, as though her cheekbones were cutting through her flesh. Even had hair growing on her face. Oh, she had been so beautiful. Ach, how I missed her."

Katie's eyes filled with tears. "Whom did she look like?"

"Your mother. And just as beautiful. Something else I remember too. Roisin used to get bits of food from the Lord's son. Lord my ass. I mean from Bosh's son, Tony. And she gave most of it to us. They were very close . . . I liked him.

"Your brothers were Danny and Sean," he continued. "I still see Danny's belly." He closed his eyes and gave out with a soft groan. "How it swelled. Like all of us, he was skin and bone, except for his stomach. Like this," he used his hands to describe an extended belly, "and hair grew all over it. One day we found him dead, lying on the hearth. The next day baby Sean passed. Oh those English bastards. What they did to us."

"Why did they wait so long to leave there?" she asked in an angry tone. Her cheeks covered with tears.

"You're crying, sister. Ya want me to continue?"

"Yes. It's time I know."

"Mom and Da had no money to buy passage. We'd nothing left to sell. They kept thinking the hunger would end. Then one day Bosh's coachman, Kieran, came to our door. I saw him give Da a piece of paper that he said would get the three of us to New York. Shortly after that we were on the *Larch* sailing for America. We never knew who provided our passage, but suspected it came from Tony. I still think of him. Of his goodness."

"What was it like? The voyage, I mean," she asked, finishing her last sliver of chocolate cake.

"You really wanna know? It wasn't nice. It was . . . it was downright horrible."

"I have to know," she said. She was totally engulfed, sitting across from him with her elbows resting on the table and her chin in her hands.

"It was a coffin, the ship that is. So many died. And the stink . . . the terrible smell in the hold. The filth. The peoples . . . buckets of crap stinking like hell 'cause we couldn't go up top at night where the privies were. The crew kept us locked in the hold every night. For short periods during the day they'd let us up on deck, a chance to slop out. But the stench never left down below where we lived. And when someone came down with the fever, then we were locked in all the time." He stopped when he saw his sister turning ashen.

"Go on," she said. The tears continued without letup.

"And the families, many with lots of children, were confined to such small spaces. At least two families in an area smaller than this little room," he said.

"Did Da suffer much?" she asked.

"I guess he did. But he never complained. Died in his sleep. And what shocked me at the time was that Mom never cried."

"Why?" she snapped.

"At first, I couldn't understand, but later on I did. She had no tears left. She'd seen so many deaths: Roisin, Danny and Sean. And so many relatives and friends back home. Every day, fresh bodies lined the roadside, waiting to be taken for burial. She saw it all over again on the ship."

* * * * *

Less than two months after Katie's graduation, three more members of the Pvt. Michael Brogan Engine Company were killed-in-action. They were felled in battle on the blood-drenched fields of a place called Gettysburg, along with many more thousands of American men and boys— many of whom were immigrants or the sons of immigrants—all blown to hell by the machinery sold to the Union and Confederate armies by the Bimsbeys of this nation. Losses on both sides were staggering.

Lincoln needed more recruits and he needed them in a hurry. The army could no longer depend on volunteers. So that spring, in order to meet the military's manpower needs, the government passed the National

Conscription Act; the draft. The mention of a draft set off tempers among the poor, the people who would have no choice in the matter but to serve. Unlike their wealthier counterparts, they didn't have $300 to buy a deferral from the government or to pay to a poor man to take his place. Naturally, most New Yorkers, the majority of who were poor, opposed the draft. They were fed up with *Lincoln's war* that had killed off or maimed so many of their loved ones. They would no longer fight this rich man's war; fight a war for their bosses who sucked the life out of them for a minimal wage while getting richer and richer. On July 12, 1863, when the draft commenced in New York, all hell broke loose. Tens of thousands of New Yorkers took to the streets, burning and looting and taking on the police. For four days they ravaged the city, only to be stopped when combat hardened Army troops, some of them native New Yorkers and some of them immigrants, arrived and opened fire. Bimsbey's hidden agenda of pitting the Yankee workingman, immigrant, and colored against each other reared its ugly head. At least twelve *coloreds* were killed by the rioters who had lost at least 1200—or as many as 20,000—from their ranks.

When the rioting and the destruction began, Johnny sounded the alarm and assembled most of his people from the fire company and the Young Immigrants, some of whom had been drinking and wanted to join the rioting. But he explained vehemently that many of the businesses being destroyed and looted provided jobs for the poor. To a man they listened to him. Instead of rioting, he got them to stand guard over the neighborhood and places where the people worked, including Macon's Beef, the gas works, Brogan's and the Shamrock Inn and Waterside. Their neighborhood suffered no losses during those bitter days.

CHAPTER EIGHTEEN

FRIDAY, JUNE 26, 1864 – A confident looking young man, decked out in a dark blue pinstriped suit and wearing a gray bowler upon his head, entered the Louvre—a rich man's *watering hole*. Taking a seat near the far end of the customerless bar, he ordered a nip of Paddys whiskey, bringing a grin to the barman's face.

"You must be Tony Bosh," said the surprised but expecting barman. "But you look so young. Should I even give you whiskey?"

Young Bosh returned the smile. "Call me Tony," he replied with a touch of an Irish accent. "And your name, sir?"

"My friends call me Batesy."

"How did you know who I am?" Tony asked, looking a bit puzzled.

"Because your teetotaler uncle, Jacob Bosh, told us to order a generous supply of Paddy's. Just for when you get here. But he didn't say you were so young."

"This youngster is twenty-four," said Tony.

"Actually, I knew it had to be you because nobody here ever drinks that Irish shit." Bates laughed, pleasantly.

"They don't know what they're missing." Tony had a hard time keeping the smile on his face.

Tony Bosh was the nephew of the textile magnate, Jacob Bosh, one of the power broker associates of Charlton Bimsbey. An elderly man, he never married and had no progeny. Recognizing he would not live forever, Jacob Bosh wanted someone to help him run the business, someone to in time take over when he retired or became incapable of working. His only choice was his nephew, the sole child of his older and only brother, Lord Hennington Bosh, who lived in Ireland. To that child Tony Bosh, Jacob offered it all upon his death. All Tony had to do was learn the business, and while doing that, he would share in the profits. Uncle Jacob promised Tony that money would never be a problem.

Jacob Bosh knew well about the disastrous relationship between his brother and his brother's son, and he wholeheartedly supported Tony. He had no tolerance for the treatment his brother, Lord Bosh, afforded his tenant farmers during the Great Hunger. And he knew Bosh senior had cut Tony off from his fortune. Jacob was only too happy to take up the slack where Tony's father left off. He respected his nephew for what he did, and the way he turned his back on his father's fortune. Besides the thirty thousand plus acres of land he owned in Skibereen, land his ancestors stole from the native Irish in the 16th century during the Cromwellian era, Lord

Hennington Bosh also produced textiles in London, where he also owned considerable property. He also had trading partners in America.

As Lord Bosh often pointed out to Tony during their many arguments: "Their crime is their Catholicism."

During the potato blight (1845-1851) Skibereen was hit hard. Of Bosh's estimated 2850 tenant farmers, most of who were children, more than 1400 perished. Many of those who survived did so by migrating to America.

Regardless of his father's explanation 'that God used the hunger to solve England's problem in Ireland: too many Irish,' Tony Bosh and his uncle Jacob never accepted Lord Hennington's cruelty in allowing so many of those Irish to die.

Tony knew from his father's ledgers that he had shipped to the colonies enough food produced on his land, other than potatoes, to feed the people twice over and still make a profit. There being no money in Ireland, the tenant farmers used their produce to pay the rent.

Tony's father, like so many other English occupiers of Irish soil, wanted to use the land to raise cattle for the colonies, which would be even more profitable. To do so, Ireland had to be depopulated.

Bosh Limited, as Jacob Bosh's textile business was known, supplied fabrics to many of the city's top fashion stores, clothing manufacturers, and suit and dressmakers, such as Brooks Brothers and Marble Dry Good Palace; even tailors who made the Police officers uniforms. He supplied most of New York's finest hotels, including the just constructed and very fashionable, Fifth Avenue Hotel, with draperies, wall coverings, bed coverings and linens. Bosh even supplied their carpeting.

"You know why I drink this Paddy stuff?" Tony asked the barman.

"Why's that, Mr. Bosh?" Bates replied.

"Because it's Irish whiskey. Those people know how to have a good time. Especially when they're tipping a few. And I like that. Oftentimes I wish I were one of them. Hell, my people are so boring. They're all about money. And please, call me Tony."

"Well, you know, Tony, it takes money to survive in this cruel world. And those donkey bastards surely don't have any of that. And they would steal whatever they get their hands on if they had the chance. So watch 'em like a hawk."

"I'm sure not every one of them is a thief. They're Christians, you know. Just like us. And I 'know' their faith teaches them right from wrong."

"Oh. How's that?" asked Mr. Bates.

"I know better. I watched them starve to death by the hundreds because they would not steal the crops they produced on me father's land . . . when the potato failed. The only sustenance they were allowed to have. All because their church told them, 'taking what is rightfully the landlord's is stealing'. The poor fools. I'd have stolen it. God knows I would of."

"Well, we still can't trust 'em. They're the agents of their pope and he wants to take over our country. I heard it's okay for them to rob, but not from their co-religionists."

Tony smiled. "You have to be kidding. Where did you hear that?" he asked.

"I read it in *The Native.*"

"Mr. Bates. I gather you don't like the Irish."

"You right there, Mr. Bosh. Tony," replied Bates. "England should have finished the job. Should have starved 'em all instead of sending them over here. We don't need those foreigners. They steal our jobs. Work for less pay."

"Maybe they got smart. Smart enough to steal to survive." Tony Bosh raised his glass and toasted the Irish. "To Paddy, I say good luck." He smiled pleasantly, holding back the glare he wanted to give the barman.

After parting ways with his father, Tony spent considerable time knocking around Dublin with his *Irish* friends. Fortunately for him, he lived well on his mother's inheritance. He envied the Irish wit, and enjoyed imbibing with them. With equal passion, he despised the dullness of his own blue-bloods. He preferred calling himself an Irishman.

A door at the back of the barroom opened and through it peeked Batesy's fly-on-the-wall, Greg Lopat, who spent considerable time at the

183

city council. Motioning anxiously to him, Lopat, the man with the broad-forehead, whispered loudly, "You better get in here."

Judging by the gravity of the look on his face, Bates knew there were problems at the city council on an issue of major importance to them. His smile disappeared as he bolted for the backroom, rudely ignoring Bosh, who also assumed something didn't go as planned. All Tony could hear through the door were muffled shouts and a loud bang on the door, like somebody punched it.

Checking out the extensive mirror and hand-carved woodwork behind the bar, Tony compared it to what he saw back in Ireland. Nothing he had seen in Dublin matched the quality and quantity of the woodwork. He also admired the wall-sized mural painting on the wall opposite the bar: a life-like painting of a great black stallion with a white diamond on its forehead, pulling an all-white, enclosed coach with the horse's name, *Blackie*, painted on the doors. A moment later, the door at the back of the barroom opened again and through it stepped Lopat, putting on a freshly pressed white apron. "How do you do? I'm Greg, your new bartender," he said, forcing a smile.

"I am impressed with that mural," said Tony. "Is that a true depiction of somebody's horse and carriage?"

"Yes. The man who financed the opening of this beautiful establishment. A banker by the name of Bimsbey," said Lopat.

As Greg introduced himself to Tony, Batesy exited the Louvre, using the rear loading dock. Discarding his apron on a stack of empty beer kegs, he leapt from the dock and dashed out onto Broadway to the Know Nothings' office, a small storefront two shops up from the Louvre. Once there, he alerted a dozen or so members that the city council meeting wasn't going the way they had planned it. The council was voting on whether or not to grant a charter to the immigrants for their new firehouse and fire company. If the charter was granted, something the Yanks had been fighting against for years, an all-immigrant fire company would become legit.

"Listen up, men," Batesy snapped. "If the council okays the charter, we'll have to round up every patriotic American for an immediate emergency meeting.

* * * * *

Tempers were still flaring at the city council. The Tammany Hall Boys were lined up behind the immigrants and the despised, old-money elites were lined up against the charter. They were conducting a verbal vote. Support for the charter led four to two. One of the moneyed council members was ranting, "You thugs, you. You have defied our laws. You have robbed the taxpayers. And now you are granting a bunch of thugs and ruffians a charter for a fire company that is not even needed."

"Order! Order," roared the council president. "Continue with the voting," he directed.

A council member, himself a bar owner, grinned from ear to ear and came right back at the other councilmember: "You. You elitist, you. You dare to call us thieves? You and your kind have made your fortunes screwing the poor workingman. Letting him starve, forcing him to live in your dumps of tenant houses where they freeze during the winter, where they fry in the summer. It is your refusal to grant the workingman a decent wage that makes him rob. He has to feed his family. But you and your ilk don't give a damn; you well-dressed, church going hypocrites!"

"How dare you speak of us in such a manner," screamed another of the so-called elites; an overweight man dressed in the finest of clothing. "You common trash you."

"Your days running this great city, your days robbing this great city . . . they are over. Now it's the workingman's turn," the bar owner continued.

"Enough, enough," cried the president, who was grinning from ear to ear. "Get on with the voting." He called out the council member's names one after the other. Those in favor held the lead throughout the voting. The charter passed 12 to 10.

"A great day for democracy. The will of the people has prevailed. Now let us go in peace," shouted the president, his smiling face held high to a loud round of applause and cheering mixed with some hissing and booing. He marched smartly from his seat up the center-aisle of the great chamber to make his exit, followed by his entourage.

Finally, the fire company and its new firehouse were legal entities. The council did what they did because many of the council members represented the poor and the immigrant people. Those citizens depended on their council members to get some of the sweetheart deals passed. And the legalization of the fire company, being named after Pvt. Michael Brogan—a local hero since his heroic and much publicized death at the Battle of Bull Run—was one of the sweetheart deals to get passed.

The news of the "immigrants' victory" reached the Know Nothing office in a matter of minutes. The decision, which Batesy and his followers called *cowardly and un-American*, sent shockwaves through the Know Nothing community, particularly the many firemen who despised the idea of an all-immigrant fire company.

And besides, this time the generation Americans were up against the new Johnny O'Hara, a politically savvy and successful entrepreneur who not only knew how to charm the powerbrokers, but also had the full backing of Brogan's immense financial empire and a tough gang of fighters.

As an aside, Johnny even *influenced* his brick and lumber suppliers—both of who were sympathetic to the Know Nothings, to provide *at cost* the necessary supplies to build the firehouse. For this, Johnny received great praise from Brogan in one of his many telegrams: "*. . . The way you acquired the materials for my brother's firehouse, from those who don't take kindly to us, was outstanding. I could not have matched your act. But your success did not surprise me. After all, I saw that talent in you. Why do you think I trusted my business to you? So enough flattery. Be careful! The new fire station has many enemies who'll want to destroy it. Be ever on guard . . .*"

Through contacts provided by Thomas Brogan and with the assistance of his stealthy agent in City Hall, Nick Tiso, Johnny met with many relevant people and had several private meetings with three of the four most influential members of the council relative to the charter, which cost Brogan a good dollar in the form of graft. One of the councilmen, Bobby Heatley, a devout Presbyterian and the son of one of the leaders of the failed uprising in Ireland in 1798 by the United Irishmen, against their English oppressor, refused money. He supported the all-immigrant firehouse out of respect for his fellow Irish Americans and in honor of the Young Immigrants killed in action during that war.

At the public debate over the charter, Heatley exclaimed clearly, "I will never permit anything that tramples the rights of our citizens, rich or poor, especially those men and women of Ireland. They have suffered long and terribly under the jackboot of English oppression. And to think that some Americans among us want to treat them the same way in this great nation is offensive. They would do well to know who these people are. They are the descendants of the very people who made up the bulk of our revolutionary army."

Heatley's tirade drove his adversaries wild. They booed and hissed; they ranted and cursed; they even pounded on their seats. But he didn't let them intimidate him.

"And they fought courageously," he waved his fists, "and died to free our nation." He roared, "Your nation! To free us from English tyranny! And today, again, the Irish immigrant is fighting and dying on our nation's battlefields. And if I may say so, they are displaying exceptional bravery. I will never turn my back on such great Americans."

Johnny began construction of the fire station well in advance of the council members committing to the charter. His gall incensed his opponents to the point of making public threats to take action against him.

Bimsbey and his cronies, with the exception of Jacob Bosh, were delighted at the granting of the charter, knowing it would fuel the antagonisms between the Americans and the foreigners.

Batesy sent his Know Nothings out to spread the word. These men were driven by anger and would make sure they contacted every supporter, knowing where and how to reach every one of them. They ran from job site to job site, from saloon to saloon, delivering the message: "Emergency meeting this evening at 7 pm. The Pavilion. Be there!" They ordered all contacts to make sure their men spread the word to all concerned. And in less than an hour's time, the word had been spread throughout the city. Batesy would have a huge audience and he would tell them about this grave affront to American patriots. By 7 pm, many hundreds of angry faces filled the Pavilion, a good few of who were under the influence of alcohol, ready for anything. The building creaked under their weight.

Thomas Brogan's employee Nick Tiso, who served as Johnny's *fly-on-the-wall,* also attended the meeting. Dressed inconspicuously so as not to draw attention when doing such work, he stood among the crowd of patriots. Tiso also befriended as many councilmen and politicians as possible, to keep Johnny, and of course his employer Brogan, in their good graces and to keep them promptly informed.

Also in the crowd, and not the least bit recognizably dressed in soiled laborer's clothing, stood Charlton Bimsbey. He wanted to witness for himself Batesy's abilities in organizing and rousing people to action; the young man he chose to put so much trust in was something Batesy would never know.

The commotion of the waiting audience, along with the shouting and chanting, was thunderous and nerve racking for anyone who might be timid. When Batesy stepped out onto the stage, he shook his head from side to side in disgust, making sure everybody knew of his great disappointment. He intended for his visible disgust to egg them on, to fan their anger. He also wanted the newspaper reporters to appreciate the full effect of the outrage caused by the city council's decision. The cheering and applause went on for several minutes before he calmed the crowd. And once the fiery orator started speaking, utter silence prevailed. The man definitely impressed Bimsbey.

"Fellow patriots. Fellow Americans. How much can we take?" he asked. He took a brief pause to allow the question to sink in. "These foreigners. Have they now taken over our city council? What happened . . . to democracy?" Again he paused, looking around the room at the many faces, setting off another uproar, which he quickly calmed by pretending to plead with them for silence.

The more Batesy spoke and manipulated the crowd, the greater the impression he made on Bimsbey.

"City hall caters to these filthy, loathsome immigrants. This must stop," he said, speaking slowly and deliberately, as he delivered a powerful blow to the surface of the lectern.

Again the crowd roared their displeasure, which he allowed to go on for almost a minute. Not only did Bimsbey love it, but so did the news reporters.

"This foreign scum. Garbage, they are," he shouted, again pounding the lectern.

"Kill the bastards. Kill them all," a voice shouted, setting off a round of loud supportive chanting: "Kill them all. Kill them all."

Tiso felt uneasy, sensing the hatred ready to explode into violence. He saw what he called *a killer instinct* in the eyes of many of the men, especially those who had been drinking.

Batesy went on about how the American workingman has been exploited. "Because of the immigrants, the Irish papists in particular, the bastards work for smaller wages and inferior conditions. They degrade our jobs then take them from us." He then roared, "We, the American patriots," he yelled while pounding his chest like an ape. "Then they defy our laws and build their own firehouse . . . without proper authority. They even set up a fully equipped fire company . . . without the proper permission to do so. Can you imagine the arrogance? The contempt for our laws. For us!"

Batesy had his audience where he wanted them, ready to attack. With a wink of his eye, one of his henchmen shouted, "Burn that firehouse. Burn it to the ground."

A moment of silence followed, then a lone voice started chanting, "Burn it down. Burn it down." In a matter of seconds, the chant, "Burn it down. Burn it down," swept through the house. Their leader, Millhouse Bates, did nothing to discourage them. Instead, he raised his hands and shouted, "If that's want you want to do, I can't stop you."

It's time to leave, thought Tiso, fearing for his safety should he be recognized. He began working his way through the frenzied crowd to the doorway while the crowd around him chanted, "Burn it down." As he proceeded, he bumped shoulders with a longhaired man dressed like a laborer. He did not get a look at his face, his long hair covered it. Little did Tiso know, but that man was Bimsbey, who he knew of from Brogan. He tried to get a good look—the long hair surrounding his head got his interest—but the rush of Batesy's supporters who didn't want to be involved in the violence, pushed him toward the door.

Once outside, Brogan's fly-on-the-wall could still hear the chanting, "Burn it down. Burn it down." *Gotta get to Johnny before they do*, he told

189

himself. Appearing unexcited, he ambled along until he reached the corner, where he turned and bolted, running as fast as his hefty frame would permit.

Johnny and the McCarthys were the only volunteers in the firehouse. But that would change shortly. Vinnie McCarthy had sounded the *emergency signal*: a rapid thirty second clanging of the firehouse bell, which he had repeated. Although the emergency signal was normally used to signal a fire, this time they used the bell to announce the great news that the Pvt. Michael Brogan Engine Company had finally been granted its charter. So in short order, the members of the company began appearing.

Meanwhile, Johnny busied himself filling out a fire report for a fire they had the night before, right in the heart of their district on Ninth and 35th, which consumed a furniture store. That loss resulted from the fire companies fighting each other to see who would put out the fire, rather than immediately fighting the fire.

The fire had started outside as a rubbish pile. *It was while the firemen were fighting* that the fire spread to the inside of the store, where it did extensive damage. Two smiling representatives of the insurance industry witnessed it all; more ammunition against the volunteers in the battle to replace them with a paid fire department. Once again the firemen were their own worst enemy.

The fighting continued after the fire was extinguished. One of the Yanks tried to throw paint on the new steam engine, but a *crack in the puss* from Battler Quinn stopped him cold. Instead, the paint wound up on the perpetrator's clothes.

Only a handful of fire companies in the city had horse-drawn steam engines. They were one of the handful and were perhaps the most advanced, considering that the building's steam boiler in the basement had a hook up to the fire engine above to keep the engine pressurized with steam.

Many of the firemen had already made it to the firehouse by the time sweat-soaked Nick Tiso arrived, panting like a dog. Johnny heard him shouting his name.

"What's up, Nick?" Johnny knew something wasn't right. It was out of character for Nick to be so upset.

"They're coming to wreck this place," Nick shouted, wiping the sweat from his brow with the back of his hand.

"Who! Who's coming!" Johnny demanded to know. He could hear the men cheering the sign over the door that was just uncovered, *Private Michael Brogan Engine Company.*

"Batesy and his Know Nothing mob. They're pissed. All worked up about the charter. And some of them are mad with drink," he shouted.

"You hear that boys," Johnny called out for all to hear.

"Hear what?" somebody shouted.

"The dumb, dumb Know Nothings are coming to wreck this place. Our new firehouse."

"Let the bastards come," roared one of the men.

"We will wreck them, the scumbags," shouted another.

"I don't think so. There's at least a hundred of 'em, I'm sure," said Nick. "When I left the hall, they were chanting, 'Burn it down. Burn it down.'"

"Nick, hustle over to the police station," ordered Johnny, his hand on Nick's shoulder. "And pray God that O'Connell's there. Tell him what you just told me."

Johnny again sounded the fire bell, this time with a greater urgency. More and more men reported in.

"Where's the fire," a man shouted.

"There's no fire yet. But there might be one right hear real soon. We gonna be attacked," said Johnny. Most of the men wore their red fireman shirts and tattered trousers, including Johnny, who'd usually be dressed in his business attire. Some donned their helmets to protect their heads.

"Who *vill* attacking us?" asked a German accented man.

"Who do you think? Batesy and his *dumb dumbs*. But they're going to have one hell of a fight on their hands. Right men?" Johnny shouted to the roars of the men.

"There's good news too. We got our charter." The men hooted and hollered, but they couldn't really enjoy the moment with the pending battle. "But forget that for now. We must protect this place. Our home. Hundreds of those bastards are on their way here."

"Over our dead bodies," one man shouted.

"Well, if we don't get ready, there may well be dead bodies," said Johnny. "Vinnie. Timothy," he motioned to the McCarthys, "Go next store and get a load of axe handles. We'll be prepared to crack some heads. Hans, get the engine hooked up to the hydrant and have a hose line in place." Johnny wanted a hose line in place ready to put out any fires they may start.

Hans and his crew pushed the engine out to the side yard through a special sliding door installed for that purpose.

By now, Batesy and about seventy-five of his drunken, club-wielding, fanatics hustled across 33rd street towards the firehouse chanting, "Burn it down! Burn it down!" Pedestrians cleared the way; parents with children hurried out of their path.

On 35th Street, outside the 20th Precinct, thirty-seven nightstick wielding, uniformed police officers wearing their plug hats, many of them big men, under the command of Sergeant Desmond O'Connell, were lined up.

Shouting commands, O'Connell called his men to attention, then ordered: "Right face," followed immediately by, "Double Time, *ho!*" Off they went across Eight Avenue heading to the firehouse. The intimidating shuffling of their feet could be heard loud and clear. They too got the attention of the excited public.

As the officers hurried along, Sergeant O'Connell shouted commands to them; his voice rang with authority and clarity. "Our orders are," he said, "to protect the new firehouse on 33rd Street and the people in it."

"But that place is not legit," shouted one disgruntled copper. "Shouldn't we be clearing it out?"

"At 4:45 this evening it became legit. It now has a charter to operate," advised the delighted looking O'Connell, dressed in a freshly-pressed uniform. "We will protect it at all cost."

"You mean we might have to attack fellow Americans?" questioned another officer.

"That all depends on who you call Americans. Are you referring to the drunken rabble on its way to attack the men that belong to the Pvt. Michael Brogan Engine Company that protects members of our community. The very fire company from whose ranks twelve men gave their lives in the war."

A hardy cheer erupted from the officers.

O'Connell sprinted ahead of his men and while still on the run, faced them to see their faces when he directed forcefully, "My orders will be obeyed. Or I swear to the Almighty, I will personally crack . . . I mean he who defies the department's orders will answer to me."

CHAPTER NINETEEN

As Batesy's mob reached the intersection of 33rd and Eight Avenue, another bunch of men joined their ranks. By now more than a hundred men were loudly chanting, "Burn it down!" Some of them were barefooted, their feet black with filth. Windows were heard opening as people looked to investigate the commotion.

The chanting was what Sergeant O'Connell and his force heard as they neared Ninth and 33rd, just before the Know Nothing's reached the intersection.

"Blocking formation," shouted O'Connell. His men maneuvered into three rows, across the intersection, blocking the path of the advancing mob; each hand holding an end of their nightsticks.

"Get the hell out of our way," shouted a voice from the mob.

Hurrying to the front of the formation, Sergeant O'Connell shouted to the mob, "Stop where ye are. Ye'll not enter this block."

A voice in the crowd shouted, "Fuck ya, ya mick. Youse ain't got no right to tells us Americans wot ta do."

"I'm authorized by the city of New York to stop ye from violating its laws. And stop ye I will," thundered O'Connell.

Batesy came to the fore of the mob, where he faced his men and waving his arms, signaled them to stop. "Officer. We are here as concerned Americans wanting only to protect our precious democratic ways."

Quickly, the public gathered at a safe distance. They were not about to miss the action.

Batesy continued, "We want to put a stop to this corruption of our system. The buying of a charter to establish a Papist fire company denies the rest of us the democracy our forefathers fought and died for in the war against the British oppressors. So get your booly dogs and go back to your precinct and mind your own business."

"That's a lot of malarkey," barked an Irish-accented cop. "Our ancestors were there, too."

Batesy waved his men forward only to be stopped by the police, who moved menacingly towards them, thrusting their nightsticks and getting ready to crack heads.

"I'm telling you right now, go back or we'll drive you back," ordered the Sergeant.

The mob started shouting and cursing, moving towards the police. They began pelting them with bottles and rocks while others rushed around the outer perimeter of the police cordon and charged towards the firehouse. Nightsticks thumped the attacker's heads as clubs clobbered the police. The sharp cracking sounds and the dull thumps of the bludgeoning of heads and torsos were sickening. A running battle raged with fists, stones, and flying bottles at the police. Faces and heads on both sides bled, some copiously, but the charge towards the firehouse continued, as did the pummeling of each other.

"Hold your positions at all costs," ordered Johnny from his position at the front of the firehouse, sounding like an officer leading men into battle. "And Hans, make sure your guys stay with the hose line. Be ready for a fire." Shaking the axe handle over his head, he shouted, "Bring it on."

Before the running battle reached the firehouse, some anxious defenders forgot their purpose and started for the attackers, but were stopped in their tracks when Johnny roared, "I said, hold your positions. Let them come to us!"

The first of the mob to reach the firehouse, an inebriate who held a lit bottle of paraffin over his head, drew back to throw the firebomb at the firehouse, but a blow on the head from the nightstick of a red-headed cop sent him sprawling unconscious on the street. The bottle shattered a few feet from him, setting the paraffin afire. But a second man managed to throw another bottle through an open second floor window, where fire flared up in an instant.

"Hans! Hans, you take care of that?" shouted Johnny, who proceeded to cold-cock that attacker.

"Don't vorry, Yonnie. Ve get it." True to his word, Hans, as much as he wanted to get into the donnybrook, held his position with the hose line. No sooner had the fire been ignited upstairs, than Hans and his crew were heading up the steps with the charged hose line to extinguish the fire.

No less than 150 men were battling it out by the firehouse. The thumping and slapping of them hitting each other filled the air, as did the sound of bodies hitting the ground. The bleeding combatants clashed on the street and the sidewalks. Woman and children shouted from their windows, cheering the Young Immigrants on, and on this occasion, they shouted support for the coppers and cursed at the enemy. Throughout the battle-royal, men, including coppers, were momentarily laid out unconscious. Everybody seemed to be using weapons of some sort.

Two more firebombs were tossed into the first floor shattering against the right side wall just beyond the house-watch desk that burst into flame. By now the flames and thick smoke gushed from two second-floor windows. Luckily, Hans and the crew had a handle on the fire upstairs; a stream of water came through the windows, knocking down the fire then showering down on the combatants on the street.

I know him. Johnny recognized the guy that threw the firebomb. *Fucking Halstrom. From USA. That sonofabitch.* "I'll get you, you fucker you," Johnny shouted, as a blow glanced off his back.

If Red was here, that wouldn't have happened, the thought flashed through his mind. While pivoting to face his attacker, he was punched on the jaw and knocked on his ass, but was back on his feet as fast as he went down. His attacker, an equally big man, lunged for him, screaming, "Foreign scum," but Johnny's reaction was quick. He drove the end of his axe handle into the man's solar plexus, knocking him out of commission for the moment. Then he slammed his bloodied axe handle against the head of another man who had just clubbed Vinnie McCarthy to the ground, making a loud whacking sound.

Meanwhile, the fire inside at the House Watch area took off. Flames rolled up the high wall and mushroomed across the ceiling, merging with the thick black smoke that rushed up the stairs to the second floor. Luckily the horses and the engine were outside on the opposite side of the firehouse.

Hans and his men gagged and coughed as they made their way back down the stairs through the thick smoke. The German accented Hans barked orders, directing his men to hurry.

Battler was charging towards two individuals crouched in the smoke and sneaking into the firehouse when he saw one of Batesy's prizefighters creeping up on two firehouse defenders. One by one, Batesy's thug worked the defenders over with his quick hands, dropping them with flurries of punches. He even dropped the redheaded cop, but Battler's equally quick hands ended his reign of terror. From behind, he delivered him a crushing blow to the kidney, causing him to squeal in pain. And when the man faced him, Battler hit him with many punches, knocking him out. When he hit the ground, his head slammed on a cobblestone, making a horrible cracking noise. "Do unto others as you'd have them do unto you," Battler mumbled.

Battler then continued his charge into the firehouse where he threw himself into the smoke, diving at the man raising an axe to chop the hose line, sending him and the axe sprawling. The surprised Timothy McCarthy came to his aid as the two of them punched it out with the enemy. Hans and Vinnie McCarthy kept the water stream flowing, knocking down the fire that had begun to take off, ready to set the whole garage ablaze.

Scores of men: cops, good guys, and bad guys hammered away at each other. Blood flew each time a club banged a head and each time a fist hit a face. Men moaned with each kick in the groin.

The defenders weren't able to block all the attackers. Another lit lantern sailed over their heads into the garage area. This, too, was thrown by

Halstrom, the man Johnny recognized as a contractor who bought building supplies from him. Fortunately, the firebomb burst in the midst of the already burned house watch area and was quickly doused by Hans and his crew. From outside the firehouse, Halstrom was heard shouting in a slurred voice, "Fuck you, O'Hara. You don't scare me."

"Ve cool da bums down," shouted Hans. "Putting da water on dem now, right now."

"Good idea," Vinnie answered.

"Maybe dat stopping the fighting. You do it now."

"Okay, boss," Vinnie replied. With a smile on his bloody face, he turned the water stream on everybody. That's right, the coppers too. Then when the shocked combatants divided, he kept the stream on the attackers, driving them back, bringing the fighting to an end. Batesy's men began their retreat back towards Ninth, shouting, "Papists scabs," "Mick bastards," as they did, while the defenders of Pvt. Michael Brogan Engine Company cheered loudly.

* * * * *

This workday morning was no different than any other morning for the young gal who stood on the stoop of the brownstone. She caught the eye of every fellow, young and old, on his way to work. Some of the smiling men even stopped and gawked. One called out, "There's the gorgeous one."

Like always, the *gorgeous one* warranted their attention. She was attired this day in a full-length, green dress that brought out the singular beauty of her face with her light-green eyes and flaming red hair. Her snug dress also revealed the many curves of her fine frame.

She stood there with her back against the stoop railing, reading her book, *Speaking Proper English*. Normally she would ignore her many admirers. But she did not ignore the orphaned newsboy, one of her very young admirers, who shouted "Immigrant Firehouse Attacked."

Shit, not again, she thought. *That's my firehouse.*

"Hey little boss, let me see that," she shouted, beckoning the newsboy with her hand. She snatched a copy of the *Herald* from his pile.

He happily complied. "Och I. Anyting for you, ya pretty ting ya," responded the little guy, getting an even bigger smile from her.

"Boy you're a cocky little guy, aren't ya?" she said, opening the paper to page two, to the story under the picture of the damaged firehouse. *Good man, Johnny. Ya did it, didn't ya?*

The *Herald* story began, "Thugs set alight the new firehouse on West 33rd, the fire company named after Pvt. Michael Brogan, hero of Bull Run. The attackers were a band of Americans outraged by the city council's decision to grant a charter to the all-immigrant fire company. John O'Hara, a local businessman and foreman of the fire company, vowed revenge. "These attackers claim to be patriotic Americans. Rubbish. They are common trash, common thugs, a disgrace to our great nation. They shot my mother dead; they attacked my closest friend in a most horrific way . . ." Her heart throbbed. *He still thinks of me.* "And they destroyed our first firehouse in '55. And now this . . ."

Johnny credited both the police officers and his firemen with saving the day. He said, "The building would have been burned to the ground had it not been for the courage and fierce fighting of the police officers from the 20th Precinct. And my firemen. They're the patriots. The people we can all be proud of."

He also praised the quick thinking of several of his men. "Expecting the attack," he said, "we had our new steamer running and a hose stretched, ready if they tried to burn it down, which they did, starting fires on the main floor and upstairs. Our men were quick to put the fires out."

Johnny went on to single out Hans Hauser and Vinnie McCarthy, who he said brought the fighting to and end by turning the water on the attackers, driving them back: "Which the attackers seemed to appreciate. By then the fight was knocked out of them," he said.

That's great, Johnny O'Hara. You're still my best friend, too. She handed the newsboy his paper. Thoughts of Johnny raced through her mind. *I'd like to see him. It's been a long time. Too long . . . wonder if he'd wanna see me. Wonder if he thinks badly of me.*

* * * * *

Besides his puffed lips and facial bruises, Johnny didn't look like himself nor did he act like himself. When at work, he usually stayed in the office area running the business; dressed meticulously in business attire. But this day he stood in the yard, wearing work clothes and enjoying the early morning breeze blowing in from the river. His people expected something would be happening, for he only wore work clothes when around the firehouse or somebody needed an ass kicking. And he wasn't working at the firehouse.

"Who today, Yonnie?" asked Hans.

"Halstrom," he said, while swinging open the squeaky yard gate and walking out to the street. "They should be here momentarily. I want to get him outside."

"Da fucker who trying to burn us?" he asked.

"Yep."

"You'll be saying goodbye to dat account," warned Battler.

"Sure, but in this case, Brogan wouldn't give a damn hell all. Halstrom went too far. Anything else, I wouldn't care."

Right on time they heard the clip clop of the horse's hoofs as it pulled Halstrom's USA truck.

"There they are," said Johnny, facing the wagon with its crew of four as they headed for the gate. Stepping out into the street, he waved his arms and bellowed, "Stop the wagon. You're not getting in here."

"What ya talking about?" Halstrom shouted back.

"Get down from there and I'll show ye." Johnny motioned him down.

Fear showed in Halstrom's blackened eyes. His skin color turned ashen, but still he got down, ready for whatever might happen. His crew got down with him and stood behind him. A few passersby stopped to watch the obvious confrontation, maintaining a safe distance. They were joined by the workers at Brogan's, who spilled out onto the street from the yard.

"What's your problem, potato?" said Halstrom.

"In a calm deliberate voice, Johnny said, "You. You tried to burn us out. Now you're going to pay the price."

With that, Halstrom snapped off a sneak punch to Johnny's temple. Johnny's legs weakened at the knees and he staggered backwards across the street. Right then, the men from both sides squared off, but did not engage each other. Seeking to keep the advantage, Halstrom rushed Johnny, but Johnny, although groggy, sidestepped him while hooking him in the gut, *forcefully deflating his lungs.* Halstrom's eyes looked like they wanted to pop out of his head. Before he could turn around, Johnny gave him a fierce punch with his ham-sized fist on the back of the head, driving him headlong toward the tenement across the street. Johnny stayed with Halstrom, grabbing the hair on the back of his head and slamming his face against the brick wall. Blood streamed from Halstrom's mouth and nose—some of yesterday's wounds were again spurting blood. Johnny spun the rubber-legged man around, grabbed his shirt collar, and twisted it to a point where Halstrom choked. Still nobody from either side got involved. Halstrom was finished without much of a fight. "Ye ever go near our firehouse again, you disgrace to America, you're dead meat. And that goes for all ye scum friends. Ye got that?" he snapped, using a pronounced Irish lilt.

Halstrom did not reply.

"You Papist bastard," barked one of the Halstrom's men, his face flushed with anger. But before he caused an incident, his co-workers silenced him.

"Answer me," Johnny shouted at Halstrom, at the same time whacking his face, splashing more blood.

"Yes! Yes," Halstrom moaned.

Oh shit, what's that, Johnny wondered, listening to running feet coming up behind him, followed by a shuffle then a thud. Sensing an attack, he stepped to his left and pivoted just in time to see a man with a brick in his hand collapse. Standing right next to the man was Hans. *Hans saved me ass. Just like Red used to do.* Johnny muttered, "Sonofabitch," and kicked the side of his attacker's face

Then he kicked Halstrom in the butt. "Get your ass out of here and don't come back," he said in his cool, deliberate way. Then he called to Hans, "I owe you, Hans."

"It not me. It vas dat guy." Hans pointed to a fast moving figure wearing a Union Army campaign hat, already half way down the block.

"Anybody see who that was?" asked Johnny.

"No," said Battler. "Happened so fast. He tooked off right away."

CHAPTER TWENTY

"Hey, wait for me," Johnny shouted, taking off at a jog. He had no idea who just saved his ass, but he had to know. Not until he closed in on the stranger did the light bulbs start going off in his head. A sense of joy tickled his gut. "I'd know that beautiful butt anywhere."

The stranger made no effort to lose Johnny. Johnny's protector slowed to a saunter.

"Red. Red Hester, is that you?"

She spun to face him. "Hello Johnny," she said in a soft all-female voice, her sparkling green eyes gazing teasingly into his. "How'd ya know it was me?"

"Once I saw that backside. I mean, how could I forget it?" he said.

"Do I detect a dirty mind at work?" She smiled, happy to see him, wanting to wrap her arms around him, but wouldn't. She didn't know if he'd appreciate it, her being what she is and being gone so long. Johnny, too, couldn't let himself go, as overwhelmed as he was with emotions: elated to see her; angry that she left him; and full of desire, wanting so much to hold her.

"Gees, Red! It's good . . . hell, it's great to see you."

For a few seconds they said nothing, only staring into each other's desire-filled eyes. Then as if rehearsed, they muttered, "Bullshyte," then stepped towards each other and embraced.

"Likewise, Johnny O'Hara. It's been a long time, hasn't it?" They held the embrace.

"Why did you stay away so long?" he half whispered, half muttered.

"My pride, I guess."

"I hope you had a good life," he said.

"Yes. We'll talk about that later," she said.

"I should have known it was you who bopped that guy. I mean 'covering my back' like the old days. If not for you, right now I'd be lying in a puddle of my own blood. He squeezed her even harder.

"Easy there boy," she said while gently moving him back. "You're gonna squeeze my insides out."

Why am I getting all excited, he asked himself. Hell, she still dresses like a man. He had to find out where she stood on men. "See you still wear men's garb. Does that mean—"

"Stop! Don't even ask. I'm as straight as a ten-penny nail? Does it make a difference to you?"

"Very much so."

She liked his response.

From their position outside the stockyard gate to the yard, Hans and Battler stood bewildered, watching Johnny repeatedly hugging this guy.

"Who the hell is that? What's with the hugs," said Battler. "Go see who it is," he said to Hans.

"No. You going. *Me* not nosy."

"Bullshit. You want to know just as much as me," barked Battler. Hans simply smiled.

"What brought you here?" asked Johnny.

"That headline in the *Herald*—"

"By the way, your English is terrific. What—"

"Let me finish," she insisted. "The headline read: 'Thirty-third Street Firehouse Attacked.' And your comment about the attackers: 'They attacked my best friend in a most horrific way.' I had to come. To check it all out. And to see you, Johnny."

Johnny flushed, the thought that she might *love him* sent a hot sensation surging through his body, arousing him, flushing his neck and face. Just the possibility overcame him. He wrapped his arms around the back of her neck, pressing his face against hers, cheek to cheek, which she didn't resist.

"Oh shit!" muttered Battler. "What da fuck's he doing? Dat's a guy he's cheeking it with."

Red laughed at the sight of the startled faces of Battler and Hans; their eyes appeared ready to pop out of their heads. "I better show my face before they drop dead." She took of her cap and stepped forward, giving the guys a big wave. She saw their faces light up with big smiles.

"Oh, crap," Johnny laughed. He turned and shouted back to them, "It's okay! It's Red!" He redirected his attention to Red and asked, "You can read and write now, can't you?"

"I was wondering when you were going to ask that question again. Yes. For a long time. Is it obvious?" she asked.

"Without a doubt. I'm proud of you." Still in awe at the sight of her, smiling, almost laughing, he couldn't take his eyes off of her. *That face. That beautiful face.*

"Stop staring at me," she said, blushing.

"But I can't resist," he replied, grabbing her hand, the touch of which shot another bolt of passion through his body. "You're blushing?"

"Yes. And you're trembling," she retorted, wondering if he detected her shaking.

"You—you'll be around for a while?" he asked.

"I got something to take care of," she said.

"Are you gonna disappear on me again?" he asked, covering his heart with his left hand. "How about after—"

"No, I'll be around," she said.

"How about we feed our faces together?"

"I'd like that very much."

* * * * *

"Back again. Seems you just left," Batesy said to Tony Bosh in the way of a greeting from his position behind the bar as he shined glasses in the customer-less Louvre. The lunch hour had not yet begun.

"Had some business to take care of," said Tony. When he noticed Batesy's black eye, he grinned and asked, "Where'd ye get the blinker?"

"Ah, had to eject some rowdy snob last night. No big deal. Now, what'll you be having? That same old Irish . . . stuff again."

This bastard's always knocking the Irish, Tony reminded himself. He found it hard not to glare at this guy. But he would not let him get away scott-free with still another dig against the Irish. He pointed to Batesy's eye and asked, "You sure it wasn't an Irishman who gave you that?" He laughed loudly, appearing to be joking, but knowing he got to Batesy. *Fuck this Irish hater.*

As much as he wanted to confront Batesy, he decided against it. "A glass of water would be more than sufficient."

"A sensible man, I see," said Batesy, forcing a smile.

Tony returned the smile and said, "You got that right. Always want *me* senses about me."

"When did your ship get in?" Batesy asked as he poured him a glass of water.

"Tuesday."

"Your uncle was all nerves about your coming. Afraid that Paddy here," he snapped a finger off the bottle of Paddys, "wouldn't be on time. Happy as a pig in shit that you came out." He placed the glass of water in front of Tony.

"Indeed," Tony said, raising an eyebrow. "And he knew me at the dock, although he'd never laid eyes on me before. Got me starting work this

Monday, bright and early. Even got a coachman to take me around the city, mind you. That's more than me father ever did for me back in the old country. And he had loads of money."

Batesy smiled. "Didn't know they had carriages in that godforsaken place."

"You're right. Very few people there had money for such lavish conveniences. Maybe an occasional donkey-drawn cart. Probably much like the outback parts of this great country. No, just the rich who'd stolen all the wealth. Those lowly, thieving bastards. They should all burn in hell. Oh," Tony grunted. "Don't get me started on that scum."

"Oh boy," Batesy said, cringing, giving him a strange look.

"I need a little information that I hope you can provide," said Tony, changing the subject. "First, I need a fine bookshop. Second—"

"Just outside the door to your left. Fabio's. A great book shop. What else?"

"A quick description of the city. Where should I not go?"

"Stay away from the west side, west of 8th Avenue," Batesy advised. "Nothing there but trouble." The question delighted him, his chance to tear apart the Irish. A chance to stick it to Bosh while pretending to help him. "Filled with immigrant scum. They'd not hesitate to slit your throat. The same type as the Five Points. Further down on Broadway."

"What's the Five Points?" asked the puzzled looking Tony.

"That's where the lowest of the lowest live. Live like animals. Go in there and you're not coming back out. Guaranteed."

"Where do most of my people settle?" Tony asked.

"That . . . to the Points or the west side."

"Where is thirty-three Westside?" Tony asked.

Batesy chuckled, lighting up a cigarette. "That's probably West 33rd. Just west of here. That's the west side. As I said, that area is bad. When you finish in Fabio's, go to your left. That's 33rd. Just straight ahead. In no time you be in the middle of the immigrant heartland: mostly Irish and German, and some Dagos. You'll see the squalor that they thrive in."

"It's got to be a better place than what they had in Ireland," said Bosh.

"If you don't mind, why all the curiosity about the Irish?"

"Because I have to find someone there. I believe if there's a fire brigade in the area—" Tony paused for a few seconds, slightly irked by Batesy's ear-to-ear grin. "Why are you laughing?" he asked.

"Oh, nothing."

"As I was saying," Tony continued, "if there's a fire brigade in the area, he'd probably belong to it."

"You might be lucky. I think there's a fire station," he grinned, "on 33rd near Tenth Avenue. A fire brigade, as you call it. Named after some donkey killed in the war. The company's made up of a bunch of street fighters. Thugs. They're not like my fire company, Know Nothing Hose Company. All solid Americans."

"Is it ya don't like the Irish now, Mr. Bates." Tony thickened his Irish accent, but kept his cool.

"That's for sure." Batesy gave him a hard look. Most Americans don't like them. Of course, we wouldn't consider you to be one of them."

"Ach, but I consider meself one of them," said Tony, returning the hard look. Tell me now, will ye? Just how big is this neighborhood of foreigners I'm going to?"

"Too big," Batesy replied. Tony's strong Irish accent had him irritated. But he too, kept his cool, more so out of fear of Tony's uncle's influence. "But not too big to find somebody. If they're not *on the run.*" He laughed aloud. "When you reach the fire station, you're dead center in the danger zone."

"Surely the fire *laddies* will protect me," challenged Tony.

"Not so. Like I told you, they're all thugs."

The tension between them mounted.

Batesy continued, "They call themselves the Young Immigrants. They'll be the ones to go after you. The bad boys. Micks and Krouts, mostly. They're causing our good, honest, native firemen real problems.

And the insurance companies are pushing like hell to create a paid fire department. They, and the bums up in Albany, want to get rid of the volleys. All because of the likes of them." He reached for a whiskey bottle and poured himself a shot. He offered the same to Tony, on the house, which he declined.

"So what's wrong with that?" asked Tony, going along with Batesy's tirade.

"First of all, the volleys have always done a damn good job putting fires out. And often gave their lives. And secondly, many of 'em would not get the job because it would be given to a foreigner. And that my friend, is bullshit!"

"Well, I certainly would agree with you there," Tony said.

In truth, replacing the volleys with a paid fire department wasn't all about anyone being too reckless and combative. For the longest time, the insurance companies had been waging a silent campaign to create a paid fire department. They wanted a fire service they could control and hold accountable. This, they felt, would eventually save the insurance industry millions of dollars in losses per annum. And money being the bottom line, a paid fire department would overcome the problem of recruiting volunteers for the growing city. The war cut deeply into their recruit pool.

"Bejasus, Mr. Bates. You sound like *me father*. True English aristocracy. He begrudged his tenants everything. Not even a simple education would he allow them. Even let them starve. I mean to death. I hope you don't share his views on immigrants?"

Batesy paused, taking a sip of his whiskey. "Good stuff," he said. A smile replaced a hint of anger. "As I told you before, they'd rob you blind if they got the chance. I wish they never came to our country."

"I hope I never need anything from you. Me *tinks* you'd let me starve. Or if me house was burning, you'd let it burn," said Tony, getting to his feet. "After all, I, too, come from Ireland."

"Oh, but you're okay, sir. You're English."

Enough of this tyrant. Let me go find me boyo. Tony left.

* * * * *

"Oh, oh! Again you're in your work clothes. Or should I say, fighting clothes?" said Battler, dropping the last of his cigarette on a pile of horse manure.

"Yah," said Hans. "I vondered dat too, Yonnie. Who dis time?"

"Because I have one more problem to resolve. And it requires me rags, if ye know what I mean." He cracked his knuckles.

"Who's next to get his ass whipped?" Battler asked.

Johnny just shook his head. "You'll probably hear about it." Looking through the front window, he saw Katie approaching. It was 1:45pm.

"Ach, the most beautiful girl in the world," he said as she stepped into the office. Her pretty face turned red.

"Beautiful girls should not be shy," Johnny said to her. "Watch the place," he told the men. "I'll be back within the hour."

Johnny grabbed her hand. "Let's go, beautiful one," he said, forcing a smile. He no more wanted to smile than a cat wanted to jump on a hot griddle. He was on his way to do a dirty deed that needed to be done.

"I'm scared, Johnny. I don't like this at all," she said, sauntering at his side.

"Well it's got to be done. No man is going to mess with *me* sister. No man," said Johnny. "Give me one of those," he said, taking one of the two food parcels she was carrying. She did voluntary duty, bringing food to the hungry elderly and the sick.

It was another July scorcher. Their heavy perspiration made their shirts cling to them.

Ironically, this day Katie was bringing food and water to two elderly women living in the same building where she and Johnny had lived with their mother.

"I wish I didn't have to bring them today," said Katie, wiping the sweat from her brow with the back of her hand in which she held a jar of water. Her other hand held a bag with sandwiches in it. "It's just too hot."

As they moved along the mostly earthen sidewalk up Tenth Avenue, they could smell the cooking from the paupers' village: an open area of land filled with little shanties. Seemed that in every little shack people were cooking the day's dinner—those who had food to cook. There were many puffs of smoke rising from the shanties. He could hear the high-pitched voice of Hans' wife, known for her dopey-looking smile, calling to him, "Hello, Yonnie," over the voices of the men and women and the children that were shouting his name.

Her brother's popularity impressed Katie. "Everybody knows you." Her face beamed with pride.

"Hold it up." They stopped in front of the building. "Let me put these on." He slipped on a pair of tight-fitting black gloves. "Onward Christian soldiers." They entered their old building. Katie started up the creaky, wooden stairs. Right behind her tiptoed Johnny. He felt bad that she had to be there—did not like for her to be exposed to violence—but so be it, he figured. *This has to be done.*

Predictably, looking up the stairwell, they saw almost total darkness except for a crack of light coming from the slightly ajar roof door. She suspected Grogan had turned off the gas lamps. As she passed through the second-floor landing and started up the stairs to the third floor, she heard Grogan's door opening on its squeaky hinges. She could see the silhouette of his half-naked body holding his penis, through the narrow ray of daylight his open door introduced to the landing. She hesitated out of fear and disgust, only to feel her brother gently prodding her forward. He whispered, "Don't be afraid."

Having to pass Grogan's apartment always scared her, but it wasn't until recently that she told her brother, and only because Grogan groped her and threatened that the next time he would pull her into his bed. She worried that Johnny would kill him and be sent to prison. But he had promised her he wouldn't kill him.

* * * * *

"Ah, will ya come in here now, little Katie, and spend a bit of time with me? Make me feel good now, will ya, me wee lassie." Grogan's voice was low and raspy. His apartment emanated a repulsive odor of urine and cigarette smoke.

"Mr. Grogan," shouted Katie, sounding fearless and older than her fifteen years. She had confidence in her brother, who crouched behind her. She repeated what Johnny had been rehearsing her to say: "Johnny has something for you."

"And what's that, me darling," Mr. Grogan groaned. With that, Johnny sprang from behind her and into Grogan's flat, closing the door behind him. This kept Katie out of sight from what Johnny had to do, but not out of listening range. He had Grogan off the floor, one of his glove-covered hands holding the hair on the back of the evil man's head and the other hand placed between his buttocks, holding his penis and testicles as he squeezed, twisted and yanked. Then holding him like a battering ram, he repeatedly slammed his head against the wall. The blood stains on the wall and filthy bedding grew larger and more numerous each time his face hit the wall.

Hearing the thumping sounds against the wall, Katie pushed open the door and shouted, "Johnny, you promised. Stop. Please stop!"

Johnny immediately dropped Grogan flat on his straw mattress, but held a firm grip on his privates. Grogan offered no resistance, simply moaned while Johnny continued twisting and yanking his manhood.

"Close the door, Katie. I'll be right out," he admonished her. She did as he demanded.

"Please, Johnny! Please," Grogan babbled in his dazed state.

"She's not your darling, Grogan," Johnny said in a soft, but terrifying way.

"Please, Johnny. That hurts terribly. Please stop," Grogan continued pleading, his voice muffled by the bedding.

"Johnny! You promised me. You promised me," Katie screamed as she opened the door. Now she was crying. "You'll kill him and leave me all alone."

With that, Johnny, now in a hurry to finish, placed his knee on the back of Grogan's neck and pressed hard. "Now, Mr. Grogan." Again he spoke in that scary tone of voice. "I love my sister dearly. She's all I got. And if anybody fucks with me sister, anybody, I will kill him." Then Johnny removed his knee and with his two massive hands, gripped the full

210

of Grogan's neck, raised his head up from the mattress and squeezed tightly. Grogan gasped, tried to talk, his eyes ready to pop, but Johnny released his grip, letting him fall limp.

"Remember, Grogan! I will kill him," Johnny snarled.

Grogan, nodded, mumbling, "Yes, yes, yes," straining to get the words out.

Johnny followed Katie out onto the landing, shutting the door behind him, where he gave her a fatherly kiss. In his calm reassuring way, he said to her, "He won't be bothering you anymore. See you later, love."

Even though the experience had terrified and almost sickened Katie, she sensed great relief in knowing that Grogan would never bother her again. As a matter of fact, she felt nobody would ever bother her again.

Resuming her mission of mercy, she continued up the stairs, feeling proud of her brother's fearlessness and his ability as a fighter.

Arriving on the fifth-floor landing, still trembling, she paused to pull herself together. *A big smile would help*, she thought.

On hot, humid days like this she regretted being a volunteer. But just like her mother, she also loved helping people. Perhaps that's the reason she never missed a day of voluntary service at Holy Cross that she had been doing since her eleventh birthday. After school every Monday and Wednesday she brought food parcels and water to the elderly or helped out with orphaned children. Presently, her assignment was the two sisters she was about to visit.

"Is that you, Katie *darlin*?" Mary Cramphorn called out from inside her flat. "Yes," shouted Katie, pushing the door in, releasing a familiar stale stench. The old gals were just too old and fragile to be up and down the stairs every time they had to relieve themselves. They used a potty.

"I—I—I didn't tink ye'd ever get here. It's so hot." Mrs. Cramphorn spoke slowly with a quivering voice.

"I'll be right in," she said, placing the food parcels inside the flat. "Soon as I open the roof door." She was up to the roof and back to the flat in a flash. The sisters, sitting on a mattress of straw, reached with fragile arms for the food.

"God loves you, child," said the other sister Matilda. "What was all that ruckus down below?" she queried.

"I think that crazy Grogan was yelling at himself," said Katie, smiling nervously.

"It's so hot. Lucky we're all not crazy," said Matilda.

*****

Tony Bosh stepped out from under the ornate entranceway to Fabio's bookstore. He carried a ten-inch thick bundle of books about everything to do with fires and their extinguishment. Those books he carried were wrapped in brown paper. *I'll find that O'Hara yet,* he told himself.

The opulence of Fifth Avenue quickly disappeared as Tony strutted west along 33rd, looking hard, looking confidant. Alert not to be a gawking tourist—something he learned while walking the back streets of Dublin—that was easy bait for the thugs that roamed the city.

Once he passed Sixth Avenue, he was in the infamous Tenderloin district, an area known for its wild nightlife. With great interest, he noted the abundance of dives and brothels, the likes of which he had never seen before. While the facades of fine buildings along Fifth Avenue were richly ornate and stylish, certain to draw the attention of daytime visitors, the fascia portion of the buildings throughout the Tenderloin appeared very dreary. They were intentionally designed to be dull during the day. But at night they had a strong lure of flashing lights that drew the attention and money of the good citizenry looking for a good time.

He found himself repeatedly aroused by the beautiful women—many of who were young girls—he saw posing temptingly outside the many three-story brownstone homes that lined the streets. *Why are there so many of them hanging out and doing nothing,* he wondered. And then thinking of his experiences in the back streets of Dublin, he quickly deduced their purpose. They were members of the world's oldest profession: they sold their bodies for sexual pleasure.

He noticed many Irish faces among them. Many even smiled at him. *Aren't they the friendly lot,* he thought. *A prerequisite of the occupation.*

"Hey, boyo? What's your fancy?" a girl with lovely black hair and sparkling eyes called out.

Another girl with an Irish accent shouted, "I'll do ya better."

"Not just now, girls," he shouted back real cocky like, wanting them to think that the twenty-four-year-old was an old pro.

At the sight of the Crystal Palace, with its fascinating array of light bulbs that shaped the loudly attractive designs on this enormous edifice, he forgot himself and his mouth dropped, no longer able to hide his fascination with New York. But he recommenced with his vigilance as he walked through the quiet street that at dusk would be wall to wall people. He remained alert enough to see the two scruffy-looking, thug-likes standing outside the Palace entranceway who were giving him bad looks. That and their threadbare clothing signaled to him that there could be trouble. Pretending to ignore them, he resumed his cocky walk. But they didn't ignore him, taking up after him.

Now what do I do? Confront them, he wondered, thinking of similar incidents he experienced while living among the Dublin paupers. He did an abrupt about-face and walked briskly right at them, staring hard into their eyes. But they did not waver. Coming face to face, he asked in a cocky-tone, with an Irish accent, "Can I help you, gentlemen?"

His accent startled them. "Are you one of us," a young freckle-faced man asked in a New York Irish accent, while tapping his chest, "or one of them?" He then pointed towards Fifth Avenue.

Two police officers appeared at the corner and immediately approached.

"That I am," Tony replied, nodding his head. He smiled and in his self-assured tone, he said, "In me heart, I've always been *one of us*, as you say. And I have nothing but contempt for *them*," he nodded towards Fifth Avenue.

As the police officers neared, the two youths, who were startled by his response, started to leave.

"Wait," Tony said. "I have a question."

The two stopped and faced him.

"Sir, are they a bother to you?" asked one of the officers, twirling his nightstick while looking suspiciously at the two.

"Not at all, officer. They were giving me directions," said Tony.

The police nodded. They took their leave to a post in front of the Crystal Palace from where they continued to observe the youths.

"What you wanna know?" the freckle-faced one asked. "And what you got in *dat* bag?"

"Books about fire brigades. Sure you wouldn't be wanting them, now, would ye? Where can I find little Johnny O'Hara?" asked Tony.

Their eyes narrowed cautiously. "Little? He not little, mister. Who wants ta knows?"

"Tony Bosh. A friend from home."

"I'll tell you *nutting*, friend or not," he replied with his hands in his pockets.

"Then where's the fire brigade?" asked Tony.

"Straight ahead." Freckle face pointed towards the North River.

Tony continued on his way, passing Eight Avenue, when a good-looking young gal stepped out in front of him.

"What's *ye* fancy, me bucko?" she said with an Irish lilt, wearing an ear-to-ear smile.

"You!" was all he said, catching her off guard.

"What does that mean?" she asked.

"I want to marry you," he said, unable to hold back a chuckle.

"Sure, you wouldn't want to marry this lassie," she replied with a laugh, at the same time eyeing his package. "You'd marry a stranger, would ya?"

"Why not?" he asked. "If she's as pretty as you."

"Sit down here," she said, gesturing for him to sit to her left on the stoop. "I'm Ellen and you're?" she asked.

"Tony Bosh." He placed his package atop of the stoop's fancy cut-stone railing right near an open window. He took a seat on a lower step, next to the young lady. That's when an arm partially clad in green reached out the window from behind a curtain, and without a sound, lifted the package.

"You do know what I do for living, I'm sure?" she asked, while positioning herself to look out to the street with him as he watched the side of her face.

"Have intercourse with men for a fee, is it?" he asked.

"Exactly. Would you want to marry someone like that, now?" she asked with a chuckle. She straightened out his tie.

"You'd never know," he said, maintaining a serious expression.

"You gotta be crazy, me bucko." Her smile changed to a more serious look. "What would a gentleman like ye be wanting with a courtesan? You'd be knocked by your people."

He rose to his feet. "It's been me pleasure, Miss Ellen. But I must get going. I bought some books for a friend I'm trying to locate," he said as he turned to get the bundle. "What the—they're gone." His startled look quickly turned to one of curiosity. "You know anything about this?"

"Not at all," she said, straight faced, emphasizing her Irish accent. "If you catch the thief, give him a good belt for me."

"I like you," he said in earnest.

He must be crazy, she thought.

"Maybe one day you'll join me for lunch?"

He is crazy. "Maybe," she replied.

When Tony reached Ninth Avenue, he ran smack into the tantalizing aroma of fine cooking. That aroma drifted from the open doors of the North River Inn and competed with the smell of horse manure. His stomach growled, alerting him to his extreme state of hunger. *Better get a bite before I go any further.*

He pressed his nose up against the large glass window of the completely remodeled North River Inn, formerly the Shamrock Inn. He saw a mixed clientele—some of who were staring back at his mug—many of who were not befitting such a fine establishment. He glimpsed a rough and tumble sort, just like many of the places he frequented while bumming around Dublin.

This is as good a place as any, he assured himself. He removed his coat and tie. "Here goes," he muttered. He pushed in the stained glass door and immediately scanned the inside for a place to sit.

Other than a few office and shop workers, the North River Inn was crowded with working men: diggers, brickeys, carpenters, and laborers of all kinds. Some ate lunch and others drank lunch. One group conversed in Irish. The guttural tone of the language got Tony's immediate attention. *There's me opening*, he thought. *Certainly they'll welcome someone that speaks the language.*

He squirmed his way through the human congestion in the dining area, ignoring several glares, right to the Irish speakers. Battler watched him with a keen eye. *Who's this big shit*, he wondered.

"Afternoon, gentlemen," Tony said with a smile, speaking in Irish and getting the Irish speakers attention.

One of them, a burly-chested man with a full white beard, acknowledged him with a nod and a Celtic grunt.

Again speaking in Irish, Tony asked, "I'm looking for my good friend, Johnny O'Hara. Can any of you direct me to him?"

"Direct you to him, is it? Does that mean, 'do we know where he is?'" another Irish speaker asked. They laughed at this selection of words.

"And who, might I ask, are you, sir?" asked the burly-chested man, again speaking in Irish.

"Tony Bosh. From home with him."

"And where might home be?" the man asked in English, sipping his drink.

"Skibereen."

"Och. So much death . . . and suffering," said the man, his eyes narrowing with anger. "And why, might I ask, does the name Bosh have a familiar ring to it?"

Before Tony could reply to the man's pointed question, a hand tugged on his right shoulder. He turned his head to find Battler's eyes glaring at him.

"Did I hear you say, Johnny O'Hara?" he asked. Battler made no effort to hide his hostility. He eyed Tony's attire with contempt.

"That is correct." Tony no longer felt safe and struggled to conceal it. He noted the many sets of eyes that followed him and Battler as they spoke. In some of those eyes he saw the same mean look his father often got from his tenants back in Skibereen.

"Your name is? And what is your business with Mr. O'Hara?" asked Battler, as if trying to provoke him.

The first thing Tony noted about Battler were the many little scars that cut through his lips and eyebrows and an obvious broken nose. *A fighter*, Tony assumed.

"Tony Bosh. And who are you, sir?" asked Tony, cracking a pleasant grin.

"The Battler. That's who," Battler Quinn responded in the distinct New York Irish accent. And I'm ready to do battle with you if you don't answer me questions. And . . . there's no sirs around here."

Tony, admiring Battler's guts, replied in as cocky a voice as he could muster, "I've just arrived from the *old sod* and I'm trying to track him down. That's all, mate."

Battler smiled, contemptuously. "Oh yeah. You're the son of that Lord *fella*.

"Yes," he said, at the same time shaking his head. "But don't hold that against me."

"You wait here and I'll check you out," warned Battler. He muttered something unintelligible to the others.

"You mean I found him?" Bosh couldn't hide his pleasure at locating Johnny.

"I didn't say that. Be back in a jiffy." Battler disappeared.

CHAPTER TWENTY-ONE

Thirty minutes later, after a hardy sandwich, Bosh was pleased to see the smiling Battler barge through the entrance of the North River Inn. He saw a happy man with his hand extended. Over the roar of the crowd he heard Battler shouting, "Why ya not tell me youse his best fren?"

Bosh returned the smile, springing to his feet. "You didn't—"

"Tony Bosh from Skibereen, welcome to Young Immigrant country," said Battler, giving him a firm handshake. "The boss is thrilled. Can't waits ta see ya. And when Johnny's happy . . . I'm happy. So git ya slicks and wez hit da bricks."

Tony grabbed his coat and tie, bid the smiling Irish crowd goodbye, and followed Battler out the door, where they darted west along 33rd Street. It wasn't long before his nostrils were flaring at the stench of a burned building; the odor hung thick in the air. "Was there a conflagration?" Tony asked.

Battler looked confused. "Con—fla—Wot da hell wuz dat?"

"Sorry, chap. Fire. Was there a fire somewhere?"

"Yep. Dat's where wez going."

Tony saw the large group of men on the other side of the street, working at a furious pace as they carried debris from inside the firehouse and placed it onto waiting wagons. Others were busy on ladders, painting the restored window frames on the second floor.

"Good God, man. The fire station? That's the last kind of building one would expect to see burned," Tony said. He shook his head in disbelief. "What happened? Who did it?"

"Some peoples doan likes us immigrants," said Battler. "Even though lots of us wuz born here."

Tony nodded. "Please. Tell me more." He could see the workers looking him over. He sensed they didn't like what they saw.

"*Dose* dimwit *nonuttins*. Da fucks wuz pissed because wez finally gots a okay for our own firehouse."

"What's wrong with that?"

"Like deys considers us all foreigners. Ya know, being catlics."

"But why?" asked Tony.

"Dey doan want us in charge of anything. Dat's da why."

"But you're an American, aren't you?" said Tony.

"All depends where our peoples cum from," said Battler. "Call us scabs too 'cause dey say wez work for less money. But wez can't git decent jobs. Wot can wez do? Gotta eat. Gots to pay da rent."

"Who's the big *shyte*?" asked Vinnie as he and some others maneuvered the heavy new garage door towards its tracks.

"He's awright. Comes from where Johnny lived," replied Battler while walking up to the men with the new garage door. Several gals scrubbed the smoke and fire blackened surfaces of the building's fascia.

"Where'd Johnny go?"

"What's his name? What's his business?" asked Vinnie McCarthy, not liking Bosh's appearance. McCarthy's detestation was obvious.

"Doan ya listen? I said from where Johnny come from. You know, Ireland," said Battler. "Tony Bosh."

Vinnie nodded, still not friendly towards the well-dressed stranger. He'd wait to see Johnny's reaction. "The kitchen."

"I wuz saying," said Battler as they stepped into the firehouse, stopping by the house-watch area. Battler checked to see if the plaque with the names of the war dead was damaged. It wasn't. "Dem fuckers cum back today when nobidy wuz in dere. Again dey put it on fire. And again, our boys put it out. And by tonight, wez have it looking like new."

"So I get it. They don't like you because of your foreign connection," said Bosh, staring at a smoke-stained memorial plaque on the wall that commemorated the death of a fireman in the line of duty. "But why would they get so angry over the charter? It doesn't make sense at all," said Bosh.

"Well dere's a lil more to it dan dat," said Battler. "The okay wuz da icing on da cake. First ya have to understand dey doan trust catlics, and as I said before, to dem wez scabs because wez works for lesser money. The only way wez can git work. Dis time dey gots mad 'cause of a story in the newspaper. It said we wuz great at a fire. And dat we wuz *one of the best, if not the best*, of New York City's fire companies."

"God, that must have boiled their blood," said Tony.

"Yeah. And as I said, less than six months ago, after years of da catlic-haters fighting against it, wez wuz about to get da okay. But when a whole bunch of dem jerks starts a yelling *no charter, no charter*, the city council putted off the vote. But last Friday they finally voted, which started some fistfights. If a bunch of coppers wuz not dere, a big brouhaha would've happened. And wez won, two votes up."

That same *Herald* account also said, "Pvt. Michael Brogan Engine Company consists of and is run by foreigners, and their American-born offspring, who happen to be mostly Irish and German." Outrage spread rapidly throughout the ranks of New York's Volunteer Fire Department. Most of the volunteers—especially those who never had the experience of working at a fire with the all-immigrant fire company—were outraged at the *Herald*. And not because they despised the Catholic immigrants, but because they were jealous over the fact that they were called *the best*."

The *Herald* had editorialized about a recent fire in a tenant house filled with immigrants at which members of the first fire companies to arrive were all Yanks, and they made no extraordinary effort to save a mother and her two children that were trapped on an upper floor of the burning building.

The newspaper acknowledged that it would have been reckless, if not suicidal, for the firemen to attempt such a rescue, but at the same time told their readers that it was not good publicity for them to not even try getting to the family."

The story described their predicament in this way: "Fire and smoke were everywhere, rolling across the underside of the staircases and hallways, eliminating any access the firemen might have had getting to the family. What the Know Nothings didn't know, but the local immigrant volunteers did know, was that the apartment the kids were in had a window facing on a small enclosed air shaft situated dead center in the building."

And here follows the paragraph that really pissed off the Yanks: ". . . Three members of the Pvt. Michael Brogan Engine Company (Johnny O'Hara, Hans Hauser and Battler Quinn) raced to the roof of an attached building, carrying a rescue rope. Once there, they lowered O'Hara by rope into the airshaft, which he described as, 'like descending into hell.' There he entered a window that billowed hot, acrid smoke. With the help of his two comrades, O'Hara pulled the three trapped victims to safety—extreme heroism rarely paralleled."

What really happened almost wrecked Quinn and Hauser's nerves. Once inside the window, their best friend disappeared for a couple of minutes that seemed like an eternity. And when he did not respond to their shouts—he couldn't breathe in the thick smoke let alone shout—they became terrified for his safety. And all they could see around them were flames whipping up over the sides of the structure. It seemed to them the whole building was ablaze and he had no way out other than the way he went in. Then to their great relief, O'Hara's soot-covered arm emerged up through the thick rolling smoke, lifting the limp form of a little child just out of their reach. To make up the distance, Battler Quinn, held by the powerful arms of Hauser, lowered himself up-side-down from the ledge of the roof just enough to grab the child and swing it up to the roof. No sooner had he gotten the child on the roof than a second one appeared out of the smoke. In the same manner, Battler also got that unconscious child to the roof.

Then there were screams and the sounds of scuffling. The terrified mother refused to climb out the window. They heard O'Hara shout, "Damn you, shut up," then, "Sorry lady," which was followed by a smack sound and then silence. "Okay, let's get her up," Johnny coughed out. The three of them pushed or pulled the woman's limp body to the roof. Then Johnny screamed, "Get me the fuck out of here. I'm burning. I'm burning."

Hurriedly, the two of them reached down and plucked him from a close call with death. It took all their strength to pull O'Hara's big frame to the roof and just as his frame cleared the shaft, flames exploded out the window, setting the airshaft afire.

By now much of the roof was in flames, lighting up the night sky as well as the street below. Nearby roofs were littered with people watching the terror and the heroics.

* * * * *

Inside, at the rear of the firehouse, a group of woman had just finished scrubbing clean the white wall tiles of the kitchen that had been discolored by the smoke. Johnny and Red entered as the women were leaving. "Those tiles look cleaner than ever," he complimented the ladies. But it wasn't the tiles he had on his mind. It was Red. Just the sight of her had him discombobulated. His eyes darted all over her body; her smiling face that melted his heart; her small breast that he often envisioned; her strong legs and broad shoulders; and a backside that buckled his knees.

"Forgive me, Red. But you – you drive me crazy," he spoke softly. "Darn it! I'm shaking."

Just as she had promised Johnny that morning, she had returned to the neighborhood. Her first time back since she had left.

"Easy, big guy. Haven't you ever seen a beautiful gal before?" she asked, cracking a smile that made her eyes glitter.

"Not like you." He turned away. Seeing her in a dress fascinated him. *Did she do all this just for me?*

She stood by the kitchen table, sporting a dark green, tight-fitting dress. She moved her well-defined figure in ways she knew would provoke desire in him, her green eyes constantly watching his reaction.

"D—d—d—dresses become you," he said, his eyes again scanning her body and trying not to be noticed, but he didn't fool her. She could hear the quiver in his voice. "You," he paused, afraid to continue. After a deep breath, he asked, "You wear girls' things . . . all the time?"

"Yes."

"Like you," he asked with reluctance, "you prefer us now?" He tapped his chest. "Oh, and I like the perfume."

She decided to have a little fun with him. Holding her chin between her thumb and forefinger, she glanced up at the ceiling as though thinking, then shook her head—solemn faced—as if saying no. As soon as his face displayed his deep disappointment, she exclaimed, "Of course, Johnny. That's why I'm here . . . to let you know I prefer men." She laughed hardily.

Next thing he knew, they knew, they were embracing each other, her grip as tight as his. "You mean you prefer men?"

She nodded. "That's exactly what I mean."

"Welcome back . . . I've missed you so much," he whispered with closed eyes.

"And I missed you," she replied, as she ran her fingers across his lips. She gently parted from the embrace. "Heard you've done a lot with the junkyard. Made it bigger. Made work for the boys. That's great."

"I've been fortunate," he replied. "Thanks to Brogan. But how 'bout you? What've you been doing?"

"A woman of the night," she said, knowingly sending terrible images through his mind; images of her having intercourse with strangers willing to pay for sex. She had to know if he still really cared and she knew saying that would do the job. She watched his face pale and his body slump. She could see he was crushed. *He cares all right.*

Turning away, he said haltingly, "God, I wish ya didn't say that."

"Gotta feed my face, Johnny."

He kept his back to her.

"Look at me," she snapped, grabbing his elbow and pulling at it. "Would you rather I sell my body?"

"Well, isn't that what ya meant?"

"Not at all," she smiled, shaking her head. "I meant *tail diving*. Cleaning out the pockets of those rich bastards. That and a few other little tricks. Dats . . . I mean, that's how I exist." The smile returned to his face, his happy eyes rolled in his head, which made her feel good.

"Still picking pockets, hah?" he asked, repeating what she said.

"Yep. But not by choice. I spent a lot of time learning to read and write. Then I learned numbers. Counting. What you say? Arithmetic, right? Taught I'd get a job *counting*." Then she paused and stepped in his face. Speaking forcefully, she said, "And ya know what? The bosses didn't want girls. Is that the kind of boss you are?"

"Not at all. Why didn't ya come to me? I'd—"

"Pride, Johnny. My pride. Besides . . . I'd become a damn good cat burglar."

Johnny turned serious. "You're kidding, aren't you?"

"Yep. I mean no. But only when I'm hired to do a job. I've done some of the craziest things. I've even climbed tall buildings."

"Stop! You're scaring me." His heart sank. He remembered how he would be terrified when she used to high dive and swing from the derricks and ships masts down by the river.

"All my swimming and rope antics paid off," she answered, flexing her arm muscles. "And I mean climbing buildings. I'd often climb many stories, sometimes as much as seven floors up. At first it scared me. But the more I did it, the more I got used to it. You know those fancy buildings with all the decorative designs on the front. The ledges and ornamental animal shapes. That all made climbing easy. And safe."

"Stop. I heard enough." He shook his head. "Why don't you work for Brogan? A job's guaranteed. Your old job, if you want it." Then he looked at her, remembering what she had said. "If you meant what you said, you should have no qualms about coming back to work with me."

"What'd I say?"

"Remember?" he asked. "We were the best of friends 'until the day we die,' if I got it right."

"You got it right. I didn't forget. And I hope it still stands."

"It does. After all, I never wanted you to leave. I know you had to find yourself, but you should have come right back when you did. I missed the hell out of you."

"Easy. Stop that mushy stuff. Now open your gift!" she insisted, changing the topic.

"You shouldn't have," he said, removing a penknife from his pocket. He cut the twine that secured the package. "Gee wiz! Where did you—" He went silent with astonishment as he laid the books out on the large, highly polished mahogany dining table. Five books in all. His attention went right to English language versions of *The Paris Fire Service* and *The LaFrance Steam Powered-Horse Drawn Fire Engine*. "I've been looking for these. How'd you know what to get?" he asked while opening one of the books. "Oh you're a doll."

"We better get out front. Before the boys think naughty thoughts of us," she said.

"That'd be okay by me," he said, staring her in the eye. "But if you insist." He led the way with a book in hand. "You don't know how happy I am, Red. To see you again."

He stopped at the horse stall and said, "Come, meet our horses." He stroked their manes while gently speaking to them. "Hey, fellas. Meet my good friend, Angela "Red" Hester." The horses 'nosed' Johnny repeatedly, returning his affections.

"Whadda their names?" she asked, rubbing one of them along the jaw line."

"Tisn't that himself?" Tony Bosh shouted, filled with excitement like a child with a new toy, hardly able to restrain himself. He wanted to run over and give Johnny a warmhearted embrace. *But how would that look to these ruffians*, he wondered. "Oh bejasus, it's good to see an O'Hara again," he again shouted.

When Johnny heard his name mentioned with such excitement in the voice, he spun like a top, making eye contact with Tony.

"Who's the big jackass wearing the fine clothes and silly hat?" quipped Red. With hands on her hips and her head cocked, she glared at Tony, as if challenging him. Bosh wisely avoided eye contact with her.

"I know that face," Johnny muttered to Red. Then he heard the man shout, "Johnny O'Hara from Skibereen."

"Tony? Tony Bosh?" asked a startled Johnny O'Hara, his face beaming with joy. Red didn't know what to think.

As if rehearsed, they stepped towards each other, calling each other's name.

"Ach, Johnny, it's good to see you," said Bosh as he hugged him.

"Likewise," said Johnny, returning the embrace. "Let me get a look at the noble Englishman," he continued.

"Good God, man. Don't call me that. I'm an Irishman. Just like you," snapped Tony.

"You look like a man of the town, Tony." Johnny stepped back to study him. "And a handsome bucko, to boot."

"By God, you certainly turned out to be a women's man yourself. And a big one at that. Surely I wouldn't want to meet you in a dark alley," he smiled.

"How the hell did you know where to find me?"

"Ya man here, Battler."

"Battler, why didn't ya tell me he was here?" asked Johnny.

"I wants to surprise ya. So I ask'd ya sister. Knew she'd knows him if he was to be knowd."

That's when Red recognized Tony as the guy she stole the books from. Embarrassed, she slithered away, back towards the kitchen. She wanted to crawl into a hole and disappear.

"Ach, you've got it already," said Tony, disappointment evident in his voice. He pointed to the copy of *Modern Firefighting* that Johnny held in his hand. "Where did you get that?"

"A friend just gave it to me."

"What a coincidence. I just purchased a copy for you. And four other titles. I knew how fond you were of the fire brigade. But they were just stolen."

She stole them, was the first thought that shot through Johnny's mind. He chuckled. "Good minds think alike." Johnny's eyes, searching the crowd for Red, caught a glance of her making a beeline for the kitchen. "I make it my business to read as many books as I can on this topic. Maybe I can help you find those books. Certainly, it would be to me advantage." He smiled. "But it's great to see you."

"And to see you too, Johnny," said Bosh.

"Come, Tony. Let's see if we can't find the books. My good friend back in the kitchen will probably be very helpful."

Upon entering the kitchen, Red approached Tony from behind and asked,, "Did you lose a package of books?" She sounded very sincere.

"Well yes I did," answered the startled Tony Bosh."

Johnny couldn't help but laugh. "Oh, let me introduce you. This is my best friend, Angela Hester, who answers to Red."

Tony shook hands with Red. He sensed the wool was being pulled over his eyes and said, "I somehow thought that my books—the package as you call it—were stolen from me. I didn't know that I had lost them."

"Oh God no," she said, insisting, "I found them lying on a stoop not far from here. And of course once I saw them, decided to give them to me best friend, Johnny. Johnny O'Hara, who is a fireman."

"Yeah, but—"

"And I'm delighted to meet you, sir," she said, again shaking his hand. "Any friend of Johnny O'Hara is a friend of mine."

"But—"

Before he could respond to Red, Johnny, with a fit of laughter, once again stressed his overwhelming joy at seeing his old friend from Skibereen. Wanting this discussion to end, Johnny asked with great enthusiasm, "How long did it take you to find me?"

"I've never been so fortunate," Tony jumped for the bait. Perhaps he, too, wanted the discussion about the books to end, seeing that Red was a close friend of his old friend. "I just started looking for you a couple of hours ago. And the first place I looked, I found you. After coming three *tousand* miles."

"How'd you know where to look?" asked Johnny.

"The barman in the Louvre told me."

"You were there?" Johnny asked.

"Yes. A classy establishment. But I can't say that for the barman. He's no friend of the Irish."

"That's Batesy. He's typical of many of the so-called *gentlemen* who hang there. He's caused us so much hurt. Isn't that right, Red?"

"I felt like hammering him," snapped Tony, cocking his fists.

"Then you bought the books at Fabio's?"

"Oh, yes, those books," he laughed, then turned to Red, shaking his head.

"Oh, I'm so embarrassed," she said. She, too, broke into a laugh. "I just can't lie to you, sir. A friend of Johnny's. I picked ya books over by Eight Avenue."

"On the stoop of a house where a gentleman was talking to a young lady?" he asked.

"Exactly," she said.

Bosh laughed. "You were good."

"That's the choice for a poor girl like me if I want to survive. Sell my body or steal. And I will not sell me body."

"No harm done," said Bosh with a look of satisfaction. He wasn't made a fool of.

"We friends?" asked Red, grabbing for his hand and shaking it. Bosh winced, looking at their gripped hands. "Wow. By golly, you got some grip there, gal."

"She told me she *picked them up* for me," said Johnny. "Apparently, that's exactly what she did; picked them up . . . off that stoop you were on. Now let's just be friends and let me say thank you, Tony."

"For what?" Tony exclaimed.

"For the food me sister fed me. That kept me alive," replied Johnny, again shaking Bosh's hand, this time with both hands. "And it was you, wasn't it, who sent good old Kieran down to the dock with the food for our voyage here?"

Bosh nodded and whispered. "Yes. And I see Roisin's face in yours. How beautiful she was," said Tony, a look of sadness in his eyes. With genuine sincerity, he turned to Red and said, "As beautiful as this woman."

"Ach. Enough of this sentimentality. We need to get together for a night out on the town. We've a lot to talk about," said Johnny.

Bosh enjoyed being in the firehouse, a first-time experience for him. He inquired about the pencil sketch of several union soldiers in field dress with their rifles in hand that hung from one of the kitchen's walls. Johnny explained who the soldiers were, one of them being Michael Brogan, after whom the fire company got its name. Tony found that very interesting, thinking it the proper thing to do, considering the man was a hero.

"Have Tony join us for dinner," said Red.

"I'd love that," said Tony, "But you'll be my guests."

"Not at all. What kind of hosts would we be if we let our guest pay? We'll be eating in one of the finest restaurants in the area. Where a lot of Irish hang out.

"I'd love it. Mingling with me own," Bosh beamed.

"Your own? You're a bloody Englishman," quipped Johnny.

"Not if I can help it. I claim to be an Irishman and I ask to be treated as such," he said in a firm voice. "And besides, I lived there longer than you did."

"Welcome to the Irish race," said Johnny, patting him on the back. "I always said you were a good man. Right Red?"

"That he did," Red confirmed.

"And one more thing, Tony and Red," Johnny said, looking at both of them. "Thanks for the books."

CHAPTER TWENTY-TWO

Charlton Bimsbey's coach cruised along as it made its way toward the Astor House for a 7 PM dinner appointment with Mitchell Fogglemeyer, a prominent banker from Chicago. Fogglemeyer had interests throughout the Midwest, including heavy investments in oil. Also attending was Rockwell Carltan, who represented railroad, insurance, and other financial interests in Pennsylvania. But first, Bimsbey had an important stop to make.

"We're here, sir. Any parking instructions?" the coachman asked as they joined the heavy traffic of Fifth Avenue.

"Not on Fifth, whatever you do. Thirty-third will be fine. Out of the flow of traffic. And people," he grunted.

As conspicuous as his over-sized Brougham coach was, Bimsbey did not like to draw attention to himself. But he loved it when people admired his one-of-a-kind coach, a serious contradiction of his need for privacy. His one-of-a-kind Brougham coach got people's attention not only because of its size, but also because of the detailed images of the giant black stallion that pulled it being painted on the doors.

He had the coach built by the Brougham Coach Company in England and shipped to the U. S.

Once past Fifth, the driver stopped the coach to let his employer out. Like a teenager, the tall 59 year-old jumped from the glossy white coach down onto the slate sidewalk. "I'll be back shortly," he said. He walked smartly and just before turning onto Fifth, he untied his ponytail and let his hair hang. He then adjusted his hair so that it covered his head and face.

The time was after six, dinnertime at the Louvre. Many coaches lined both sides of Fifth, keeping a dung wagon and its operator busy.

Just inside the Louvre, Bimsbey bumped into his front man, Bill Bailey, who greeted customers there. The startled Bailey jumped to attention and began straightening out his tie that didn't need any straightening; his mouth moved as if to talk, but he said nothing.

"Calm yourself," said Bimsbey in a soft but firm tone. "Don't draw any attention."

"Yes, sir. Shall we go to my office?" asked Bailey.

"Yes."

Unnoticed, they wormed their way through the crowd to Bailey's office. There must have been a hundred men at the bar at least two to three deep. The loud buzz of chatter filled the barroom.

Right in the middle of it all were several gents arguing loudly over a recent illegal boxing match between two popular pugilists: Yankee Sullivan, the favorite of the immigrants, and Tom Hyer, the American favorite. The lone fan of the Irish warrior, Yankee Sullivan, was catching a hell of a verbal lashing.

Once in the office, Bimsbey got down to business. "That's Batesy behind the bar, isn't it?" he asked Bailey.

"Yes sir. Is there a problem?" Bailey asked, looking very uneasy.

"Not at all. His eyes," said Bimsbey, "they command respect. I listened to him at the Pavilion last night, but I didn't get a good look at him. That man's a good choice. A natural leader."

Bailey was aghast. "You were there, sir?"

"Yes. I had to see your man in action. He's good. Had them raging mad in no time. I read the reports of the fighting by the firehouse. Hell, his followers took on the police for him. He'll be able to use the charter issue for a while longer. Then there'll have to be something else. Something else to keep them at each other's throats." By then Bailey looked confused, but his confusion quickly disappeared. "The workingmen that is. You see the courage in battle of the Irish Brigade, that 69th. Bull Run, Fredericksburg, Gettysburg, everywhere they fight. They're gaining a lot of respect. I mean, who cannot but admire such courage. There's nothing in our wartime history to compare with their bravery at Mayre's Heights. Nothing. Maybe we should run him for city council. That's a sure way to keep the people divided. You know, us against them." Bimsbey chuckled.

"I've been thinking of that," said Bailey. "I know he'd be interested."

"Good. Now make it your business to get him on the council," said Bimsbey, sounding like he was ordering him.

* * * * *

The immigrants' modern firehouse fascinated Tony. The latest of materials were used in its construction, including electric lights and a gas stove in the kitchen. And the up-to-date bathroom on the second floor had three showers. That wasn't all. A horse drawn fire engine with ladders, many lengths of hose with all the fittings and nozzles they could use, and seating for nine firemen. And, of course, the steam engine was connected to the furnace in the basement, keeping the steam engine always at the ready.

"By golly, man. The stove in the kitchen. I've never seen the likes of that before. How do they cook?"

"Gas. Gas that's piped in right from the street, which is piped underground all the way from the gas works down by the river. Just recently, all these streets were dug up and the gas lines laid. The same with the lighting. It's what they call *electric.* And it runs throughout the building, providing what they call *incandescent* light." Johnny showed him wires that came in through the kitchen wall. "Those wires there. They bring the electric in from the street. From the poles out front that you asked about. You'll find it in many parts of the city now. But don't ask me how it works. Just say it's magic."

"How the hell did ya get permission to bring the gas and incandescent . . . whatever you call it, lighting in here?" asked Red.

"We didn't. We took it on our own to do it. As a matter of fact, most of this place was up before we got the okay to build," said Johnny.

"I'm proud of ya. That's the only way to get what we need. Take it. Hold it. And if they come after it, fight like hell to keep it," said Red, with a low growl. "That's the only way we'll get ahead around here."

Bosh said nothing, but he liked the aggressive attitude of these people. He admired Red's outburst.

Johnny continued, "This is one of the first firehouses in New York to have public sewer and fresh water lines. The water pipes also run under the street. Comes all the way down from up in the country. A place called Croton. The Croton Reservoir. That's what enabled us to have lavatories with running water on both floors. Hell, we even got showers up there," said Johnny, pointing at the ceiling.

"Enough of this. Time to enjoy each other's company," said Red. "Let's go get drunk."

"Think I'll love this place," said Tony.

* * * * *

"What possessed those bloody fools to burn this place?" asked Bosh as they made their way towards the North River Inn. Together, they picked their steps along the mucky, wood plank sidewalk, avoiding the cobblestone piles and pallets of slate earmarked for the new roadway and sidewalks.

"They're Know Nothings. They hate everything foreign. Everything Catholic," said Johnny. "Sound familiar?"

"We're the Papists. And they're the Anglo-Saxons. You know," Red chuckled, poking fun at him. "Just like in Ireland."

"Yes. But like I said, I'm one of you," Bosh replied. "But why?" he pressed.

"In this case it has to do with the firehouse. Yesterday, after many years and many fights, the city council granted us a charter, finally making our *all-immigrant* firehouse legal. The attackers don't want foreigners running fire companies. They don't mind us being firemen, but not leaders. You see, the heads of the fire companies usually become very influential in their communities, often getting elected to the council. In our case, we could knock a native or two out of the box," said Johnny. "Maybe more."

"Screw the humps," barked Red. "They better be afraid. This here man," she pointed to Johnny, "is gonna be running this town one day. And the fire department too. And I'll be right beside him. Right, Johnny?"

"In more ways than one, I hope," he said, making Red blush and bringing a smile to Bosh's face.

"I think I'd want to be on your side, Red. And I mean that," Bosh uttered.

"That's up to you. If you ever get talking to these jerks, tell 'em most of us are native born. Born and raised right here in good old Amerikay." She nodded at Johnny. "And if they don't like it. Well, screw 'em."

Tony took the tough-talking little redhead serious, observing a couple of small scars that cut through her eyebrows and lips; and a u-shaped scar on the cleft of her chin.

"My uncle tells me that the Americans do have legitimate gripes," said Tony.

"Right. And that's what they should be fighting for," said Johnny. "The truth be told, every time the American worker betters his work conditions, along comes the immigrants, who'll work harder and longer. And for less pay. Hell, they should be pissed off. And then comes the coloreds, who undercut the immigrants. It's those no-name humps with the big money that are the problem. They keep us at each other's throats.

"The lot of us, natives, immigrant, and colored alike, should join together and go after the no-names. But the whores would never let that happen."

"Yeah," Red cut in. "But the Yanks don't mind us doing the street cleaning. Picking up all the shit and animal waste. Never heard them complain about that."

"I'm impressed with your logic, old friend," said Bosh, himself several years older than Johnny. "But they still have the right to be pissed."

"You're right. But blaming us is not the answer. Collectively we must bring the benefactors to their knees. Can that be done?"

"Me uncle shares your views on this," said Tony.

When they turned the corner and Red saw the remodeled Shamrock Inn, and the large neon sign with the green lettering, which she knew nothing about, she stopped in her tracks, causing the others to pile up on her.

"Oh, boy! What do we got here? Am I good enough to go in there?" she asked with a chuckle, then answered herself, "Ya damn right I'm going in. Let somebody try to stop me."

"W—w—w—wow! Loo—loo—loo look at this," she sputtered out as she stepped into the completely remodeled entranceway that was a maze of fancy woodwork and stained glass. "Man, I'm gonna like this place."

"You'll always be welcome here," Johnny said. "At least as long as we own it."

"Who's we, Johnny?" she asked.

"Brogan and meself."

Red's entry startled her old friends; especially those who had not seen her earlier wearing the dress. That's why she raised her fists as a warning, then shouted, "I know what you're thinking, and if you know what's good for you, you better not say it."

There were many turned heads, bright smiles and shouts of welcome, but no comments about her dress. One after the other, they stepped forward to greet her. There were hugs and kisses.

"It's great to see you guys too . . . and I really mean that," she said in response to the warm welcome they gave her.

She quickly changed the conversation, not wanting to show emotion. "I don't believe this place," she continued. "All new and shiny. Classy like the Louvre. Look at all the mirrors. Hell, I think I'd eat off the floor."

"Where ya learn da fancy talk, ah?" asked Battler, smiling from ear to ear.

"From the books. The books . . . and a good friend," she answered.

The ceramic floor, looking like a million black and white octagon checkers with shamrock and harp designs mixed in, looked a lot different to the worn wooden floors she remembered. The fancy gas lamps throughout the place gave off a lot of light rather than being dimly lit like it had been under Brady's dominion.

Many voices greeted Johnny, which he acknowledged with his broad smile and a wave of the hand.

"Wow, Johnny," she said in a low voice. "You're a popular guy. You should think about running for alderman."

"Why don't you?" he countered. "You got the looks to be the first woman in the council." They both laughed. "Wait 'til you see the woman's toilet," he continued. "I mean la-va-tory."

"Ya mean shithouse, don't ya?" Battler interjected.

"You're so uncouth," she shot at Battler. "You haven't changed one bit." She smiled when Battler asked, "Wot the hell does dat word mean?"

"What possessed the old man to fix it all up?" she asked, standing in front of the mirrors, patting her thick red hair into place.

"Uh, uh. He's dead and buried," Battler volunteered.

"Sorry to hear that," she said, her smile disappeared. "He was a good man."

An anxious waiter rushed to their side, leading the three of them to Johnny's favorite corner table. "Good to see you, Mr. O'Hara," said the older German immigrant. He was dressed in a black vest over a white shirt and black tie, and a short white apron over black pants. On reaching the table, the smiling waiter reached for O'Hara's favorite chair, but Johnny stopped him. "That won't be necessary," he said.

"Vat you be drinking?" the waiter asked while placing menus before them.

"Get us the best, Karl. Paddys and a lager for each of us," said Johnny.

When Tony skipped off to the bathroom, Johnny slid his chair against hers. He put his arm around her and gave her a gentle squeeze. "Battler was right about the way you speak. I mean I'm impressed. Like you're English is perfect. I'm so damn proud of you." His eyes locked on hers. He pecked her on the cheek, which she affectionately returned.

She felt herself melting in his grip. She wanted to kiss him. She wanted to make love to him right then and there. "Oh thank you, Johnny dear," she gasped. *What's coming over me? And where the hell is that Tony?*

"But now tell me why you bought this place?" she asked, while pushing him back with her elbow. "Doesn't running the yard take up all your time?"

He replied in a whisper, "Between you, me, and the wall, I am running for the city council, for alderman as you called it. It's Brogan's idea. And I got the support of just about all the foreigners. Of all nationalities. When I told him I want to run the fire department, he told me that at the end of the day he would get me appointed as commissioner of the fire department. When it becomes a paid fire department."

"Now I'm really proud of you. My best friend's gonna be a big shyte. Wow," she said.

The waiter arrived with the drinks. Tony returned, slipping almost unnoticed into his chair. Red's eyes were too busy admiring the glass of lager in her hand. "Ya have good beer, Johnny," she said. "Not often ya get a head like this."

"We serve Schafer here. Only the best," said Johnny. "And only the best with the whiskey, too. Paddys and Jamiesons Irish. But we do carry some of that Scotch stuff. Just in case." He stopped to look around at his guests, then said, "We were looking to open a new place near Broadway. We knew it would be risky. Too close to the enemy. But felt we had to take the chance if we were to penetrate the American voters. While we knew Brady's had long been up for sale, we had no interest in it. But my supporters kept pushing me to buy it and make it my headquarters. 'It's in the heart of 'O'Hara Country,' they kept insisting. Then Mulvihey and Sergeant O'Connell told me of Mrs. Brady being bankrupt and that in order to survive she had to sell the place. The rest is history."

As an afterthought, he added, "Remember when me mother passed? Brady offered the place for the wake. Even put up food and drink."

"Indeed, I do," Red said with a nod.

"Speaking of old men, how's yours?" Johnny asked Tony.

"Still about. But as far as I'm concerned, he's dead and buried. And I am sorry to hear about Mrs. O'Hara."

"And Da. Thank you, Tony," he nodded, appreciating the sincerity of his condolences.

"How do you find the time to keep everything going?" Red asked.

"You're right again, Red," said Johnny. I don't have the time to run everything."

"Whadda ya gonna do about it?" she asked.

"Up 'til now, I didn't know. My problem has always been Brogan's absence. While he's a good boss and partner, his being in Colorado is of no help to me here. That forces me to have to run the show by meself. But if there was a third partner—"

"Oops! Time for me to leave?" asked Tony.

"Stay where you are," insisted Johnny. "Someone I could depend on. Capable of keeping our secrets. Someone I can trust to cover my back." He leaned his long torso across the table and put his face inches from Red's. His hands crept up from his lap and cupped hers, sending a charge through both of their bodies. "Well? What about it?"

With a startled look in her eyes, she asked, "You asking me . . . to be a partner?"

"Exactly."

"You gotta be kidding. With what?"

Without answering her, he turned to Tony and said, "Now back to you, my friend, who is your uncle?"

"Jacob Bosh."

"Not *the* Jacob Bosh of textile fame?"

"That's him, old boy," said Tony.

"The brother of the cruel Lord Hennington Bosh?" asked Johnny, astonished.

"Yes, and to save you having to ask the question, no, he's not like me father. Jacob's a gentleman. Fair to the people who work for him. And he treats Americans and immigrants as equals."

"Bartender," Red shouted, waving her hand. "These glasses are empty."

"What brings you to the states?" asked Red.

"My uncle Jacob. He wants that I should work for him. He respects my decision to walk out on his brother. And that I turned my back on his fortune. He, too, despised my father for how he treated his tenants. How he could let so many starve . . . die."

The waiter arrived with fresh drinks and removed the empty glasses. "Are you ready to order?" he asked.

"Can I suggest the T-bone?" said Johnny, as the three of them downed their Paddys.

Red gulped her beer to cool the burn of the whiskey. "Why not? You're picking everything else for us," she laughed, raising her empty whiskey glass and half-finished lager.

Johnny turned beat red, momentarily lost for words. Then he laughed hardily. "I love it. I love it," he said, baffling Red.

"Love what? What ya talking about?" she snapped.

"I just love that horseshoe," he quipped.

"What horseshoe?" asked Red, not having an inkling of what he was talking about.

He paused for another hardy laugh that she didn't appreciate. "The one on your chin," he said as he reached over and touched the u-shaped scar. "How did ye get that one?"

Even though she looked angry, she burst into laughter. "Probably a toe or a heel," she said, again with a robust laugh.

Red and Johnny's laughter had Tony confused. "How's that funny? What do you mean 'a toe or a heel?'" he asked, sparking even more laughter.

"She got kicked in the face and doesn't remember if it was the toe of a boot or the heel."

"My God," said Tony, shaking his head. He found nothing funny about it. "How can you laugh at that?"

"But she's still as beautiful as ever. And I— "

"Barman, you can bring another round," Tony shouted after the waiter.

"When's the last time you saw your father, Tony?" asked Red.

"Must be two years. And we've not communicated since."

"That's interesting," said Johnny. "We're all without family. Red here's been on her own since she was nine." He smiled. "Luckily, she had me as her best friend. Right?"

"Yeah, best friends. *'Til* the day we die . . . and I didn't lose my mother. She abandoned me."

* * * * *

At 7 pm sharp a smartly-dressed waiter seated Charlton Bimsbey. Already seated at the odd-sized table in their private dining room inside the Astoria House were his two associates, Mitchell Fogglemeyer and Rockwell Carltan, both with their gold-colored napkins in place. The three of them were fellow Republicans and big-time supporters of President Lincoln. Like Bimsbey, their money, too, had tentacles that spread everywhere in the business world. Most of these tentacles found specialized connections that benefited from the wartime economy, producing anything and everything the military needed. All part and parcel of their support for Lincoln.

The redwood dining table they sat at was unusual in size, each side being nine feet long. Fogglemeyer did not like to be crowded while he ate and drank his lager. He needed room around him.

"Charlton, I must advise you that I am partaking in this discussion under protest," said the highfaluting Rockwell Carltan, raising Bimsbey's eyebrows.

"I beg your pardon. Just what does that mean?" challenged Bimsbey.

"This table is criminal. Never again invite me to dine with you over a redwood table."

"And what is this all about, my dear friend?" asked Bimsbey.

"The Redwoods are a national treasure," Rockwell continued. "I am a dead serious backer of the campaign in Washington to stop the destruction for profit of the Redwoods. That whole area in California must be declared a Federal preserve. Those magnificent trees must be left to nature. Many of them are over one thousand years old."

"Why, that's the height of hypocrisy? You, who cares nothing about the welfare of his employees and you, who led the successful charge in Philadelphia to create a paid fire department—like me, of course—is concerned about the welfare of a bunch of damned trees."

"That's the way it is, my dear friend, Charlton. So the next time we meet, just make sure there's no redwood furniture about. I thank you."

"It won't be long now until we have a paid fire department right here in New York. Tell me, how is your new fire department progressing in Philly?"

"It took a while," said Rockwell, "but they're proving to be quite effective and problem free. They put the fires out and are saving us considerable money."

"That's great," said the visibly pleased Bimsbey. "I'll make sure that information gets to Albany, where the legislature is considering a measure to create a paid fire department for the city, the Metropolitan Fire District. But enough of that. Let us get on with our business," said Bimsbey, his eyes on the half a roast duck he was pulling apart with his hands. "These worker's unions are becoming a real problem. They must be stopped. Crushed if need be. By that I mean the working people must be kept divided. I am talking about all of them, the Americans, the immigrants and the coloreds. You see how the hotel and restaurant waiters, both white and colored, joined together and have won concessions and higher wages. That's no good!" He pounded the redwood.

Rockwell agreed with a nod and said, "Amen. They are striking at two of my plants and that damned mayor will not send the police in to crush them."

"Well, in all fairness to those people," said Bimsbey, "they are entitled to share in a small way the big, big profits we are making from the war? And remember, we are only talking about union members. Not the immigrants and certainly not the coloreds. This will work to our advantage. A small increase in wages will further divide them."

"You call that fairness, Charlton? Next thing you'll be asking that Brogan's man, that O'Hara person, gets a top post in the new fire department."

"Never," snapped Bimsbey. "I'd never support a papist for such a position. Especially an Irish one. Never."

Rockwell knocked over his half-full glass of wine. "Damn it," he snapped. Still looking at Bimsbey, he motioned with his fingers to the waiter to clean up his mess. "You were saying, Charlton."

"I would recommend that you and all your patriotic associates make certain you hire immigrants and where possible, coloreds. Isn't that what that man there would want us to do?" Bimsbey directed their attention to a large portrait of President Abraham Lincoln that hung above a monstrosity of a fireplace.

His eyes half closed, the sly looking Fogglemeyer asked, "Well, what's that supposed to mean?"

"They don't strike. They take what they can get. And it will serve as a lesson to our American boys. They better not push for better wages or they might lose their jobs to an immigrant. And I'm talking about across the board. All jobs."

"Were you involved in any way with that fire house incident last night?" asked the wily-eyed Fogglemeyer.

"Let's just say that people are being groomed for important political positions that will enable us to keep the turmoil stewing between the working classes. Politics and education is the way forward."

"Meaning what?" asked Rockwell.

"Simple. Keep them uneducated and make sure they don't hold political office. You see, times are changing. It's no longer just a clean-cut issue of Americans versus foreigners. The war has changed all that. That "Fighting 69th with all its heroes. Most of them were Irish. Even the Rebs praised them. By the time this war's over, they'll be pretty well accepted by society. The immigrants will have proved themselves as Americans."

"Democracy doesn't really mean anything when it comes to money. It's the rich against the poor," said Rockwell.

Fogglemeyer then asked, "I assume New York's big money is all together on this?"

"Yes," Bimsbey chuckled aloud. "The *no names* are united. All but one. Jacob Bosh. But I don't think he'd intentionally go against our wishes. I've been advised that his sole heir, who is just like him, is now with him. And I understand that although he's an Englishman by birth, he purports to be an Irishman. He has to be watched if he remains here."

"I have the fullest respect for that man," said Bimsbey looking up and pointing at Lincoln's portrait. "I pray that the North wins and Lincoln puts an end to that scourge of slavery; A curse that has torn our nation apart. And shame on my native England for bringing it to this great nation."

* * * * *

The waiter removed their empty dishes. Not a morsel of food remained other than the three meatless bones and a few breadcrumbs. Red ordered another round of drinks, the same. They were feeling the Paddys.

"Does he have a job for you," asked Johnny.

"Yes," Tony said. "I'll take over when he retires or passes on. I have my own coach and driver to chauffeur me around the city for business and pleasure."

"Shyte," Red laughed. "You got a carriage too, right Johnny?"

He nodded his head. "Yeah. When I need one."

"When am I *gonna* – going to have one?" she asked.

"Good evening, Johnny O'Hara," said a woman in passing, who he graciously acknowledged.

"I'm sure if you were my partner in this place, it wouldn't be long before you'd have your own coach."

"How could I afford that?" she asked in a serious tone.

"Oh, I'm sure you got enough stashed away, knowing how good you were in your recent line of work, from which you since *retired*. Am I right or wrong?"

"Wise guy, hah?" She grinned, finishing her beer. By now her voice had a slur to it.

"Tony," he asked, "That bartender at the Louvre. That Batesy guy. I'll give you a little advice. He's bad, bad. Hurt a lot of people. He organized that attack last night, just as he did back in '55 when me mother was shot dead."

Tony gasped. "Good grief, man! I'm so sorry." He joined his hands as if praying.

"It's a long time ago, now. He didn't do the shooting. One of his men did. But he makes these things happen. So be careful with him," Johnny warned.

"Did they catch the killer?"

"No!" Red cut in. "Like he disappeared off the face of the earth. By the way, the food was delicious."

"Sure the empty plates will attest to that," laughed Tony.

"As much as I miss the old man, I don't miss the dirt of the place," said Red. "Right, boss? Hell, we can eat off this floor."

"You probably could, but please don't try it."

"Well, no fault to the company, but I'm bushed," said Tony.

"Don't be a party pooper," Red cut him off. "Have one more before we call it quits."

"No. Not for me. I need a good night's sleep. Tomorrow's to be a busy day. But before I go, tell me how you snatched me books without me seeing you?"

Red laughed. "Easy. You weren't even sitting yet. You'd just left the books down and turned to sit by Ellen. She made sure you would not see me. I just reached out from inside the window and lifted the package."

He laughed. "Yes, she is a good looker. Hmmm. Maybe I'll see her on my way back. That's if I can find my way back."

"Don't concern yourself. Battler and Hans will do the honor. Just tell them where to take you."

"How 'bout me?" asked Red.

"I'll be your escort," said Johnny. "If ya don't mind me taking care of some business at the yard?"

"I'm in no hurry," she said. "I'm sure we got a lot to talk about."

* * * * *

Brogan's office was adorned with fancy woodwork, dark baroque wall covering and carpeting, including a few expensive looking paintings. And rightly so, this office was also used for entertaining customers.

Johnny offered her a drink, which she accepted.

"I don't have any business here. Just wanted to be alone with you," he said as he walked over to the bar. "Just want to stare at your face. That lovely face I've missed seeing for so long."

She smiled. "Well, you got your wish. What do you want to talk about?"

"About you. What did you do for a living while you were away?" he asked. He set two glasses on the bar top, poured the liquor into them, and then added a splash of water, stirring each with his finger.

"Different things."

"Be specific," he said, licking his finger and handing her a Paddys and water.

"Why . . . why talk about me?" she said.

"Why? Because I missed you. Missed talking to you."

"Missed you too. Enough to realize I'm not a fairy."

"At least I have a chance now," he said.

"A chance for what?"

"To be more than just a best friend."

"Looking for something, Johnny?" she challenged him, insulting him.

"God, you're a tough one. Yeah, maybe I am." He wanted to be angry, but couldn't help thinking of her bad history with men.

"What's that, Johnny? My womanhood?"

"Yeah. That's exactly what I want," he barked. Then, with the help of the Paddys, he gripped her shoulders and pulled her to him. "But not without your heart."

She did not resist, keeping her eyes on his.

He kissed her hard on the lips then snapped his head back all apologetic.

"Oh I'm so sorry. Red. I—"

She put her finger to his lips. "Stop, before you make a fool of yourself. It's okay, Johnny." In that instant she realized how much he meant to her, how much she wanted him. She wanted to scream out: Take me. Take my heart."

"Did you ever think about me . . . in that way?" Johnny asked.

"Yes. Often. That's why I'm here."

Their breathing grew shallow as their bodies trembled with desire.

"Better change the subject. Or we'll need the fire department," she chuckled, taking a deep breath.

"I'm," he groaned. "I'm running for alderman. Against our old adversary."

"Adversary?" she questioned. "I don't know that one yet."

"Our enemy. Hear he's got big money behind him. But I got Brogan behind me. And a lot of support in the community. Just being foreman of the fire company alone could get me elected. Actually, my campaign will be starting in a couple of days. Let me show you."

She followed him into an adjoining room. With a twist of a silver colored gas valve, he brightened the glow of three gas lamps.

"As I told you before, all I want out of it is to run the department. Chief Engineer John O'Hara."

"I figured that," she said. "Just because I've been away doesn't mean I haven't been following the fire company . . . and what you were doing. I read the newspapers. I am just as concerned about the plight of the volunteers. I know they wanna get rid of us. And I'm smart enough to know that those bums with all the money usually get what they want."

"Although I am a volley at heart, I am realistic, too," he said. "The insurance companies are losing too much money because of our recklessness. Volleys would rather fight each other than fight the fires," he laughed. "Insurance wants a fire department that would be answerable to the mayor and city council. I would give it all to be chief engineer. Of course, that is with you by my side as my deputy."

"And I'd be your biggest supporter, Johnny," she said. "But is it possible? Where's your clout?"

"Brogan's me clout. With his money, anything is possible. And he's already told me he would back me fully, regardless of the outcome of the election."

"But in a paid fire department with only men, I'd never get to fight a fire again. I wouldn't like that," she said.

"You'd be too busy between being my assistant here in the firehouse and running the saloon."

Rubbing her fingers together, she asked, "How much of this would I need?"

"Half. Half of what I paid. How much ye got?" he asked.

"What was your share of the partnership?" she asked.

"Two thousand," he lied.

"I can handle half," she said. "How much for the work you've done on it?"

"We can work that out," he said, his face aglow. He couldn't hide his delight. As a partner, she would always be nearby and that's what he wanted. "Shall I call you partner?"

"Sure." She smiled broadly, feeling the effects of the alcohol.

Again he pulled her to him, embracing her; instantly aroused by the feel of her.

Feeling safe, she returned his embrace, resting the side of her face against his powerful chest. She could feel his hardness against her stomach.

He kissed the top of her head, then her forehead. Then their lips met, but only briefly, before she pushed him back. "It's getting awful hot in here. Do you feel the heat, Johnny?"

"Oh God I do," he said, his voice slurring a bit.

Again she smiled, but said nothing.

"Where're you staying tonight? You're welcome to stay with me," he said.

"Johnny. You crazy? I'd probably I wind up having a baby."

"Ah, but Katie lives with me," he said. "We best get outside before I attack you."

"As long as Katie's there, I'd love to stay. Just like old times. You got me something to rest me head on?" she asked.

"In deed. A proper bed just for you, in a private room," he said.

"Where the hell do you live?"

"In a new building. Even has a tub for a bath. Not like the old days." He laughed. "It's one of the buildings I partner with Brogan."

"You've done well, haven't you? I mean a saloon, partners in a couple of tenements."

"And I'm sole owner of another."

"Damn, I feel jealous."

"Why the hell did you have to leave?" he snapped. "You could have been part of it all."

They were both feeling their liquor, which loosened their lips.

"Well. Maybe one day what I have will be yours, too." He stared at her, waiting for an answer.

"What does that mean?" she asked.

"You know what I mean. Aw shit! I'd better shut me mouth."

Again she smiled, but said nothing.

"Let's get out of here before we get in trouble," he said.

"Good idea."

"One more thing. Here's what I wanted to show you." He opened a closet door, revealing shelves stacked with handouts and posters. "This is just the beginning."

"What's all this?" she asked.

"For my campaign." There were thousands of handbills and hundreds of placards and posters.

* * * * *

This is far enough, gents. I must see that young lady," said Tony, his index finger pointing at Ellen across the street.

"Ya knows who she is?" asked Battler. "Wot she does, I mean?"

"Yes. I met her on the way over," he said as they departed. He ran across the street, avoiding a couple of fast-moving carriages.

"Good evening, Ellen," he shouted, feeling good from the drink.

"And good evening to you," she said. "To what do I owe the pleasure of your presence?"

"My package of books that were stolen here today. I thought you'd want to know that I reclaimed them."

"You did, did you?" she said. She perked up, crossed her arms as if getting real serious.

"And guess where I found them?"

She gave him a guarded look, not knowing what to expect. "Where might that be?"

"On the kitchen table in the new firehouse."

"How did the books get there?" she asked, playing dumb.

"Your lovely friend, Red, gave them to Johnny O'Hara as a gift. Believe it or not, but that's the very same reason I procured them, to give them to him as a gift. I knew Johnny when we were kids. The science of fires and their extinguishment always fascinated him."

By now she knew he knew. "I'm very happy that you found them. I have to get inside," she said, trying to get away from him.

"Oh, please let me finish. I know you were the decoy who set me up."

She started for the door, but he stepped in front of her in a most unthreatening way. "But that's not why I am here."

"Oh yeah. Then why are you here?"

"Because I still want you to join me for lunch. What do you say?"

She laughed. "You got some line there, boyo." She paused, contemplating his request. "Why not? I'll be here tomorrow at noon."

* * * * *

"Tony, today you're going to meet some of the people who run this town," said his uncle Jacob Bosh. "Soon enough you will be one of them." The senior Bosh spoke from his simple wooden swivel chair that faced his seventh-floor office window, overlooking the North River.

Tony's eyes narrowed. His lips moved before the words came out. "I don't . . . understand. Be one of them?" Tony moseyed over to the window to take in the view. "My God, we're so high up. It scares me," he said, gasping as he stepped back.

"You'll get used to it, young man," said Jacob.

"Of what? Being one of them, or the height."

"Both, I guess."

"Soon, when I retire . . . I'll expect you to take over much of the daily operations of my interests." Jacob watched Tony's reaction, looking for fear in his eyes. To his pleasure, he saw none. "You will be in charge."

Tony stared at him. Again, his mouth moved as if speaking, but there were no words forthcoming. Just "hum-a-hum-a-hum-a."

"Well, say something, young Bosh. Say what's on your mind."

"You . . . you don't even know me. You don't know if I'm even capable of what you expect," said Tony. "Oh, I'm honored by your confidence. And I certainly want to fulfill your expectations of—"

"Well, can you meet my expectations?"

"I assure you I can. Totally." Tony's expression of self-confidence satisfied Jacob Bosh.

"Settled, Mr. Chairman . . . of the Board that is. We have a 1:30 appointment with Charlton Bimsbey."

"Oh no! I have an important appointment at noon," pleaded Tony. He gave Jacob a pathetic look.

"Do what you have to do, but be back here no later than one." The old man was firm in his warning.

"Bless you, Uncle—"

"Stop that nonsense," Jacob snapped. "Just don't be late."

"Who is Bimsbey?" asked Tony, stepping in front of a wardrobe mirror for a last minute check of his attire. *This is an odd place for a wardrobe*, he thought.

Jacob laughed. "One of those faceless, nameless bastards who run the economy. Who keeps workingmen at each other's throats."

"Is he richer than you, Uncle Jacob?"

Jacob, not known to have a sense of humor, forced a smile. "Go on. Get out."

* * * * *

Tony was determined to be on time for his lunch date. The looks of that lady of the night and her wit brought back precious memories of his reckless days living amongst Dublin's destitute. He would value her company.

Again, he hurried west on thirty-third street, expecting to find her on the stoop, but from the distance he didn't see her there, knocking the wind out of his sails.

Shit a prostitute standing me up. I don't believe this, he thought.

251

By the time he got to her stoop, he was thoroughly annoyed. "The bloody bitch!" he muttered. "Why, I'm gonna—oh shit!"

All she saw from inside the doorway when their eyes met was his angry puss. "What's wrong there, Tony?" she asked, with an ear-to-ear smile. "Did ya think I wouldn't show?"

Tony stood silent for a moment with his mouth open, then answered, "Yes. Precisely. But you're here and that's what counts."

She saw genuine gratitude on his face. *This guy's really happy to see me*, she thought. *He must be horny as hell.*

"Well, come up to my room and we'll get on with it," she said.

"Now you are insulting me. I thought we were going to lunch?"

"Lunch!" She was taken aback. Her surprised look turned to a pleasant smile. "You were serious, weren't you?"

"Where do you prefer to eat," he asked.

"The Rambling House. Good food. Good folks."

"By the way, are you giving out your last name?" he asked.

"I don't mind telling you. It's McBride. Ellen McBride. But ya still got to pay for me time, you understand? No freebees here," she said. Immediately, she sensed his hurt. "Now, what's the puss for?"

Snapping his head back, he mimicked a pleading child. "You're breaking my heart, Miss Ellen. I'm here for the pleasure of your company. That's all."

"Sorry, Tony. But this is my work time. I gotta get paid for my time. I got bills to pay, too, you know. Maybe some other time. But not during me work hours."

"How much do you get for intercourse?" he asked, speaking bluntly.

She laughed as she responded. "Ten big ones."

"What's so funny?" he asked.

"You're so proper. 'How much do you get for intercourse?' We call it a 'lay' or 'a shag.'"

"Here's for your time," he said, handing her a ten-dollar bill.

"I don't want your charity, boyo," she snapped, her neck stiffening.

"Now you're offended," he said. "Don't you understand, I just want the pleasure, yes, I mean the pleasure . . . of your company. I enjoyed very much the few moments we spent chatting the other day."

"You're really serious, aren't you?" she asked. "Oh what the hell." She smiled. "Why not? But first, get rid of that coat and tie. *Dem* duds would cause you problems where we're going." She took the garments and left them somewhere inside, beyond the foyer door.

"First you have to promise me my duds won't wind up in Red's hands."

She smiled, then asked in jest, "Red who?"

Unlike his previous trip through the area, this time there were many people about. All of a sudden he sensed people watching him as if they knew he was going to 'have intercourse with this prostitute.' Then in a flash, he cleared his mind of those thoughts. *Bloody hell! Who gives 'a damn hell all' what they think?* He smiled and proudly held his head high all the way to the diner.

The Rambling House was a workingman's place all right. It was lunch hour and some of the dirtiest of the dirty workingmen sat amongst men wearing suits with white shirts and ties, and nobody gave a damn who sat next to them.

* * * * *

"So, Jacob, this is the young man you've been telling me about?" asked Bimsbey. "He'll certainly get the attention of the fair sex." He watched Tony, waiting for his reaction, to begin feeling him out. He never offered to shake young Bosh's hand.

"I'll have to keep that in mind, Mr. Bimsbey. Especially when I'm turned down by those young ladies." Tony laughed and so did the others.

"He has a sense of humor. Not like you, Jacob," said Bimsbey. Grinning pleasantly, he motioned them to take seats at a long, rectangular conference table at the other end of the large room that also served as his office.

The extreme grandiosity of the office enthralled Tony. Right away he compared it to the starkness of his uncle's office. Both offices were identical in size and layout. Yet Bimsbey's office looked like a totally different room.

It was the plushness and flamboyance of everything in the office that impressed Tony; everything was luxurious. All the chairs in the office were colored white and over-stuffed with their backrests shaped like diamonds and studded with gold-colored buttons. The dark, multi-colored drapes were separated wherever there was a window.

An exceptionally thick Oriental rug covered an area of the floor thirty feet by thirty feet. With the exception of the wall behind his desk, the corner walls that consisted of side-by-side windows were trimmed with a gaudy, dark red and green floral design wallpaper that also covered the windowless walls. Through the winding flowers passed vertical lines.

Every piece of wood trim, whether used as baseboards, casings or decoration, was elaborate and hand carved, unusually large and ornate, and painted bright gold. With its two huge crystal chandeliers hanging from the ceiling, Tony imagined the room as a mini-ballroom. He found it all to be strange and overpowering.

He noticed that Bimsbey kept glancing up at a painting of a young woman with red hair that hung behind his desk.

My God, she's lovely, thought Tony. "Who's that beautiful, wee lassie?" he asked.

"The Angel," Bimsbey replied.

"I just met a spitting image of that face," said Tony, picturing Red's face. "Also with red hair. The resemblance is unbelievable."

"Where?" asked Bimsbey in the most serious of tones. His face paled; his smile disappeared. "Where did you see this face?"

Bimsbey's reaction startled Tony. "By the new immigrant firehouse," he said, his eyes glued to the painting. "Bloody hell. They're identical." Then the painting next to Angel's caught his eye. *I've seen that before. But where,* he wondered. Then it came to him: a duplicate rendering, the mural over the bar in the Louvre. The black stallion pulling that humongous white carriage with an image of the stallion painted on the door and *Blackie* over it.

"That's a strong Irish accent you have?"

"I spent most of my life in Ireland," answered Tony.

"Is this why we're here? To talk about your female fantasies, Charlton?" snapped Jacob, who had no time for his *meaningless banter*. "If I remember correctly, the purpose of our meeting is for me to introduce you to my partner. My first partner ever, who will be an equal partner in every way, including our meetings on the future of industry and labor here in New York and elsewhere." He tapped a pencil against a glass of water.

"Poor Jacob. I hope your nephew does not share your lack of humor." Bimsbey raised his glass of water to his mouth and took a swallow.

There were soft taps on the office door.

"Come in," Bimsbey grunted. The door opened.

"Mr. Morgan, sir," said Miss Bentley, a matronly middle-aged woman, sounding very formal.

"Ah Leonard, my good man. C'mon in and meet our new associate, Jacob's nephew," said Bimsbey.

"Tony Bosh is the name, sir," he said in a very self-confident manner. "It is indeed a pleasure, or should I say honor, for me to meet such people as yourself and your equally esteemed associate, Mr. Bimsbey."

"Listen to him, will you. Brash. Full of self-confidence. I love it," said the pleasantly surprised Morgan, a short, squat man who was conservatively dressed in an unsullied brown pinstriped suit.

Tony, who was himself taken back by his sudden forcefulness, saw the delight in both Morgan and Bimsbey's reaction.

"Jacob. You know how to pick 'em. Assertive. That's what we're all about," said Bimsbey, his eyes still glued to Tony. "Young Bosh, we are what you call the faceless, nameless few; the people who shape the lives of the society we live in. We create the economy that produces the jobs the working trash fight over."

Bimsbey expected Tony to comment and when he didn't, Bimsbey goaded him. "You understand, young man?"

That's how it works here. I thought this was a democracy. For the people, by the people, and with the people, is it? Tony sensed all eyes were on him. "Trash sir. Just whom might I ask is the trash? Are you referring to the lords and politicians, sir?" Tony laughed.

"Ha, ha, ha." Bimsbey and Morgan feigned a hardy laugh.

"A great sense of humor," said Morgan, as he looked toward Bimsbey, still wearing a smile.

"No, not at all," said Bimsbey, his smile hardening. "The politicians, most of those scoundrels are our friends. The trash I refer to is the workingman. Like the people you met over at the new firehouse." Bimsbey paused, staring at Tony and awaiting his reaction. When there was none, he said, "Those people who want to take from us what is ours." Again he looked at the painting on the wall of the young lady behind his desk. Motioning his head, he said, "Like her. That poor thing wanted what wasn't hers."

So far, Tony did not like Bimsbey. But he had no problem hiding his feelings. Wisely, he maintained his cheerful demeanor; his youthful smile. He did not want to let Uncle Jacob down, nor did he want to ruin it for himself.

"Jacob, didn't you tell him there are no lords over here? That we chased them back to England," said Bimsbey, still smiling.

"You sound just like an Irishman," said Morgan. "Are there any Irish left in Ireland or did they all come here to good old New York?" He laughed with scorn, flaunting his dislike for the Irish.

"Please! Let us get on with our business," demanded Jacob Bosh. Frowning himself, he challenged Morgan, "Leonard, if I didn't know better, I'd think you are trying to provoke my nephew."

"Yes," said Morgan. "It is important that he be convinced of just who the enemy is. I sense that Tony is a little thin-skinned when it comes to the Irish. The very people who would love to take from us what is rightfully ours. I am talking about our hard-earned wealth."

Tony nodded. "Yes sir, Mr. Morgan. That's becoming clear. Very clear." He reacted in such a way as to make them think he supported their anti-workingman rhetoric. He knew well that his every reaction to every view articulated by Jacob's business associates was being closely monitored. He well knew that any negative reaction on his part could be his downfall. He intuitively sensed that he could do much more good for his friends by being part of this group, than not. And besides, he owed his cooperation to his uncle, who he knew would be his mentor.

"Another point you must be aware of," Morgan cut in, "is the threat posed to us by these upstart labor unions. I am sure Jacob has filled you in on them."

"Yes. Yes," said Tony. "The workingman uniting to bring pressure on their employers."

Morgan continued, "How do you perceive them?"

"As a detriment to us all, of course. What else? That is the vehicle they would use to try to steal from us our hard earned wealth." Tony nodded toward Bimsbey, which he returned. "But won't our friends in government take appropriate measures to keep them in check?"

"Not necessarily. Like I said, not all of them are our friends," said Bimsbey.

"I've noticed also," continued Tony, "there are two, maybe three groups to be concerned with, and please tell me if I am wrong. There are the Americans, the immigrants, and soon to be in the workplace freed slaves. Or the darkies. Whatever they're called."

"Very astute, I must say," said Bimsbey. "God forbid these people ever join forces and come after us. I don't know if we could keep the upper hand. After all, I mean manipulating and controlling them is how we make our fortunes."

"It's obvious we must keep them divided. Am I right, fellow gentlemen?" asked Tony.

"Right you are," said Bimsbey. "I think young Bosh is going to do very well."

Morgan signaled agreement as to his satisfaction with this young man they have apparently welcomed into their group.

Bimsbey changed the course of the discussion. "We'll put Bailey's man, Batesy, up for the special election for alderman."

Bloody hell. Does he mean that barman, Tony wondered.

"Tony. You're frowning. Do you know Batesy? You've a problem with the man?" asked Bimsbey.

"Sure he'd not get one Irish vote. He hates them with a passion. Can't hide the fact neither," said Tony. His eyes beaming, he glanced sideways at Bimsbey and said in his finest Irish accent, "Sure he doesn't have the charm of an Irishman. And sure an Irishman can steal the heart away."

Tony's rhetoric raised Bimsbey's eyebrows. "Ahhhh," groaned Bimsbey, nodding his head, and at the same time, feeling his ponytail as if looking for something to do with his hand.

"What special election?" Jacob cut in.

Bimsbey, looking like the devil he was, replied, "That Mulvihey fellow dropped dead. His seat has to be filled and we have two months to fill it with one of ours."

With furrowed eyebrows, Bimsbey asked Jacob, "Who would you propose?"

"Someone who could garner immigrant votes. And to answer your next question, no I don't have any suggestions."

"I'd be a good Irishman," said Tony. "I have the charm and the wit, you know."

"You wouldn't be pushing yourself, would you?" said Morgan with a chuckle.

"No. But if I were drafted. Forced to run by popular demand, that is, I'd have no choice."

Tony saw this as an opportunity to split Batesy's support.

"Tony. What in God's creation are you doing?" snapped the mesmerized Jacob Bosh.

Again Bimsbey shook his head. "I don't believe this," he said. "Up until a few minutes ago, I didn't know you existed. Now I'm considering you as a likely candidate for an important elected position that I must control. Ugh, pardon me; that we must control." He smiled, looking at both Morgan and Jacob. Bimsbey had no intention of backing the young, unknown Bosh, even though he would make it look like he would if Tony wanted it.

"Who'll be his opponent?" asked Morgan.

Bimsbey said, "I'm sure that our Irish associate has already picked someone. With that said, I must adjourn this meeting. I have other pressing matters that also require my attention. Good day, gentlemen."

He walked with them to the door. "Young Bosh, can I have a private moment with you?"

"Yes sir." He remained in the room. When the door shut, Bimsbey stepped close beside him and speaking softly, not quite whispering, said: "I didn't think it would be possible for there to be another woman that could look like her," poking his chin at the woman's portrait. "What's the young lady's name?"

"Angel Hester. She's known as Red," he replied.

Bimsbey did an instant about face, looking away from Tony. "Please, leave," he snapped, his face turning pale, his legs wanted to give out from under him. It wasn't easy to unnerve Bimsbey, but on hearing Red's name, he was shaken to his core.

What's his problem, wondered Tony, feeling brushed aside.

CHAPTER TWENTY-THREE

"The best of lighting. And a ceramic floor. It's all good. Just like the Louvre," he added, staring at the highly polished flooring. "Many say better."

"How'd you know that?" asked Johnny.

"*Ya* think I was never there?" asked Brogan. "Remember. If you have money, everybody's your friend. Even your declared enemies. Everybody with money visits the Louvre."

"I hope I didn't go overboard on this place?"

"Not at *'tall*. You've done a hell of a job," said Brogan. "This is big time."

Thomas Brogan checked every nook and cranny in the North River Inn. He loved it and admired all the newest conveniences, including twice as many wall-hung gaslights along the walls. They gave off a much brighter glow than the old style and the flame in each of them could be adjusted—to be dimmed or brightened at will—with the turn of one knob. "And it will help your campaign immensely. Just about every voter from the ward will be stopping in. Ya know why?" Brogan slapped his shoulder.

"Tell me," said Johnny.

"To meet the Democratic Party's candidate." Brogan poked Johnny's chest. "Our next alderman, Johnny O'Hara."

Johnny shook his head. He trusted Brogan's insight. "Already I feel like a winner."

"And at the right time I'll get a story placed in the *Herald*. That will draw many curiosity seekers."

* * * * *

The crowd was unusually low-keyed as the big man and Johnny moved about the Inn. No matter what the crowd appeared to be doing, they all kept an eye on the big man, Thomas Brogan, who most of them knew well, and he, likewise. His immense wealth had given him a God-like status in the community. Some of the people who knew him well, now stayed out of his path, which Brogan did not appreciate. But being tired from the long trip, he didn't much mind. He just wouldn't have the time to socialize with everyone. But to show his good nature, he treated the house to lunch and a drink.

"Do you really think the folks over at the Louvre would come here?" asked Johnny.

"Oh absolutely. If they want my support with their questionable projects they want pushed through at the council. As a matter of fact, some of our enemies are over there talking you up."

Johnny chuckled in disgust. "Where's their loyalty? Seems like people in power, regardless of their positions in life, seems are all bull-shyte. Nothing more than *liars.* "

Brogan smiled. "Correct. They are all like politicians. Self-serving whores. With few exceptions." He waved a hundred dollar bill. "This is their loyalty."

"You mean in Batesy's home base they're talking me up?"

"Exactly."

"Whores. I mean they're sickening," said Johnny.

"Exactly. That's the common criminality of politics. Now, to change the subject, those chandeliers. Waterford I'm sure. They're the finest I've ever seen and grander than that English shit they have over in the Louvre. And not because they're Irish. This place belongs over on Fifth . . . I'd say the North River Inn is now the finest club in the ward. Old man Brady would flip in his box. And with me and Red running your campaign, you can't lose."

"But you'll remember, won't you, Tom? At the end of the day, I want to be top man in that new fire department they keep talking about," Johnny asserted.

"That will come to pass. And you will be on top. But first you have to become well known and popular, not just in your home ward, but throughout the city. And the way to do that is to hold a prominent office. And to do things in the council that gets you written up in the newspapers."

Johnny shook his head. "Can I afford this campaign?"

Brogan raised his hand. "Hold it, boyo. Who said anything about spending *your* money? The Party and I will finance it. That's the way it works. Of course, you'll be expected to give preferential treatment to those who helped you get elected." Brogan hunched his head and nodded.

"I will not be a yes man. Please, Thomas. Don't—"

Again, with a wave of the hand, Brogan silenced Johnny. "I will always try to respect your honor and that of the name O'Hara. And do the right thing for the poor. But," he waved his finger warningly, "this is politics and like you said, 'whores and criminals'. Of course we would never call it that . . . but good politics is about compromise. You give and you take."

"There's Red," said Johnny, his eyes brightening. "Red," he shouted, with a wave of his arm.

Hell, that's the big man himself. He's not even dressed like the big shot he is, Red thought as she headed towards them, her pretty face smiling broadly.

"Mr. Brogan, it's a pleasure to see you, sir. When did you get in?"

"Just this morning," he said. "You're doing a great job running this place, future Alderman O'Hara here tells me. Tough on the men and all that. That's good. Ya have to run a tight ship . . . or you'll sink."

"Where are the fancy clothes? I mean, the big suit, the fancy shoes, and the big hat?" asked Red as she looked him over.

"I was waiting for somebody to pass that remark." Brogan laughed aloud. "I wouldn't feel comfortable dressed like that in *me* neighborhood. Hell, they'd laugh me out of the neighborhood. They'd probably call me a big jerk."

They had a good laugh when Red reminded them of her reaction to Tony, the first time she saw him dressed in the fancy suit and big hat. "That's exactly what I called him, 'A big jerk.'"

* * * * *

With his hair masking his face, Bimsbey secreted himself into the Louvre through the back door—always mindful of protecting his nameless/faceless image. And as arrogant as always, he pushed open the door without knocking.

"Charlton!" yelped Bailey, placing his hand over his heart. "Don't give me a heart attack." Bailey did not like him barging in, but he did not show his distaste.

Bimsbey cracked open the lounge door to sneak a peek at the impressive image of his horse Blackie and his Brougham carriage. He grinned with admiration. "I just love it. Your man did a great job on the mural." When about to shut the door, he spotted Batesy serving drinks. "Your man should not be working behind the bar," he snapped. "He should be in proper attire at all times and mingling with the clientele or out on the streets. He's to be selling himself to the voters. Not selling liquor."

"But, but . . . ." Bailey hesitated. "You mean pay him for that? And hire another barman?"

"His backers will have to cover the expenses. And for God sake," he snapped again, "get them dammed posters up in there. And everywhere. You do want him to win, don't you?"

"Yes. Yes. Of course, sir," Bailey replied meekly.

"O'Hara will be tough to beat. He's got big money behind him. And I hear he's got a real charmer at his side much of the time when he's out canvassing. We've only two months to get our man the support he needs to take Mulvihey's seat."

Again Bimsbey peeped out at the lounge. "And tell him to get rid of that hard look. It takes more than rhetoric to win elections. Smiles go a long way. Tell him that."

Bimsbey shut the door and sat in Bailey's seat at his paper-strewn mahogany desk. He motioned for Bailey to take a seat.

"Is that fellow with the broad forehead still about?" Bimsbey asked, cracking his knuckles. All he got from Bailey was a blank stare. "He was the comrade of that big blond kid that disappeared a few years back," he continued. "You've got to know him. He worked with Batesy for years."

"Oh, yes. Yes, of course. That's Lopat. The man you thought had something to do with the disappearance of your beautiful girl friend. Angel."

"That's the man, alright. But he had nothing to do with it, I was assured," said Bimsbey. "Is he still around?" Bimsbey drummed his fingers on the cluttered desk.

"Yes. Should I get him?"

"That would be just fine. It's important. Very important. I want to see him here tonight. After you close shop." Bimsbey spoke authoritatively, giving him an order, as he rose from his seat and readied to leave.

"Yes sir," snapped Bailey, rising to his feet.

"Now get Batesy out from behind that bar and on the campaign trail. We want a winner on Election Day. Not a loser." As he held the doorknob of the back door, another thought came to him: "Bailey. Has anyone ever recognized Blackie or the Brougham?"

"Nobody ever brought that to my attention. No, nobody."

"Let's keep it that way." Bimsbey made a hasty exit out the back, not bothering to shut the door, another of his arrogant traits that pissed Bailey off.

* * * * *

Just past midnight, Bimsbey stood across the street from Bailey's place and waited in the shadow of a shop entranceway well out of range from the glow of the nearest street lamp. Once certain the last of the Louvre's customers had left, he would make his entry through the rear door, where he knew the anxious Lopat awaited him.

It was quiet in Bailey's office, except for the sharp thumps of the heels of Lopat's shoes hitting the floor as he paced back and forth and the sound of wrinkling paper as Bailey leafed through the *Herald*.

Batesy had literally forced Lopat to be there. After all, Lopat's livelihood depended on him. Although he never had anything to do with Bimsbey, Lopat knew of him and had haunting memories of him.

Lopat sat near the backdoor. Looking at his timepiece, he asked Bailey, "You sure we got the right time?"

At that moment they heard the metal against metal sound of the doorknob turning and the door push open. The sight of Bimsbey with his shoulder-length hair covering most of his face, stunned Lopat. A rush of images he wanted to forget flashed before him, among them a large black horse and a white coach. Then he envisioned the faces of Chuck Jansen and Angel Hester. A cold sweat formed on his ashen face and his hands began to tremble. Nausea overcame him. *This is the guy. This is the guy,* he told himself.

"You look like you've seen a ghost," chuckled Bimsbey, motioning Bailey to get up from his seat behind his desk into which Bimsbey plopped himself, at the same time making sure his hair covered his face.

"Ye, ye, yes." Like I saw you a long time ago. Like in another life."

"Oh yeah?" asked Bimsbey, his partially hidden face souring. "When was that?" He crossed his legs and rested his clasped hands on his chest.

Shut your mouth, Lopat told himself. "Probably in a dream. That's all. Is this about Batsey's campaign?" Lopat wanted to change the course of the conversation."

"No. Not at all," Bimsbey silenced him with a wave, then paused while staring at him.

Lopat returned the stare with a steady grin, telling himself, *I'm not gonna let this big shit scare me.*

"It's about all the good work you've done for the organization, for which I want to congratulate you."

Lopat smiled nodding pleasantly, but said nothing. He could see Bimsbey grinning through his hanging hair. But he did not notice Bailey leaving the room until he heard the door close behind him.

"I know you're the eyes and ears of the organization. One of its most trusted people."

"Well, I don't know about that," Lopat replied, rubbing his fingertips across the palm of his hands.

"You're the man that infiltrates the enemy. Those immigrant swine. Because of you we know what they are doing and sometimes what they are planning. Isn't that right?"

"Well sometimes, but—"

"Isn't it you that got us the leg up on O'Hara's campaign? About the big money behind him." He paused for Lopat's reaction. There was none. He continued, "I think you should be earning more than you are. You are

265

too valuable to us not to be." Bimsbey again paused for his reaction. This time he did respond favorably, going by the look on his face. "Should I ask Bailey to make sure your salary is doubled?"

"I wouldn't mind that at all. I'd be delighted. Any strings attached?"

"All you have to do is put more time into Millhouse's campaign. Spend more time in the firehouses talking him up with the men. Walk the streets with him. Perhaps you can hook him up with a popular young lady to tag along on his vote-getting strolls."

"Done," replied Lopat.

Bimsbey got to his feet in silence, straightening out his jacket, while ignoring Lopat. He started for the door, but turned to face Lopat again.

"Oh, there's something else you can do for me," Bimsbey said in a near whisper.

"What's that?"

"You know that red-headed gal that hangs with O'Hara?"

"Yes. Red."

"I'd love to get into her pants."

So this is what it's all about, thought Lopat. *Now he wants the daughter.*

"There's fifty in it for you, if you can set me up with her."

Lopat's eyes lit up. "I'll give it my best shot."

CHAPTER TWENTY-FOUR

Out front of the Louvre three upbeat musicians played patriotic music, entertaining a fast expanding crowd of passersby and campaign workers. The campaigners were dressed in red, white, and blue jackets and wearing the same color hi-hats. When they finished, a distinguished-looking gentlemen joined them, readying to sing.

Inside the Louvre, Batesy and Lopat put the final touches to their dressed-to-kill attire, which included large, red, white, and blue *Vote American Vote Batesy* buttons. They were ready to hit the streets on the campaign trail. Batesy stomped his foot in rhythm with the music. Shortly, they would step outside to greet and charm the good patriotic citizens of the ward. Batesy would drive home his nutshell message to all within earshot: Put an American back in office. By that he meant return things to normal— a White Anglo Saxon Protestant elitist political machine that screwed the workingman whether they are the so-called nativist, the immigrant, or the colored. He would classify Alderman Mulvihey's death as Divine Intervention: that the Good Lord gave the good citizenry a chance to cleanse the district of *immigrant scum corruption* by voting for him. They would step outside when the vocalist began singing the Star Spangled Banner.

But first Lopat had a bone to pick with Batesy. "You know who you had me meet last night?"

Batesy saw the anger in his eyes and did not like a challenge coming from a subordinate.

"I mean, like, do you know who this guy Bimsbey is?" Lopat continued.

"I didn't know you were meeting him. I was doing Bailey a favor," answered Batesy, returning the hard look. "Said somebody important wanted to meet you. He didn't say who or why. Why! What's the big deal?"

"He's a manipulator trying to set me up. That's the big deal. Tells me how important I am and all that good shit. Even said he'll get me a bigger salary."

"Bimsbey," he said with stunned surprise. "The guy probably owns half the city. He'll get you more money. Wait and see."

"Yeah. Somebody else's."

"What's wrong with that?" asked Batesy, shaking his head.

"That's not why he wanted me," said Lopat. "The moment I saw the hairy bastard, images of that night eleven years ago flashed before me . . . when that Hester woman got killed. He's the one. She's dead because of him. That," he pointed at a mural over the bar depicting a black stallion and a coach. "That's his. That big white coach. And that monster of a horse.

267

Jansen and me, we picked it up from him. And took her away. He used his long hair to hide his face. Just as he did last night."

"You're crazy. Get it out of your mind," Batesy insisted.

"Yeah. Then why did the bastard ask me if I knew her daughter? You know who she is? O'Hara's redheaded friend. Said he'd like to screw her. That there'd be a fifty in it for me to make it happen."

"So what? She's a good looker."

"Damn you. She's Angel Hester's daughter and looks just like her. Would he kill her too?"

"What do you care?"

Outside, they were playing the National Anthem. "C'mon, there's my cue. Let's get out there. Get my campaign underway."

They stepped out onto the stoop. Batesy stood rigid, looking good before the large cheering crowd of campaign workers and interested public. Two dozen or more campaigners, men and woman, were either handing out Batesy handouts or holding and pumping over their heads, large red, white, and blue placards with the *Vote American, Vote Batesy* slogan.

Batsey stood at rigid attention on top of the entry stoop, making sure all could see him. As soon as the vocalist finished the anthem, his overly enthusiastic supporters—who were on the payroll—began chanting, "Batesy for alderman. Batesy for alderman."

He greeted them with a big smile—unusual for him. In a few words the fiery orator captivated his audience, reiterating his consistent message: "Put an American in office." He told the supportive crowd they must get rid of the corrupt immigrant scum, a message the crowd heeded with passion. He then addressed his campaigners who were shouting with great enthusiasm. "I am indeed grateful to all of you for your vital support. It is your efforts that will win the day; that will put this council seat and the council itself, back in American hands."

Lopat divided the campaigners into groups of four with two people handing out handbills and two chanting and pumping the posters. "It's important to get these into the hands of everybody in your path," he stressed.

268

Bailey cut Lopat's rhetoric short when he appeared at the open entrance door and shouted with urgency, "Come here. I have something to tell you." He surprised Lopat. They huddled in the doorway. "You have to go to O'Hara's place, right now."

"But how 'bout the campaign?" asked Lopat.

"Don't worry about it. There's plenty of help. Besides, I want you to get started right away on the redhead. This is very important to me. Of course, that faceless fucker is on my ass. I won't say anymore other than that Bimsbey is a very necessary influence in all our lives. We must keep him happy."

Lopat wanted nothing to do with this subterfuge. In the few hours since he'd met Bimsbey, he'd sized him up to be despicable; a person who used people as disposable tools. He felt the same about Batesy who he knew would never be there to back him up should he need him.

"What do you want me to do?" Lopat asked.

"I don't know. Befriend her. Bullshit her. Just get her to come here," said Bailey. "I'm sure you'll figure some way."

The campaigners took off towards 32nd street, chanting over and over: "Vote American, Vote Batesy: Vote American, Vote Batesy."

A pissed Lopat started on his mission; a mission and a group of people he wished he could just walk away from, but that couldn't be. They were his livelihood. He cursed himself. *What am I gonna do?* It still ate at his conscious what happened to Angel Hester and the attack on her daughter. Even though he'd been an unwilling accomplice on both occasions, he still felt guilty.

Once he passed Eight Avenue, where the real pauperism started rearing its head, the tenant houses and shanties were plastered with *Vote O'Hara* placards. On several corners there were volunteer firemen dressed in their red shirts and helmets, shouting into bullhorns, urging people to be sure to turn out for the election and to vote for Johnny O'Hara. Their urging also stressed the importance of his victory. Lopat smiled, thinking O'Hara may well beat his boss. "Good luck, Irish," he whispered. *Maybe I can get an honest job with him.*

The more Lopat penetrated poor-man's country, the more he feared for his safety. He wore fancy clothes while many of the locals were dressed in rag-tag clothing, some with tattered shoes, some shoeless. He could sense the envy and resentment in the people's eyes. In one fast maneuver, he removed the Batesy button from his lapel. At the same time, he felt the blackjack in his hip pocket.

He did not appreciate seeing so many children in their bare feet playing on the unpaved surfaces.

Up ahead, several older teenage boys stepped from a doorway, intent on blocking his path. Hiding his fear, he headed right for them, his hand firmly gripping the blackjack. Sergeant O'Connell watched it all from behind the window of Tobin's green grocery. He stepped out into the street.

"Mr. Lopat," he shouted, defusing the situation. "Is it fun you're looking for? Or is it mischief?" O'Connell wore a friendly smile.

The youngsters stopped nearby, close enough to monitor the conversation.

"You'll find no trouble with me, Sergeant. Just heading to the new North River Inn. Looking for my acquaintance Mr. O'Hara and his redheaded friend."

With that the boys took off to Ninth Avenue to warn Johnny.

"Your side has the money to run a great campaign for the wrong guy," said O'Connell. "But we have the numbers. I predict a victory for Johnny on Election Day."

"I must say, I agree with you. Going by what I see here today. The man seems to have great support. Everywhere."

"That he does," said O'Connell. "And I hope it's a peaceful day. You might want to pass that on to Mr. Bates. Tell him that any display of violence to keep the voters away from the ballot box will be brutally crushed. No matter what gang of thugs they send to the voting centers."

"Well, I'll certainly see to it that he gets your message. Now, if you could tell me of Johnny's whereabouts?"

"Certainly. Come. I'll walk you there."

The two men sauntered side by side toward Ninth Avenue along the newly installed slate slab sidewalk, the good sergeant twirling his nightstick in a way not many officers could. As always, the public enjoyed his twirling display; there were many smiling faces.

"You're good with that stick, Sergeant O'Connell," shouted a man from his stoop. "I wouldn't want ye to be bringing it down on me noggin." The man tapped his head with his knuckles.

The sergeant smiled as the man's friends laughed. Lopat enjoyed it too.

"When's the last time you've been to the Inn?" asked O'Connell.

"Not lately, I assure you. I don't think I'd be too safe there. Heard it's a real fine place."

Lopat knew well that Johnny had taken over the Shamrock Inn and of the magnificent renovation job he had done on it. He knew too that Angel Hester's daughter had returned. After all, that's what he got paid for, knowing what the *enemy* was up to.

The time was 10 am when they reached the Inn, its door still locked at this early hour. O'Connell rapped the door's brass knocker plate with his nightstick, making a loud whacking sound that echoed throughout the block and inside the establishment. The curtains parted, revealing the porter's smiling face, a face that sported some scar tissue. In the dining area at to the rear of the bar where a meeting was taking place, Johnny also heard the familiar sound of the nightstick hitting the knocker plate.

"That's probably for me. Take over the meeting, Red," he said. There were a dozen or so people sitting at two tables joined together in the dining area.

The porter cracked open the door enough to poke his head out. "Ach. If it's not the good Sergeant. Good morning to ye. And how can I help you this fine morning?" The porter gave Lopat a not too friendly look, but nodded out of respect for a fellow brawler. Lopat greeted him in the same manner.

The porter well remembered Lopat from the pitched battles their gangs fought against each other.

"'Tis Johnny about? There's a gentleman here to see him," said O'Connell.

He opened the door. "Come in and I'll fetch him for ya." But before he could get to O'Hara, Johnny was standing at his side.

What's his business, wondered Johnny. "You move fast," he said, letting Lopat know he knew he was coming. After determining his business, he and O'Connell led Lopat to the meeting.

Lopat paled when he saw Red's face amongst the crowd. His stomach fluttered, his legs weakened.

"Mr. Lopat," said Johnny, extending his hand for all to see. "Welcome." He was setting the tone for his associates.

Lopat's body stiffened, surprised by Johnny's friendliness.

"Well, thank you," he said, returning the handshake. He kept glancing over at Red. Couldn't help but see her look hardening.

She suddenly sprang to her feet, knocking her chair over, and made a beeline for him. He braced himself for whatever. "You got some pair coming into my turf," she bellowed, pushing Lopat, causing him to stumble backwards.

Her associates got to their feet, but Johnny quickly said, "Gentlemen, please. Stay in your seats. Everything's okay. Mr. Lopat is my guest."

"Back off there, lady," Lopat snapped at her.

"Miss Hester!" O'Connell smiled, stepping between them. "That's no way to treat a guest."

"Guest, my ass," she barked. "This sonofabitch—" She then silenced herself as if her jaw locked.

"It's okay, Red." Johnny interjected himself, tightly wrapping his arms around her.

"What do ya mean it's okay?" she growled, struggling in vain to free herself from his grip.

"First hear what he has to say," Johnny replied.

"I didn't come here for your bullshit, lady," Lopat barked. "Either you let me talk, or I'm out of here." He turned as if to leave. As much as he wanted to get this off his chest, he was not about to let her belittle him.

"Hold it up. She wants to hear what you got to say," said Johnny.

"In private," said Lopat, looking at Sergeant O'Connell and the others.

"That okay, Johnny?" asked O'Connell.

"That would be fine, Sergeant," Johnny agreed.

"Why don't ye give me that blackjack you got in your back pocket? I wouldn't want anyone getting cracked upside the head with it, now."

Lopat smiled, shaking his head. "How'd you know?" He handed it over.

"I'll be right outside should ye need me," said O'Connell.

"I assume you have something to tell my dear friend," said Johnny, with a cold look about him as he stood towering over Lopat.

Lopat gave him a nod. "It's time I get this off my chest."

"We'll use the banquet room," said Johnny. "Come with us, Red."

Johnny opened the nine-foot high, stain-glass pocket doors, sliding them into their walled pockets. The room was a maze of light; the sun's rays beaming through the pitched, glass paneled roof, reflected brightly off the dozen four-foot wide Waterford Crystal chandeliers equally spaced throughout the room, and the numerous mirrored wall panels. Directly across from the banquet room entrance stood a large statue of St. Patrick in an equally large recess in the wall.

Lopat tried to, but could not hide his surprise at the lavishness of the Inn, which eased somewhat Red's anger. She even chuckled. *What's on his mind,* she wanted to know. *Did it have to do with her mother?*

They took the first table they came to.

"I did not forget how you welcomed me at the firehouse that graduation day," Lopat said to Johnny. "I liked that. The family thing was great. Never went to one of them. Really, it was good."

273

Johnny nodded, a pleasant look on his face, but remained silent.

"And . . . and working that fire with you guys. Awesome. And it felt good helping those people." His sincerity showed on his face. "They were just like anybody else."

"Sounds like you have a good side," said Johnny.

"What's this all about?" asked a confused Red.

"While you were away, he paid us a visit. He wound up saving my butt at a *good one* right down the block from the station."

"Why are you here?" she asked.

"To invite you, Miss Hester, to meet the richest man in the whole city. Charlton Bimsbey."

"Bimsbey! Why does that name sound so? Oh no." She froze, then stumbled backwards. A deathly pale covered her face as she plopped down on a chair. A vision of two men throwing her mother into a large white carriage appeared to her. Then she spoke in a soft voice, as if whispering: "Bimsbey. He's the guy that my mother dated." Tears flowed freely down her cheeks. "He was with my mother on that last night." She went silent and began sobbing.

"I'm also here to spy on your campaign, which we know is well organized and financed. You got Brogan money behind you. You can't hide anything—," he chuckled.

Spinning to her feet, Red screamed, "You got no right to come into our turf and talk like that." But again, Johnny blocked her.

"Let him finish," said Johnny. "You're so anxious to do the wrong thing here."

She didn't like Johnny snapping at her and eyed him accordingly.

"Damn you, Hester. You and your mom have been my cross all these years."

Red and Lopat glared at each other.

"I'm here for good reasons. To bare my soul to you. About the night your mother disappeared." He paused, checking her reaction. "Should I continue?" he snapped and took his seat.

"Yes."

"You want every detail?"

"Yes. And I still *wanna* get that big sonofabitch for what he did to me," she insisted, sliding her finger across her throat. "Where is he?"

"I'm also here on another mission . . . which I will explain later." Lopat continued. "Don't think you'll ever get Jansen. Haven't seen him since I last saw you all." Lopat shook his head, his eyes watched for her reaction. "Thought you'd know where he is."

"Oh yeah? Why would you think that?" asked Johnny, surprised by Lopat's challenge.

"That morning I met youse, I met Jansen too. That was supposed to be his last day in the city before heading to Staten Island, to hide 'til things blowd over. But first he wanted to apologize to you, Miss Hester." Then he tipped his chin at Johnny. "You, he wanted to kill."

Red's stomach knotted. "Ye gotta be kidding," she growled. "You believed him?"

"Wha-wha-wha," Lopat stammered, as his eyes darted from face to face, suddenly sensing a threat to his safety.

"Wha-wha, your ass. Ya fucking buddy raped me. If I'd gotten him I'd of done him good." Again she ran her finger across her throat.

"But he promised," muttered Lopat, his voice wavering, unable to look either of them in the eye, "not to hurt you." Then in an angry outburst, muttered, "Just like your mother, Angel. The prostitute."

Before Red could react, Johnny had his arms around her chest pinning her to the chair. "Please. Just listen. I beg you."

"I mean you no harm. But that's fact," continued Lopat.

"What about my mother?" Butterflies fluttered in her gut.

"That night he lied. Ruined my fucking life." Lopat became very uneasy, remorseful, looking as though he would shed a tear.

"What did he do to her?" she pumped him. Her hands gripped the chair as if ready to spring from it.

Looking at the floor, Lopat mumbled, "He's a killer."

"Wait. Wait a minute," Johnny cut in forcefully. "If you're going to talk about a murder and you're really sincere about this, you got to tell Sergeant O'Connell?"

Lopat froze in place, saying not a word. He never expected to be in such a predicament, faced with talking to the police about the murder of Angel Hester. But after a long moment, he barked loud and clear, "Fuck him. The liar. The fucking killer."

Red sagged in her chair, a surge of lightheadedness rushed through her. She began to relive that night many years earlier, seeing her mother's face as plain as day.

"Then your answer is yes?" said Johnny.

"Yes," said Lopat. "I know this is my death warrant. But so what?"

"I'll be right back." Johnny hustled out of the room.

Red's look softened. Suddenly she felt compassion for Lopat.

Although sensing a measure of relief after having for the first time spoken about his role in Angel's death, he still felt overwhelming guilt. In a crazy way he hoped they would beat the shit out of him, wanting to be punished for his role.

Through the door came Johnny with the sergeant.

"Greg, you already met Sergeant O'Connell. If you'd please continue."

"Raped her. Then killed her," Lopat mumbled.

"Start at the beginning," said Johnny.

"Jansen told me we were to beat her a bit. Her mother." He nodded at Red. "Scare her, you know. He picked me up outside the Louvre after he'd left off the rich banker. It was Bailey, the owner of the Louvre and his nephew Batesy, the bartender, that hired Jansen and me. To carry out that dirty deed for Bimsbey."

"Whoa! Whoa!" said Red. "Who's Bailey?"

"We know him," Johnny cut it. "Let him continue."

"Jansen was decked out in a coachman's suit with the hat and all. He hardly stopped to get me. I had to run and jump in. Then I saw the woman. Tied up. Scared stiff. Her face beaten and bloody. Before I knowd it, we were hurrying down to the river. He told me that he and the banker had beaten her because she had tried to blackmail the banker. That we were to take her to the river and beat her again and leave her there. He said nothing about killing her. I swear to you. But when we got there, he dragged her out and dropped her on her back. Picked up her legs, she kicked like hell. He tore her knickers off and did his dirty deed. Things got nasty as hell. He must of broke her neck. Whatever. She was dead . . . I'm so sorry."

Lopat sobbed, burying his face in his hands.

"The banker is Bimsbey?" asked O'Connell.

He mumbled through his hands, "Yes. I found that out last night. A bit of a weirdo. When I first saw him years ago, when I didn't knowd him, he kept his hair tied at the back of his head. I'm sure of that. Last night it hung all over his face."

"That's the guy who picked her up that night with the big coach. Hair all over his face." She closed her eyes and took a deep breath. "Where ye bury her?"

"In the old hayshed," said Lopat.

"Where? By the river?" she asked.

That news stunned them.

"Yeah. Right where you lived all those years." He nodded at her. "He even carved a cross in a timber support that stood just over the hole where he put the body. For years I wanted to tell you. The guilt's been unbearable. I tried to tell you that day by Macon's Beef. You remember?"

"Yes." Johnny nodded.

"But I lost my nerve. I've carried it with me ever since."

He then got to his feet and faced Red, who had just sprang to her feet, with clenched fists. "Please, please," he appealed to her. "I don't wanna fight you. I just wish that you'd forgive me. Or at least tell me you believe me when I tell you I am so sorry."

Red was taken aback by his sincerity. No outsider had ever treated her with such respect. *How can I not believe him*, she wondered. In an equally sincere voice, she replied, "If you're telling me the truth—and I believe you are—you've done nothing." Emotions and memories clouded her thinking.

Somebody knocked on the door. Johnny shouted, "Come in."

As if prearranged, the porter came in with a pot of tea and four mugs."

"Right on time," said Johnny.

He offered them something stronger to drink, which the four of them declined, then left.

"And what else did you want to tell us," Johnny continued. Sergeant O'Connell purposely refrained from questioning him, not wanting to jeopardize his collaboration.

"He's got a crush on you, Miss Hester. Wants me to con you into a date with him. Must really be crazy 'bout you. He heard you look just like your mom. He'll see to it that my wages are doubled if I can get you to date him."

She shook with anger. "I wouldn't let him kiss . . . kiss my . . . ah shit," she growled. She pounded the table.

Sergeant O'Connell stepped forward. "Mr. Lopat, you . . . you seem sincere."

Lopat waited for the question he knew was coming.

"Would ye consider helping us get him?"

Red jumped to her feet. "If at all possible. What the hell's that supposed to mean?"

"Miss Hester. Again I ask you to listen." O'Connell gazed calmly into her eyes. "Do you think that with his money—that with all the jobs he creates—do you really think he'd go to jail?"

Her lips moved, but no words came forth. She turned away for a split second, then barked, "Who the hell's side you on?" Before O'Connell could respond, she uttered in a low, deliberate voice, "Then I guess I'll have to take care of him."

"I didn't hear that," said O'Connell. And before she could repeat herself, which she intended to do, O'Connell explained: "Red, God knows I'm on your side. I'd love to be the one to put him in prison."

Lopat seized the moment to befriend her. "If Miss Hester wants me to take care of him," he said. "I owe that to her. Besides, I'm already a goner."

"Not while you're on our turf," said Johnny, speaking with conviction.

"Well then let me know what I can do to help," said Lopat.

By now all eyes were on O'Connell, anxious to hear his proposal.

"Red. Would you consider meeting Bimsbey?"

"Under these circumstances, I can't say no."

"Then you can start the ball rolling," he told Lopat. "Go now and tell him Miss Hester would love to meet him," O'Connell smiled, realizing Red, whose neck suddenly turned red, was taking him serious.

"Easy," he said before she could react. "Where's ye sense of humor? This is strictly strategy. Ya know, what we call blarney."

"Can you be back here by six with his answer?" asked O'Connell.

"One way or the other," said Lopat, while getting to his feet.

"Good. And while ya gone we'll work on a plan of action. Oh," the sergeant continued in a stern tone, "Tell him somebody will be with her and there's no give on that."

Lopat smiled, nodding in agreement. "I feel good already. Like, for once I'll be doing something good."

PART III

CHAPTER TWENTY-FIVE

T he lunch hour had arrived. Every seat in the North River Inn was occupied with hungry, thirsty souls. Johnny, Red, O'Connell and Tony kept themselves incognito in the privacy of the banquet hall, again sitting at the same table and perusing their menus.

"Sergeant O'Connell, this is Tony Bosh, a dear friend from the old country," said Johnny. The two complimented each other as they shook hands. Right off the bat, Tony was impressed with the smart-looking sergeant.

"The sergeant's a godsend to this community," said Johnny.

While the waiter took their order, Tony compared the vaulted wooden ceilings of the banquet room to some of the ballrooms he'd been to in Dublin.

When the waiter disappeared, Red explained to Tony the circumstances surrounding her mother's death and how Lopat linked Bimsbey to the killing. With that O'Connell jumped into the exchange.

"And Tony, with your position dealing directly with Bimsbey, you can be a great help proving his guilt. If he is indeed the culprit."

Nodding his head, Tony accepted. "Sure, if it's proper by Johnny, it's proper by me."

"I thought you'd say that," the sergeant said. "You've met Bimsbey, I understand."

"Yes. And others of enormous wealth. A Leonard Morgan who has financial interests in many states. I can't even imagine their worth. They talked like they were responsible for many thousands of jobs."

Nobody recognized the name Morgan or Jacob Bosh. And until recently, they didn't know Bimsbey either.

"My uncle, Jacob Bosh, is one of them, but he is an honorable gentleman. He's associated with them because of his wealth. There are others in the group, including an Irishman, mind you. But he'd not been one of the attendees. And their names weren't disclosed."

They were all taken back with the news of the Irishman.

"An Irishman?" asked Johnny, obviously surprised.

Red followed up with, "Any idea of who he is?"

"No. Like I said, they don't disclose names. You have to meet these people," said Tony.

"Well, what did they want with you?" asked O'Connell.

"I'd say because of my aging uncle, who I'll eventually be replacing within the group. Guess they wanted to study me. And might I add, I told Bimsbey that I had met a wee lassie that looked just like the woman whose painting hangs behind his desk. That seemed to upset him, yet excite him. Strange," Tony added.

"What do these people do? What's their purpose as a group of financial leaders?" O'Connell continued his questioning.

"I'd say they function to protect their financial interests and to increase their wealth along with their influence. Or should I say power. And how they do that, it appears to me, is by keeping the workers at each other's throats. It was the man Bimsbey who said, 'As long as they're fighting each other, they're not coming after us.' He also said that years ago 'he had an all-immigrant fire house burned to the ground.' He also boasted about instigating numerous other attacks by the Americans against immigrant neighborhoods."

"Wait a minute. Who said that . . . about burning the firehouse?" asked Red, as every muscle in her face tightened.

"The leader of the group. The one called Bimsbey. Charlton Bimsbey."

"Then he's also responsible for me mother's death." Johnny closed his eyes, reliving the day Jansen shot his mother dead.

"Yes. But let's not jump to conclusions. Besides, we know he did not pull the trigger. As a matter of fact, we know nothing for sure. Let's stick to Red's mother for now." O'Connell then explained to Tony, word for word, the many details not covered by Johnny about Angel Hester's violent demise.

Tony looked at Red. "I could not believe the resemblance between you and your mum. You're the image of her. An extraordinarily beautiful woman if I may say so," he said.

"Minus a few scars," said Red. "Wait a minute. It's my mother's painting he has on the wall?"

"Yes. Behind your man's desk. I thought it was you. I wondered why he had you there."

"So he's the Bimsbey that picked my mother up that night. The big banker. The hairy bastard."

"What makes you so sure, Red?" O'Connell pressed.

"I'll never forget that carriage or the horse."

"With the name Blackie on it?" asked Tony.

"Yes."

"This could be a coincidence," said O'Connell.

"I wouldn't think so," said Tony. "Bimsbey hardly took his eyes off the painting."

"Is his hair as long as she said it was?" asked O'Connell.

"Not when I saw him, sir. But it's possible. His hair was kept in a tail."

"And the carriage you spoke of," continued Tony Bosh, a surprised look on his face. "There's another painting behind his desk. A giant canvas of a black stallion and a great white carriage."

"Then it's no coincidence," said O'Connell. There was a look of devilment in his eyes.

"Why you staring at me, Sergeant?" she asked, running her fingers through her short hair.

"Because we got work to do. And you're the main player."

"What's the plan then?"

"I'll sum it up for ye. You have to get Bimsbey to take you to his office, get him drunk, and get him to attack you. Physically, I mean. Sinister I know."

"Whoa! Wha—whadda ya crazy?" insisted Johnny, holding his hands up and motioning him to stop.

"Hold ye horses," said O'Connell. "We'll be there to stop him. Mr. Bosh, am I correct that your uncle's office is right above Bimsbey's?"

Bosh nodded yes.

"I'm sure your uncle will let you use it the night of Red's rendezvous?"

"I'm sure we can work that out," said Tony. He chuckled, as did Red and the others.

"Can you keep your uncle out of the loop?"

"Under these circumstances, yes. He'd want Bimsbey to pay for his sins."

After a lunch break, they resumed their strategy session on laying out the plan of how Red would set up Bimsbey. O'Connell insisted that Johnny O'Hara be excluded from that part of the meeting. "You are not to have any foreknowledge of the plan," the sergeant said. "I'm afraid you won't be able to handle it." She jumped on the proposal. Besides, she liked a good physical challenge, a chance to once again apply her gang fighting logic: "No man too tall, no man too small. I will dump them all." *Besides*, she thought, *it might provide me an opportunity for sweet revenge.*

* * * * *

It was still lunch hour when Lopat caught up with Batesy's campaign team at the corner of 23rd and Broadway. The sidewalks were alive with people, many of them were sitting wherever they found a place to sit and eat their lunches. Likewise the streets were overwhelmed with horse-drawn coaches, delivery wagons, and the shouts and curse words of frustrated drivers. Lopat walked with a cockier than ever stride, heading straight for Bailey, who he delighted with the news that Angela "Red" Hester would meet Bimsbey. Now Bimsbey would be off Bailey's back.

A large crowd of people eating their lunch had also gathered around Batesy's campaign team to listen to the rhetoric of a young man using a bullhorn, telling the people why Batesy must be elected. Dispersed among the crowd were tough-looking hecklers, working for the O'Hara team.

"Isn't your man Batesy a street fighter? Isn't he a man who has had people badly beaten?" one of O'Hara's men shouted. "Isn't he a man who turns workingmen against each other?" He got the attention of the crowd.

Instead of responding to him, the campaigner, waving his fist in the air, shouted, "If our man loses, we all lose. If Mr. Bates loses, the thugs win." Then he pointed to the man who shouted the criticisms and yelled, "Is this who you want running our city? Thugs?"

Then another detractor shouted, "Answer the man's question, sir. Is your man a divider or a *uniter*?"

Then a woman's voice joined in, calling on him to answer the question.

"He'll unite the Americans. Not the foreigners."

There were some boos, cheers, hisses, and clapping. Several people walked away.

Another heckler challenged him. "But he burned businesses, wiping out jobs and even burned down a firehouse." There was a sigh from the crowd.

"Rubbish. He's a true American," shouted the campaigner.

"But I was there, sir. I saw him and his gang start the fire. I swear to God I tell the truth. His men were shooting guns, too."

"Thank you Ladies and Gentlemen. Don't forget to vote this Friday. And vote for America's survival. Vote for Mr. Bates."

The campaign team cheered and applauded, then took up the chant, "Bates is the man, Bates is the man," as they stepped off, heading to another location, followed by the tough-looking hecklers.

CHAPTER TWENTY-SIX

That evening the four of them waited for Lopat at the North River Inn, where a strong odor of boiling cabbage wafted from room to room. He arrived on time, popping up right in front of them like a jack-in-a-box. Escorting him were two tough-looking teens he had met that morning.

There were no menus or waiters to wait on them. As a group they stood in line to get their pre-determined dish of grilled beef with boiled cabbage, and potatoes. They were there supporting a *Johnny for Alderman—O'Hara Night* fundraiser: one dollar a head. Everybody got the same dish.

Again, they were in the banquet hall, but this time they had no privacy. There were too many people packed into every corner of the building. And they were all O'Hara supporters, drinking and making a lot of noise that overwhelmed the music of the Jimmy Crum band as it played "Beautiful Dreamer."

Just like its predecessor, the Shamrock Inn, the North River Inn had been designated a voting station, thanks to the influence of Mulvihey and his cronies in the council. The nativists wanted the voting station located in their territory, knowing full well that many of O'Hara's supporters would not risk their safety going into Batesy country.

Lopat smiled when he saw the large posters on walls everywhere throughout the establishment: *O'Hara Night*. He could actually feel himself not only wanting O'Hara to beat Batesy, but wanting to help him do it.

"Get your plates. We'll eat in the office," said Johnny. "At least in there we can hear ourselves think." But it wasn't much better in the office. The loud, disjointed noise of so many people talking and shouting passed right through the walls of the office that sat right behind the portable stage his supporters had set up for the night, just for Johnny to speak. The office had two doors, one situated right behind the stage, and the other on the opposite wall that opened behind the bar.

An odd but unique painting on the far wall instantly caught Lopat's attention. He shook his head in wonderment. "What's the purpose of that painting?" he asked. "I mean, don't you see enough poverty right here? Do you need reminders?"

"Yes. Constant reminders. Of what we," —Johnny nodded in O'Connell's direction— "*our* people had to endure during *The Hunger* because of a people who despised us."

"Because of our religion," said O'Connell.

"Those scrawny, emaciated images represent what our families looked like during *The Hunger*. Of course, I mean the survivors." He pointed to the hovel. "That small mud hut along the side of the road represents what many of us had to live in after we were chased from our land at the point of a rifle and its bayonet; the land the English elite stole from us." Johnny pointed to two small images. "See that? They were the corpses of the latest members of that family to die from hunger or hunger-related diseases, waiting to be picked up for burial. Buried in mass graves. And you know what? The American elites are prepared to do the same thing to us if need be to achieve their goals. But here at least we have unions to fight for us. We must be prepared to fight to the death to protect those unions." Then Johnny smiled and faced the group.

Red cut in. "Wouldn't it be wonderful if," she waved her hand, "we could rid ourselves of those cockroaches?"

"I won't ask what you mean by that wishful thinking," said the sergeant. "Be real, Red. We need the jobs they create. There has to be another way."

"What happened to that family, and many tens of thousands more like it, is the reason I am here in this country," said Tony, abruptly cutting in. "My father bears the responsibility for many of those deaths. I am ashamed of him. All for greed."

"Good man," said Sergeant Desmond O'Connell, who also lost family to The Hunger.

"Something tells me I'd be on your side," said Lopat.

They gave him a cautious look.

"Mr. Lopat, do you have any news for us?" O'Connell asked.

Lopat turned his head to the side and covered his mouth with the back of his hand and gave out with a noisy yawn. "This sofa makes me wanna sleep. Yes I do. He said any place, any time."

Having finished his meal, Lopat hesitated to put his dirty dish down on the serving table with its highly-polished, black marble surface that rested on a pedestal shaped like a goblin. There were at least a dozen of them throughout the room.

"Oh, go 'head. Put it down," said Red. "We ain't no faggot *ee-ly-tists*, you know." She looked at the wall clock, a fancy piece of woodwork with gold trimming. "A few minutes more and you'll be on, Johnny."

Lopat wiped his mouth and hands with his napkin, then dropped it on the plate.

The office was a new addition to the Inn, placed there as part of the renovation. Like everything else in the building, it had the finest of equipment and the latest of fixtures and conveniences; even the most elaborate of wall covering and the most expensive of imported carpeting. They had brought in the "paper man" himself, Benny Kinucane; a well-known decorator from the town of Haverstraw where Johnny got all his bricks. Finucane contributed big money to the O'Hara campaign.

"Any suggestions as to where this romantic encounter should take place?" asked O'Connell, who answered his question with a question. "How about Hernon's? Neutral country where nobody would know ye." O'Connell paused then asked, "Well, what do ye think?"

"No. Too neutral is right. I want it where I got friends I can depend on."

"Make a suggestion, then."

"The Waterside. Next Thursday, nine sharp," she said, "That's the where and when of it. Gotta be after the elections."

The noise level from the banquet room easily passed through the hollow plaster-frame wall, beginning to interfere with their conversation. By now they were very nearly shouting at each other.

Even the floor shook. And that became worse when the crowd of several hundred people began stomping their feet calling for Johnny: "We want Johnny. We want Johnny."

Red sprang to her feet. "It's time for Alderman O'Hara," she barked, herself all fired up. "They're waiting for you Johnny, dear, to pump 'em up. Now, go on out there and get them ready for Friday." She knew Johnny listened to her; that she inspired him and gave him strength. And now she asserted herself.

"Get on that stage and remind them of who the enemy is; what they did to our people in Ireland; what they've done to us here. And tell them just like you told us. We must be ready to fight. That it would be over our dead bodies before they'd ever trample us again. And you can tell them we'll be right at your side, whether the fight's at the voting place or on the street."

Red asserted herself in a way none of them knew her, not even herself. She captivated them. The fire in her voice had them all startled. Even Lopat.

"Quite the orator," said O'Connell. He too moved towards the door.

"Like I said before, if there's to be a fight, I'll be on your side," Lopat repeated himself.

"Let's hope it doesn't come to that," the sergeant said, breaking a slight grin.

"Johnny," Tony got O'Hara's attention. "You sure you don't' want her to give your speech?"

Johnny shrugged his shoulders. "It would be easier on me." He smiled at Red. "Damn, it's good to have you covering my back again. Just like the old days."

Out of sight of the others, she blew him a kiss.

"Just make sure you stress the importance of them casting their votes on Friday," she continued in her aggressive tone. "And they're not to be intimidated at the voting place by Batesy's bullies." She punched her hand. "Let them know that our boys will be there to protect them. And I'll be right in the middle of it. Just like the old days." She laughed hardily. "Like I'm looking forward to a good donnybrook."

They all cast her a look of admiration.

The banquet hall had a capacity crowd with standing room only. It seemed everybody showed up, the Italians, the Germans, the Irish, a group of Han's Jewish friends, even a few Arabs, and a small group of coloreds and Orientals who worked in the kitchen. Not all of them were eligible to vote but they all supported Johnny. He treated them fairly and got them memberships in the waiters union, whose members were both white and colored.

As soon as Jimmy Crum's band finished playing, "The Star Bangle Banner," Johnny started out to the banquet room, following his entourage: Battler, Hans, the McCarthy brothers and Tony, with the green-eyed, flaming redhead and the sergeant at the forefront. A thunderous applause greeted them. Red stepped up onto the portable stage, bringing with her Jimmy Crum's' bullhorn.

"Hey! Whadda ya doing with my horn?" Crum challenged.

"What about it?" she snapped at him, her voice carrying to the crowd. "Can't ya see I'm Johnny's introducer? You got a problem with that?" Her voice carried over the horn.

The crowd erupted with loud laughter.

"Okay. Okay," said Crum, wisely backing off. Crum and his band left the stage.

"Awright! Awright!" Red's voice boomed through the horn; she didn't sound like a sweet little girl. Immediately the roar of the crowd fell silent. "It's time to hear what the big guy has to say. So shut your yaps and let him use his. Awright?"

"Who the hell are you?" somebody shouted. But before she could answer the heckler, somebody else shouted, "Shut ya trap and let the redhead say her piece."

"First things first. Don't forget, we'll be doing our voting right here," she jabbed her finger repeatedly at the floor, "just as we did when it was Old Man Brady's place, the Shamrock Inn. That's right. Right here." She spoke forcefully. "Okay. Now let's get on with the show," she shouted, her face aglow with her radiant smile. "It's my honor," she tapped her chest, "to introduce to you the next alderman for the ward; the man who made a lot of jobs for our people." She paused then shouted, Johnny O'Hara."

She handed the bullhorn to Johnny then stepped down from the stage.

"Thank you, Miss Hester. It's a lucky candidate that has such a beautiful gal at his side to attract all the good voters." Reluctantly, he shifted his eyes from her smiling face to the audience. "Sure it does my heart good to see you all here tonight, lending me your support . . . for this most important election, this Friday." He looked around the room and shouted, "Do I have your attention?" There was total silence. "Yes. Friday's election is most important because if I lose it, we all lose. The hard-fought-for gains Alderman Sean Mulvihey won for us during his reign will be lost.

"That's right. Everything Mulvihey gained, we will lose." He paused to give them a moment to reflect on what he said, then shouted, "Everything, if Bates is elected to alderman, and not me. So you know what you have to do." He spoke slowly and deliberately. "Every one of you, and all the eligible voters you know, *must*, I repeat, must . . . turnout and vote. And I warn you . . . do not be intimidated by their thugs. On every block in the district where our people live our lads will be there watching and ready to step in, to defend you. And our good friend Sergeant Desmond O'Connell," the sergeant raised his hand and waved repeatedly, "has assured me that the police will also be out in great numbers. My opponent and his moneyed supporters want you to be scared off. They know that's the only way they can win . . . if you don't show up and vote. And we will not give them the election. Am I right?" he shouted into the horn, and the crowd roared back, with many different messages of support.

"There is something dear to me that not all of you will want to hear." He felt Red tapping his leg, and when he turned to her he saw her, shaking her head and whispering, "Don't get into that shyte."

"Sorry, Red," he whispered back.

"After I am elected, one of my plans is to bring us all together."

Somebody shouted from the floor, "Who da hell is 'us?'"

"To begin with, I mean all the so-called immigrant people joining forces with the Americans."

Lopat, who had remained in the office, smiled when he heard Johnny talking about working together. *He's crazy*, he thought.

Then another voice shouted, "And wot does dat mean: 'to begin wid?'" The question prompted a lot of shouts from people who shared the man's concern.

Johnny saw Red shaking her head as she muttered, "I told you."

"Listen to me," he shouted. "Like it or not, we are all workingmen. We are always fighting over the same pool of jobs. Us against them."

"Wait a minute. Wait," the same voice cut in again. "Yeah. And then the Americans will take our jobs. Wot ye say is bull-shyte!"

The room became very quiet.

"McGinty, let me finish what I have to say, okay?" Johnny shouted into the horn. "We are forced to work for lesser wages than our American counterparts. In other words, we are forcing wages down instead of up. We are wiping out the gains their labor organizations fought so hard to get. We are undermining them. You hear me? Let me repeat that: We are undermining what they, and their fathers before them, worked so hard for; improvements in wages and working conditions. Can anybody tell me that's the right thing to do?" His remark prompted a lot of grumbling and shouts of protest. Somebody with their own bullhorn shouted back, "But we have families to feed, Mr. O'Hara?"

"The owners know exactly what they're doing when they keep us fighting each other. It's planned that way. They know you'd do anything to feed your family . . . many of whom are often starving, I might add. Only the owners and their butt-lickers profit from the disunity; the fighting. This war is making them even richer and they're not sharing it with us." He looked around the room at the many faces.

"Next ting ya be saying, we gotta work wid dem coloreds," another voice shouted. An angry roar erupted from the crowd.

Red yanked the cuff of Johnny's trousers, getting his attention. She reared her head back and hollered, "Johnny. What the hell ya doing? Ya gonna blow it."

"Well," Johnny continued, "if we all worked together instead of fighting each other, we'd be able to force the bosses to treat us all equally. The owners just love to see us at each other's throats. As I just said, 'That's how they keep our wages down.' But if we were one united body, immigrant and American, black and white, working together, fighting the bosses for fair wages and decent working conditions, we'd all be winners." To Johnny and Red's surprise, only a few people booed. As a matter of fact, a few people even applauded.

"Of course, there are inherent dangers in what I propose," he continued. "From within ourselves and from outsiders. Surely some of our own would be bought off with a few pieces of silver. Judases doing the enemy's bidding. And, of course, the bloody newspapers won't do us justice. Most of them would take the bosses side. Imagine if we had our own press . . . one newspaper read by all the workingmen? Throughout the country. Sure we'd all think and act the same when it comes to what's good for the country and its people. Hell, we the people, the democratic majority would run the nation. The way it's supposed to be in this democratic republic. Instead of the elites." The banquet room erupted into cheering and foot stomping, alleviating Red's fear that Johnny had gone too far. Johnny paused until the crowd went silent, then continued.

"But remember my friends, until all the workingmen are working together, I will fight like hell for you and your families. But, of course, I won't be able to help anybody if you don't turn out right here," he continued while pointing to the floor, "in this building and cast your vote . . . for me. My success, I mean our success, depends on you."

"Yeah. Vote early and vote often," somebody shouted. Again the hall erupted with laughter.

Over the shouting and clapping of the people, Red bellowed into the bullhorn: "That's Johnny O'Hara for alderman. And if anybody tries to stop ya from voting, hit 'em a shot with this." She waved a blackjack. "This is a *Vote for O'Hara* blackjack and you can pick yours up at the door when you're leaving."

Suddenly, what sounded like an explosion of shattering plate glass came from the bar area. The crashing noise that scared the hell out of many of O'Hara's supporters seemed to last forever, when, in fact, it lasted for a matter of seconds.

"Dynamite!" "It's an explosion!" people shouted.

There was no explosion. O'Hara's opponents had sent a barrage of cobblestones and bricks through all the nine-foot by twelve-foot plate glass windows that covered the entire front of the Inn. Out in the bar, large and small shards of glass, flew through the air like daggers seeking human targets to carve up. Luckily, the bar area had cleared out when Johnny began speaking in the banquet hall.

Johnny's supporters scattered. Some sought escape through the kitchen, some remained in place, and of course, some rushed towards the bar to investigate.

"Stay in here! Stay in here!" Red shouted into the bullhorn. Meanwhile, Johnny, Battler, Hans and the McCarthys became a human barrier between the banquet room and the bar.

"For God's sake," Johnny shouted, "don't go out there, people. You'll get cut to pieces. And don't leave the building."

Raising his fist in the air, an old man shouted, "The bastards will never stop me from voting."

* * * * *

On Election Day Johnny O'Hara won with a sizable majority. Not only did his own supporters turnout in great numbers to back him, he even won support from people who were not friendly to immigrants, including a few of the big shits from Fifth Avenue. And, surprisingly, very few voters complained of voter harassment, which, of course, probably had something to do with the presence of police patrols moving about the Ward as a deterrent to Batesy's boys. Sergeant O'Connell saw to that. Of course, the groups of club wielding Young Immigrants must have also served well as deterrents. Some *unknown* police source apprised those club-wielding groups of the streets that the police would not be able to cover.

CHAPTER TWENTY-SEVEN

For a quarter of an hour, Red stood in the doorway of Friedman's, a green grocery diagonally across the street from the Waterside, where she avoided a sudden, torrential downpour. Old man Friedman asked if she wanted to step inside and wait, but she declined. She did not want to miss her signal that Bimsbey had arrived. So heavy had the downpour been that it flattened and almost completely washed away several mounds of horse droppings, before it abruptly stopped.

She was dressed in a tight fitting dress that clung to her body. The dress was not her idea. She wasn't used to dressing that way and she felt ill at ease. Hell, she had always dressed like one of the boys. As Battler had told her on the way over, "I wish I didn't knowd Johnny. I'd give him some stiff competition."

* * * * *

She gawked at the new look of the Waterside, a place she remembered since childhood as a dark spot on the block; a ramshackle dump of a place where the windows were always missing a pane or two; a place that always needed a coat of paint. Presently, it served as a bright spot on the block. It had a professionally made *Waterside* sign above its large multi-paned cottage window. Its front had been completely done over with brick, the window framing painted in a shiny white, and its entranceway painted with glossy red and white colors. A slate sidewalk replaced the earthen one. All because Mr. Dagastino's wife Maria insisted: *"The placea gotta be cleaned upa."* Not long after the renovation, a story had circulated about the bricks used to redo the storefront might have come from a load of bricks that disappeared from the site of a tenement recently put up on 34th street. Whatever the truth be, the Waterside had to be upgraded. It looked terrible standing not far from all the freshly painted fences and commercial structures that lined the street. .

The Waterside had been more like Macons slaughterhouse. That stinking slop shop still begged to be cleaned up, although the stench of the animal waste was gone.

Much of the "fresh look" of the area resulted from Mulvihey's relentless fight with the council's anti-Catholic bias. He got them to pave

Ninth, Tenth, and Eleventh Avenues with cobblestones, replacing the filth-covered earthen streets that were often muddy. He also instituted street cleaning into the area. Several times a week the dung wagons, manned by locals employed by the City, visited the neighborhood, cleaning up the horseshit and decaying animal entrails from Macons, causing a noticeable lessening of the rancid pong that contaminated the atmosphere, making it a safer place to live.

As the story goes, "When Mulvihey died, he took the smell with him."

Red waited for the signal that Bimsbey had arrived at the Waterside. While standing in the entryway, many of the workers on their way home from Macons gave her their best of smiles. No less than a half-dozen of them remarked about her looks. The most common remark being, "If only I be single." She enjoyed it all.

Battler appeared at the entrance to the Waterside, drawing on a cigarette, her signal that Bimsbey had arrived.

She stood just inside the establishment and eyeballed the joint, hardly believing her eyes. Everything appeared to have been updated. Where there used to be a counter consisting of planking on top of barrels that served as the bar, there now was a highly polished counter and top permanently affixed to the floor. New stools for patrons lined the bar. The walls were dark purple or maroon; one of those preferred Italian colors. And all the dimly lit wall gaslights were new, adding a romantic touch. Dagastino even added some lights to the dining area and converted that area into a proper dining room. Looked real cozy. Large display windows lined the rear wall, enabling the patrons to view the river and watch the passing boats. There was even a small deck out back for mild days.

Mr. Dagastino greeted her. "Ah Red," he shouted, in his Italian accent. "Come with me." As preplanned, he led her to a corner table, all the time being closely watched by Battler and Hans.

From his isolated corner where he sat in the dark, Bimsbey got Dagastino's attention.

"Is that Miss Hester?"

"Yes. And who are you?" Dagastino asked, pretending he didn't know him.

"An old friend," he nodded, stepping out of the dark.

He got to his feet and headed for Red. Before she knew it, he towered over her. She showed no sign of being phased by his presence. She simply jabbed her chin at him and asked, "Can I help you?"

"Miss Hester?"

"Who wants to know?"

"I'm Mr. Bimsbey," he replied, extending his hand to her, which she limply shook. "I am delighted that you joined me. Truly." He reeked of alcohol.

"Hey Red," shouted the fast approaching Battler. "Damn, it's good to see you." They shook hands. All prearranged. "Stop by and say hello. Hans is over there. And who's ya friend?"

"Oh yeah. Battler Quinn, this is Mr. Bimsbey." Bimsbey did not acknowledge him.

"Mr. Bimsbey, you didn't say hello to my friend."

"Oh I'm so sorry. How thoughtless of me. Hello, Mr. Quinn," he said, never taking his rapt-looking eyes off of her. *She's a hard one.* "I assume you got that name because you are a street fighter?"

"Ya could say dat. But it would be more right to say dey call me dat 'cause I'm weal good wid my hands," answered the cheery-eyed Battler. Neither he nor Bimsbey moved to shake hands. "See ya later, Red."

"I would be grateful if nobody knows who I am," Bimsbey said.

Battler sensed a warning in his tone. "I hope I remember that." He chuckled as he took his leave.

By then Red had detected a bit of a slur in Bimsbey's speech. *This guy's a drinker.*

"Please join me, Miss Hester?" he asked, gesturing to where he had been sitting. "We'll have something to eat." Her presence overwhelmed him. With several drinks under his belt, he felt as though the love of his life,

Red's mother, was again with him. He struggled to hide the tremors surging through his body; kept his trembling hands on his thighs. He wanted to plow her right there and then.

"What's wrong with right here?" She wanted to be disagreeable, but knew that such behavior would serve no good purpose.

"I have private things to tell you . . . about your mother. If you don't mind. And besides, I don't like to be seen in public."

She stood and asked, "How'd you git here? In ya big white wagon?" Her question surprised him.

"I walked," he replied. "Walking is good for the body . . . if not the soul." *How did she know about my coach,* he wondered.

They returned to his dark nook, keeping himself and Red out of sight and away from the only other couple eating dinner. Playing the gentleman, he sat her first.

"The proprietor recommends the striped bass," she said. "Right out of the river. Try it. You'll like it. Comes with veggies and spuds."

"If it's good enough for you, it's good enough for me," he said, grinning pleasantly.

"Mr. Dags," she shouted. "Two stinkies will do."

"Coming up! Two stinkies just for Red and her friend," Mr. Dagastino sang back in a melodious Italian accent.

"Why did you call them stinkies?" he asked.

"You know the stink of fish when—"

"Ugh," he cut her off, waving his hand and wincing his nose. "No details, please."

"Well, what is it you have to tell me about my mother?" she asked in a business-like tone.

"When I first saw you . . . I thought . . . I thought I was seeing things. I thought you were your mother. Angel. Who I loved so dearly."

"Spare me the bull-shyte, mister." Red thrust forward, leaning across the table. Through clenched teeth she growled, "You sonofabitch. My

297

mother is dead because of you. Who you kidding? You loved her? Don't you know I saw you? Your hair was just like it is now. Covering most of your face."

"What did you see?" He pulled back, wide eyed.

Mr. Dagastino arrived with two glasses of wine. He had a white towel draped over his arm. "Only the best for my friend," he said with a big smile that flaunted a fine set of white teeth.

When the owner left, Bimsbey came right back. "You are wrong if you think I did your mother," he said. "So wrong." At the same time he reached for her hand.

Frowning, she jerked her head back and snarled, "Don't you dare touch me."

Who the hell does this trash think she is talking to? "I wasn't with her when she . . . when she passed. It was that fool I hired. Batesy's man. A real villain, and I needed someone like him to scare her. You hear me? To scare her." He spoke in a firm whisper.

"Keep talking," she said.

"Your mother was with child. Mine. And I didn't want a baby. Not only were we not married, but your mother . . . well, what can I say."

"A prostitute. Is that what you won't say?"

"Yes. I told her she'd have to terminate it. She refused. She wanted me to marry her. I refused . . . which I've regretted ever since. Then she threatened to go public, which I just could not let happen. Being a businessman, such publicity would have destroyed me."

"Then you killed her?"

"No, I told you." He raised his voice, but quickly checked himself. "I had nothing to do with her death. Nothing. I only wanted to scare her. That's all. Yes, I did strike her several times as did that big blond-headed thug."

Visions of the actual assault that she had buried deep in her memory for all these years, suddenly flashed through her mind. She was waiting to pounce should he lie. But he didn't. Instead she saw remorse in his eyes, even in his speech.

"Then we shoved her into the coach," he said, with an apologetic shrug of the shoulders. She quickly corrected him: "You mean you threw her." He gasped, then nodded, reluctantly acknowledging his guilt. He scowled on hearing Battler give out with loud laughter, then grunted angrily at a nearby steamer when it blew its foghorn.

"I saw it all from my window. You with your giant horse and carriage. I'd seen them so many times before. And I saw you and your partner attack her. Then for two days and nights I waited for her to return. When she didn't, I knew she wouldn't return. So I left. I never did find out what happened to her. I know the police considered her dead. But they never found her. So I wasn't sure."

"That was the end of my involvement," he said, looking relieved. "After that, I had the thug, the one called Jansen, drop me off. He then picked up another goon. They were to take her down by the river. To tell her that if she persisted, they'd tie her hands and throw her into the river. I figured that would put an end to her threats."

She smiled at him, which he right away returned. *This guy has to pay for this.*

Gazing out at the water, he whispered, "I loved your mother." Then he turned and looked her in the eye. "I have never loved anyone since."

She crossed her arms and settled back in her seat. "Did you try to find her?"

He shifted in his seat. "As painful as it was for me, I couldn't do anything. I had to protect my interests." Then he pleaded, "Surely you understand."

"No I don't," Red snarled. "Obviously she didn't mean that much to you. Did she?" She stared hard into his eyes.

"But I thought you'd understand," he said, narrowing his eyes.

Again she detected a slur in his voice. "What did you do to Jansen and his partner?"

"As I said, I could do nothing." He downed his drink and banged the glass on the table, signaling for another refill.

"You could have had one of your boys, or goons as you call them, take care of them."

With eyes nearly bulging and a handful of fingers pressing against his chest, he asked, "You mean for me to be associated with violence. Oh, God, no!"

"Well, what happened to them?" she persisted. She leaned forward on the table.

"I met the Lopat guy the other night. The goon that got you here. That was the first time I ever set eyes on him. And Jansen," he smiled, "well after that day, I never saw him again, nor did I ever hear anything of him."

In truth, Bimsbey never did see them again. That's the way he operated to keep himself above the law. He and his kind indirectly made known to certain underlings who are capable of terrible things, what they'd like to see happen. They never ordered anyone to do anything. They remained aloof, knowing the likes of Bailey and Batesy would get people to carry out their wishes. People such as Jansen served that purpose.

Dagastino served their dinners. They ate in silence. Once finished and the dinnerware was removed, they continued talking. As they did, Red sucked pieces of food free from between her teeth and Bimsbey used his fingernails for the same purpose. The one thing they agreed on was that they both enjoyed the meal. In his words, the meal, "Proved to be outstanding, actually," to which she quipped, forcing a smile as she did, "There's something good about us common folk, hah?" She winked at Hans who moseyed past them.

"Why don't you tell your friends to stay in their seats," Bimsbey said, shaking his head. "You're safe with me."

"I'm sure you told my mother the same thing."

"I would love to show you her portrait. A masterpiece of beauty." His breathing became rapid.

She nodded her head, agreeing. "When?" she asked.

He reached for her arm but was warned off. "No need to be touching me." She waved over to Battler, who hardly took his eyes off of Bimsbey.

"What's with him?" Bimsbey asked while returning a hard look.

"My protector. Have you forgot? That last time a Hester woman met you, she disappeared."

She found it difficult to play along with this man, a person whom she hated. He found her resistance to his advances most unbearable. He wasn't used to not having his way.

"But I told you what happened." He contended he only struck her a few times. "And softly at that." He insisted he deeply regretted doing so. "Well, I guess I can understand your friend's concern, especially since you all thought I did something real bad to your mother. But now you know I didn't. You're safe with me." Again he reached for her arm.

This time she glared at him. "Don't. Don't touch me," she said snarling, waving her finger.

The tough-skinned Bimsbey did not back off. He knew what he wanted and like a dog in heat, nothing would prevent him from getting it— as always. "Sorry about that. How about Monday. I'll show you the portrait. After dinner, of course?"

She nodded her agreement. Her hard look softened, which pleased him. He would not have been so pleased if he knew that her sudden cheerfulness was born from the thought of getting revenge for her mom. She finished her wine and declined another glass.

"How can ya sit there and tell me," she tapped her chest with her thumb, "you got nothing to do with violence? I know well who you are, you know. I know of all the trouble and suffering you and your kind have caused the workers." Then she leaned forward, her eyes locked on his, and muttered, "Even though you were not *directly* involved."

"Stop! You've said enough," he snapped in a hushed tone, trying hard to hide his anger. "Speak to your leader. He's one of you. Let him answer your question."

She laughed. "You gotta be kidding. Honest Johnny O'Hara. You gotta—"

Bimsbey laughed. "You are not as smart as you think you are, young lady."

"Who then! Who you talking about?"

"Now I got you." Again he laughed. He clasped his hands, bringing them up under his chin. "Well, when you find out, you ask him who caused all this trouble and suffering."

CHAPTER TWENTY-EIGHT

Old man Bosh placed a pile of folders on the desk in front of Tony. "These are some of American Textiles' best accounts. Study them. That'll keep you busy while your friends wait to pounce on Bimsbey." Tony had no choice but to tell the old man, whom he swore to secrecy. Jacob surprised him when he replied that he'd have no problem helping to hang that degenerate.

"Treat these clients with the utmost civility," he continued, staring out the window at the dark of night.

Tony made it a habit of working late since starting with his uncle, wanting to learn his functions and responsibilities quickly, which old man Bosh admired.

"The customers are always right. They keep the cash flowing in. And I want you to regularly visit them to make sure they are completely satisfied with our products and service. That's why I am providing you with a carriage and driver."

"For that I am deeply grateful, Uncle Jacob."

Just below Bosh's office, Red and Bimsbey sat in two different sofas—she was almost lost in hers, the cushions were so thick—sipping glasses of wine. Already he felt numb, having had several shots of whiskey with his dinner. He couldn't take his eyes off of her, making her uneasy. Several times she instinctively felt for her trusty knife. *I hope they're paying attention up there,* she thought of the Boshs being ready to intervene.

"Come. Let me show you the painting." She heard quivering in his voice; in his quick breathing. *Hell, this guy is ready to attack me. I just know it.* When he opened the door for her and she stepped into his office, she saw him feel himself..

Just outside the building, Sergeant Desmond O'Connell, a building passkey in hand, stood beside his partner Police Officer Ernest Zelle and looked up at Bosh's and Bimsbey's windows, waiting for the signal. In Bosh's office, where Tony studied the accounts, he and his uncle also awaited the signal, Red's scream.

At the sight of her mother's image, Red broke into a sweat. She collapsed in the nearest seat, feeling faint; a strange feeling she never experienced before. *My God,* she thought, *I look just like her.* She became misty eyed. "God, she was beautiful."

"Look at her hair. Just like yours," he said, his breathing intensified even more. "You're the image of her." She felt his arms encircling her; one hand forcing its way between her legs, the other cupping a breast. She screamed as he pressed her face down over the desk. With a handful of her hair, he held her down while his other hand lifted her dress and pulled at her panties. "Oh Angel," he shouted. "I love you. I miss so much."

Tony sprang from his seat shouting, "That's it. That's Red." He bolted for the stairs and Jacob rushed to the open window where he shouted to O'Connell and his partner who were already charging through the building's already-opened entrance. They too had heard her screams. Jacob Bosh hurried behind Tony. "Now we can watch the rat squirm," he barked, with a chuckle.

It delighted Tony that the old man wanted to be involved, to be a witness. Red's screams and the sounds of struggle, the furniture being knocked around, were easily heard. They also heard the pounding of the coppers footsteps as they rushed up the stairwell.

Meanwhile, Red's fingernails clawed at his throat with little effect. Bimsbey's hands were too busy pulling at her panties. She kept screaming. As much as she wanted to pull the knife and use it, she knew that would ruin everything. *Where the hell are they? I think I'm gonna throw up.*

Bimsbey slapped Red drawing a little blood from her lip. She dug her nails into his cheeks breaking his skin. Her dress was up, his pants' were down, her panties were ripped off, and his penis was in his hand, and that's what the coppers and the Bosh's saw when they barged through the office door.

"Stop in the name of the law," O'Connell demanded.

"Get this drunken bum off me," Red shouted, as she shoved at her stunned attacker.

"We heard the screaming," said the old man. "We were upstairs working late. Thank God we were there."

Red feigned surprise when they entered, yet could not hide her gratefulness at their arrival. She didn't look to good, her hair a mess, her face reddened from his slap. "He tried to rape me," she shouted. "The bastard ripped my underwear off," she protested, holding her undergarment in her hand.

Tony went to her aid. "Are you okay, Red?" he asked while the startled older Bosh stared at Bimsbey.

"What kind of an animal are you, Charlton?"

"She's lying. She tried to blackmail me. Just like her mother," he shouted in his defense.

"But, Charlton, your pants are down. And you had your pee-pee in your hand." Jacob shook his head.

"Get your clothes on. I'm taking you in," said O'Connell, sounding official.

"Don't you dare, officer. You don't know who you're dealing with," Bimsbey threatened.

"Just doing me job, mister," O'Connell replied, emphasizing his Irish accent.

* * * * *

They stood in the lobby of the 20th Precinct in front of the sergeant's desk, a highly polished oak desk that was taller than Red, and waited for the desk sergeant.

Red and her protectors were not long there when a distinguished looking, loudmouthed man charged into the lobby and rudely took over the conversation.

"Charlton, my good man. What in God's name is happening here," said the smartly-dressed G. Parnell, Bimsbey's attorney.

Parnell and his associates were well known for their work defending the swindlers of Wall Street. Not surprisingly, they rarely lost a case.

The desk sergeant appeared at that time. He was a big beefy man with a graying handle-bar mustache and long thick sideburns. He hustled into the lobby, ready to silence the loudmouth. But when he saw who it was, he chose to remain silent. Right then a nervous looking police commissioner and an assistant to the mayor entered the police station lobby. Without a word, they adjourned to a private room with Bimsbey in tow.

"I knew this would happen," said O'Connell. "You gotta be ready for anything," he told Red. "And please, don't do anything you might regret. This man, as evil as he is, is very important to this city's economic wellbeing. Like I told you before."

Jacob Bosh reiterated what O'Connell said. He then took his leave, advising them it would be best if he left. "And, young lady, I would advise you to listen carefully to what the good sergeant tells you."

No sooner had Jacob Bosh left than Bimsbey and company came out of the room. They were all smiles. "Thank you, gentlemen," he said. Then, along with his attorney, Mr. Parnell, he proceeded to leave the police station.

As soon as the top cop and the mayor's assistant stepped out of the room, the desk sergeant separated O'Connell from Red and Tony, then led the two of them into the room Bimsbey just came out of.

The Commissioner motioned for O'Connell to join him and the Mayoral assistant who were standing off to the side of the lobby.

"Sergeant, I am advised that you are a fine example of a police officer. A credit to the department," said the commissioner, who spoke softly so as not to be overheard; his eyes darted around the lobby. He had difficulty maintaining eye contact with the sergeant.

"Why, thank you, sir." O'Connell knew the commissioner had more to say.

"I am happy to hear he did not rape the prostitute," he said, as he looked at the mayor's assistant. "Just a little harmless groping. Isn't that what happened?" the commissioner said with insistence.

"Sir, this woman's no prostitute." O'Connell struggled to hide his anger. "Sure he had her dress up and had her *bloomies* ripped off. And besides, he slapped—"

"But he didn't rape her. Isn't that right?" said the commissioner.

"But that's only because we prevented him. Besides he assaulted her . . . and molested her. Those are criminal—"

"Stop. Stop," whispered the top cop, now shifting from foot to foot. "Didn't you hear what I said happened? This man is one of our most important citizens. He has created many, many jobs in this city. Thousands of them. Nobody really knows how many. But the number is staggering, I am advised. And he employs both immigrants and Americans. Such a scandalous story could destroy him and many of those jobs. We just can't go heavy on him."

O'Connell knew this would happen, just as he already suggested to Red.

"Is the young lady going to get some kind of satisfaction?" he asked. At the same time, a shout came from the desk sergeant: "Can I help you, sir?" A big man, but light on his feet, he was up and out of his seat and down on the floor in a flash, intercepting a man who'd barged through the door. He knew that man to be a reporter.

"I'm Don Kappo from the *Herald*. We've received word that a rapist has been arrested?"

"I'm afraid you either got the wrong word or the wrong stationhouse. We've had a quiet night here. So far." The smiling desk sergeant chuckled.

"You sure sergeant? I just saw some newsworthy people leaving here. Two of the town's most influential people. Why would they be here?"

"I think you better take my word for it." The smile left his face. "So out the door with you, Mr. Kappo." With that, the reporter departed, but warned, "The *Herald* won't take it lightly if you are suppressing the news."

The commissioner nodded approvingly to the sergeant. "It's not over yet, Sergeant O'Connell. Don't utter another word about this. If the reporters ever get wind of it, there will be hell to pay. I wouldn't want to be in that woman's shoes." With that said, the commissioner and the mayor's man left.

O'Connell met Red and Tony outside the precinct. "I'll meet ye across from the Inn in half an hour.

CHAPTER TWENTY-NINE

Albany's decision to create the Metropolitan Fire District came as a surprise to nobody, just as the angry uproar from the volunteers surprised no one. Their days as volunteer firemen were numbered. As of July 1865 there would be a paid fire department protecting the city of New York run by a board of commissioners appointed by the governor; the volunteer fire companies would be disbanded and all their apparatus, equipment, and firehouses would have to be turned over to the new department.

When Nick Tiso informed Brogan of the legislature's overnight decision to quickly vote on the issue of a paid fire department, he caught the first train back to New York. He feared very much that the volunteers would react violently, which to him meant the Pvt. Michael Brogan Engine Company would be right in the middle of any disorder. And that meant Johnny O'Hara's chances of leading the new department would be negated.

To his great satisfaction, when midway back on his trip from Colorado, he learned that his good friend John Dexter, the head of the Volunteer Fire Department, had successfully defused the possibility of a violent outburst. Brogan would now use the opportunity to secure the top position of chief engineer for Johnny O'Hara.

He would also use his return to the home turf to deal with Red's threat to go to the *Herald* with the Bimsbey story, if the police did not bring charges against him. Brogan knew she would be in great danger if she persisted. He had to get her to back off. Bimsbey's people would not hesitate to silence her for good.

* * * * *

"It's three weeks already and I've not heard a word from anyone in the department," said O'Connell. He took a seat in the North River ballroom, where they usually conducted their business. "Not that I expect the commissioner to change his mind."

"I'm not going to let this pass." Red growled softly.

"And every time I bring it up," the sergeant continued, "I'm told to remember what the *Commish* told you. That you should expect nothing."

"Bullshyte! Over my dead body," Red roared, jumping to her feet. "I am not going to let him get away with it." She stomped across the floor, looking for something to kick.

Everybody sat silent, their eyes following her every move. They shared her anger and frustration. Then Tony spoke up. "Listen to me. Although my uncle is part of the economic inner circle, he despises that Bimsbey. He agrees he belongs in jail and wouldn't mind seeing him there. But he knows that would never happen. He implores you, begs you that is, to forget it and to get on with your life."

"Where is this thing called justice?" she asked. "What's so good about this democracy? People with money can take a life and get away with it. They don't have to fight in the wars they create. Like all they have to do is profit from our blood and heartache. I mean, are we just cannon fodder, put on this earth to serve them? I mean if I had my way, I'd get rid of them all. Especially the ones that use and abuse the people."

"What good would that do? Other vultures would quickly fill the void," said Johnny.

"Well," she laughed out loud, "At least I'd have the joy of killing them."

"Oh, Miss Hester," O'Connell pleaded. "Please listen to Mr. Bosh. He is a man that believes in the working people. He treats his employees with dignity. Believe me, he would not steer you wrong. And like I said, the department wants it to die. Let it go."

With a loud thump, the double doors swung open. Through it stepped the big man himself: Thomas Brogan—startling everyone—dressed to kill in a fine dark suit, spats, and all. Even a Fedora, but no tie.

"What the hell is going on here?" Johnny shouted.

Everybody jumped in place. Red gawked with an open mouth. Even Sergeant O'Connell responded with surprise.

"Thomas . . . what . . . what are you doing here?" asked Johnny.

"I'm not here for my health, I assure you. It was one hell of a nasty trip. But I had no choice but to come."

"What do you mean," Johnny asked.

"I told you she'd be trouble."

"Mr. Brogan. Tom. She hasn't been any trouble at all. She's been my backbone. I—"

"Hold it, Johnny. Mr. Brogan, are you talking about that Bimsbey?" she asked, restraining her anger.

"Exactly."

"What's it to you? I mean, why did come all the way back here?" she asked.

"Let's just say I'm concerned for your safety. People will kill for him. Will kill you, is what I mean. Their survival depends on him. Too many jobs depend on that sonofabitch. You'll go to your grave before he'd go to prison."

"I'll take him with me," she snapped back.

"Easy. I'm on your side." Brogan told them all to sit as he took a seat at the table. Before he sat, he opened the lower three buttons of his vest to relieve the pressure from his slightly enlarged gut. "Who is this gentleman?" he asked Johnny.

"Tony Bosh. Nephew of Jacob Bosh. Good people. He's involved with us and if it's okay by you, Mr. Brogan, I'd like him to be part of this discussion."

"Ach, Jacob Bosh. A fine man. If he's at all like his uncle, we'll get along just fine," Brogan responded.

"Look Red, just listen to what I have to say," Brogan continued. "First, I want to make sure you understand what I just said. I am on your side and well aware of what happened, and I knew about it the day after it happened."

"How do you know about this," she wanted to know.

"It's my business to know everything important that happens in this city. At another time, I will explain myself more clearly. Regardless of what this man did to you, even his culpability with the deaths of your mother . . . and Johnny's, he will never have to pay for his crimes. Do you know why?"

"Yes, he told me why," she said pointing to the sergeant. "But what are *you* telling me. Telling Johnny? That our mothers' deaths don't mean anything. That he can have people killed and get away with it?"

"Yes."

Red again jumped to her feet. "Who do you think you are?" she roared. "Now you're like Bimsbey. Treating us like we're nothing. Is that it, Mr. Brogan?"

Before she could finish, Johnny jumped to his feet and wrapped her in his arms.

"No, daughter of Angel Hester. I am not on their side. Remember what I just told you. I'm on your side and I mean that. It's the powers that be and their henchmen who do the dirty work. And he didn't shoot Johnny's mother nor did he break your mother's neck. Remember, it was that Jansen fellow. The one that disappeared." With the back of his hand, he wiped the sweat from his brow.

"How did you know that?" she snapped.

Brogan displayed the coolness of a man on a mission. "I knew that shortly after your mother disappeared. And when they didn't find her body, not that they looked hard, they let the case die. Even the newspapers kept silent. Not because they loved him, but because of what he circuitously represented."

"But how did you find all this out?" she pushed, her temper cooling.

He paused to look each of them in the eye, contemplating just how to answer her. Then out it came. "Because I'm one of them. One of the no names and have been for several years. I am one of New York's wealthiest citizens, a member of the city's inner circle. Our survival assures the economic survival of this town. Putting Bimsbey behind bars, in public view, will cost many jobs. Something this city cannot afford and *will not tolerate*. And Johnny, the time has come for you to make up your mind. Do you want to run the new fire department? And if you still do, in what capacity? In a civilian or uniformed capacity." He then turned back to Red. "You see, Miss Hester, if you go after Bimsbey, you will knock Johnny boy, my friend and partner, out of the box. He wouldn't have a chance of getting appointed."

"That . . . that's wrong. Bullshyte." She was flustered. "Once again, they got us over the barrel. I'm sick of this crap."

"We'll meet again, shortly. After I meet with the no names. Then we'll figure something out."

* * * * *

At noon, Broadway by city hall was thronged with people. Most were gawking tourists. Mingled in with the crowd were workers sitting on benches or the plush green grass while eating their lunches. Many different noises could he heard. There were people shouting, horses neighing, and coaches, wagons, and trucks of all sorts making rattling and grinding sounds as they rolled over the cobblestones. And, of course, the *clippidy-clop* of horseshoes. Added to all the commotion were the shouts and whistles of a police officer trying to keep the traffic moving. In the middle of all that chaos stood a dung wagon with its crew cleaning up after the horses. The copper yelled at the operators of the dung wagon, "Do ye have to do that now?"

"Read all about it," shouted the cocky little, black-headed, blue-eyed newsboy as he held up the *Times* with its prominent headline;: *Lee to*

Surrender. "The war is over," he continued in his childish voice. The papers flew out of the kid's hands.

Brogan grabbed a copy, handed the kid a fiver and told him, "Keep the change."

"At last. Too bad it took so long," he muttered. His heart sank with the thought of his brother being killed at Bull Run, along with the other boys from the neighborhood. *And the rich became richer,* he reminded himself. Personally, he had no investments in the war machine.

"Yes. Big Mike should be here with us," said Tiso, a sympathetic look on his face. "All those precious souls blown all to hell."

Yeah, thought Brogan. *Fodder for the cannons.* For a moment he pictured Michael's smiling face, one of the first from the neighborhood to be *killed in action.*

"Good news for some, but not for all. Those men working war jobs will soon be on the soup lines," said Brogan.

Tiso followed the big man through the gateway into the peaceful, country-like sanctuary of City Hall Park, away from the hustle and bustle of Broadway and Centre Streets.

"I hope you got some good news from Albany."

"Yes. Yes, I did," said Tiso. "The governor has selected a board of commissioners to organize the new Metropolitan Fire Department and he put your good friend, C.C. Pinckney, in charge."

"Who did he appoint as chief engineer?"

"Your man, Kingsland."

"They know about Johnny, right?"

"That's all taken care of. He's on tap to be the next chief engineer," said Tiso.

"Great," Brogan said, throwing a handful of peanuts to a score of waiting pigeons and a squirrel. "That's great news, Nick. Just what I need to get those two to listen. Both of them are set well right now and I want them to stay that way.

Tiso nodded his head in agreement.

"But if they push hard to get revenge on Bimsbey, they will pay a dear price. For one thing, Johnny will not get the appointment. They'll never buck the system that's there to protect the Bimsbeys, and not the O'Haras and Hesters of this city."

"Personally," continued Brogan, "I'd like to take the Brit bastard to the roof of his building and throw him off. You know, to see *shit fly*. But that's not the way it's done. Johnny, and even Red, have set good examples for the kids of the neighborhood. They are looked up to by their friends and neighbors because they're successful. And thanks to his generosity, look at all the work Johnny's sister has done with organizing the education program for the hoped-for orphanage, and the advanced study program she put together at Holy Cross." He crossed his fingers for good luck while nodding in the direction of city hall. "And Johnny's proposal will be a godsend for the war orphans *when it passes this morning*. And just in time. The war has softened somewhat the Protestant reluctance to hire our people. Johnny's sister is already turning out well-educated young men and women. And they are being hired. And right now she's up in Albany for a week with other reps from the Catholic school system, lobbying for financial assistance."

"I guess you're involved in that, too?" asked Tiso, starting to bite a fingernail.

"Not really. Johnny now has a lot of influence with the old money. Look at the support they gave him in the election."

A group of scowling aldermen left city hall in a hurry. Among them were several snob-likes, acting as though they were *God-like creatures put on earth to save the common folk*. A second group of aldermen left the building, most of whom were bright-eyed and smiling. O'Hara walked with that group. The common council had just finalized a scheme—opposed by a few of its members—that made available a grant of $75,000 for the construction of an orphanage for the orphans of Catholic soldiers killed in the war. At the time, there were available only Protestant-run orphanages that usually welcomed all orphans, including Catholics, but with every intention of converting them into Protestants.

"Before Johnny gets here, I got something to tell you that I don't think you'd want him or Red to know about," said Nick. "It's Bimsbey.

He's been checking out the neighborhood, looking for Red. Incognito. Nobody has seen him. At least not yet. He's been drinking heavy and hooking up with local prostitutes."

"What's that about prostitutes?" quipped Johnny as he approached them.

"Just comparing New York with the mining towns out west," said Brogan, keeping a casual expression on his face.

"Hi Johnny," said Nick, getting to his feet. He shook Johnny's hand and congratulated him. "Going by your very contented look, I'd have to assume we got the grant."

"You got that right," said Johnny, his face beaming like a child seeing Santa Claus, as he shook hands with his boss.

"Congratulations on a job well done," said the thrilled Brogan. "I'm proud of you, me boyo. Complete success on your first proposal. That's great."

Johnny continued, "You should have seen the faces on the opposition. And you know who orchestrated the whole campaign?"

"I have my suspicions," said Brogan.

"Well, if you suspect her, you're correct. She's good. Damn good."

With that, Tiso disappeared into city hall to carry out his *fly-on-the-wall* function for Brogan.

"Sit. We still have much to talk about. I know you guys were upset with me being one of Bimsbey's business associates. It's not by choice, I assure you. It's out of necessity. The quickest way to lose your fortunes is to operate by your lonesome. Especially with vultures like him working against you. I despise them as much as you guys do. As much as Jacob Bosh does."

"I've thought about it," said Johnny. "I understand. Just that it came as a shocker to us. I know you, Tom. I trust you. Hell, everything I have, I have because of you. The same for Red."

"You made your point. And remember, you guys worked your butts off for what you got. Now let's talk about Bimsbey. It's obvious you guys still want revenge."

"No, no," said Johnny. "Not me. It's Red. And she scares me."

"Then you have to change her thinking. Going after him is very risky. Especially now, since he's been hitting the bottle. I understand he's nasty as hell when he's drinking. And that's quite often now. She'd be risking her life, and needless to say, her success. So with that said, I strongly urge her to let it go. The system will never go against him. Too many people depend on him. People in such powerful positions will destroy others, no matter what it takes, to protect their interests." He ran his finger across his throat. "You know what I mean."

Brogan scattered another handful of peanuts on the red cobblestone walkway. "You have to get her to understand." Brogan paused to watch a daring young pigeon hop up onto his shoe beseeching him for more food. "What do you think, Johnny? Can you get her to back off? I don't want anything to happen to you guys." He paused, throwing his last few peanuts to the pests, and again asked, "Can you get her to back off?"

Johnny's eyes narrowed. "I hate that man."

* * * * *

The enchanting tone of Red's Ulliean Pipes never failed to pierce Johnny's heart, filling him with conflicting emotions, both joyous and sorrowful. The eerie tenor brought back hidden memories of Skibereen and of the loved ones and friends who perished during the Great Hunger. Of course, the sound of the pipes always refreshed his undying love for her. This *love of his life* that had messed up his mind when she did not know if she could ever love a man. He softly hummed the air she played.

He remembered when they were kids, when he used to hear the sounds of her pipes drifting down from the roof to where he lived, and how he would dash up the stairs to be with her and how happy it would make her.

Not a sound could be heard in the North River Inn, where she performed for a full house. So captivated were the people by her music that

315

when the leg of a chair moved, causing a screech, a communal *shhhhhh* erupted.

It had been a long time since she played publicly to a large crowd. Normally, she would play on the spur of the moment for small groups at the North River Inn or the Waterside. But this time everybody knew she would be performing at the North River.

Johnny admired her confidence. It made him proud of her and cognizant of his love for her, this girl that since he could remember had been his only love. He hummed along with the tune.

The hour-long, sweat-bath of a show finally ended, but it was well worth it. The crowd jumped to their feet cheering and clapping. They loved her. And she loved the recognition.

"As much as I love the music, it makes me so lonely for my mom," she told him. "So sad. I gotta go right now and pay her my respects. Will ya come with me, Johnny? Then we can go for a swim, all right?"

"Sure, I'll go with ya, but I ain't going into no water."

They withdrew to the office. There, he removed his shirt and tie. She stepped behind a privacy curtain and donned a pair of trousers, removed her sweaty shirt and bra and put on a fresh pullover.

"Gotta get in that water. I'm all sweat," she said.

Even after rubbing her face dry with the shirt, fresh beads of sweat quickly replaced the ones she had wiped away. They departed through the ballroom via the privacy of a backdoor.

"You know we've been so busy with everything else, we haven't had any time for ourselves," he said, pulling her to him. Right away she felt his bulging manhood pressing against her navel.

"What are we gonna do about it?" he asked.

"Nothing exciting. Just find my mom's grave and go for a swim. That's all for now, lover boy," she said with a smile.

He replied, "That's not what I had in mind," he paused, letting his frustration show. "I'm still crazy about you."

She pecked his lips. "Like I said, the grave, the swim."

A few moments later they were walking along the river's edge, retracing their footsteps to the shed they once called home. She saw so many changes; so many schooners, even more docks.

Sadly, she noticed that the MacAdam's family summer home had been raised. *Damned progress,* she thought. In its place were stacks of lumber and several large warehouses under construction nearby. Also Macon's had doubled in size. Seemed as though the only bit of shoreline that remained untouched by the progress was the former hobo colony and the area where the shed once stood.

But the one thing that didn't change was the beauty of the river that was well lit up by the reflection of a full moon off the river's tranquil surface.

At times he slowed his pace to let her get in front of him just so he could look at her from behind.

"I don't see that big old crane anymore. That you used to jump from," he said, shaking his head. "You always scared the hell out of me. You were crazy."

"Guess there's no need for it anymore," she said with a laugh, slapping her hand at the air. "Ain't nobody crazy enough to use it. Ya remember that night I swung from it and you thought I drowned? And I sneaked up behind ya. Scared ya." They laughed hardily.

When they came to where the shed should have been, Red sighed and her heart sank. All she saw in the dark of night was a black mass of over grown weeds and brush right where the shed should have been. "Johnny, it's gone. The grave. Where is it?"

"C'mon!" He commanded, taking her by the hand. Through the man-sized bushes they marched. In a few steps they were standing at the edge of a large hole in the ground. "That must be it," he said, kicking a stone down into the black pit that returned a splash.

For a long moment they stared into it, reminiscing the fun and misery of that life they shared. Then they thought of Jansen, then her mother.

"I've been telling myself to get my mother a proper grave. I hope I didn't wait too long." She began to sob, and when she sensed Johnny

317

coming to her, she quickly silenced herself, just a little too late. He wrapped his arms around her in a comforting gesture.

"Why you doing that?" she asked, pushing him back, without much success. "I'm not crying."

"I know that," he said, at the same time staring into her moist eyes. "I just want you to know you're not alone any more. And to assure you that we'll find your mother's body. Even if I have to dig up this whole place."

She cherished the moment in his powerful arms, feeling a security and comfort she hadn't experienced since childhood when her mother used to hold her.

The shed itself had vanished, the wood probably used by paupers to build shelters or for firewood.

She remembered what Lopat had said about her mother being buried towards the back of the shack. That Jansen had carved a cross on a nearby supporting column. She pointed to where the rear would have been, about where she figured Jansen's remains were, right by a remaining column. He rubbed his fingers across its weather beaten surface feeling for an impression. "Feel this," he said.

"It's a cross alright. I don't believe this," she said. "Her killer's buried right next to mom."

"And we put him there."

Red said a silent prayer while Johnny muttered: "Our Father, who art in heaven . . ."

"You have to let it go," he said. "No matter what we do, we'll never get 'em back. Your mom or mine. I hope you listened to what Brogan said? What O'Connell said? If we persist on bringing him down, we'll wind up in the grave."

Red reacted with a simple utterance, "Come on. I'm going for a swim." She grabbed his hand.

Once at the riverside, she kicked off her shoes. "Oh this is going to feel good." She dove into the water with hardly a splash. Her strokes were swift and strong. In no time she made it halfway across the river.

"Be careful. Please," he shouted after her. "You're scaring me again."

She enjoyed his concern and took advantage of it by disappearing from sight for a good while and listened to him calling her. She enjoyed the near panic in his voice. But before he panicked completely, she reappeared, shouting to him. And she could not help but laugh aloud.

She swam to a point about thirty feet out where she pulled her top off and threw it to him, shouting, "Get that."

Oh my God, she's half naked. He fumbled as he grabbed for her top.

"Come on out," she shouted, reaching with her arms. "Come on. Put your arms around me."

And if that wasn't enough, he could swear he heard her calling in a soft almost inaudible, teasing voice, "Come and get me, Johnny. I'm all yours." The man was on fire, but what could he do, being afraid of the water. Then she faced him, baring her breasts. "These are for you, Johnny. Only you."

A burning desire for her raged within him. Suddenly he was knee deep in the water, shoes and all. *What am I doing,* he asked himself. But when she again called out, "Take me. I'm yours, Johnny O'Hara," he found himself chest-high in the water, with Red in his arms. He kissed hard against her lips, quickly moving down to her breasts, while his hands pulled at the cheeks of her butt. That's when he popped, embarrassing himself and shortchanging Red. He apologized, shaking his head.

"I love you," he told her. I've always loved you." He lowered her, her bare breasts rubbing his face, his chest. "Everything about you. Every inch of you."

She put her hand over his mouth. "And I love you. And have always loved you. Even when I didn't know who I was."

"Then make me the happiest man in all the land," he whispered. "Marry me."

She smiled, showing no surprise. "I'd be glad to," she said, then kissed his lips.

"Oh shit! What am I doing?" he shouted, his eyes abruptly filled with fear. "I'm gonna drown."

* * * * *

Johnny didn't like what he saw in her sparkling green eyes. Pure anger. He had again asked her to abide by Brogan's advice, to forget about Bimsbey.

"How can you ask me to do that?" she asked. "I want the revenge I deserve."

"I'm begging you, Red. Don't push him too far. With all his drinking, he might do anything. He won't think twice about having you killed."

Brogan had warned Johnny that Bimsbey had become a madman since his war industries collapsed after the war, causing him great financial losses.

"Not if I get him first," she shot back.

"Then how about me? What would I do without you?" he pleaded. "Do you want me to beg you?" He started to kneel."

"Stop. Get up," she snapped at him, anger still in her eyes. "Guess I have no choice then. But only if we give the story to the boss's newspaper friends out west. That'll hurt him and protect me."

"You're not fooling me, are you?" asked Johnny.

"No I'm not, Johnny O'Hara. When I was out there in the water, I thought about how good life is right now. Got a good job, a good home. Three squares a day and a proper bed to sleep in. Do I want to throw it all away? Especially now," her eyes sparkled, "that Johnny O'Hara wants to marry me."

"Sleep with me tonight?" he insisted. "Katie's in Albany."

She pecked him on the lips. "Do you want me pregnant before we marry?" She gave him a puzzled look. "Come on. Let's go meet Tony and Ellen."

* * * * *

"Look," Bimsbey barked with a slight slur, a contemptuous look on his face. "Our token Irishman has finally arrived. Late, mind you. Don't you know—" But before he could finish his insult, Brogan was in his face, towering over him with clenched fists. In a calm voice he muttered, "Shut your obnoxious mouth . . . you Brit bastard."

Brogan arrived late intentionally. He wanted to provoke Bimsbey.

Their wide-eyed associates were dumb-founded, frozen to their seats, not knowing what to expect. Yet one of them seemed to know what was happening, Jacob Bosh, who cracked a smile.

"I'm not in the mood for your bullshit. And I don't particularly care about your losses. You should have known this would happen with the end of the war. And there's another point I want to make. Do your associates know what you did to my dear friend, young Red Hester?" He paused, glaring at Bimsbey. "I'm sure the name Hester rings a bell with you. You knew her mother very well. That most beautiful woman. Who's no longer with us." He glanced at Morgan, Santan, and Rothchilder.

"We have business to conduct," insisted the ashen-faced Bimsbey, while glaring back at Brogan. But Brogan ignored him and continued his tirade. "Who the hell do you think you are to trample on my friend?"

The men were gathered in the Astoria House's Oak Room to discuss the financial problems of the city—the nation was in the midst of a prolonged recession since the war's end—but instead they were in the midst of what could quickly become a free-swinging brawl, unless one of them interceded. Actually Brogan had no intention of hitting the smaller man, just wanted to shake him up, which the grinning Bosh seemed to comprehend.

The recession has cost Bimsbey more than half his worth.

"We got more important things to talk about than a common whore," snapped Bimsbey, while stepping back from Brogan. But Brogan quickly closed the gap, at the same time removing his jacket. Their colleagues stepped between the two.

"Gentlemen, please," said Leonard Morgan, his voice quivering. "This is not how we resolve our differences."

"You see gents," barked Brogan, "where I come from we do our own fighting. When we do somebody wrong we're prepared to pay the price. We don't have others pay for our crimes."

"Mr. Brogan," Bosh cut in. "Is there not another way that we can settle Mr. Bimsbey's offense against that beautiful young lady."

Bimsbey's glare turned to Bosh.

Bosh continued, "If I may say so myself, I know if I were her man I'd be looking for blood. But that's not the way for us to resolve things."

Bimsbey went to his desk, turned his back to everyone and raised a flask to his mouth. He completely ignored Bosh.

"Whatever you say, Jacob. But get this . . .get him to agree to an acceptable resolution. Here! Today!"

A sick looking Bimsbey sat at the head of the table. "Let us get on with the business." Brogan sat directly across from him, where he kept eye contact.

"Yes and this issue will be part of our itinerary," Bosh insisted. "The first order of business."

"Well then," said Morgan. "What do you propose?"

Bimsbey glared at Bosh.

"I know one sure way to try to resolve this," Bosh said, speaking slow and deliberate.

"And what's that?" asked Morgan.

Bosh continued, "That young lady you so brutally violated is prepared to go to the press with it, if no action is taken by the courts. And she wants action now."

"What are you going to do?" snapped Brogan.

"Damn, Charlton! Do something . . .now," demanded Prago Santan. "Get it behind us. We don't need public scrutiny and I am afraid if this drags on that's exactly what is going to happen."

Rothchilder and Morgan rose from their seats as if rehearsed, and shouted their agreement loud and clear: "Yes, yes, yes."

"I'll take care of it," Bimsbey uttered softly while glaring at Brogan. "Even though she was the seducer."

"What does that mean?" asked Bosh.

"That's for me to decide."

"I'll be around for a while to make sure you do the proper thing," said Brogan. "And speaking of the proper thing, at our last meeting in '64 we all agreed that Alderman O'Hara would be appointed to the new fire department's board of commissioners if he wanted it. He has decided that he wants first to serve as the chief engineer, then later on the board. He wants to lead the new department in a firefighting capacity, which I fully support. I know he will be a damned good leader. If there's no objection, I will contact Chief Kingsland."

Elisha Kingsland had taken over as head of the department from the chief of the volunteers, John Decker, who reluctantly stayed on during the transition from a volunteer force to a paid fire service.

CHAPTER THIRTY

Months passed and nothing happened. Charlton Bimsbey insisted on paying a thousand dollars and Red refused, demanding $10,000. Then suddenly it all came to a head, and not the way Red and Johnny wanted it. An incident occurred that made them painfully aware of just who and what they were up against: Brogan's warning, "You'll never beat the system or Bimsbey."

Early one morning, after closing down the North River Inn for the night, when Red and Vinnie McCarthy were on their way home, a speeding coach mounted the sidewalk behind them. The coach skimmed the side of the building, its axel ends ripping apart two of the inn's large plate glass windows, sending heavy shards of glass through the air—instant guillotines—almost decapitating McCarthy. Red jumped into a doorway, suffering only minor injuries. Her worst injury was to her emotions. She felt terrible and guilty, for the brutal death of her long-time friend, Vinnie, who was run over. The driver disappeared into the night. Suspicion fell on

323

Bimsbey's people. But the police department deemed the incident "an accident," thereby closing the case. Ironically, that's when Bimsbey agreed to the payout of $10,000, even though he still claimed innocence. It didn't make Red any happier, but she accepted, telling herself, *justice will never be achieved. Might as well take the money.*

* * * * *

After finishing her swim across the river and back, Red couldn't get air in her lungs fast enough. Her gasping scared Johnny. "Why are you breathing like that?" he asked. He had been waiting at the shoreline, as he frequently did. For some illogical reason he felt his presence made her safe, even though he still couldn't swim.

"Either I'm getting old or that current's stronger than usual."

Johnny stepped forward, taking the towel from her. "Let me have the pleasure."

He held her close as he rubbed her down, taking certain liberties that only a future husband or lover would do. He loved holding her perfectly shaped frame.

"Oh, I shouldn't be doing this," he groaned, a quiver in his voice. He thrilled at her well-toned body; her shoulders, legs and arms still well defined. "The wedding can't come fast enough."

She stepped into a pair of trousers, one of the only neighborhood gals her age to wear pants anymore.

"By the way," he said, "what are you going to do when you lose your little beach?"

"What do you mean?"

"You didn't hear, then? In another few weeks Macon's going to double the size of their dock. At the same time, on the McAdams property, some shipping company from Netherlands is planning to set up a cross-Atlantic operation. They'll be building a large pier and complex that will fill the McAdams property."

"We'll find a way, Johnny, me boy."

PART IV

CHAPTER THIRTY-ONE

Chief Kingsland had advised a select few of New York's top elites about his plans to step down as head of the Metropolitan Fire Department, but he would not tell them when. He did not inform Bimsbey, with good reason. He despised his heavy drinking, fearing he might do something stupid. He was especially concerned about his boasts that he would *screw* Red Hester, which Kingsland had learned from Leonard Morgan.

At a private meeting in Bimsbey's office, according to Morgan, while Bimsbey was drinking heavily, he had pointed to the portrait of the Hester woman and boasted, "I had her and soon I will have her daughter."

One of the favored candidates to replace Chief Engineer Kingsland was Johnny O'Hara. So, as a favor to Mayor John Hoffman, Chief Kingsland decided to step down on O'Hara's wedding day, December 16, 1866, so that the mayor could announce his appointment at the wedding. It would be his wedding gift to the bride and groom. Nobody knew of his decision other than himself, the mayor and Thomas Brogan.

The Mayor had planned to make the announcement at the wedding service in St. Patrick's Cathedral, but Archbishop John McCloskey put a damper on that: "There will be no politicking in the House of God."

After the wedding service, they left the Holy Cross Church, where Johnny's sister had done so much for the school. The mayor and the O'Hara's riding in a giant, glass-sided wedding coach, led the parade of coaches and a couple of fire trucks up to the North River Inn, getting the mayor plenty of public attention on the way. At the reception he wasted no time. Right after the newlyweds were introduced, Hoffman took the floor and the O'Hara's took seats behind him at the head table, expecting a long speech. Johnny hardly heard a word of what Hoffman said, having something more pressing on his mind. Whispering in Red's ear, he asked, "Are you pleased with how everything went at Woodlawn?"

"Of course I am," she whispered back. "Especially now that she's resting in peace."

Then he coughed, clearing his throat, ready to get to what really concerned him. "You still scare the wits out of me."

"Why's that, dear hubby?" she asked, looking him squarely in the eye.

"Tell me you're finished with Bimsbey."

"Oh sure," she said, not at all persuasive.

"That's real good. Then you won't be having those revenge nightmares anymore. You got the money you wanted and everything is settled. Right?" She didn't get to answer him. The mayor called on them, "Will the newlyweds please join me?"

"Let's go," she said, elbowing Johnny. "His highness wants to toast us."

With champagne in hand, he toasted, "God bless the newlyweds with good health and good fortune, and plenty of little ones," which got a big cheer. He then raised the champagne glass to his lips and drank, as did everybody. Then he paused, allowing the people to silence themselves and to take their seats. Then resting his hand on Johnny's shoulder, he shouted for everybody's attention. At that moment the proud, smiling Thomas Brogan got to his feet.

The mayor continued, "Today's a great day, not only for the O'Hara's, but for the great city of New York. Especially for our young fire department." He paused, looking around the room. "Ladies and gentlemen, fellow New Yorkers, I am privileged and honored to introduce the next head of the Metropolitan Fire Department, your alderman, Chief Engineer . . . Johnny O'Hara."

After a brief moment of befuddlement, the house erupted with applause and cheers, hooting and hollering, led by none other than Thomas Brogan. Everybody sprang to his or her feet. Jimmy Crum's drummer wailed on his drums a long roll. The loudest hooting came from several members of the department that were former members of the Young Immigrant Engine Company. Even Johnny lost his cool, albeit momentarily; he raised his fists over his head in a victory symbol and gave out with some hooting and hollering of his own. Red jumped up and down, gave Mayor Hoffman a hug and a kiss, then wrapped her arms around Johnny's neck and kissed him. Suddenly Johnny calmed himself, then approached the mayor like a professional and thanked him while shaking his hand.

"I will build the greatest fire department of them all," Johnny shouted for all to hear.

The next day the *Herald,* even the *Times,* gave the wedding and O'Hara's appointment prominence in their society sections. The *Herald* included a front-page story about O'Hara becoming chief engineer of the MFD with its 13 chief officers and 552 company officers and men. It also included a photo of the mayor congratulating O'Hara *and his beautiful bride*, as in the words of the reporter who covered the story.

* * * * *

At 8 AM sharp Monday morning, after a ten-day honeymoon at *The Beloe House* in Atlantic City, Chief Engineer O'Hara was standing tall in the temporary department headquarters' on Mercer Street in the quarters of Engine One. There he met his 13 chief officers, checked fire records and other pertinent materials, checked the membership rolls, and, of course, picked up the chief engineer's wagon, which he would garage at the former Young Immigrant Fire Company's quarters that was now part of the paid department. The governor had ordered all volunteer firehouses and equipment turned over to the department.

He made meeting his men, the brothers as he called them, one of his top priorities. To do so he planned to respond to as many fires as permissible, day and night, and to visit the firehouses.

Everything worked just the way he wanted it, with one exception, Red wanted to be an active part of the Metropolitan Fire Department. She wanted to be a fireman, but that could not be. The department hired only men. But where there's a will, there's a way. The solution, they determined, she would be his chauffeur and would wear the metropolitan uniform. To accomplish that, he appointed her as the department's sole auxiliary fireman. Her duties were limited to driving and administration. But to her that did not mean she could not be a firefighter if need be. For that reason, they stored on the chief's wagon an extra set of firefighting gear.

* * * * *

Broadway's business district was no place to be on a Saturday, not after midnight—deserted, dark and eerily silent—even though people were still celebrating the Christmas season and goodwill filled the air. The few streetlamps were almost useless. Only drunken visitors that had lost their way and the people that preyed upon them wandered the area. It took nerves of steel to roam those streets, even for a lone copper.

Yet a lone silhouette that wasn't a copper's, maneuvered along Broadway, hugging the walls and doorways, keeping the silence and staying out of sight. From time to time the figure looked back to make sure no one followed. Then it stopped at the alleyway of the Bimsbey Building and again made sure no one followed. Suddenly, what sounded like a solid piece of hardwood cracking against a brick wall echoed through the canyons of the tall buildings. Or was it a lone copper whacking his nightstick against a building?

But the silhouette's presence was detected by a couple of dogs in the horse stable behind Bimsbey's building. They started barking, making a hell of a racket, only to be roared at by their master, telling them to *shut up*. The shouting and barking spooked the horses and they bucked and stomped. The figure took advantage of the commotion and sprinted past the stable to the underside of the fire escape at the rear of the building.

Besides the dim light coming from the stable doorway, the only other light was a solitary flicker of light at a fifth-floor window, where a man's voice was heard, shouting incoherently, which at times sounded like sobbing. Red recognized the voice to be that of Charlton Bimsbey. *Why's he still here?*

Like a light-footed gymnast, she scaled the wall and the underside of the fire escape, then up over the railing where she hustled up the narrow rungs to the fifth floor. There she extended her head above the landing, just enough to allow her to peer in the window and get a glimpse at her nemesis. And what she saw startled her. He was drunk as a lord, stumbling around his desk, crying like a baby. Stewed to the mickey was the only way to describe the man. Holding on to his desk, he downed a glass of whiskey. *Why's he crying,* she wondered.

After whaling like a banshee in mourning, he called out, "Angel my love," then roared, "Please, leave me alone."

At first his rambling baffled her, wondering who was he talking to, but when he reached out and touched the painting behind his desk, it dawned on her: the target of his ramblings was the painting of her mother. She froze. Hurt filled her gut.

"Please," he pleaded in his stupor. "I only told them," again he whaled, "to scare you." He motioned as if to throw the glass at her image, but dropped it to the floor. "I'm so sorry. I miss you terribly."

My gosh. He must have loved her. She was stunned. *What the hell is this all about?* Suddenly she felt sorry for him; her desire for revenge turned to confusion. She began to question her motives. *Why am I here?* No longer did she want to burn out his office. Instead she wanted to disappear, knowing that if anything happened to him and she was seen, she would be an instant suspect.

She watched him stagger to a door leading to a private rear stairway that opened on to the rear yard, across from the stable, where she assumed he would be going. How else would the legless man get home? She decided to stay put until he entered the stable. *Did he regret not marrying her?* She even wondered how different her life would have been as the stepchild of such a rich man.

The clang of an iron door slamming against the building's brickwork brought her thinking back to the moment, to the sound of Bimsbey's incoherent blabbering as he stumbled out of the doorway towards the horse stable. Pounding on the stable door, he kept babbling, but then he clearly commanded, "Open that damned door you imbecile you. It's your employer." Then more pounding and shouting of expletives. Never once did he call his hack, Mr. Malding, by his name. The man opened the door. Once the two of them were inside with the door closed, Red dropped from the fire escape and took off for the street. Between Bimsbey's shouting and the dogs barking, the commotion blocked out any noise she made.

Malding's screams stopped her in her tracks. "No, no, don't," she heard him shout. Then she heard glass shattering.

"You're crazy," Malding shouted.

Shocked by what she saw, a red-orange flame quickly spreading within the wood-frame structure, she darted back to the stable, her ears rebelling against the death squeals of the horses. When she opened the stable's double door super-heated smoke reached for her. Dropping to the floor, she found Malding sprawled just to her front with the legs of his trousers smoldering. And just past him she saw an image she'd never forget: three fire-engulfed horses leaping convulsively before dropping dead, and an odor she'd not forget, the smell of so much burning flesh.

The former vengeance-seeker turned hero was operating on pure adrenaline-fueled instinct. She snatched a blanket from just inside the door, crawled to Malding's side and covered his legs with the blanket. She then pulled the fair sized man to safety with her exceptional strength, keeping just ahead of the fast spreading fire that quickly filled the inside of the structure. The last nightmarish sight she had to endure before making her escape, which made her puke, was the flame-covered image of Bimsbey—squealing like a pig—stumbling through the fire and smoke.

By then the flames were through the roof, being fed by strong winds. Won't be long before they're setting Bimsbey's building ablaze. It would be only a matter of time before the glass panes shattered, allowing the flames and heat to enter.

After pulling the fire alarm box, she sprinted across the street and disappeared in an alley, so not to be seen. From there she would watch the fire's progress and await the fire department and her husband, the head of the department, and to concoct a cock-and-bull story as to how she had arrived so quickly.

"Oh shit," she muttered upon hearing a cop's whistle sounding real close by. Then there he stood, a big man wearing sergeant stripes looking the image of Sergeant O'Connell. He stood by the alleyway to the fire, whacking his nightstick against the brick wall. It sounded just like the banging sound she had heard a short time ago. *I should have known it was a copper.*

Another police officer's whistle sounded, coming from nearby.

The smell of the smoke and fire permeated the area.

"Damn hell all, I hope he didn't see me," she whispered. Already her eyes were watering from the smoke.

With the exception of a single dog yelping, and the deathly roaring sound of a large fire burning out of control, the area was otherwise silent. But that silence was soon broken by the clanging of bells and galloping hoof beats, and the shouts of the men on the fast approaching fire trucks.

Thick smoke began billowing from the alley, chasing the cop back out to the street.

They can't get here fast enough, she told herself as she watched the column of smoke getting bigger and bigger.

An engine truck pulled in first followed closely by a ladder truck. Men were heard shouting orders back and forth. Peeping out from her hiding place, she saw the chief's wagon—her husband—pulling up, almost blocking the alleyway in which she hid. *Good cover,* she thought.

More bells clanged as more fire companies rushed to fight the blaze. Her adrenaline pumped at max. In their excitement, the horses shook their heads, neighed, and fidgeted about. Firemen rushed ladders to the rear yard. Others hooked the fire engines up to water plugs and stretched hose lines into the alleyway. The sergeant took off with the firemen before Red could see his face.

Red blended in with the action, going straight to Chief O'Hara's wagon, where she opened the trunk and donned her fire gear of booths, rubber coat, and helmet. After an affectionate rub of the horse's snoot, she walked up behind her husband, tapped him on the shoulder, and said, "I'm here ready to serve."

He looked relieved when he saw her. "Glad you're here. Going to need you for this one."

"Shall I get Engine 18 to protect the exposure?" she asked, wide-eyed with excitement.

"Yes and make it quick." As she took off running, he shouted after her, "How'd you know what's going on back there?"

"It's obvious," she shouted back. "There's a lot of fire back there."

She saluted the officer of 18. In her most masculine of voices, she directed, "Get a line and follow me." They pulled lengths of hose from their hose bed and hustled with her to the rear of the building, where she brushed against the sergeant who was blinded by the smoke. Teary-eyed and gagging, Sergeant O'Connell was helping get Malding to the street. Malding kept yelling, "Bimsbey's in there. Bimsbey's in there."

By that time a strong updraft drove the thirty-foot high flames against Bimsbey's building, causing windows on the third-floor to shatter. Flickering orange glows quickly became visible inside the third floor. Red rushed to update O'Hara on the situation. Upon hearing what she had to say, he directed her to transmit a third alarm." She ran to the alarm box, tapped in the third alarm for Station 359, and returned to the rear of Bimsbey's building to again check on the fire's extension. What she found was large, whipping flames shooting up the side of his building. Smoke was everywhere. Firemen shouted back and forth, some sounding overly excited. Shattering glass rained down on them, forcing the men back into the alley, preventing them from discharging the water most effectively.

Using his bullhorn, O'Hara ordered the next two companies to the third floor of the exposure to attack the fast moving interior fire.

Red was gasping when she returned. "Heavy fire . . . on the third floor with possible . . . extension to the fourth." Red was delighted with herself, playing such an important role in fighting this fire.

To their horror, smoke began billowing from several front windows on the third floor. "Transmit a fourth," O'Hara ordered. She took off.

More companies rolled in. These companies he sent into the exposure, which was now his priority. The sound of the shattering glass of the main entrance to the exposure pleased him. He knew then that in a few moments the men would be putting out the fire. Now he could concentrate on putting out the stable fire that still raged out of control, with flames now reaching forty plus feet into the air. Two hose lines were fighting that fire, while Engine 18's line was protecting the exposure from further extension. He ordered the next two hose companies to arrive to also attack that fire.

While waiting for the ambulance, O'Hara stepped over to Malding and questioned him about what had happened. The excited man replied, "He was drunk as a lord. He killed my horses."

"Who was drunk ? Who killed your horses?" asked O'Hara.

"Bimsbey that sonofabitch."

O'Hara cringed. "Bimsbey?"

"Yes. He killed my darlings. All three of them."

"Where is he now?" O'Hara continued.

"In there." Malding pointed back towards the stable."

O'Hara's jaw dropped. "What . . . what happened?"

"He smashed the lanterns and set the place ablaze."

* * * * *

Bimsbey's sparse remains were uncovered later that morning, under the charred ruins of the stable. The authorities wouldn't release any information about his death, not until they had verified his demise. The authorities also *warned* Malding, whom they considered the only witness that he was not to talk to anyone. Of course, another person had witnessed his death, Red. But she chose to remain silent, and besides, she thought differently of him since hearing him profess his love for her mother.

It wasn't until seventy-two hours later that the O'Haras finally had an evening together. Johnny had been up to his neck with the police investigation of the fire. After all, one of New York's leading citizens had been killed, which provoked the question: was he murdered? Red too had been busy, looking after the family businesses. So too, she hadn't had much sleep. Her nights had been filled with nightmarish visions of Bimsbey's burning figure and endless thoughts of his ramblings about loving her mother. Two secrets she had chosen to keep to herself, but then a mean guilt trip changed her mind. *I can't keep secrets from him.*

They wanted to be alone that evening and enjoy a good, hot meal together. What better place for privacy and a good T-bone steak dinner than the back deck of the Waterside, right on the river. They began their time together with a glass of wine, actually two glasses each, and small talk. "I missed you terribly," he said and she replied, "I missed you, too. Terribly." Then he spoke about the investigation, giving her a few details about it, which he expected her to question, but she didn't. Instead, she updated him on the businesses. They chewed food through the first minutes of their chat.

With a sliver of steak in his mouth, he said what was really on his mind, "Well, I guess you can say we got our revenge." But he didn't get the response he'd expected. She looked despondent, saying not a word. "Why are you so upset?" he asked. "I thought you'd be happy, especially when we had nothing to do with it." It puzzled him that she still didn't respond. Then he recalled that when he first saw her at the fire, she had known a fire company would be needed to protect the rear of Bimsbey's building from the stable fire. *How had she known that and how did she get there so fast?*

"You know, my love, I don't understand how you got there so fast. Or how you knew we'd need to protect the exposure."

Putting her knife and fork down, she nodded her head and spoke. "Yes. I was back there. I'm the one who sent in the alarm." She paused and leaned back on her chair, resting her hands in her lap.

His eyes widened. "What are you talking about?"

"I went to his office. I don't even know what I intended to do. But I wanted to do him some harm," she said.

"Oh, no. Don't tell me you did it, please," he gasped, but then sighed with relief when she replied, "God, no. I had nothing to do with it." His eyes rolled back in his head.

She began her story with the minutest of details: how she walked the lonely streets, keeping in the shadows to avoid being seen; how quiet and scary the streets were, how the dogs started barking when she had stepped into the alley; even how the stable master yelled for the dogs to shut up.

Johnny's transfixed eyes hardly blinked. "How'd you get into the building? It had to be locked up."

"I resorted to my old tactics. I used the rear fire escape adjacent to the stable. From the fire escape I saw him in his office and watched him in his drunken stupor, stumbling and mumbling. I hated the sight of him. But then," she paused, "he started scolding my mother's image. You know that picture behind his desk. Yelling, 'Leave me alone.' He begged her to forgive him. Then he began sobbing, even whaling, telling her how sorry he was. That he didn't want her killed. He only wanted her scared."

Johnny realized she was choking up. "Are you feeling sorry for this guy?"

"Let me finish. Bimsbey guzzled a whiskey. Then more sobbing and whaling. Then he shouted that he'd loved her and that he still misses her."

Johnny cut in, "But how did he wind up in the stable?"

A passing ship's foghorn blasted, silencing her. Twice more the foghorn blasted when she attempted to answer him. Then it went silent.

"He used a private stairwell to the rear yard. I watched him from the fire escape. Watched him staggering as he headed to the stable. He kept shouting at the stable master, real angry like, demanding he open the door. Me, I just stayed where I was 'til the guy Malding let him in. Once inside, he continued shouting, getting the dogs barking again, even got the horses started up. That's when I rushed down the stairs and cleared the fire escape. Once again, I used the commotion to hide any noise that I made."

Neither of them had since touched another morsel of food.

"But how about the fire?"

"Well, when I took off out of there, I heard screaming. At the same time, I heard glass shattering and that made me stop. Had to be the lanterns. When I turned to look, I saw flames. Looked like the place exploded with fire."

"Was it you who the stable master saw? The person the coppers want to question."

"Guess so. But Malding never saw my face. I made sure of that. Besides, a person couldn't see in that smoke. Too thick."

"Yeah, that's what he said too. Alright, so continue."

"In an instant, the place was roaring. So I rushed back to do what I could. I flung open the doors and crawled in under the smoke and heat and grabbed Malding and pulled him out. The horse's screams sounded awful. I watched them as they burned alive. Horrible. I felt sick. And if that wasn't bad enough" she shook her head, "then I saw Bimsbey burning up. Heard

335

his screams. Just dropped . . . dead. And you know, I felt sorry for him. Can you imagine that? Sorry. I couldn't understand. It was later that I realized I saw him differently, knowing he had loved my mother."

"We better eat before everything is cold," he said. They both fed their faces.

"After that, I sent in the alarm and hid in the alley across the street until you arrived. Then I . . . I just blended in and joined you."

CHAPTER THIRTY-TWO

Bimsbey's drunken rambling about Angel Hester had a lasting effect on Red. Her bitter hatred of him eased, she even regretted his death. She began to mellow towards him. At first Johnny thought her transformation was a passing thing, but several months had passed since the fire and the changes continued. The new Mrs. O'Hara delighted him.

First she started doing her work—taking care of their business affairs—mostly from home, a real shocker to him. She had loved working at the Inn. It was her social life. He observed, too, that she took a much greater interest in their home, going as far as having it repainted. They had it painted just before their wedding six months earlier. At that time she couldn't even tell him the colors used, except that the ceilings were white.

There's got to be something else going on with her, he told himself. When they first got married, she'd only cared about a good bed and a sturdy dinner table. He had assumed that her current changes were temporary, but when she began to vigorously furnish their new home, he realized what she was doing would endure until she was satisfied. What sealed it for him was when she converted two of their nine rooms into a proper office.

He arrived home from headquarters one evening wearing an ear-to-ear grin. He wrapped his arms around her, just as he always did, but this time he lifted her up over his head like a paper doll. As she yelled, "Easy there, boy," he shouted, "I just love the new Mrs. O'Hara." He was so upbeat.

"What do you mean, 'the new Mrs. O'Hara?" She loved the feel of his powerful arms around her.

"You're so content."

"What are you talking about?" she asked.

"You're a new person. Even better than before."

"Are you looking for something?" she asked, giving him a quizzical smile.

"No, not now. I'm serious, my love. For one thing, you're doing the company's business from here. I didn't think that would last. You even set up an office here, which is great." He put her down and hung his coat in the closet. He turned back to her and said, "And you're even furnishing the rest of the place. What a change. Heck, all you ever worried about was a good bed and kitchen table."

"So you finally noticed?"

"Not really," he said. "I knew all along, but didn't think it would last." Then he pointed towards the different rooms. "You had the place repainted. A short time ago I didn't think you even knew what colors were on the walls. God knows, it looks a lot nicer."

"Life is so good," she said. She was delighted with Johnny running the new fire department, and she no longer lived with the bitterness she had carried so long for the man she thought had her mother killed.

"Yes my love, that's the new me," she replied, then planted a kiss on his lips.

"God knows you've mellowed." He looked her square in the eye and asked, "And I haven't the slightest idea about what brought it all on.

"For one thing I'm Chief O'Hara's wife."

"I love it," he said.

"Another is finding out that he had actually loved my mother. That meant so much to me. All that hatred and bitterness is gone. I actually regret he's dead."

Johnny just looked, but said nothing.

"And I got a big surprise for you," she added. "I'm going to paint one of the bedrooms pink."

"Why? You just got the whole place painted." Then his eyes lit up. "You're . . . you're with child?"

With a nod and a smile, she whispered, "Yes, my dear." Her face beamed, her green eyes glowed.

Again he lifted her off her feet and shouted, "We must celebrate. We're going to be a family. I'm going to be a father."

"How about me?"

"Well if it's a girl let's hope she's a red-headed, green-eyed beauty like its mother.

* * * * *

Johnny loved Battler's suggestion that the celebration take place in Fraunces Tavern. "Such a special occasion calls for a special place," Battler had told him. Both Hans and Tony were quick to ask what was so special about the Tavern, to which Battler answered, "For ya efacation you foreigners—"

"Edification," interjected Johnny.

"Whatever," replied Battler. "Fraunces Tavern was George Washington's hangout during the revolution. That's where he said goodbye to his generals. You know, Tony, when we threw the damned Brits out."

"Amen," said Tony. "How do we get the bastards out of Ireland?"

* * * * *

The O'Haras were taking their closest friends to Fraunces Tavern to celebrate their good fortune. Johnny hoofed it from Headquarters while Red and the rest of the crew traveled by coach from the Inn. "It's a twofold celebration," Johnny had told Battler. "Not only was Red with child, but she's finished fighting fires until after she gives birth." He wanted her to resign permanently, but she wanted none of that. "She told me she's too young to give up such a great calling."

Johnny arrived before the others, looking like a million dollars, sporting a new gray suit, a gray shirt with a black tie, a Fedora, and spats. *She'd never recognize me,* he reckoned.

"Chief O'Hara," a familiar voice called. He turned to see Greg Lopat standing at the entrance door to the Tavern. "Will we be having the honor of your company tonight?"

O'Hara and Lopat shook hands. "What are you doing here?" O'Hara asked.

"I decided working for a living was a good thing. Besides, money's good here. Get to meet influential people. How 'bout you? Why are you here?"

"My wife's getting ready to grow our family."

Lopat smiled. "Well congratulations." He excused himself to hold the door for a large group of well-dressed buyers and sellers of beef."

"Who are they?" asked O'Hara.

"Cattlemen. They're making their deals with each other."

"Ah, here they come now."

The coach rolled up outside the tavern. Tony, the proper gentleman, jumped to the street, turned and grabbed his date, Ellen McBride, by the waist and lowered her. He then reached for Red, but she laughed. "You gotta be kidding. I can handle this myself."

"Please love, will you allow him to let you down?" Johnny pleaded. "You're almost three months already."

She gave him a challenging look, but complied. "Honey, you worry too much."

She looked gorgeous. The only sign of her being pregnant was the glow on her face that matched her striking green eyes and red hair. Johnny grabbed her in his arms and planted a kiss on her lips. "Watch my lipstick," she yelped, a big smile pasted on her face.

"Where's Yelda?" Johnny asked Hans.

"Och. A schmuck. Not like the drinking. So I don't bring her," he replied. The two bachelors, Battler and Timothy, patted him on the back. "Good move. Now we can have fun," said Battler.

Heads turned and the chatter level rose when the big man came through the door. "Welcome Mr. Councilman," somebody shouted. "You mean the head of the fire department," the owner clarified, "with his lovely wife, Red. We are honored." He led them to a private room, which Johnny had requested when he made the reservations.

A stout, squeaky-clean waiter arrived with their drinks, mugs of lager and shots for everybody. He then took their food order—steaks for everyone except salmon for Ellen—which included another full round of drinks.

"Real pronto like," said Battler.

A few moments later the waiter returned and placed the tray of fresh drinks on the table.

"Just in time," quipped the cheery Battler, as he finished his beer.

Johnny ordered another round, but this time only beer.

"What's that Lopat guy doing here," Red asked Johnny.

"I'm the official greeter," Lopat said with a loud voice, as he stepped through the door. "Nothing like an honest living."

Red nodded, giving him a hesitant smile.

"I have a message for you, Mrs. O'Hara," he said. "A Mr. G. Parnell would like to see you. He said you'd know him. Bimsbey's attorney."

Her smile turned to a look of puzzlement. "Yeah, I know who you mean. What does he want?"

Lopat shrugged his shoulders and flashed his hands. "Didn't say. Just that it's important."

What's he want with me, she wondered.

"I'll be right back." She tapped Johnny's shoulder, then nodded to Lopat, and said, "Show me the way."

The main room was crowded and so noisy that even though she could see somebody banging on the piano, she hardly heard their music. The bar itself was two to three deep with sitting and standing patrons, all of who seemed to be talking at the same time. *Does anybody ever listen,* she wondered. Most tables were occupied. Hairy-headed bartenders with handlebar mustaches and thick sideburns rushed back and forth behind the bar.

"Who the hell are these loudmouths?" she asked Lopat.

"They're the cattlemen. A big convention at the New Yorker. Pains in the ass, but big tippers," he said.

Mr. Parnell rose to his feet as Red approached his table. He immediately pulled up a chair for her to sit. "Mrs. O'Hara. Please have a seat," he said. They exchanged greetings. He introduced himself as Graham Parnell.

"What is it that's so important?" she asked, getting right down to business. Her only experience with this man was not a good one. He was Bimsbey's attorney, who appeared for him at the police station and made certain nothing happened to him the night he attempted to rape her. No charges were ever filed. But this evening he was all smiles.

"It's about Charlton Bimsbey. I won't be but a moment. You probably don't know this," he spoke with sincerity, "but he loved your mother and never stopped loving her. Contrary to what you believe, her death almost destroyed him."

"Yes, I'm aware of that. Is that all?"

"There's more. In his sober moments he regretted very much what he tried to do to you." He then put his hand inside his suit coat and retrieved a sealed envelope. "His last will and testament stipulated that you be given this. It is part of his will." She stared blankly at the envelope, not knowing what to expect. On its face she saw her name, *Angela "Red" Hester*. She thanked him, took the envelope and departed.

When she returned to the table, her friends were louder than when she left, shouting and laughing. The alcohol was doing its job. Battler had just started telling a joke:

"There was a man who suspected his wife was cheating on him. Fearing he would lose her altogether, he hesitated to confront her. When the man finally got the nerve to challenge her, he said, 'I feel that I'm playing second fiddle to someone else, to which his wife replied, 'You're lucky you're still in the band."

A waiter placed a glass of champagne before each of them.

Battler raised his glass. "Okay, listen up. I'm making a toast, so raise your glasses," he said. "Here's to two of the best people I ever knowd. Johnny and Red. I hope dey have a healthy and happy baby. Drink up." They touched glasses and drank up. Battler, having an afterthought, shouted, "Oh yeah . . . and may dey have a lot of kids." He laughed aloud.

Finally, they got to enjoy their dinners, but not without laughter and loud conversation.

"Parnell gave me this," she told Johnny while opening the letter for the first time. He watched her as she read it and saw great surprise in her eyes. "What is it?" he asked. She handed him the short note without a word.

"Oh my God. You're rich now. Can't believe this. It's all here. His love for your mother; his apology to you."

"Look at the way he worded his bequeath to me," she said.

He read from the letter, "let me see, he leaves you . . . the picture of your mother. He goes on to say that it should hang in the living room." He paused to read on. "Do you believe this: 'I had promised to your mother that she would one day own real estate.' Who's he kidding?"

"Read on before you say another word."

He stared at the letter in awe, then slowly repeated what he silently read, "'Of course she passed away before that ever materialized. The least I can do is confer the properties to you." Johnny became quiet, staring into her eyes as though deep in thought, then continued, "The concerned holdings are: 414 and 424 Fifth Avenue, and the Bimsbey Building. G. Parnell will handle all the details."

He looked her in the eye and shook his head in disbelief. "You're rich now."

NO IRISH NEED APPLY

A young fireman appeared at the door. His nervous mien gave away the serious nature of his business. He made a beeline to O'Hara. "Sir, a third alarm on arrival has been transmitted for station 448."

"Ah, hell. I got to go. Duty calls," O'Hara told the group.

"What's up?" asked Red as Johnny hugged and kissed her.

"There's a general alarm fire," he replied while getting to his feet.

"Bullshit! You're not going without me," she said with determination in her voice.

"But you're finished with fire. At least 'til after the baby."

"That starts tomorrow."

CPSIA information can be obtained
at www.ICGtesting.com
Printed in the USA
BVOW11s0038030616

450481BV00009B/81/P